THE RANCHER'S BABY

BY
MAISEY YATES

MILLS
BOON

First Published in Great Britain 2018
By Mills & Boon, an imprint of HarperCollins*Publishers*
1 London Bridge Street, London, SE1 9GF

© 2018 Harlequin Books S.A

Special thanks and acknowledgement are given to Maisey Yates for her contribution to the Texas Cattleman's Club: The Impostor series.

ISBN: 978-0-263-93586-8

51-0118

MIX
Paper from
responsible sources
FSC® C007454

This book is produced from independently certified FSC™ paper to ensure responsible forest management.

For more information visit: www.harpercollins.co.uk/green

Printed and bound in Spain
by CPI, Barcelona

Maisey Yates is a *New York Times* bestselling author of more than thirty romance novels. She has a coffee habit she has no interest in kicking, and a slight Pinterest addiction. She lives with her husband and children in the Pacific Northwest. When Maisey isn't writing she can be found singing in the grocery store, shopping for shoes online and probably not doing dishes. Check out her website: www.maiseyyates.com.

One

My fake ex-husband died at sea and all I got was this stupid letter.

That was Selena Jacobs's very dark thought as she stood in the oppressive funeral home clutching said letter so tightly she was wearing a thumbprint into the envelope.

She supposed that her initial thought wasn't true—strictly speaking. The letter proclaimed she was the heir to Will's vast estate.

It was just that there were four other women at the funeral who had been promised the exact same thing. And Selena couldn't fathom why Will would have made her the beneficiary of anything, except maybe that hideous bearskin rug he'd gotten from his grandfather that he'd had in his dorm at school. The one she'd hated because the sightless glass eyes had creeped her out.

Yeah, that she would have believed Will had left her. His entire estate, not so much.

But then, she was still having trouble believing Will was dead. It seemed impossible. He had always been so…so *much*. Of everything. So much energy. So much light. So much of a pain in the ass sometimes. It seemed impossible that a solemn little urn could contain everything Will Sanders had been. And yet there it was.

Though she supposed that Will wasn't entirely contained in the urn. Will, and the general fallout of his life—good and bad—was contained here in this room.

There were…well, there were a lot of women standing around looking bereft, each one of them holding letters identical to hers. Their feelings on the contents of the letters were different than hers. They must be. They didn't all run multimillion-dollar corporations.

Selena's muted reaction to her supposed inheritance was in some part due to the fact that she doubted the authenticity of the letter. But the other part was because she simply didn't need the money. Not at this point in her life.

These other women…

Well, she didn't really know. One of them was holding a chubby toddler, her expression blank. There was another in a sedate dress that flowed gently over what looked to be a burgeoning baby bump. Will had been too charming for his own good, it seemed.

Selena shuddered.

She didn't know the nature of those women's relationships to Will, but she had her suspicions. And the very idea of being left in a similar situation made her skin crawl.

There were reasons she kept men at arm's length. The vulnerability of being left pregnant was one of them. A very compelling one.

As for the other reasons? Well, every woman in this room was a living, breathing affirmation of Selena's life choices.

Heartbroken wives, ex-wives and baby mamas.

Selena might technically be an ex-wife, but she wasn't one in the traditional sense. And she wasn't heartbroken. She was hurt. She was grieving. And she was full of regret. She wished more than anything that she and Will had patched up their friendship.

But, of course, she had imagined that there was plenty of time to revive a friendship they'd left behind in college.

There hadn't been plenty of time. Will didn't have any more time.

Grief clutched at her heart and she swallowed hard, turning away from the urn to face the entry door at the back of the room.

The next visitor to walk in made her already battered heart jolt with shocked recognition.

Knox McCoy.

She really hadn't expected him to come. He had been pretty scarce for the past couple of years, and she honestly couldn't blame him. When he had texted her the other day, he'd said he wouldn't be attending the funeral, and he hadn't needed to say why.

She suspected he hadn't been to one since the one for his daughter, Eleanor.

She tried to quell the nerves fluttering in her stomach as Knox walked deeper into the room, his gray eyes locking with hers. She had known the man for more than a decade. She had made her decisions regarding him, and he…

Well, he had never felt the way about her that she did about him.

He looked as gorgeous as ever. His broad shoulders, chest and trim waist outlined perfectly in the gray custom-made suit with matching charcoal tie. His brown hair was pushed back off his forehead, longer than he used to keep it. He was also sporting a beard, which was not typical of him. He had deep grooves between his dark brows, lines worn into his handsome face by the pain of the past few years.

She wanted to go to him. She wanted to press her thumb right there at those worry lines and smooth them out. Just the thought of touching him made her feel restless. Hot.

And really, really, she needed not to be having a full-blown Knox episode at her ex-husband's funeral.

Regardless of the real nature of her relationship with Will, her reaction to Knox was inappropriate. Beyond inappropriate.

"How are you doing?" he asked, his expression full of concern.

When he made that face his eyebrows locked together and the grooves deepened.

"Oh, I've been better," she said honestly.

A lopsided smile curved the corner of his mouth upward and he reached out, his thumb brushing over her cheek. His skin was rough, his hands those of a rancher. A working man. His wealth came from the chain of upscale grocery stores he owned, but his passion was in working the land at his ranch in Wyoming.

Her gaze met his, and the blank sadness she saw in his eyes made her stomach feel hollow.

She wondered if the ranch still held his passion. She wondered if anything did anymore.

"Me, too," he said, his voice rough.

"Will is such an inconsiderate ass," she said, her voice trembling. "Leave it to him to go and die like this."

"Yeah," Knox agreed. "His timing is pretty terrible. Plus, you know he just wanted the attention."

She laughed, and as the laugh escaped her lips, a tear slid down her cheek.

She'd met Knox at Harvard. From completely different backgrounds—his small-town Texan childhood worlds away from her high-society East Coast life—they had bonded quickly. And then... Then her grandfather had died, which had ripped her heart square out of her chest. He had been the only person in her family who had ever loved her. Who had ever instilled hope in her for the future.

And with his death had come the trust fund. A trust fund she could only access when she was twenty-five. Or married.

The idea of asking Knox to marry her had been... Well, it had been unthinkable. For a whole host of reasons. She hadn't wanted to get married, not for real. And her feelings for Knox had been real. Or at least, she had known perfectly well they were on the verge of being real, and she'd needed desperately for them to stay manageable. For him to stay a friend.

Then their friend Will had seen her crying one afternoon and she'd explained everything. He had offered himself as her solution. She hadn't been in a position to say no.

Control of her money had provided freedom from her father. It had given her the ability to complete her education on her own terms. It had also ended up ruining her friendship with Will. In the meantime, Knox had met someone else. Someone he eventually married.

She blinked, bringing herself firmly back to the present. There was no point thinking about all of that. She didn't. Not often. Her friendship with Knox had survived college, and they had remained close in spite of the fact that they were both busy with their respective careers.

It was Will. Whenever Will was added to the mix she couldn't help but think of those years. Of that one stupid, reckless decision that had ended up doing a lot of damage in the end.

For some reason, she suddenly felt hollow and weak. She wobbled slightly, and Knox reached toward her as if he would touch her again. She wasn't sure that would be as fortifying as he thought it might be.

But then the doors to the funeral home opened again and she looked up at the same time Knox looked over his shoulder.

And the world stopped.

Because the person who walked through the door was the person who was meant to be in that urn.

It was Will Sanders, and he was very much alive.

Then the world really did start to spin, and Selena didn't know how to stand upright in it.

That was how she found herself crashing to the floor, and then everything was dark.

* * *

Fucking Will. Of course he wasn't actually dead.

That was Knox's prevailing thought as he dropped to his knees, wrapping his arm around Selena and pulling her into his lap.

No one was paying attention to one passed-out woman, because they were a hell of a lot more concerned with the walking corpse who had just appeared at his own funeral.

It was clear Will was just as shocked as everyone else.

Except for maybe Selena.

Had she loved the bastard that much? It had been more than ten years since Will and Selena had been married, and Selena rarely talked about Will, but Knox supposed he should know as well as anyone that sometimes not talking about something indicated you thought about it a whole hell of a lot.

That it mattered much more than the things that rolled off your tongue with routine frequency.

As he watched the entire room erupt in shock, Knox was filled with one dark thought.

At the last funeral he had attended he would have given everything he owned for the little body in the casket to come walking into the room. Would've given anything to wake up and find it all a nightmare.

He would have even traded places with his daughter. Would have buried himself six feet down if it would have meant Eleanor would come back.

But of course that hadn't happened. He was living a fucking soap opera at the wrong damned moment.

He looked down at Selena's gray face and cupped her cheek, patting it slightly, doing his best to revive her. He didn't know what you were supposed to do when a woman fainted. And God knew caregiving was not his strong suit.

His ex-wife would be the first to testify to that.

Selena's skin felt clammy, a light sweat beading on her brow. He wasn't used to seeing his tough-as-nails friend anything but self-assured. Even when things were terrible, she usually did what she had done only a few moments ago. She made a joke. She stood strong.

When Eleanor had died Selena had stood with him until he couldn't stand, and then she had sat with him. She had been there for him through all of that.

Apparently, ex-husbands returning from the beyond were her breaking point.

"Come on, Selena," he murmured, brushing some of her black hair out of her face. "You can wake up now. You've done a damn decent job of stealing his thunder. Anything else is just showing off at this point."

Her sooty eyelashes fluttered, and her eyes opened, her whiskey-colored gaze foggy. "What happened?"

He looked around the room, at the commotion stirring around them. "It seems Will has come back from the dead."

Two

Will wasn't dead.

Selena kept playing that thought over and over in her mind as Knox drove them down the highway.

She wasn't entirely clear on what had happened to her car, or why Knox was driving her. Or what she was going to do with her car later. She had been too consumed with putting one foot in front of the other while Knox led her from the funeral home, safely ensconced her in his rental car and began to take them… Well, she didn't know where.

She slid her hand around the back of her neck, beneath her hair, her skin damp and hot against her palm. She felt awful. She felt… Well, like she had passed out on the floor of a funeral home.

"Where are we going?" she asked.

"To your place."

"You don't know where I live," she mumbled, her lips numb.

"I do."

"No, you don't, Knox. I've moved since the last time you came to visit."

"I looked you up."

Knox hadn't come back to Royal since his divorce. She couldn't blame him. There was a lot of bad wrapped up in Royal for him. Seeing as this was where he'd lived with his family most of the year when he'd been married.

"I'm not listed." She attempted to make the words sound crisp.

"You know me better than that, honey," he said, that slow Texas drawl winding itself through her veins and turning her blood into fire. "I don't need a phone book to find someone."

"Obviously, Knox. No one has used a phone book since 2004. But I meant it's not like you can just look up my address on the internet."

"Figure of speech, Selena. Also, I have connections. Resources."

She made a disgusted sound and pressed her forehead against the window. It wasn't cold enough.

"You sent me a Christmas card," he said, his tone maddeningly steady. "I added your address to my contacts."

"Well," she said. "Damn my manners. Apparently they've made me traceable."

"Not very stealthy."

"*And* you're rude," she said, ignoring him. "Because you did not send me a Christmas card back."

"I had my secretary send you something."

"What did she send me?" Selena asked.

"It was either a gold watch or a glass owl figurine," he said.

"What did she do, send you links to two different things, and then you said choose either one?"

"Yes."

"That doesn't count as a present, Knox. And it certainly doesn't equal my very personal Christmas card."

"You didn't have an assistant send the card?" he asked, sounding incredulous.

"I did not. I addressed it myself, painstakingly by hand while I was eating a TV dinner."

"A TV dinner?" he asked, chuckling. "That doesn't jibe with your healthy-lifestyle persona."

"It was a frozen dinner from Green Fair Pantry," she said pointedly, mentioning the organic fair-trade grocery-store chain Knox owned. "If those aren't healthy, then you have some explaining to do yourself."

She was starting to feel a little bit more human, but along with that feeling came a dawning realization of the enormity of everything that had just happened.

"Will is alive," she said, just to confirm.

"It looks that way," Knox said, tightening his hold on the steering wheel. She did her best not to watch the way the muscles in his forearms shifted, did her best to ignore just how large his hands looked, how large *he* looked in this car that was clearly too small for him. One that he would never have driven in his real life.

Knox was much more of a pickup truck kind of man, no matter how much money he made. Little luxury vehicles were not his thing.

"I guess I don't get his bearskin rug, then," she said absently.

"What?"

"Don't you remember that appalling thing he used to have in his dorm room?"

Knox shot her a look out of the corner of his eye. "Not really. Hey, are you okay?"

"I am… I don't know. I mean, I guess I'm better than I was when I thought he was ashes in a jar." She cleared her throat. "I'm sorry. Are you okay, Knox? I realize this is probably the first—"

"I don't want to talk about that," he said, cutting her off. "We don't need to. I'm fine."

She didn't think he was. Her throat tightened, feeling scratchy. "Okay. Anyway, I'm fine, too. My relationship with Will… You know."

Except he didn't. Nobody did. Everyone *thought* they did, but everyone was wrong. Unless, of course, Will had ever talked to anyone about the truth of their marriage, but somehow she doubted it.

"How long had it been since you two had spoken?" Knox asked.

"A long damn time. I don't believe all the things Rich said to me before the divorce. Not anymore. He was toxic."

As little as she tried to think about her short, convenient marriage to Will and what had resulted after, she tried to think about Will's friend Rich Lowell even less. Though she had heard through that reliable Royal grapevine that he and Will had remained friends. It made her wonder why Rich wasn't here.

Rich had been part of their group of friends, though he had always been somewhat on the periphery, and he had been…strange, as far as Selena was concerned. He had liked Will, so much that it had been concerning. And when Will had married Selena, Rich's interest had wandered onto her.

He had never done anything terribly inappropriate, but the increased attention from him had made her uneasy.

But then… Well, he had been in their apartment one night when she'd gotten home from class. He'd produced evidence that Will was after her trust fund—the trust fund that had led to their marriage in the first place. And she needed that money. She needed it so she would never be at her father's mercy again. The trust fund had been everything to her, and Will had said he was marrying her just to help her. She'd trusted him.

Rich had been full of some weird, intense energy Selena hadn't been able to place at the time. Now that she had some distance and a more adult understanding, she felt like maybe Rich had been attracted to her. But more than a simple attraction…he'd been obsessed with Will. It almost seemed, in hindsight, as if he'd been attracted to her *because* he thought Will had her.

And what Rich had said that night… Well, it had just been a lot easier to believe than Will's claim that he wanted to help her because they were friends. Trust had never been easy for her. Will was kind, and that was something she'd wanted. Not because she was attracted to him, but because she had genuinely wanted him to be a real friend. After a life of being thoroughly mistreated by her father, hoping for true friendship was scary.

Selena had spent most of her childhood bracing herself for the punch. Whether emotional or physical. It was much easier to believe she was being tricked than to believe Will was everything he appeared to be.

She and Will had fought. And then they had barely limped to the finish line of the marriage. They'd waited until the money was in her account, and then they'd divorced.

And their friendship had never been the same.

She had never apologized to him. Grief and regret stabbed her before she remembered—Will wasn't actually dead.

That means you can apologize to him. It means you can fix your friendship.

She needed to. The woman she was now would never have jumped to a conclusion like that, at least not without trying to get to the bottom of it.

But back then, Selena had been half-feral. Honed into a sharp, mean creature from years of being in survival mode.

The way Knox had stuck by her all these years, the kind of friendship he had demonstrated... It had been a huge part of her learning to trust. Learning to believe men could actually be good.

Her ability to trust hadn't changed her stance on love and marriage. And she fought against any encroaching thoughts that conflicted with that stance.

It didn't really matter that Knox sometimes made her think differently about love and marriage. He had married someone else. And she had married someone else. She had married someone else first, in point of fact. It was just that...

It didn't matter.

"I know this dredges up a lot of ancient history," Knox said, turning the car off the highway and onto the narrow two-lane road that would take them out to her new cabin. Now that she had the freedom to work remotely most of the time—her skin-care company was so successful she'd hired other people to do the parts that consumed too much time—she had decided to get outside city limits.

Had decided it was time for her to actually make herself a home, instead of living in a holding pattern. Existing solely to build her empire, to increase her net worth.

Nothing had ever felt like home until this place. Everything after college had just been temporary. Before that, it had been a war zone.

This cabin was her refuge. And it was *hers*.

Nestled in the woods, surrounded by sweetgrass and trees, and a river running next to her front porch.

Of course, it wasn't quite as grand as Knox's spread in Jackson Hole, but then, very few places were.

Besides, grandness wasn't the point. This cabin wasn't for show. Wasn't to impress anyone else. It was just to make her happy. And few things in her life had existed for that reason up to this point.

Having achieved some happiness made her long for other things, though. Things she was mostly inured against—like wanting someone to share her life with.

She gritted her teeth, looking resolutely away from Knox as that thought invaded her brain.

"Which is now a little bit annoying," she pointed out. "He's not even dead, and I had to go through all that grief, plus, you know…"

"Thinking about your marriage?"

She snapped her mouth shut, debating how to respond. It was true enough. She had been thinking a lot about her marriage. Not that it had been an actual, physical marriage. More like roommates with official paperwork. "Yes," she said finally.

"Divorce is hell," he said, his voice turning to gravel. "Believe me. I know."

Guilt twisted her stomach. He thought they shared this common bond. The loss of a marriage. In reality, their situations weren't even close to being the same.

"Will and I were only married for a year," she commented. "It's not really the same as you and Cassandra. The two of you were together for twelve years and…"

"I told you, I don't want to talk about it."

Blessedly, distraction came in the form of the left turn that took them off the paved road and onto the gravel road that took them to her cabin.

"Why don't you get this paved?" he asked.

"I like it," she said.

"Why?"

That was a complicated question, with a complicated answer. But he was her friend and she was glad to be off the topic of marriages, so she figured she would take a stab at it. "Because it's nothing like the driveway that we had when I was growing up. Which was smooth and paved and circular, and led up to the most ridiculous brick monstrosity."

"So this is like inverse nostalgia?"

"Yes."

He lifted a shoulder. "I understand that better than you might think."

He pulled up to the front of the cabin and she stayed resolutely in her seat until he rounded to her side and opened the door for her. Then she blinked, looking up into the sun, at the way his broad shoulders blotted it out. "What about my car?" she asked.

"I'm going to have someone bring it. Don't worry."

"I could go get it," she said.

"I have a feeling it's best if you lie low for a little bit."

"Why would I do that?"

"Well," he said. "Your ex-husband just came back from the dead, and both of you cause quite a bit of media interest. You were named as beneficiary of his estate along with four other women, and that's a lot of money."

"But Will isn't dead, and I don't care about his money. I have my own."

"Very few people are going to believe that, Selena," Knox said, his tone grave. "Most people don't acknowledge the concept of having enough money. They only understand wanting more."

"What are you saying? That I'm…in danger?"

"I don't know. But we don't know what's going on with Will, and you were brought into this. You're a target, for all we know. Someone is in an urn, and you have a letter that brought you here."

"You're jumping to conclusions, Knox."

"Maybe," he said, "but I swear to God, Selena, I'd rather have you safe than end up in an urn. That I couldn't deal with."

She looked at the deep intensity in his expression. "I'll be safe."

"You need to lie low for a while."

"What does that mean? What am I supposed to do?"

Knox shrugged, the casual gesture at odds with the steely determination in his gray eyes. "I figured I would keep you company."

Three

Selena looked less than thrilled by the prospect of sticking close to home while the situation with Will got sorted out.

Knox didn't particularly care whether or not Selena was thrilled. He wanted her safe. As far as he was concerned, this was some shady shit, and until it was resolved, he didn't want any of it getting near her.

All of it was weird. The five women who had been presented with nearly identical letters telling them that they had inherited Will's estate, and then Will not actually being dead. The fact that someone else had been living Will's life.

Maybe none of it would touch Selena. But there was nothing half so pressing in Knox's life as his best friend's safety.

His business did not require him to micromanage it. That was the perk of making billions, as far as he was concerned. You didn't have to be in an office all the damned time if it didn't suit you.

Plus, it was all…pointless.

He shook off the hollow feeling of his chest caving in on itself and turned his focus back to Selena.

"I don't need you to stay here with me," she said, all but scampering across the lawn and to her porch.

"I need to stay here with you," he returned. He was more than happy to make it about him. Because he knew she wouldn't be able to resist. She was worried about him. She didn't need to be. But she was. And if he played into that, then she would give him whatever he wanted.

"But it's a waste of your time," she pointed out, digging in her purse for her keys, pulling them out and jamming one of them in the lock.

"Maybe," he said. "But I swear to God, Selena, if I have to go to a funeral with a big picture of *you* up at the front of the room…"

"No one has threatened me," she said, turning the key and pushing the door open.

"And I'd rather not wait and see if someone does."

"You're being hypervigilant," she returned.

"Yes," he said. "I am." He gritted his teeth. "Some things you can't control, Selena. Some bad stuff you can't stop. But I'm not going to decide everything is fine here and risk losing you just because I went home earlier than I should have."

She looked up at him, the stubborn light in her eyes fading. "Okay. If you need to do this, that's fine."

Selena walked into the front entrance of the cabin and threw her purse down on an entryway table. Typical Selena. There was a hook right above the table, but she didn't hang the purse up. No. That extra step would be considered a waste of time in her estimation. Never mind that her disorganization often meant she spent extra time looking for things.

He looked around the spacious, bright room. It was clean. Surprisingly so.

"This place is… It's nice. Spotless."

"I have a housekeeper," she said, turning to face him, crossing her arms beneath her breasts and offering up a lopsided smile.

For a moment, just a moment, his eyes dipped down to examine those breasts. His gut tightened and he resolutely turned his focus back to her eyes. Selena was a woman. He had known that for a long time. But she wasn't a woman whose breasts concerned him. She never had been.

When they had met in college he had thought she was beautiful, sure. A man would have to be blind not to see that. But she had also been brittle. Skittish and damaged. And it had taken work on his part to forge a friendship with her.

Once he had become her friend, he had never wanted to do anything to compromise that bond. And if he had been a little jealous of Will Sanders somehow convincing her that marriage was worth the risk, Knox had never indulged that jealousy.

Then Will had hurt her, devastated her, divorced her. And after that, Selena had made her feelings about relationships pretty clear. Anyway, at that point, he had been serious about Cassandra, and then they had gotten married.

His friendship with Selena outlasted both of their marriages, and had proved that the decision he'd made back in college, to not examine her breasts, had been a solid one.

One he was going to hold to.

"Well, thank God for the housekeeper," he said, his tone dry. "Living all the way out here by yourself, if you didn't have someone taking care of you you'd be liable to die beneath a pile of your own clothes."

She huffed. "You don't know me, Knox."

"Oh, honey," he said, "I do."

A long, slow moment stretched between them and her olive skin was suddenly suffused with color. It probably wasn't nice of him to tease her about her propensity toward messiness. "Well," she said, her tone stiff. "I do have a guest room. And I suppose it would be unkind of me to send you packing back to Wyoming on your first night here in Royal."

"Downright mean," he said, schooling his expression into one of pure innocence. As much as he could manage.

It occurred to him then that the two of them hadn't really spent much time together in the past couple of years. And they hadn't spent time alone together in the past decade. He had been married to another woman, and even though his friendship with Selena had been platonic, and Cassandra had never expressed any jealousy toward her, it would have been stretching things a bit for him to spend the night at her place with no one else around.

"Well," she said, tossing her glossy black hair over her shoulder. "I am a little mean."

"Are you?"

She smiled broadly, the expression somewhere between a grin and a snarl. "It has been said."

"By who?" he asked, feeling instantly protective of her. She had always brought that out in him. Even though now it felt like a joke, that he could feel protective of anyone. He hadn't managed to protect the most important people in his life.

"I wasn't thinking of a particular incident," she responded, wandering toward the kitchen, kicking her shoes off as she went, leaving them right where she stepped out of them, like fuchsia afterthoughts.

"Did Will say you were mean?"

She turned to face him, cocking one dark brow. "Will didn't have strong feelings for me one way or the other, Knox. Certainly not in the time since the divorce." She began to bustle around the kitchen, and he leaned against the island, placing his hand on the high-gloss marble countertop, watching as she worked with efficiency, getting mugs and heating water. She was making tea, and she wasn't even asking him if he wanted any. She would simply present him with some. And he wouldn't drink it, because he didn't like tea.

A pretty familiar routine for the two of them.

"He put you pretty firmly off of marriage," Knox pointed out, "so I would say he's also not completely blameless."

"You're not supposed to speak ill of the dead. Or the undead, in Will's case."

He drummed his fingers on the counter. "You know, that does present an interesting question."

"What question is that?"

"Who died?" he asked.

"What do you mean?"

"There were ashes in that urn. Obviously they weren't Will's. But if he's not dead, then who is?"

Selena frowned. "Maybe no one's dead. Maybe it's ashes from a campfire."

"Why would someone go to all that trouble? Why would somebody go to that much trouble to fake Will's death? Or to fake anyone's death? Again, I think this has something to do with those letters. With all of the women in his life being made beneficiaries of his estate. And this is why I'm not leaving you here by yourself."

"Because you're a high-handed, difficult, surly, obnoxious…"

"Are you finished?"

"Just a second," she said, taking her kettle off the stove and pouring hot water into two of the mugs on the counter. "Irritating, overbearing…"

"Wealthy, handsome, incredibly generous."

"Yes, it's true," she said. "But I prefer beautiful to handsome. I mean, I assume you were offering up descriptions of me."

She shoved a mug in his direction, smiling brilliantly. He did not tell her he didn't want any. He did not remind her that he had told her at least fifteen times over the years that he did not drink tea. Instead, he curled his fingers around the mug and pulled it close, knowing she wouldn't realize he wasn't having any.

It was just one of her charming quirks. The fact that she could be totally oblivious to what was happening around her. Cast-off shoes in the middle of her floor were symptoms of it. It wasn't that Selena was an airhead; she was incredibly insightful, actually. It was just that her head seemed to continually be full of thoughts about what was next. Sometimes, all that thinking made it hard to keep her rooted in the present.

She rested her elbows on the counter, then placed her chin in her palms, looking suddenly much younger than she had only a moment ago. Reminding him of the girl he had known in college.

And along with that memory came an old urge. To reach out, to brush her hair out of her face, to trace the line of her lower lip with the edge of his thumb. To take a chance with all of her spiky indignation and press his mouth against hers.

Instead, he lifted his mug to his lips and took a long drink, the hot water and bitterly acidic tea burning his throat as he swallowed.

He really, really didn't like tea.

"You know," she said, tapping the side of her mug, straightening. "I do have a few projects you could work on around here. If you're going to stay with me."

"You're putting me to work?"

"Yes. If you're going to stay with me, you need to earn your keep."

"I'm earning my keep by guarding you."

"From a threat you don't even know exists."

"I know a few things," he said, holding up his hand and counting off each thing with his fingers. "I know someone is dead. I know you are mysteriously named as a beneficiary of a lot of money, as are a bunch of other women."

"And one assumes that we are no longer going to inherit any money since Will isn't dead."

"But someone wanted us all to think that he was. Hell, maybe somebody wanted him to be dead."

"Are you a private detective now? The high-end

health-food grocery-chain business not working out for you?"

"It's working out for me very well, actually. Which you know. And don't change the subject."

A smile tugged at the corner of her mouth.

He was genuinely concerned about her well-being; he wasn't making that up. But there was something else, too. Something holding him here. Or maybe it was just something keeping him from going back to Wyoming. He had avoided Royal, and Texas altogether, since his divorce. Had avoided going anywhere that reminded him of his former life. He'd owned the ranch in Jackson Hole for over a decade, but he, Cassandra and Eleanor hadn't spent as much time there as they had here.

Still, for some reason, now that he was back, the idea of returning to that gigantic ranch house in Wyoming to rattle around all by himself didn't seem appealing.

There was a reason he had gotten married. A reason he and Cassandra had started a family. It was what he had wanted. An answer to his lifetime of loneliness. To the deficit he had grown up with. He had wanted everything. A wife, children, money. All of those things that would keep him from feeling like he had back then.

But he had learned the hard way that children could be taken from you. That marriages crumbled. And that money didn't mean a damn thing in the end.

If he'd had a choice, if the universe would have asked him, he would have given up the money first.

Of course, he hadn't realized that until it was too late.

Not that there was any fixing it. Not that there had

been a choice. Cancer didn't care if you were a billionaire.

It didn't care if a little girl was your entire world.

Now all he had was a big empty house. One that currently had an invitation to a charity event on the fridge. An invitation he just couldn't deal with right now.

He looked back up at Selena. Yeah, staying here for a few days was definitely more appealing than heading straight back to Jackson Hole.

"Okay," he said. "What projects did you have in mind?"

He never said he didn't like tea.

That was Selena's first thought when she got up the next morning and set about making coffee for Knox and herself. Selena found it singularly odd that he never refused the tea. She served it to him sometimes just to see if he would. But he never did. He just sat there holding it. Which was funny, because Knox was not a passive man. Far from it.

In fact, in college, he had been her role model for that reason. He was authoritative. He asked for what he wanted. He went for what he wanted. And Selena had wanted to remake herself in his mold. She'd found him endlessly fascinating.

Though she had to admit, as she bustled around the kitchen, he was just as fascinating now. But now she had a much firmer grasp on what she wanted. On what was possible.

She had felt a little weird about him staying with her at first, which was old baggage creeping in. Old feelings. That crush she'd had on him in college that had never had a hope in hell of going anywhere. Not because she thought it was impossible for him to desire her, but because she knew there was no future in it. And she needed Knox as a friend much more than she needed him as a...well...the alternative.

But then last night, as they had been standing in the kitchen, she had looked at him. Really looked at him. Those lines between his brows were so deep, and his eyes were so incredibly...changed. Physically, she supposed he kind of looked the same, and yet he didn't. He was reduced. And it was a terrible thing to see a man like him reduced. But she couldn't blame him.

What happened with Eleanor had been such a shock. Such a horrible, hideous shock.

One day, she had been a normal, healthy toddler, and then she had been lethargic. Right after that came the cancer diagnosis, and in only a couple of months she was gone.

The entire situation had been surreal and heartbreaking. For her. And Eleanor wasn't even her child. But her friend's pain had been so real, so raw... She had no idea how he had coped with it, and now she could see that he hadn't really. That he still was trying to cope.

He hadn't come back to Texas since Eleanor's death, and she had seen him only a couple of times. At the funeral. And then when she had come to Jackson Hole in the summer for a visit. Otherwise...it had all been texts and emails and quick phone conversations.

But now that he was back in Texas, he seemed to need to stay for a little while, and she was happy for him to think it was for her. Happy to be the scapegoat so he could work through whatever emotional thing he needed to work through. Knox, in the past, would have been enraged at the assessment that he needed to work through anything emotionally. He was such a stoic guy, always had been.

But she knew he wouldn't even pretend there wasn't lingering damage from the loss of his little girl. Selena had watched him break apart completely at Eleanor's funeral. They had never talked about it again. She didn't think they ever would. But then, she supposed they didn't need to. They had shared the experience. That moment when he couldn't be strong anymore. When there was no child to be strong for, and when his wife had been off with her family, and there had simply been no reason for him to remain standing upright. Selena had been there for that moment.

If all the years of friendship hadn't bonded them, that moment would have done it all on its own.

Just thinking of it made her chest ache, and she shook off the feeling, going over to the coffee maker to pour herself a cup.

She wondered if Knox was still sleeping. He was going to be mad if he missed prime caffeination time.

She wandered out of the kitchen and into the living room just as the door to the guest bedroom opened and Knox walked out, pulling his T-shirt over his head—but not quickly enough. She caught a flash of muscled, tanned skin and…chest hair. Oh, the chest hair. Why was that compelling enough to stop her in her tracks? She didn't even have a moment to question it. She was too caught up. Too beset by the sight.

Genuinely. She was completely immobilized by the sight of her best friend's muscles.

It wasn't like she had never seen Knox shirtless before. But it had been a long time. And the last time, he had most definitely been married.

Not that she had forgotten he was hot when he was married to Cassandra. It was just that…he had been a married man. And that meant something to Selena. Because it meant something to him.

It had been a barrier, an insurmountable one, even bigger than that whole long-term friendship thing. And now it wasn't there. It just wasn't. He was walking out of the guest bedroom looking sleep rumpled and entirely too lickable. And there was just…nothing stopping them from doing what men and women did.

She'd had a million excuses for *not* doing that. For a long time. She didn't want to risk entanglements, didn't want to compromise her focus. Didn't want to risk pregnancy. Didn't have time for a relationship.

But she was in a place where those things were less of a concern. This house was symbolic of that change in her life. She was making a home. And making a home made her want to fill it. With art, with warmth, with knickknacks that spoke to her. With people.

She wondered, then. What it would be like to actually live with a man? To have one in her life? In her home? In her bed?

And just like that she was fantasizing about Knox in her bed. That body she had caught a glimpse of relaxing beneath her emerald green bedspread, his hands clasped behind his head, a satisfied smile on his face…

She sucked in a sharp breath and tried to get a hold of herself. "Coffee is ready," she said, grinning broadly, not feeling the grin at all.

"Good," he said, his voice rough from sleep.

It struck her then, just what an intimate thing that was. To hear someone's voice after they had been sleeping.

"Right this...way," she said, awkwardly beating a path into the kitchen, turning away from him quickly enough that she sloshed coffee over the edge of her cup.

"You have food for breakfast?" he asked, that voice persistently gravelly and interesting, and much less like her familiar friend's than she would like it to be. She needed some kind of familiarity to latch on to, something to blot out the vision of his muscles. But he wasn't giving her anything.

Jerk.

"No," she said, keeping her voice cheery. "I have coffee and spite for breakfast."

"Well, that's not going to work for me."

"I'm not sure what to tell you," she said, flinging open one of her cabinets and revealing her collection of cereal and biscotti. "Of course I have food for breakfast."

"Bacon? Eggs?"

"Do I look like a diner to you?" she asked.

"Not you personally. But I was hoping that your house might have more diner-like qualities."

"No," she said, opening up the fridge and rummaging around. "Well, what do you know? I *do* have eggs. And bacon. I get a delivery of groceries every week. From a certain grocery store."

He smiled, a lopsided grin that did something to her stomach. Something she was going to ignore and call hunger, because they were talking about bacon, and being hungry for bacon was much more palatable than being hungry for your best friend.

"I'll cook," he said.

"Oh no," she said, getting the package of bacon out of the fridge and handing it to Knox before bending back down and grabbing the carton of eggs and placing that in his other hand. "You don't have to cook."

"Why do I get the feeling that I really do have to cook?"

She shrugged. "It depends on whether you want bacon and eggs."

"Do you not know how to cook?"

"I know how to cook," she said. "But the odds of me actually cooking when I only have half of a cup of coffee in my system are basically none. Usually, I prefer to have sweets for breakfast. Hence, biscotti and breakfast cereals. However, I will sometimes eat bacon and eggs for dinner. Or I will eat bacon and eggs for breakfast if a handsome man fixes them for me."

He lifted a brow. "Oh, I see. So you have this in your fridge for when a man spends the night."

"Obviously. Since a man did just spend the night." Her face flushed. She knew exactly what he was imagining. And really, he had no idea.

That was not why she had the bacon and eggs. She had the bacon and eggs because sometimes she liked an easy dinner. But she didn't really mind if Knox thought she had more of a love life than she actually did.

Of course, now they were thinking about that kind of thing at the same time. Which was…weird. And possibly responsible for the strange electric current arcing between them.

"I'll cook," he said, breaking that arc and moving to the stove, getting out pans and bowls, cracking eggs with an efficiency she admired.

"Do you have an assignment list for me?" he asked, picking up the bowl and whisking the eggs inside.

Why was that sexy? What was happening? His broad shoulders and chest, those intensely muscled forearms, somehow seeming all the more masculine when he was scrambling eggs, of all things.

There was something about the very domestic action, and she couldn't figure out what it was. Maybe it was the contrast between masculinity and domesticity. Or maybe it was just because there had never been a man in her kitchen making breakfast.

She tried to look blasé, as though men made her breakfast every other weekend. After debauchery. Lots and lots of debauchery. She had a feeling she wasn't quite managing blasé, so she just took a sip of her coffee and stared at the white star that hung on her back wall, her homage to the Lone Star State. And currently, her salvation.

"Assignment list," she said, slamming her hands down on the countertop, breaking her reverie. She owed that star a thank-you for restoring her sanity. She'd just needed a moment of not looking at Knox. "Well, I want new hardware on those cabinets. The people who lived here before me had a few things that weren't really to my taste. That is one of them. Also, there are some things in an outbuilding the previous inhabitants left, and I want them moved out. Oh, and I want to get rid of the ceiling fan in the living room."

"I hope you're planning on paying me for this," he

said, dumping the eggs into the pan, a sizzling sound filling the room.

"Nope," she said, lifting her coffee mug to her lips.

Knox finished cooking, and somehow Selena managed not to swoon. So, that was good.

They didn't bother to go into her dining room. Instead they sat at the tall chairs around the island, and Selena looked down at her breakfast resolutely.

"Are you okay?"

"What?" She looked up, her eyes clashing with Knox's. "You keep asking me that."

"Because you keep acting like you might not be."

"Are you okay?"

"I'm alive," he responded. "As to being okay…that's not really part of my five-year plan."

"What's your five-year plan?"

"Not drink myself into a stupor. Keep my business running, because at some point I probably will be glad I still have it. That's about it."

"Well," she said softly, "you can add replacing my kitchen hardware to your five-year plan. But I would prefer it be on this side of it, rather than the back end."

He laughed, and she found that incredibly gratifying. Without thinking, she reached out and brushed her fingertips against his cheek, against his beard. She drew back quickly, wishing the impression of that touch would fade away. It didn't.

"Yes?" he asked.

"Are you keeping the beard?"

"It's not really a fashion statement. It's more evidence of personal neglect."

"Well, you haven't neglected your whole body," she said, thinking of that earlier flash of muscle. She immediately regretted her words. She regretted them more than she did touching his beard. And beard-touching was pretty damned inappropriate between friends. At least, she was pretty certain it was.

He lifted a brow and took a bite of bacon. "Elaborate."

"I'm just saying. You're in good shape, Knox. I noticed."

"Okay," he said slowly, setting the bacon down. His gray eyes were cool as they assessed her, but for some reason she felt heat pooling in her stomach.

Settle down.

Her body did not listen. It kept on being hot. And that heat bled into her cheeks. So she knew she was blushing brilliant rose for Knox's amusement.

"I'm just used to complimenting the men who make me breakfast," she said, doing her best to keep her voice deadpan.

"I see."

"So."

"So," he responded. "There's nothing to do other than work," he said. "Lifting hay bales, fixing fences, basically throwing heavy things around on the ranch. Then going back into the house and working out in the gym. It's all I do."

Well, that explained a few things. "I imagine you could carve out about five minutes to shave."

"Would you prefer that I did?"

"I don't have an opinion on your facial hair."

"You seem to have an opinion on my facial hair."

"I really don't. I had observations about your facial hair, but that's an entirely different thing."

"Somehow, I don't think it is."

"Well, you're entitled to your opinion. About my opinion on your facial hair. Or my lack of one. But that doesn't make it fact."

He shook his head. "You know, if I had you visiting in Jackson Hole I probably wouldn't work out so excessively. Your chatter would keep me busy."

"Hey," she said. "I don't chatter. I'm making conversation." Except, it sounded a whole lot like chatter, even to herself.

"Okay."

She made a coughing sound and stood up, taking her mostly empty plate to the sink and then making her way back toward the living room, stepping over her discarded high heels from yesterday. She heard the sound of Knox's bare feet on the floor behind her. And suddenly, the fact that he had bare feet seemed intimate.

You really have been a virgin for too long.

She grimaced, even as she chastised herself. She hated that word. She hated even thinking it. It implied a kind of innocence she didn't possess. Also, it felt young. She was not particularly young. She had just been busy. Busy, and resolutely opposed to relationships.

Still, the whole virginity thing had the terrible side effect of making rusty morning voices and bare feet seem intimate.

She looked up and out the window and saw her car in the driveway. "Hey," she said. "How did that happen?"

"I told you I was going to take care of it. Ye of little faith."

"Apparently, Knox, you can't even take care of your

beard, so why would I think you would take care of my car so efficiently?"

"Correction," he said. "I don't bother to make time to shave my beard. Why? Because I don't *have* to. Because I'm not beholden to anyone anymore."

Those words were hollow, even though he spoke them in a light tone. And no matter how he would try and spin it, he didn't feel it was a positive thing. It seemed desperately sad that nobody in his life cared whether or not he had a beard.

"I like it," she said finally.

She did. He was hot without one, too. He had one of those square Hollywood jaws and a perfectly proportioned chin. And if asked prior to seeing him with the beard, she would have said facial hair would have been like hiding his light under a bushel.

But in reality, the beard just made him look…more masculine. Untamed. Rugged. Sexy.

Yes. Sexy.

She cleared her throat. "Anyway," she said. "I won't talk about it anymore."

Suddenly, she realized Knox was standing much closer to her than she'd been aware of until a moment ago. She could smell some kind of masculine body wash and clean, male skin. And she could feel the heat radiating from his body. If she reached out, she wouldn't even have to stretch her arm out to press her palm against his chest. Or to touch his beard again, which she had already established was completely inappropriate, but she was thinking about it anyway.

"You like it?" he asked, his voice getting rougher, even more than it had been this morning when he had first woken up.

"I… Yes?"

"You're not sure?"

"No," she said, taking a step toward him, her feet acting entirely on their own and without permission from her brain. "No, I'm sure. I like it."

She felt weightless, breathless. She felt a little bit like leaning toward him and seeing what might happen if she closed that space between them. Seeing how that beard might feel if it was pressed against her cheek, what it might feel like if his mouth was pressed against hers…

She was insane. She was officially insane. She was checking out her friend. Her grieving friend who needed her to be supportive and not lecherous.

She shook her head and took a step back. "Thank you," she said. Instead of kissing him. Instead of doing anything crazy. "For making sure the car got back to me. Really, thank you for catching me when I passed out yesterday. I think I'm still…you know."

"No," he said, crossing his muscular arms over his broad chest. "I'm not sure that I do know."

Freaking Knox. Not helping her out at all. "I think I'm still a little bit spacey," she said.

"Understandable. Hey, direct me to your hardware, and I'll get started on that."

Okay, maybe he was going to help her out. She was going to take that lifeline with both hands. "I can do that," she said, and she rushed to oblige him.

Four

Knox was almost completely finished replacing the hardware in Selena's kitchen when the phone in his pocket vibrated. He frowned, the number coming up one he didn't recognize.

He answered it and lifted it to his ear. "Knox McCoy," he said.

"Hi there, Knox" came the sound of an older woman's voice on the other end of the line. She had a thick East Texas drawl and a steel thread winding through the greeting that indicated she wasn't one to waste a word or spare a feeling. "I'm Cora Lee. Will's stepmother. I'm not sure if he's ever mentioned me."

"Will and I haven't been close for the past decade or so," he said honestly. Really, the falling-out between Will and Selena had profoundly affected his friendship with the other man.

In divorces, friends chose sides. And his side had always clearly been Selena's.

"Still," Cora Lee said, "there's nothing like coming back from the dead to patch up old relationships. And, on that subject, I would like to have a small get-together to celebrate Will's return, just for those of us who were at the service. You can imagine that we're all thrilled."

If she was thrilled, Knox wouldn't have been able to tell by her tone of voice. She was more resolute. Determined. And he had a feeling that refusing her would be a lot like saying no to a drill sergeant.

"It will be kind of like a funeral, only celebrating that he's not dead. And you'll be invited. He said he wanted you to come."

"He did?"

"Not in so many words, but I feel like it is what he wants." And Knox had a feeling it wouldn't matter if Will did want it or not. Cora Lee was going to do exactly what she thought was best. "And he wants that ex-wife of his to come, too. He says you two are close."

"Which ex-wife?" He had gotten the distinct impression that there was more than one former Mrs. Sanders floating around.

"The one you're close to," Cora Lee responded, her voice deadpan.

Reluctantly, Knox decided he liked Will's stepmother. "Well, I'll let her know. She went to the funeral, so I imagine she'll want to go to this." He wasn't sure he particularly wanted to, but if Selena was going, then he would accompany her. He was honestly concerned that the other women who had been named beneficiaries, or whoever was responsible for sending the letter, might take advantage of a situation like this.

"Good. I'll put you both down on the guest list, and I'll send details along shortly. You have to come, because I wrote your names down and there will be too much brisket if you don't."

And with that, she hung up the phone. He looked down at the screen for a moment, and then Selena came in, her footsteps soft on the hardwood floor.

He looked up and his stomach tightened. Her long black hair was wet, as though she'd gotten out of the shower, and he suddenly became very aware of the fact that her gray T-shirt was clinging to her curves a little bit more than it might if her skin wasn't damp. Which put him in mind to think about the fact that her skin was damp, which meant it had been uncovered only a few moments before.

What the hell was wrong with him? He was thinking like a horny teenager. Yeah, it had been a few years since he'd had sex, but frankly, he hadn't wanted to. His libido had been hibernating, along with his desire to do basic things like shave his beard.

But somehow it seemed to be stirring to life again, and it was happening at a very inappropriate time, with an inappropriate person.

The good thing was that it must be happening around Selena because she was the only woman in proximity, and it was about time he started to feel again. The bad thing was... Selena was the only woman in proximity.

"Who was that on the phone?" she asked, running her fingers through her hair.

"Will's stepmother. She wants us to go to a non-funeral for him in a few days."

"Oh."

She was frowning, a small crinkle appearing on her otherwise smooth forehead.

"Something wrong?"

"No. It's a good thing. I'm glad to be asked. I mean, I was thinking, when I assumed he was dead, that it was so sad he and I had never...that we had never found a way to fix our friendship."

"You want to do that?" He was surprised.

"It seems silly to stay mad at somebody over something that happened so long ago. Something I know neither of us would change."

"The marriage?"

She laughed. "The divorce. I don't regret the divorce, so there's really no point in being upset about it. Or avoiding him forever because of it. I mean, obviously there was conflict surrounding it." She looked away, a strange, tight expression on her face. "But if neither of us would go back and change the outcome, I don't see why we can't let it go. I would like to let it go. It was terrible, thinking he was dead and knowing we had never reconciled."

Knox pressed his hand to his chest and rubbed the spot over his heart. It twinged a little. But that was nothing new. It did that sometimes. At first, he had thought he was having a heart attack. But then, in the beginning, it had been much worse. Suffocating, deep, sharp pain.

Something that took his breath away.

No one had ever told him that grief hurt. That it was a physical pain. That the depression that lingered on after would hurt all the way down to your bones. That sometimes you would wake up in the middle of the night and not be able to breathe.

Those were the kinds of things people didn't tell you. But then, there was no guidebook for loss like he had experienced. Actually, there was. There were tons of books about it. But there had been no reason in hell for him to go out and buy one. Not before it had happened, and then when Eleanor had gotten sick, he hadn't wanted to do doomsday preparation for the loss he still didn't want to believe was inevitable.

Afterward...

He was in the shit whether he wanted to be or not. So he didn't see the point of trying to figure out a way to navigate more elegantly through it. Shit was shit. There was no dressing it up.

There was just doing your best to put one foot in front of the other and walk on through.

But he had walked through it alone, and in the end that had been too much for him and Cassandra. But he hadn't known how to do it with another person. Hadn't really wanted to.

Hadn't known how he was supposed to look at the mother of his dead child and offer her comfort, tell her that everything was going to be okay, that *anything* was going to be okay.

But now they had disentangled themselves from each other, and still this thing Selena was talking about, this desire for reconciliation, just didn't resonate with him. He didn't want to talk to Cassandra. It was why they were divorced.

"It's not the same thing," she said, her voice suddenly taking on that soft, careful quality that appeared in people's tones when they were dancing around the subject of his loss. "Mine and Will's relationship. It's not the same as yours and Cassandra's. It's not the same as your divorce. Will and I were married for a year. We were young, we were selfish and we were stupid. The two of you... You built a life together. And then you lost it. You went through hell. It's just not the same thing. So don't think I'm lecturing you subtly on how you should call her or something."

"I didn't think that."

"You did a little. Or you were making yourself feel guilty about it, and that isn't fair. You don't deserve that."

She was looking at him with a sweet, freshly scrubbed openness that made his stomach go tight. Made him want to lift up his coffee mug and throw it down onto the tile, just to make the feeling stop. Made him want to grab hold of her face, hold her steady and kiss her mouth. So she would shut up. So she would stop being so understanding. So she would stop looking at him and seeing him. Seeing inside of him.

That thought, hot and destructive, made his veins feel full of fire rather than blood. And he wasn't sure anymore what his motivation actually was. To get her to stop, or to just exorcise the strange demon that seemed to have possessed him at some point between the moment he had held her in his arms on the floor of the funeral home and when they had come back here.

He had his life torn apart once, and he wasn't in a hurry to tear up the good that was left. At least, that was what he would have said, but this destructive urge had overtaken him. And his primary thought was to either break something or grab hold of her.

He needed to do more manual labor. Obviously.

"I'm not sure you're in a great position to speak

about what I do and don't deserve," he said, the words coming out harder than he'd intended.

"Except you're here at my house because you want to protect me, and you just replaced all my cabinet hardware, and it looks amazing. So I guess I would say you deserve pretty good things, since you're obviously a pretty good guy."

"Cabinet hardware isn't exactly a ringing endorsement on character," he said.

He needed to get some distance between them, because he was being a dick. It was uncalled-for. Selena wasn't responsible for his baggage. Not for making him feel better about it, not for carrying any of the weight.

"What about the work you need done outside?" he asked.

"Sorting through the shed. But we're going to need a truck for that."

"Do you have one?"

"I actually do. But I don't drive it very much."

"Why do you have a truck?"

"Extravagance?"

He didn't believe her, since Selena didn't do much for the sake of extravagance. If she had wanted to do something extravagant, he knew she could've gotten herself a big McMansion in town. Some eyesore at the end of a cul-de-sac. God knew she made enough money with that skin-care line of hers. But instead she had buried herself out here in the boonies, gotten herself this little cabin that wouldn't be extravagant by anyone's standard.

"To try and make friends," she said. "It's really helpful when you have something for people to use when they move. You'd be surprised how popular it makes you."

"Honey, this is Texas. I don't think there are enough people around without a pickup for that to be true."

"You'd be surprised," she said. "And my best friend hasn't been back to Texas in so long that I had to resort to making new friends any way I could."

Now she was making him feel guilty. As if he didn't already feel guilty about the illicit thoughts he'd just had about her.

"Well, you're probably better off," he said, keeping his tone light, brushing past her and heading out the front door.

To his chagrin, she followed him, scampering like a woodland creature out onto the porch behind him. "I don't know about that."

"Do you have the keys to the truck?"

"I can grab them," she said.

For some reason, he had a feeling she was stalling, and he couldn't figure out why. "Can I have them?"

"How about I go with you?"

"Don't you have other things to do? As you reminded me yesterday, you have your own money, and therefore don't need Will's estate, because you're a multimillionaire. Not from nothing, though. You actually run a giant business."

"We both do. And yet here we are. I can afford to take some time off to visit with you, Knox."

That made him feel like an ass. Because he was trying to put some distance between them.

All you do is put distance between yourself and people these days.

Well, he could do without that cutting observation from his own damn self.

"Fine." He didn't mean to grunt the word, but he did, and Selena pretended to ignore it as she went back in the house, reappearing a minute later with keys dangling from her fingertips.

She was grinning, to compensate for his scowl, he had a feeling.

"I will direct you to the truck," she said, keeping that grin sparkly and very much in place.

"You made it sound like you had an old pickup truck lying around," he said when they approached the shiny red and very new vehicle parked out back.

"I told you I bought it partly for extravagance. I couldn't resist."

Unlike himself, Selena had actually grown up with money, but he had always gotten the feeling her father had kept a tight leash on her. So whatever cash had been at her disposal hadn't really been hers; her life hadn't really been hers.

In contrast, he had grown up with nothing.

No support. No parent who had even bothered to try and be controlling, because they hadn't cared enough.

All in all, it was tough to say which of them had had it worse.

"Just because?"

"Because I do what I want," she said, confirming his earlier thought.

"Yes, you certainly do," he said.

She always had. From going to school, starting her own business, marrying Will when it had seemed like such a crazy thing to do. They had still been at Harvard at the time, and he hadn't seen the damned point in rushing anything.

But she had been determined. And when Selena Jacobs was determined, there was no stopping her.

"I'll drive," she said.

He reached out and snatched the keys from her hand. "I'll drive."

"It's my truck," she protested.

He paused, leaning down toward her, ignoring the tightening feeling in his stomach. And lower. "And I'm the man, baby."

She laughed in his face. He deserved it, he had to admit. But he was still fucking driving.

"That does not mean you get to drive."

"In this case it does," he said, jerking open the passenger-side door and holding it for her.

She gave him the evil eye, but got into the truck, sitting primly and waiting for him to close the door.

He rounded to the driver's side and got in, looking down at the cup holders, both of which contained two partly finished smoothies of indeterminate age. "Really?" he asked, looking down at the cups.

"I have a housekeeper," she said. "Not a truck keeper."

He grunted. "Now, where am I going?"

"You should have let me drive," she said, leaning toward him. And suddenly, it felt like high school. Being in the cab of the truck with a girl who made it difficult to breathe, knowing what he wanted to do next and knowing that he probably couldn't.

Except back then, he would have done the ill-advised thing. The dick-motivated thing. Because back then he didn't think too far ahead.

Well, except for two things. Getting the grades he needed for a scholarship to Harvard and getting laid.

Those things were a lot more compatible than people might realize. And the bad-boy facade made it easy to hide the fact that he was on a specific academic track. Which had been good, in his estimation. Because if he had failed and ended up pumping gas, no one would have been the wiser. No one would have known that he'd had a different dream. That he'd wanted anything at all beyond the small Texas town he had grown up in.

Fortunately, Harvard had worked out.

He had become a success, as far as everyone was concerned.

He wondered how they talked about him in Royal now. Probably a cautionary tale. Evidence of the fact that at the end of the day not even money could protect you from the harsh realities of life.

That you bled and hurt and died like everyone else.

All in all, it wasn't exactly the legend he had hoped to create for himself.

After Eleanor's funeral, someone had told him that you couldn't have everything. He had punched that person in the face.

"Just head that way," she said, waving her hand, clearly not too bothered with being specific in her directions.

He drove across the flat, bumpy property until he saw a shed in the distance, a small building that clearly predated the house by the river. He wondered if it had been the original home.

"Is this it?" he asked.

"If I were driving, you wouldn't have to ask."

"You are a prickly little cuss," he said, pulling up to the outbuilding and putting the truck in Park.

"It's good for the pores," she said, sniffing.

"So it's not all your magic Clarity skin care?"

"That works, too, but you know, a healthy lifestyle complements all skin-care regimens," she said, sounding arch. Then she smiled broadly, all white teeth and golden skin, looking every inch the savvy spokeswoman that she was.

"Question," he said as they got out of the truck.

"Possible answer," she quipped as the two of them walked to the shed.

"Why skin-care products? Is that your passion?"

"Why organic food?" she shot back.

"That's an easy answer," he returned. "That mom-and-pop place I used to go to for deli food when I had a late-night study session was doing crazy business. And it didn't make any sense to me why. When they wanted to retire, I ended up talking to the owner about the business. And how good food, health food, was an expanding market. I mean, I didn't care that it was healthy—I was in my early twenties. I just liked the macaroni and cheese. I didn't care that it was from a locally sourced dairy. So when the opportunity came to buy the shop, I took it. It was a risky business, and I knew it. It could have gone either way. But it ended up growing. And growing. And before I knew it, I owned a chain of grocery stores. And it became a billion-dollar industry. All because I liked the macaroni and cheese."

They got out of the truck, slamming the doors in tandem. He looked around at the scenery. He could see why Selena had bought the place. It was quiet. Remote, like his ranch in Wyoming. There was something to be said for that. For being able to go off grid. For being able to get some quiet.

"Now you," he said, prompting her.

She wrinkled her nose, twisting her lips to one side. "I guess it's similar for me. I knew I wanted a business that was mine. I knew I wanted to do something that was under my control. And I did a lot of research about profit margins and low overhead start-up. You know I got a business degree, and I also took all of that chemistry. Just as a minor. The two things are compatible. Skin care and chemistry. And like you said, natural organic products were on the upswing."

"So you're not particularly passionate about skin care."

She lifted a shoulder. "I find that you can easily become passionate about a great many different things. I love having my own money. I love controlling my life. I really like the fact that what I do empowers women in some regard. Skin care is not a necessity, but it's nice. When you feel good about yourself, I think you can do more with your life. Mostly, my passion is in the success." She smiled. "I feel like you can relate to that."

He wasn't sure. Things had changed for him so dramatically over the past few years. "Once you make a certain amount of money, though," he said, flinging the doors to the shed open, "it really is just more money."

"More security," she said. "All of this has to go." She waved a hand around as if it was a magic wand that might make the items disappear.

He looked down at her and smiled. She was such an imperious little thing. Sometimes he could definitely tell she had come from a wealthy family, a privileged background. She gave an order, and she expected to be followed. Or maybe that was just Selena.

"Not necessarily," he said, the words coming out a lot more heavily than he'd intended as he picked up what he thought might be part of an old rocking chair.

"I'm sorry" came Selena's muted reply. "I wasn't thinking when I said that."

"I wasn't thinking of the past either," he said. "It's just that money doesn't let you control the whole world, Selena. That's a fact."

"Well, my father sure thinks it does. And he thought he could use it to control me." She cleared her throat. "That was why… It was why I had to marry Will."

Those words hit him square in the chest, almost like one of the large stacks had fallen square on him. "What do you mean you had to marry him?"

"I just… My grandfather died my freshman year. Do you remember that?"

"Of course I remember that. You were distraught."

She sucked in a deep breath. "He was the only person who ever believed in me, Knox. He was the only person who acted like I could do something. Be something. I loved him. So much. He was also definitely an antique. And there was a trust fund. A trust fund that was set aside for me, but I couldn't access it until I was twenty-five, which was when he figured I would be an adult. Really."

"Twenty-five? That seems…"

"Or I could have gotten married." She looked up at him then, her eyes full of meaning. "Which is what I did."

Her meaning hit him with the force of a slap. He

was in shock. And the way he responded to that feeling was by getting mad. He growled and walked out of the shed, heading toward the pickup and flinging the piece of chair into the truck bed. Then he stalked back inside and picked up something else, didn't matter particularly to him what it was. "So you had to marry him because you needed the money?" he asked finally, his heart pounding so hard he was sure it would gallop out of his chest.

All this time he'd thought she'd fallen in love with Will. And that had truly put her off-limits, even after the marriage ended. She had chosen another man when Knox was right there. There wasn't a stronger way to telegraph disinterest.

Their friendship had been too important, way too important, to act on any attraction on his end. Particularly when she'd made it clear how she felt when she'd married Will.

Except she hadn't loved Will. Hadn't wanted him.

"Yes," she said. "I remember that you thought it was crazy when we got married. When we didn't just live together. Well, that was why."

"You didn't tell me," he said, his tone fierce and a hell of a lot angrier than he'd intended it to be. "I'm supposed to be your best friend, Selena, and you didn't tell me what was happening?"

"You had your own stuff, Knox. You were dealing with school. And you were on a scholarship to be there. I didn't want to do anything that would interfere with your grades. And that included bringing you into my drama."

"I was your best friend," he reiterated. "I've always taken your drama. That's how it works. How the hell could you underestimate me like that?" He shook his head. "No wonder the two of you got divorced. You married because of a trust fund."

"I don't want to rehash the past with you," she snarled, picking up a bicycle tire and stomping out of the shed. "It doesn't matter. It doesn't matter what happened between me and Will. Not now. The marriage ended, end of story. It was definitely a bad idea. Don't you think I know that? We divorced. It completely ruined our friendship."

"Why?"

"Are you and Cassandra friends?" she asked.

"No," he said. "But as you have pointed out several times, my marriage to Cassandra was not the same as your marriage to Will. So let's not pretend now. Why did it ruin your friendship with Will?"

She bristled visibly. "Because of Rich Lowell."

"That guy who used to follow Will around? The tool with the massive crush on you?"

"That tool only got interested in me when he thought Will was. And after we married he said some things to me... They didn't seem completely far-fetched. He asked me why Will would suddenly want me when...when he didn't before. He implied Will only wanted my money. Of course, Rich didn't know the details of the trust fund, he only knew I came from a wealthy family, but he made me question... Why would Will agree to marry me only to help me get my trust fund? It was so hard for me to believe he was doing it because he was my friend. That he was doing it because he cared about me. I couldn't imagine anyone doing that.

"When you grow up the way I did... When you

have to walk on eggshells around your father, you kind of fold in on yourself. And you focus on surviving. That was what I did. I became this creature who only knew how to scrabble forward. I was selfish, and I couldn't imagine anyone *not* being selfish. So when Rich asked me those questions…it just seemed more likely that Will wanted something from me than that he actually wanted to help me. I got mad at Will. I told him I didn't want anything to do with him. That if he thought he was getting any of my money he was completely insane." She laughed, the sound watery. "You know, that's why it was extra hilarious that he left me that inheritance. I mean, I guess he didn't. Because he wasn't dead. Because he didn't even really write the letter."

Knox had some sympathy for her. He truly did. Because he could remember Selena as she had been. It had been so hard for her to trust. So difficult for her to believe anyone wanted anything for her that wasn't a benefit to themselves.

For a kid from the wrong side of the tracks, knowing Selena had been somewhat eye-opening. He'd discovered that people who lived on the other side of the poverty line still had problems. They could be half-feral. They could be insecure. They could have real, serious life-and-death problems. He had always imagined that if he had money he could buy off all of life's bullshit. Meeting Selena had been his first realization that wasn't the case.

But even with the sympathy he felt, there was anger. So much damned anger. Because he hadn't deserved to be lied to for the better part of the last decade. She had never told him any of the truth, and he couldn't quite stomach that.

The nature of her relationship with Will had always been a secret from him.

He whirled around to face her and she squeaked, taking three steps backward, her shoulder blades butting against the side of the shed.

"You lied to me," he said.

"Well," she shot back, her acerbic tone reminding him of the past. "I didn't realize all of my baggage affected your daily life to this degree, Knox."

"You know it doesn't," he said.

"So why are you acting like it does? Why are you acting like it matters at all? It doesn't. It's ancient history. If I'm not upset about it anymore, then why are you?"

"Obviously, you and Will are upset about it, or the two of you would still speak to each other."

"The rift in our friendship has nothing to do with our divorce. It has everything to do with the fact that I accused him of being a gold digger." She sighed heavily. "You can imagine he was not thrilled with that. He pointed out that he didn't need money, of course. And I said being from rich parents didn't mean you didn't need money. I was exhibit A."

"I understand why that would bother him, but he couldn't forgive you for that? Will was not the kind of guy who took himself that seriously back then, and I can't imagine he's changed all that much in the years since."

She grimaced. "I never asked him to."

"You never asked him to forgive you?" he asked,

incredulous. "Even though you accused him of some-thing when he was trying to help you?"

She made a sound that was halfway between a growl and a squeak. "It doesn't matter."

"Then why are you so defensive about it?"

"Why are you acting like this? You're pissed because I didn't talk to you?"

"Because you didn't trust me," he said, moving nearer to her.

She shrank back slightly, turning her head. And her reaction just about sent him over the edge. He knew she'd had a rough past, but that was a long time ago. And he was not her father. He didn't use physical threats to intimidate women, and he had damn sure never done it to her.

He had been nothing but careful with her. And she had lied to him all these years about her feelings for Will. She hadn't trusted Knox back then. And she was acting like he might do something to hurt her now, when he was here because he wanted to make sure that she was safe and protected.

He reached out, gripping her chin with his thumb and forefinger, forcing her to look up at him. "Don't act like that," he said, his voice hard. "Don't look at me like I'm a damn stranger."

She tilted her chin up, her expression defiant. And then the wind picked up and he caught that sweet smell that spoke *Selena* to him. Lavender and the Texas breeze, and why the hell that should affect him, he didn't know. But it did.

"Then don't act like a stranger," she said.

His blood reached the boiling point then, and before he knew what he was doing, he had leaned in closer, his nose scant inches from hers. "I'm not acting like one," he said, his voice rough. "But I'm about to."

She had never really wanted Will. She had never chosen Will over Knox.

That changed things.

And then he closed the distance between them and pressed his lips to hers.

Five

Knox was kissing her.

She was sure she was dreaming. Except it was nothing like one of her typical dreams. In those fantasies—which she had always been quite ashamed of—they were always having some nice moment, and then he would capture her lips gently with his before pulling her into his warm, comforting embrace.

In those fantasies, he always looked at her with his lovely gray eyes, and they would soften with warmth and affection before he would lean in.

In this reality, his gray eyes had been hard. He had not been smiling at her. And his lips were… This was not a sweet foray over the line of friendship. No. This was some kind of barbarous conquering of her mouth by his.

This was an invasion. And there were no questions

being asked. He was still holding her chin, the impression of his thumb digging into her skin as he tugged down and opened her mouth wide, angling his head and dipping his tongue deep. Sliding it against hers. And she wanted to pull away. She wanted to be angry. Wanted to be indignant.

Because he was angry at her, and he'd been yelling at her. And she was angry at him. He had no right to question her when he had no real idea of what she had lived through. No real idea of what she'd been trying to escape.

Not when he had no idea that the reason she hadn't told him the truth wasn't because she didn't trust him, but because she didn't trust herself. Because what she had really wanted to do, even back then, was ask *Knox* to marry her. But she had known, deep down inside, that with him, a marriage could never be fake. That with him, she would always want everything. And his friendship was so special, she had never wanted to risk it.

Her feelings for him had always been big. Somehow, she had known instinctively that if she made him her husband it would be easy for him to become everything. As painful as it had been, as suspicious and horrible as she'd behaved with Will over their friendship…

Giving in to wanting Knox, to having him…that would have destroyed the girl she'd been.

So she'd kept a distance between them. She'd done what she'd had to do to guard her heart and their friendship. And now he was demolishing all of that good work. That restraint she had shown, that diligence she had practiced all these years.

She was furious. Something more than furious. Something deeper. Something that compelled her to do what she decided to do next.

She shifted, grabbing fistfuls of his shirt, and angled her head, tasting him.

Because it wasn't fair that he was the one who had done this. When she was the one who had spent so long behaving. When she was the one who had worked so hard to protect what they had—to protect herself.

He had no regard for her. No regard for her work.

And he had to be punished for that.

She nipped his lower lip and he growled, pressing his hard chest against her breasts as he pinned her to the side of the shed. He gathered her hands, easily wrapping one of his hands around both her wrists, holding them together and drawing her arms up over her head against the wall.

Bastard.

He was trying to take control of this. Trying to take control of her.

No. He was the one who was ruining things. He was the one ruining *them*. She hadn't gotten the chance to do it. She had been good. She had done her best. And now he wanted all the control?

No. Absolutely not.

She bit him again. This time her teeth scraped hard across his lower lip, and he growled louder, pressing her harder against the wall.

His teeth ran across the bottom of her lip. He nipped her. And somehow, the anger drained out of her.

There was something primal about having her best friend's tongue in her mouth. She had to simply surrender. That was all. Beginning and end.

A wave of emotion washed over her, a wave of need. The entire ocean she had been holding back for more than a decade.

Knox. It had always been Knox that she wanted. Always.

She had messed up everything when she married Will. *Everything.* And when they had divorced it had been too late. Knox had been with Cassandra. And their relationship had been real and serious.

That still bothered her. He had found something real with someone else. She never had.

It would never be the same. Because she had never… She had never loved anyone but him.

And he had loved someone else.

That internal admission hurt. More than that, it made her heart feel like it could shatter into a million pieces with each beat.

But then it just beat harder, faster as Knox shifted, curving his arm around her waist and drawing her against him. She could feel his hardness. Could feel the insistent press of him against her hip that told her this kiss wasn't about teaching her a lesson. Wasn't about anger.

Yes, it had started with anger. But now it was just need. Deep, carnal need between two people who knew each other. Two people who knew exactly what each had been through. There were no explanations required between her and Knox.

That isn't true. There are no explanations required on his end. But I haven't been honest with him. And he knows it. It's why he's angry.

She squeezed her eyes shut and ignored that internal admonishment, parting her lips and kissing Knox deeper, harder.

She was ready for this. Ready to let him undo her jeans, push them down her thighs and take her virginity right there against the side of the shed.

And there was a phrase she had never imagined herself thinking.

Her virginity. Oh, *damn it*. That would be a whole other conversation.

But then suddenly, the conversation became irrelevant, because Knox wrenched his mouth away from hers and wheeled back, his lips set in a grim line, those gray eyes harder than she could ever remember seeing them.

"What?" she asked, breathing heavily, trying to act as though her world hadn't just been tilted on its axis.

"What the hell?"

"You kissed me, Knox. You got mad at me and you kissed me. I'm sure there's some kind of Freudian horror that explains that kind of behavior, but I don't know it."

"You bit me," he pointed out.

"And you pinned my wrists against the wall." She gritted her teeth and turned away from him, hoping to hide the mounting color in her cheeks. Hoping he wouldn't know just how affected she had been by the whole thing. She was dying. Her heart was about to claw its way out of her mouth, her stomach was turning itself over, and she was so wet between her thighs she didn't think she would ever live down the embarrassment if he found out.

"I didn't realize," he said.

"That you pinned my hands?"

"That *that* was there."

"What? Attraction?" She tried to laugh. "You're a hot guy, Knox. And I'm not immune to that. I mean, maybe I'm not up to your usual standards…"

"What usual standards?" he asked. "I was married for ten years, Selena. I had one standard. The person I made vows to. I haven't been with anyone since."

"Oh," she said. "So I guess that explains it." Her stomach twisted in disappointment, then did a free fall down to her toes. "You are super hard up."

"I was angry," he said.

"Awesome," she said, planting her hands on her hips. "Angry and hard up apparently translates into kissing women you didn't know you were attracted to!"

"I knew I was attracted to you," he said. "But I don't dwell on it."

She paused for a moment, tilting her head to the side. "You…knew you were attracted to me."

"Yes. I have been. Since college. But there's never been any point in exploring that attraction, Selena. You were not in a space to take that on when we first met."

She knew what he was saying was true. She had been attracted to him from the moment they'd met, too, but she'd also built a big wall around herself for a reason.

"I wanted to focus on school," she said, the words sounding lame.

"Until Will and a trust fund came into play?"

"Whatever. You didn't make a move on me. And then our friendship became the thing. And…our friendship is still the thing." No point spilling her guts about what a sad, insecure person she was.

"Yes," he said.

"That's good. I can have sex with any guy," she said, waving her hand as if she had simply hundreds of men to choose from to satisfy her appetites. "You're my only best friend. You've known me for so long and let's just not… Let's not make it weird."

"I just think…"

"You haven't had sex in a while—I get it," she said. Which was pretty damned laughable since she hadn't had sex ever and he was the one who had jumped on her.

"I'd like to think there was more to it than that," he said. "Because there's more to us than that."

She lifted a shoulder. "Fine. Whatever. I'm not that bothered by it. It was just a kiss. Nothing I can't handle."

She was dying inside. Her head was spinning and she was sure she was close to passing out. She would be damned if she would betray all those feelings to him.

She felt like her top layer had been scraped back, like she was dangerously close to being exposed. All of her secrets. All of herself.

She cared about Knox, she really did, but she kept certain things to herself. And he was poking at them.

"So that's it?" he asked. "We kiss after all these years of friendship and you're fine."

"Would you rather I light myself on fire and jump into the river screaming?"

"No," he said closely, "and that's an awfully specific response."

"Knox," she said, "you don't want me to be anything but fine. Believe me. It's better for the two of us if we just move on like nothing happened. I don't think either of us needs this right now."

Or ever.

She wanted to hide. But she knew that if she did hide, it would only let him know how closely he'd delved into things she didn't want him anywhere near. Things she didn't want anyone near.

"Yeah," he said. "I guess so."

"You don't want to talk about our feelings, do you?" she asked, knowing she sounded testy.

"Absolutely not. I've had enough feelings for a lifetime."

"I'm right there with you. I don't have any interest in messing up a good friendship over a little bit of sex."

Knox walked past her, moving back into the shed. Then he paused, kicking his head back out of the doorway. "I agree with you, Selena, except for one little thing. With me, there wouldn't be anything little about the sex."

Knox wasn't sure what had driven him to make that parting comment to Selena after they had kissed against the shed wall. But she had been acting strange and skittish around him ever since.

Not that he could blame her. He had no idea what in hell he'd been thinking.

Except that even though he was angry at her, she also looked soft, and tempting, and delicious. Finding out she had violated his trust, that there were things about her he didn't know, made him feel like their friendship was not quite what he had imagined it was. And in light of that realization, it had been difficult for him to figure out why he shouldn't just kiss her.

Asshole reasoning, maybe, but it had all made perfect sense in the moment. In the moment when he had brought his lips down on hers.

Yeah, it had all made perfect sense then.

The next few days had been incredibly tense, in a way that things never usually were between them. But he could at least appreciate the tension as a distraction from his real life. It was strange, staying with Selena like this in close quarters—that kiss notwithstanding. Because it reminded him a lot of their Harvard days. It wasn't like he'd been blind to how gorgeous she was then. But he'd made a decision about how to treat their friendship, due in large part to Will.

In many ways that decision had made things simple. Though the kiss was complicated, it was nothing compared to loss or divorce or any of the other things he had been through since.

But now they had that party for Will, and they had to actually go be in public together. And she had to try and act like she was at ease with him rather than looking at him like he might bite her again.

Though *she* had started the biting.

Knox buttoned up his dark blue shirt and tried not to think overly hard about all the biting. And the fact that it had surprised him in a not-unpleasant way.

Damn. He really *did* need to find a woman.

But every time he thought about doing that he just felt tired. He didn't want to cruise bars. He didn't want to find strangers to hook up with.

If he was that desperate for an orgasm he could use his right hand.

He had been in love with Cassandra, once upon a time. Though it was hard to remember the good times. Not because they had faded into memory, but because they hurt.

They also ruined the idea of anonymous sex for him.

He was over that. Done with it. He knew what sex could be like when you *knew* someone. When you had a connection with them. He didn't have any interest in going back to the alternative.

He knew a lot of guys who would kill to be in his position. Away from the commitments of marriage. Knox just didn't see the appeal.

He had never found it monotonous to be with the same person. He had thought it offered far more than it took. To know somebody well enough that you could be confident they were asking for what they wanted. To just know what they wanted at a certain point.

He'd been with his wife for over a decade. The only woman for all that time. It had never seemed a chore to him.

The idea of hooking up—that seemed like a chore.

But damn, he needed to get laid. He was fantasizing about getting bitten by his best friend, so obviously something had to change.

That was the funny thing. Because while he remembered and appreciated the married sex he'd had with Cassandra, he didn't specifically fantasize about *her*. Possibly because she was bound up in something too painful for him to fully relive.

He and Cassandra were over. Done. Everything in him was done with what they'd had.

But he still found himself in the midst of a sex paradox.

He gritted his teeth, walked out of the bedroom he was occupying at Selena's and stopped still.

She was standing in the middle of the living room wearing a bright red dress that conformed to her glorious figure. Her long black hair was styled in loose waves around her shoulders, and she had a flower pinned on the side, part of her hair swept back off her face. She looked beautiful, and effortless, which he knew wasn't the case.

She had spent a good while affecting that look, but she did a damned good impression of someone who hadn't tried at all.

He wanted to kiss the crimson lip color right off her mouth. Wanted to pull her into his arms and relive the other day.

And he knew he couldn't. Knew he couldn't touch her again, and he couldn't look like he was standing there thinking about it, because they had to get to that party. And he had to manage to get there in one piece, without Selena chewing him up and spitting him out because he was acting like an ass.

He reached over and grabbed his black cowboy hat off the shelf by the door. "I'm ready," he said, positioning it on his head. "Are you?"

"You're wearing jeans," she said.

He lifted a brow. "I'm a cowboy, honey. We wear jeans to parties. Plus, it's Texas."

"I'm wearing *heels*," she said, sticking out one dainty foot and showing off the red stilettos and matching toenail polish on her feet. As if he hadn't already taken stock of that already, with great interest. "The least you could have done was throw on a pair of dress pants."

"I have cowboy boots on," he returned. Then he stuck his arm out, offering it to her. "You go with me as is or you go by yourself, babe. Up to you."

She sighed, an exasperated sound, and reached out, taking hold of his arm before moving to the front door with him. This was the first time she had touched him since the kiss. And damn it all if he didn't feel a hard shock of pleasure at the delicate contact of her hand against his arm, even though it was through fabric.

Selena, for her part, seemed unaffected. Or at least, she was doing a good impersonation of someone who was.

"I'll drive," she said, producing her keys and moving to her little red car before he could protest. He had a feeling he would hate butting up against Selena's temper right about now even more than he hated letting someone else drive, so he didn't fight her on it.

"You can drive in those shoes?" he asked when Selena turned the car out onto the highway.

She waved a hand. "You know, Ginger Rogers did everything Fred Astaire did backward and in heels. I can drive a car in stilettos, Knox," she said, her tone crisp and dry like a good Chardonnay.

He would like very much to take a sip of her.

"Good to know," he said.

"You're not impressed with my logic," she said, sounding petulant.

"The fox-trot isn't driving, so no."

"Don't worry, Knox." Her tone was the verbal equivalent of a pat on the head. "I'll get us there safely. You can be my navigator."

He grumbled. "Great."

"The Chekov to my Kirk."

"Come on," he said. "I'm Shatner. Everyone knows that."

She laughed. "No one knows that. Because it isn't true."

"Clearly I'm the captain of the starship *Enterprise*, Selena."

"O Captain! my Captain! I'm the one driving."

"Technically, as you are the one in red, I would be very concerned by the metaphor."

"This is going into serious nerd territory, Knox." She chuckled. "Do you remember we used to stay up all night with the old *Star Trek*, eating ice cream until we were sick when we were supposed to be having study group?"

"We studied," he said. "We all took it pretty seriously."

"Yeah," she said. "But at a certain point there was just no more retaining information, and we ended up vegging."

"Our college stories are pretty tame compared to some."

"Yeah," she said. "But I don't think you and I ever wanted to compromise our good standing at the university by smoking a lot of weed. We had to get out there and make our own futures. Away from our families."

"True," he returned.

"Which is why we are the successful ones. That's why we're the ones who have done so well."

He felt like he was falling into that great divide again. He wasn't sure what those words meant anymore. Hadn't been for some time. "I guess so."

Tough to think that he had spent all that time working like he had. Through school, and in business, only to reach existential crisis point by thirty-two. It was surprising. And a damn shame.

"Well," she said. "I think anyone who ever doubted us has been proved wrong. How about that?"

He shook his head, watching the familiar scenery fly by. It was so strange to be back here in Royal. He'd met Cassandra in Royal when visiting Will, and he'd decided he'd move there after college to be closer to her. They'd started their life here, their family.

He took it all in. The great green rolling hills and the strange twisty trees. So different from the mountainous terrain in Wyoming. So different from the jagged peaks that surrounded his ranch, which he'd always kept even during the time he'd lived in Royal. The ranch made him feel like he was closed in. Protected. In another place. In another world. Rather than back here where time seemed too harsh and real.

"True enough."

At least he had found a way to talk to Selena again. At least, they'd had a moment of connecting. A moment where the weirdness of the kiss hadn't been the only thing between them. They had a history. She'd known him as a college kid, out of step with the privileged people he was surrounded by, determined to use that opportunity to make something of himself. She'd known him as a newlywed, a new father, a grieving man. A newly single man.

Selena was one of the most important people in his life.

"I know you think you're the captain," she said softly. "Just like I know you don't like tea."

A jolt went down his spine. "What?"

"You don't like tea."

"I...know. I didn't think you knew. You serve it to me all the time."

"And you never say anything."

"My mama would have slapped me upside the head," he said.

He didn't talk about her much, and for good reason, really. WillaMae McCoy was a hard, brittle woman who had definite ideas about right and wrong, until it came to the men she shacked up with and the bottle of liquor she liked best to dull the heartache of losing them.

"Really?" Selena asked.

"Yes. She was big on 'Yes, ma'am,' 'No, ma'am.' Good posture and holding the door open for a lady. And I certainly wouldn't have been allowed to turn down a cup of tea."

"Even if you didn't like it?"

He lifted a shoulder. "Manners."

"Well. Don't do that with me. You can always tell me."

Finally, they arrived at Will's family ranch, the place decked out for a big party. The lights were all on inside the house and he could make out a faint glow coming from behind the place.

And just as he had told Selena, most of the men were in jeans and button-up shirts, wearing white or black cowboy hats. It was Texas. There was no call to put on a tie. Though some of the men wore bolos.

"You okay?" he asked. Because lost in all the strangeness of the past few days, lost in the revelation that Will and Selena had married for reasons other than love, had been the fact that Will was her ex-husband. And it was possible that—even though they had actually gotten married for the trust fund—she was still hurt by the entire thing.

She hadn't said she wasn't, and she had spent all these years avoiding Will. Seeing as she'd gone to his funeral, she'd imagined she'd missed the chance to ever connect with him again.

But look how that had turned out.

"I'm fine," she said, forcing a smile. "It's a good thing," she said. "Getting to see Will. I'm glad that I got this chance."

"All right," he said.

Without thinking, he rounded to her side of the car and opened the door for her, taking her hand and helping her out of the vehicle.

Then they walked into the party together. He placed his hand low on her back as he guided her through the front door of the massive ranch house. She whipped around to look at him, her eyes wide.

He removed his hand from her back. He hadn't even thought about it, how possessive a move it was. He had just done it. Because it had felt reasonable and right at the time.

He could tell by the expression on her face that it had actually been neither.

He stuffed his hand in his pocket.

The housekeeper greeted them and then ushered them out into the yard, where Cora Lee was waiting, greeting them with open arms and kisses on both cheeks.

When she pulled away, Knox had that sense again that she was the kind of woman you didn't want to cross. Sweet as pie, but there might be a razor blade buried in the filling.

Or at least, if there needed to be one, there would be.

"So good of you to come," she drawled.

"Of course," Selena said. "I'm just thrilled that Will is okay."

"So are we all, sugar," she said.

They moved back through the party and Selena shivered. He fought the urge to put his arm around her again. Obviously, she wasn't having that. Clearly, she was not open to him touching her. In spite of the fact that they had been friends for years.

It was that kiss.

And as he stood there, conscious of the newfound boundaries drawn in their relationship, he asked himself if he regretted that kiss.

No, sir. He sure as hell did not.

Because it had woken up some things inside of him he hadn't thought would ever wake up again.

And those thoughts put his mind back at the place it had been while he was getting ready for the party. He wasn't sure how he was going to move forward.

But maybe the desire for anonymous sex would come next.

He damn sure hoped so. Because relationships… Marriage. None of that was ever happening again.

And that, he realized, standing there in this crowded, loud Texas party with country music blaring over the speakers, was the real tragedy.

He had reached the point that so many people idealized. He had crawled out of the gutter, bloodied his knuckles getting there. He'd found love. He'd gotten married. He'd had a child.

And it had all come crashing down around him.

He knew what it looked like to achieve those things,

and he knew what it looked like standing on the other side of losing them.

They were nothing but heartbreak and rubble.

He didn't want them again. He just couldn't do it.

He took a step away from Selena. He was not going to touch her again. That much was certain.

Six

Selena felt Knox's withdrawal.

Although he had taken only a slight step to the side, she could sense that something had changed.

His eyes were distant. And he looked a lot more like the sad, wounded man she had first seen after his daughter's funeral than he looked like the friend she'd reminisced with in the car about their nerdy college life.

She started to say something, but he spotted someone they both knew from college and gave her a cursory hand gesture before walking away.

She felt deflated.

She knew she was acting a bit twitchy. But damn, Knox looked handsome in that outfit. In those jeans that hugged his muscular thighs and ass. And that hard place between those muscular thighs that she had felt pressed up against her body just the other day.

The cowboy hat. Oh, the cowboy hat always made her swoon. Cowboys weren't her type. If they were, she would have her pick. She lived in Texas.

No, sadly *Knox* was her type. And that had always been her tragedy.

She was brooding, and pretty darned openly, too, when her friend Scarlett McKittrick spotted her from across the lawn and headed her way. Scarlett being Scarlett, she *bounded* across the lawn, her eyes sparkling with determination in the dim light. She was like a caffeinated pixie, which was generally what Selena liked about her, but also part of why she'd been avoiding Scarlett since Knox had come to town. She didn't want her friend to grill her on why he was hanging around, or to start asking questions about what was happening between them. She'd end up telling Scarlett everything and confessing she wanted Knox. She just didn't want to have that conversation.

It made her feel a little guilty since Scarlett's adoption of her son had just been finalized and she knew Scarlett might feel like the baby was why Selena wasn't hanging around as much. But that wasn't the reason. She and Scarlett had been friends for years, even though the bond wasn't as intense as the one Selena shared with Knox, which was unsurprising, since Selena didn't secretly harbor fantasies about making out with Scarlett.

"Hi," Selena said, trying to sound bright.

"Hi, yourself," Scarlett said, her eyes assessing Selena in her overly perceptive manner. "I have escaped by myself for the evening, so I'm feeling good." She ran her hand through her short hair and grinned. "Thanks for asking."

"Sorry," Selena said. "I'm a terrible friend."

Scarlett waved a hand. "Yeah. A bit. But I'll live. What's happening with you and Knox?" The subject change nearly gave Selena whiplash.

"Nothing," Selena said, lying through her teeth.

"He seems… I mean, I haven't seen him *since*."

"I know," Selena said. "He's made himself scarce."

Scarlett bumped her with an elbow. "So have you recently."

"I'm sorry. I've been dealing with all the stuff with Will. And Knox came to stay at my house after the funeral that wasn't and he hasn't exactly left."

Scarlett's eyebrows shot up. "Really?"

"Yes," she said. "Don't go thinking weird ideas about it. There's nothing weird."

"If you say so. But he looked… He doesn't look good, Selena."

She took a deep breath of the warm night air, catching hints of whiskey and wildflowers, mingling with smoke from a campfire. "I know. He's not the same. But how could he be?"

"Yeah. I guess if he was, you'd be forced to think he was pretty callous. Or in denial."

Selena shook her head. "Well, I can say he's not in denial. He's pretty firmly rooted in reality."

Except for that kiss. That kiss had been a moment outside of reality. And it had been glorious.

"Anyway," Selena said, "he's feeling paranoid because of everything with Will. I mean, *someone* faked Will's death. And *someone* wanted me and everyone else at that memorial service. It's weird. And it is nice to have Knox here just in case anything goes down."

"Yeah. I questioned the wisdom of having a party

tonight, even though the only people Cora Lee invited
were those of us at the service when Will walked in.
But also, it's Texas, and at least eight percent of the
people here have a sidearm, so anyone who tried to
cause trouble would end up on the wrong side of a
shoot-out."

"No kidding."

"Hey," Scarlett said, obviously ready for a new
topic. "When are you guys coming out to Paradise
Farms? Or if you'd rather do something different, the
ranch next door to mine is doing a thing where you
can go glamping."

Selena blinked. "I'm sorry—what?"

"You know—" Scarlett waved her hand around "—
glamorous camping."

"I don't know anything about that. Mostly because
I don't know anything about camping, Scarlett. As
you well know."

"It's not like regular camping. Yes, you ride horses,
and go on one of the long trails that takes two full
days to complete, and there's an overnight check-
point. But the food that's included is amazing and
the tent that's set up is a really, really nice tent, luxurious even."

"I… I don't know." The idea of being alone with
Knox on an abandoned trail, riding horses, sleeping
under the stars—or under the canvas top of a very nice
tent—all seemed a little bit…fraught. And by fraught,
she meant it turned her on, which was probably a very
bad thing considering their situation.

"Well, think about it. It'd be a great way to take a
break from all the drama here in town. The invitation
is open. Because it's new, the schedule is really vacant.

And I know they'd be happy to have testimonials from both of you. You can come out to Paradise Farms and use my horses. Right now, people are bringing their own to ride the trail."

Selena tried to smile and not look like she was pondering Knox and close quarters too hard. "I'll think about it."

"Do that." Scarlett grinned. "And text me. I'm dying at home buried under diapers and things. Babies are a lot of work."

"Okay. I promise."

Scarlett shifted. "Okay. Well, do text me. And…if anything…comes up. If you need to talk about *anything*. Please remember that you can call me."

"I will. Promise."

That left Selena standing alone as Scarlett went off to talk to someone else. She tapped her fingers together, and a passing waiter thrust a jar of what she assumed was moonshine into her empty hands.

She leaned forward, sniffing gingerly, then drew her head back, wrinkling her nose.

"I'm surprised you came."

She turned to see Will Sanders, her ex-husband— sort of. They hadn't spoken in so long it was weird to have him here next to her, talking to her. And it also made the years feel like they had melted away. Like there had been no fight. No stupid marriage. No accusations. Like greed and money—her greed—had never come between them.

"Yeah," she said, "fancy meeting you here. Especially since I thought you were dead."

"I would've thought you were pretty psyched about my demise, gingersnap."

"I've never understood that nickname. I'm not a redhead."

He winked, but it was different somehow than it had been. "No, but you're spicy with a bit of bite."

"Right. I guess I bit you a time or two." But not the way she'd bitten Knox. Not the way Knox thought she might have bitten Will. Her mind was terminally in a gutter right now.

"Yeah. But that's water under the bridge. A lot is thrown into perspective when you've been through what I have." She examined him for the first time. The hard line of his jaw, the slightly sharper glint to his eyes. He was not the same man he'd been. That much was certain. She could make out faint scarring on his face and wondered how much surgery he'd had to have to get himself put back together. She'd heard someone mention that Will had been in a boating accident in Mexico and left for dead. He'd been recovering and trying to make his way home all this time.

She wondered if there was anything that could put his soul back together.

"I'm sorry," she said. "And that was so easy to say it makes me seriously question why I didn't do it earlier."

"I know why you didn't do it earlier. Because you were angry. Because you were scared. It's fine, Selena. I'm not the kind of guy you need in your life anyway."

"Oh, I know," she said. "But it would be nice to be on speaking terms with you."

"I'm sorry if I hurt you," he said.

"You did not hurt me," she said, making a scoffing sound.

"I thought that was why you got so angry at me. Because you were in love with me."

In spite of herself, in spite of the absurdity of the situation, Selena let out a crack of laughter. "Will Sanders, you thought I was in love with you?"

"Yes."

"You are so full of it!" she all but exploded. And for some reason, she felt lighter than she had in days. Weeks. *Years.* "I was not in love with you."

"You asked me to marry you to help you get your trust fund. And then you got mad at me…"

"Because I thought our friendship was too good to be true, Will. I didn't have it the easiest growing up. I didn't have people in my life I could trust. I trusted you. And when Rich planted that seed of doubt…"

Everything in Will's body went hard like granite. Right down to his expression and the line of his mouth. "Right. Well. Rich has a lot to answer for."

"I just…" She tapped the side of the jar. "I wanted so badly to believe that what we had was real friendship. I guess maybe that wasn't super common for you with women, but it meant something to me."

"So—" he frowned "—you weren't in love with me?"

She laughed. "No."

"Then why did you ask me to marry you? You could have just as easily asked Knox. Did I win a coin toss?"

Unbidden, her gaze drifted across the expanse of lawn, and her eyes found Knox. Effortlessly. Easily. Her eyes always went right to him.

"I see," he said, far too perceptive. Old Will would never have been so perceptive. "Well, this does make a few things clearer."

"I'm sorry I was such a terrible friend," she said. "I'm sorry I let my issues drive us apart. And I'm sorry

I listened to Rich when you had never given me a reason to mistrust you. You would make a horrible gold digger, Will, and I see that now."

"Yeah, well, nothing like dying and coming back to life to make people think better of you," he commented. "Of course…the thing with my life at the moment is I can't have it back."

"What?"

"Someone has been living it for me, Selena. I didn't write you that letter. I didn't write letters to anyone."

"Will…" She stared at him, at the changes in his face. "What happened, Will?"

"Not talking about that yet," he said, his voice tight. "I don't know what's actually going on and until then… until then I'm just keeping watch on everything."

Silence settled between them, and Selena swallowed hard and nodded. "Well…well, I'm glad you're okay. And I'm really glad you're not dead."

Suddenly he smiled, and she thought she saw a glimpse of the Will she'd once known. "You know, when this is over I think I'm going to start a line of greeting cards. The Awkwardly Interrupted Funeral line. *So glad you're not dead. Hey, you rose from the grave and it's not even Easter.*"

"That sounds great," she responded, laughing.

Well, at least one relationship in her life wasn't a total mess.

"I have to make the rounds. As a reanimated corpse, I'm extremely popular." He stuffed his hands in his pockets and winked again. It seemed a little try hard at that point, but she could understand.

Will's life couldn't be totally normal at the moment, all things considered.

"Great," she said, a smile tugging at her lips.

She wrapped her arms around herself and looked at who was attending the party. She caught sight of Will's stepbrother Jesse Navarro, who was always a dark and sullen presence. Selena didn't know him personally, but she knew of him. She had moved to Royal after college, lured by Will's tales of it as some sort of promised land.

And it always had been for her. She'd found a sense of home here. Part of that was because at first she'd had Knox, since she and Will hadn't been on speaking terms. But even after Knox had left…

The town was special to her. Even if she was a latecomer.

She had seen Jesse at events before. Even without being a member of the Texas Cattleman's Club, it was impossible to move in the moneyed circles in Royal and not have some clue about who the people were in your age bracket.

She also saw the woman who'd had the child at Will's funeral. And she wondered if that was Will's baby. Wondered if she knew the truth about anyone.

Because the fact remained that if Will was the one responsible for all that heartbreak she'd been standing in the middle of at the funeral, as much as she might like him, he had a lot to answer for. A lot to atone for, now that he was back.

Suddenly, Jesse's gaze landed on that woman, and his eyes sizzled with heat.

Selena felt like she had to look away, like she was witnessing an intimate moment.

When she looked back, whatever connection she

thought she'd spotted seemed to be gone. And the woman hadn't seemed to notice at all.

She looked around again, trying to get a visual on Knox, and saw that he was gone. Then she saw a figure standing just outside the lights on the lawn, holding a bottle of beer. She knew that was him. She knew him by silhouette. That wasn't problematic at all.

She ditched the moonshine in the jar and reached for a bottle of her own beer, walking gingerly across the grass in her heels, making her way to where he was standing.

"Hi," she said.

He didn't jump. Didn't turn. As if he had already sensed her. That thought made the back of her neck prickle. Was he as aware of her as she was of him?

"Hi," he returned, lifting his bottle of beer to his lips. He took a long, slow pull. And she was grateful for the shroud of darkness. Because had it not been so dark, she would've watched the way his lips curved around the bottle, would have watched the way his Adam's apple moved as he swallowed the liquid.

And her whole body would have burned up. A lot like it was doing now, just imagining such things.

"I talked to Will," she said.

"Did you?" he asked, the words laden with a bite.

"I think we made amends, for what that's worth. It was something that needed to happen. There's a lot of stuff in my past, and I'm all bound up in it. No matter how successful I get, no matter how far I move forward, it's just there."

He lifted a shoulder. "I can relate to that."

Except she knew he was talking about something a lot more grave, and she felt instantly guilty.

"Why aren't you at the party? Don't you want to talk to Will?"

"I decided I wasn't really in a party mood once everything got going."

"All right." She wrapped her arms around herself to keep from wrapping her arms around him. "Do you want to leave?"

"That's fine. If you're having fun."

"I'm not sure I would call laying a ghost to rest fun. Just potentially necessary."

"Right."

Then she did reach out and touch him. Her fingertips brushed his shoulder, and she felt the contact down to her stomach, making it clench tight. "Knox."

His name was a whisper, a plea. But she didn't know what for. For normalcy? For an explosion?

His muscles tensed beneath her touch, and she felt like her stomach had been scooped out. Felt like she had been left hollow and wanting, aching for something that only he could give her.

She remembered what it felt like when his mouth pressed against hers. Finally, after all that time. She had kissed other men. Half-hearted attempts at finding a way she could be attracted to somebody who wasn't her best friend. It had never worked. It had never excited her.

This kiss haunted her dreams. It haunted her now.

She wanted to kiss him. She wanted to give him comfort. In any way she could. And they were out here in the darkness on the edge of this party. Where Will Sanders had come back from the dead and everything was just freaking crazy.

So she decided to be crazy, too. She slid her hand

upward to his neck, curving her fingers around his nape. And then she brought herself around to the front of him, placing her palm on his chest, directly over his heart, where it was raging hard and fast.

"Selena," he said, a word of warning. A warning she wasn't going to heed.

She stretched up on her tiptoes—because she was still too short to just kiss him, even in these heels—and a rush of pleasure flooded her, a rush of relief, the moment their mouths met.

She was lost in it. In the torrent of desire that overtook her completely as his scent, his flavor, flooded her senses.

It was *everything*. It was everything she remembered and more. Kissing him was like nothing else. It was like every fantasy colliding into one brilliant blinding firework.

Oh, how she wanted him. How she wanted this. She wrapped her arms around his neck, still clutching the bottle of beer tightly, and then he dropped his bottle, grabbing hold of her hips with both hands and tugging her heat against his muscular body. She could feel his arousal pressing against her stomach, and she wanted…she wanted to ride it.

She wanted to ride *him*.

"Please," she whispered.

She didn't know what she was begging for, only that if she didn't get it she would die.

He moved one hand down to her side, then down her lower hip around to the back of her knee. Then he lifted her leg and drew it up over his hip, opening her to that blunt masculine part of him.

She gasped and tilted her hips forward, groaning

when a shot of pleasure worked its way through her body. She tilted forward, riding the wave of pleasure. Allowing herself to get caught up in this. In the rapturous glory of his mouth on hers, of his hard, incredible masculinity.

She would let him take her here, she realized. Let him strip her naked on the edges of this party and lay her down in the damp grass. Sweep her panties to the side and thrust inside of her, even though she'd never let another man do it before. She wasn't afraid. Not even remotely.

This was Knox McCoy and she trusted him with all that she was. Trusted him with her body.

I don't trust him. There's so much I haven't told him.

But if she told him everything, then he wouldn't look at her the same. What if he saw the same abused girl she always saw when she looked in the mirror, rather than the confident businesswoman she had become?

She couldn't stand for that to happen. She truly couldn't.

So maybe if there was this first. Maybe they could both find something in it. Something they needed.

He drew away from her, suddenly, sharply, his chest heaving with effort. She wished she could see his face. Wished she could read his expression. Then he slowly released his hold on her thigh, and she slid an inch or so down his body. Not the most elegant dismount, that was for sure. She was grateful for the darkness, because he couldn't see the fierce blush in her cheeks, couldn't get an accurate read on the full horror moving through her at the moment.

"I'm not sorry," she said, pulling her dress back into place.

"Did I ask you to be?" he bit out, his words hard.

"No," she said, "but you stopped."

"I stopped because I was close to fucking you right here at a party. Is that what you want?"

"I…" She was dizzy. She couldn't believe she was standing here listening to her friend say those words, directed at her. "That's a complicated question, Knox."

"No." He shook his head. "It's really not. Either you want to get fucked on the ground at a party by your best friend or you don't."

She looked away, feeling self-conscious even though she knew he couldn't see her expression. "Maybe not…on the ground…at a *party.*"

"Selena," he said, gripping her chin, leaning forward and gazing at her with his dark, blazing eyes. "I can't give you anything. I can't give you anything other than sex."

"I didn't ask you for anything," she said, her voice small.

"We're friends. And that means I care about you. But I'm never, ever getting married again."

"It's kind of a long leap from fucking in the grass to a marriage proposal, don't you think, Knox?" she asked, self-protection making her snarky, because she needed something to put distance between them.

"I just meant this doesn't end anywhere but sex, baby. And I need our friendship. I haven't had a lot of bright spots in my life lately, and I hate to lose the one I have."

"But you want me," she said, not feeling at all awkward about laying that out there. Because he did. And she knew it.

"That doesn't mean having."

And then he just walked away. Walked away like they were in the middle of having a conversation. Like her heart wasn't still pounding so hard it was likely to go straight through her chest. Like she wasn't wet and aching for satisfaction that he had denied her, yet again.

And that was when she made a decision. She was going to have Knox McCoy. Because there was no going back now. They wanted each other. And she had been holding on to all those feelings for him for so long that she knew a couple of things for certain. They weren't going away, and no man could take his place as it was.

She had known a lot of girls in college who had thought they needed to get certain guys out of their systems, which had always seemed to her a fancy way to excuse having sex when you wanted it, even though you knew it was a really bad idea and the guy was never going to call. It had always ended in sadness, as far as she had seen.

But Knox had been in her system for so long, and there was no other way he was getting out of it. She knew that. This wasn't a guy she had met in class a few weeks ago, a guy she had exchanged numbers with at a party.

She had known Knox for the better part of her adult life and she wasn't just going to wake up one morning and not want him.

So maybe this was the way forward.

She pulled her phone out, still not ready to go back

to the party, to go back into the lights where people might see her emotional state. Where they might be able to read what had just happened. And she texted Scarlett.

So, about that glamping.

Seven

Knox had stuck it out at the party just to be a stubborn cuss. By the time he and Selena got back in the car and started to drive to the ranch, he expected her to unleash hell on him.

Instead, she didn't. Instead, she was silent the entire way, and he didn't like that. He didn't like it at all. He'd enough of hard, sad silences. He preferred to be screamed at, frankly. But Selena didn't seem to be in the mood to give him what he wanted.

And he said nothing.

Then when they pulled in the driveway and finally got out, heading into the house, she spoke. "We're going glamping tomorrow," she said, her expression neutral, but vaguely mischievous.

"What?"

"Scarlett suggested it. We're going on a trail ride. And we are staying overnight in a luxury tent."

"I was going to head back to Jackson Hole," he said, lying, because he had no plans to do that at all. And for the first time, he questioned why.

He didn't like that all these interactions with Selena forced him to do things like ponder his motivations.

"I don't care. Change your ticket. You're rich as God, Knox. It's not like it's a problem."

"No," he said slowly.

"You're coming glamping with me, because you're still not okay, I'm clearly not okay, and we need to do something to get back on track. We are not leaving our friendship here. You are not going off to Wyoming for however the hell long and not seeing me. Because it's going to turn into not seeing me for months, for years, as we avoid all the weirdness that has sprung up between us."

Oh, he was personally all right with avoiding the weirdness. But obviously, she wasn't.

"Okay," he found himself agreeing, and he couldn't quite fathom why.

"It'll be fun," she said, grinning at him, all teeth. And it made him damn suspicious.

"I'm not overly familiar with fun," he said, purposefully making his tone grave.

"Well," she said, "this will be."

He had his doubts, but he also knew Selena Jacobs on a mission was not a creature to be trifled with. And not one easily derailed.

So they would go on a trail ride. They would go camping.

Once upon a time he'd liked to ride, he'd liked to camp. Why the hell not?

Maybe she was right. Maybe it would remind him of some of the things he used to like.

Although, privately, he feared that it would go much the same way as the party had gone. That all it would do was reinforce the fact that he couldn't enjoy things the way he used to. That he had nothing left to look forward to in his life.

Because he couldn't think of a single dream he hadn't achieved. Then two of them he lost. And one of them just didn't mean a thing without the others.

And he had no idea where the hell you went from there.

Camping, it seemed.

He shook his head and followed Selena into the house.

By the time they were saddled up and ready to ride, Selena was starting to have some doubts. But not enough to turn back.

They were given a map and detailed instructions on how the trail ride would work, and then she and Knox were sent off into the Texas wilderness together. Alone, except for each other.

And the condoms Selena had stuck in her bag.

Because this was a seduction mission more than it was anything else, and she was completely ready to go there.

Well, except for the nerves. And the doubts. There were those. But that was all virgin stuff.

Oh, and the fact that she was going to see her best friend's penis.

The thought made her simultaneously want to giggle and squeeze her thighs together to quell the ache there.

Her cheeks heated as she realized the rhythm of the horse's gait did a little something for it. Her face flamed, her whole body getting warm.

Knox McCoy had turned her into a sex-crazed pervert. And they hadn't even had sex yet.

He might not want to have sex with me.

Yes, that was the risk. She might get Knox alone in a tent, around a romantic campfire, and she might strip herself completely naked and get denied. It was possible. It was not a possibility she was hoping for. But it might happen. The idea did not thrill her.

But there was no great achievement without great risk. And anyway, if there was one thing she had kind of learned from this whole experience with Will's death-that-was-not-actually-a-death, it was that time was finite.

She had stood at Will's funeral and had regretted leaving things bad between them. She didn't want to regret Knox.

Somewhere in the back of her mind she knew that if this ruined her friendship with Knox she was going to regret that. She was going to regret it a whole hell of a lot. But at least she wouldn't wonder. Right now, it seemed worth the risk.

Maybe on the other side it wouldn't. But she wasn't on the other side yet.

She squared her shoulders and they continued to ride down the trail.

It was beautiful. The land was sparse, filled with scrub brush and twisty, gnarled trees that were green in defiance to their surroundings. She had been told that the trail would wind toward some water, and that it would get shadier and greener there, which was why it was good to do this leg early in the morning, before the sun rose high in the sky and the heat and humidity started to get oppressive.

But the view around her wasn't her primary reason for being here, anyway. It was him. It was Knox.

"So," she said, "it's nice out."

"Yeah," he responded, taciturn like he had been last night.

It was funny, how she had gone from the one being all angry about the kiss to him being all angry. What a delight.

She hoped that banging him was slightly more delightful.

The thought made her nerves twitch.

"So, how many hours is it to camp?" he asked.

"About six," she said.

"That seems a little bit crazy," he responded.

"I know," she said, and then she frowned. Because she hadn't really considered that. The fact that she was going to launch a full-out seduction after having been on the back of a horse all day. Honestly, there was a sweat situation that might be problematic. Not that she minded if he was sweaty. She was all okay with that. It was pheromones or something. She had always liked the way Knox smelled when he'd been sweating. After he had gone for a run in college and he would come back to hang at her dorm for a while, steal some food off her and her roommate. He had walked by her, and her stomach would go into a free fall.

It was so funny, how she had buried that reaction

down deep, and how it was all coming up now. Bringing itself into the light, really.

She had been in full denial of her feelings for him for so long. While she had definitely known they were there, she didn't focus on them. But now she was admitting everything to herself. That she was a sucker for the way he smelled. That his voice skimmed over her skin like a touch. That in so many ways she had been waiting for him. Waiting for this. And that excuses about how busy she was, how important the company was, were not really the reasons why she didn't date.

It was because no man was Knox, and never would be.

As she made idle chatter for the rest of the ride, she fought against cloying terror. She was headed toward what was her undeniable destiny and almost certain heartbreak.

But she'd come too far to turn back now. She simply couldn't.

Eventually, they did come to that river, and they found themselves beneath the canopy of trees as the sun rose high in the sky. They arrived at camp before the sun began to set, a glorious, serene tent out in the middle of nowhere right next to the river.

There were Texas bluebells in the grass that surrounded it. A little oasis just for them. There was a fire pit, places to sit. It really was the most civilized camping she had ever seen.

"I am going to jump in the river," Knox said. He got off the horse and stripped his shirt off over his head.

And she froze. Just absolutely froze as the shirt's fabric slowly rolled up over his torso and revealed his body.

Lord, what a body.

"What?" he asked.

Well, great. She'd been caught staring openly. At her friend's half-naked body. Talk about telegraphing her seduction plans.

"Nothing." She blinked. "I'll go… We can get the horses settled and then I'll get my swimsuit."

But her gaze was fully fixed on his broad, bare chest. On all those fantastic, perfect muscles. Which she had felt through his shirt a time or two in the past few days. But now… Seeing it like that, dusted with just the right amount of pale hair, glistening with sweat… She wanted to lick him.

She imagined the rules of friendship generally prevented that. But she was fully violating those anyway, so she was just going to embrace the feeling.

"Come on," he said, nodding once. "Let's get the horses into the corral."

She went through the motions of leading the horses into the gated area and making sure there was fresh water in the trough, but really, she was just watching Knox.

The way the sun glinted on his golden hair and highlighted the scruff on his face—she wanted so badly to run her fingers over it. The way the muscles in his forearms went taut as he removed the horses' bridles and saddles…

He bent down low, setting about cleaning their hooves, his body putting on a glorious play of strength and sculpted masculinity that took her breath away.

He was such a familiar sight. But in context with desire, with what she wanted to have happen later, he was like a stranger. And that both thrilled and excited her.

When they finished taking care of the animals, he straightened, and she was momentarily struck dumb again by his beauty. It was a wonder she'd ever managed to get to know the guy. His looks were a serious barrier to her ability to form cogent thoughts and words that were more than noises.

"Why don't you go on in and get your suit?" he asked, handing her her pack.

His fingers brushed against hers and she felt the touch like a bolt of lightning. All the way through her body.

Selena scurried into the tent, barely able to take in the glory of it. There was an actual bed inside, seating, a woodstove, all surrounded by beautifully draped canvas. The bed was covered in furs and other soft, sumptuous things. It was the perfect place to make love to a man you had been fantasizing about all of your life.

And when darkness fell, she was going to do just that.

The corners of her lips turned upward when she realized there was only one bed in the place. And she wondered if Scarlett was matchmaking. If Selena had been that damned transparent. She changed quickly into a black bikini, ignoring the moment of wishing it covered more of her body, and headed outside.

She was gratified when Knox's expression took on that similar "hit with a shovel" quality she had been pretty sure her own had possessed a few moments ago when he had stripped off his shirt.

"Nice suit," he said.

He was wearing a pair of swim shorts that she wondered if he'd been wearing beneath everything else the whole time. Or if he had just quickly gotten naked outside.

And then she thought way too long and hard about that.

"Thank you," she said.

The shorts rode low, revealing every sculpted line just above that part of him that was still a mystery to her. She was doing her best not to look like a guppy spit out onto the shore. Gaping and gasping. She had a feeling she was only semi-successful.

"There's only one bed," she commented. "I didn't realize that."

As if that mattered. She was planning to seduce him anyway.

"Oh," he said. "Well, I can sleep on the floor."

"Let's worry about that later," she said, because she hoped that both of them would be completely all right with the fact that there was only one bed just a little bit later.

They went down toward the river, and in spite of the heat, when she stuck her toe in the slow-moving water, she shuddered slightly.

"Oh, come on," he said. "It's not that cold."

As if to demonstrate all of his masculine bravado, he went straight into the water, wading in up to his hips and then lying flat on his stomach and paddling out toward the center of the wide body of water.

She took a deep breath and followed suit, screeching as the water made contact with the tender skin on her stomach. "It is cold," she shouted at him.

"You're a baby," he responded, turning over onto his back and paddling away from her.

"I am not a baby," she said. She swam toward him and then splashed at him. He laughed, reaching out and grabbing her wrist, drawing her against him. She didn't know what the intent had been. Maybe to stop her from splashing him, but suddenly, her legs were all tangled up with his and her breasts were pressed against his bare chest. The wet swimsuit fabric did absolutely nothing to provide a barrier between them. Her nipples were hard, sensitive, partly from the chill of the water and partly just from him. From her desire for him.

"Knox," she said. "If you don't like it, tell me. I don't want to be tea."

"You're not tea," he said.

"Good. I'd hate for you to sleep with me because of good manners. A girl wants to be wanted."

And something in his eyes changed. His jaw was tight, the lines by his mouth drawn, deep. And she could see the struggle there. The fight.

"I don't need forever," she said. Her seduction plan had just gone out the window. This electricity between them was sparking right now. And she was going to make the most of it. She was going to take it. "I just need you. For a little while. I've wanted you… Always. I have. This isn't new for me. And it's not going away." She raised her hands, trusting him, trusting his strong, steady hold to keep her afloat. She traced those deep lines on either side of his lips with her thumbs, stroking him. Touching him the way she had always dreamed about touching him. Freely, without holding back.

That was the sad thing. She felt a whole hell of a lot for him, and yet she'd always, always held it back, held back a part of herself.

She was tired of that. And she was surrounded by reminders of why it was wrong. Time wasn't infinite. She'd thought she'd missed a chance to apologize to Will.

She wasn't going to miss this chance.

"You want this?" he asked, his voice rough. "You want me right now? Let me tell you, Selena, all I can give you is selfish. I haven't had sex in two years. A little bit more, maybe. Because it's not like there was a whole lot going on during the divorce. During the grief. And I… I don't have any control left in me. I wanted to do the right thing. I wanted to be honest with you about what I could and couldn't give you, but if you keep offering it to me…"

"If I keep offering it to you then you need to trust me." She met his gaze and held it. Tried to ignore her breathlessness, her nerves. "I'm your friend. I've been your friend for a long time. Haven't I always taken what you've given to me? Haven't we always been there for each other? That's what this is. I want to be there for you. And I want this, too. This isn't pity sex, Knox. I want it. I want you. I think you want me. So let's… Let's just trust that we'll find our way. Because we are friends. We've been through hell together. It wasn't my hell, Knox, but I walked alongside you. Trust me. Trust me to keep walking with you."

She was on the verge of tears, emotion clogging her throat, and crying wasn't what she wanted. It wasn't what this was supposed to be. It was supposed to be physical, and it was becoming emotional. But too late she realized, as she clung to him while he treaded water for them both, with Knox it was never going to be anything but emotional. Because they cared for each other.

And emotion was never going to stay outside of the sex. It was never going to be sex in one column and friendship in the other. They were bringing sex into a friendship. And that was big and scary, and not something she could turn away from.

"Trust me," she said, a final plea before he closed the distance between them.

Eight

Knox had known he was lost the moment she had come out of the tent wearing that bikini. He hadn't even given himself a chance. When he had grabbed hold of her in the water… It hadn't been to stop her from splashing him. It had simply been because he couldn't stand to not touch her anymore. He had to do it. He'd had to bring her against his body. Because he couldn't stand to not have his hands on her.

And as he held her he had the fleeting concern that this was going to be the most selfish sex on the face of the planet, and he was going to treat his best friend to it. She didn't deserve that. She deserved more. She deserved better. But he didn't have control. Not anymore.

He was a man stripped of everything. Life had simply stolen every fucking thing from him in the last two years. He couldn't fight this. Not with what he had left.

He just wanted. And he was so tired of wanting. There were so many things he couldn't have. He could not have Eleanor back, no matter how much he wanted her.

He couldn't fight death. No matter how he wanted to. How he wished that there was a sword he could have picked up so he could do battle with death. Instead, he'd had to stand by helplessly, not able to do a damn thing. For a man who had never accepted the limits of life, losing to death with such resounding finality had been incomprehensible.

But he could have this. He could have Selena.

He didn't have to fight it, and he damn sure wasn't going to. Not anymore.

So he kissed her. He kissed her like he was drowning in this river and she was the air. He kissed her like there wasn't going to be anything after it. Because for all he knew, there wouldn't be. Life was a bitch. A cruel, evil bitch who took as much as she gave, so he was going to take something of his own.

Maybe anger at the world wasn't the way to approach a seduction. Maybe it wasn't the way to engage with his best friend, but he couldn't help himself. Couldn't do anything but lean into it. Lean into her. When she parted her lips and slid her tongue against his, he forgot to keep kicking, and they sank slightly beneath the water, the surface slipping past their shoulders. "We need to get out of here," he said, paddling them both toward the shore.

"There's that bed," she said softly, stroking her hand over his face, over his shoulders, the slide of skin against skin slick from the water.

He looked into her dark eyes to get a read on what she was thinking. "Did you plan this?"

"No," she said, looking very much like the picture of pristine innocence. In a black bikini that looked like sin.

"You didn't." Her eyes sparked with a little bit of heat, and a lot of the stubbornness he thought was cute about Selena at the best of times. It was cuter now, considering he was holding her nearly naked curves.

"Well." Her smile turned impish. "I didn't know there would be one bed. But I did know that I wanted you. And I figured this was as good a way as any to go about having you."

"Minx," he said, kissing her again. Kissing her until they were both breathless, out there in the bleached Texas sun.

Then he swept her up and carried her back toward that tent.

He didn't bother to dry either of them off when he deposited her on the plush bed at the far side of the canvas wall. He stood there, looking at every delicious inch of her. Those full breasts, barely contained by the swimsuit top, her small waist and firm stomach. Those hips. Wide and delicious, and her thighs, which were full and lovely. Shaped like a delicious pear he definitely wanted to take a bite out of.

He pushed his wet shorts down his thighs, careful with his straining arousal. And it was gratifying to watch her mouth drop open, to watch her eyes go wide.

She squeezed her thighs together, drawing one leg up slightly, biting her lip.

"See something you like?" he asked.

She nodded. "Yeah," she said. And it was rare for Selena to not have a snarky comment follow.

"Do you want this?" he asked.

"Yes," she said, the word breathless. "I want it so much." She rolled to her side, her wet hair falling over her shoulder, her eyes wide. "Don't change your mind."

He glanced down at his extremely prominent erection. "Oh, I'm not in a position to change my mind. Or to do much of anything with my mind at the moment, especially thinking."

She settled back into the blankets, looking satisfied with that statement. "I'm okay with that."

He got onto the bed, moving over her, kissing her again, reaching behind her neck and undoing the tie on her bikini top in one fluid motion. Then he did the other one, taking the wet cups away from her breasts.

His breath caught in his throat as he looked at her. At that glorious, golden skin, her tight, honey-colored nipples.

He leaned forward, flicking the tip of one sensitive bud with his tongue, gratified when she gasped and arched against him. He sucked her deep into his mouth, lost completely in his own desire. His need to feast on her, to gorge himself on her beauty.

He wasn't thinking about anything in the past. Wasn't thinking about anything but this. But her. There was no room for anything but desire inside of him. There was nothing else at all.

He smoothed his hands down her narrow waist to those full hips, gripped her bikini bottoms and tugged them down her legs. And he groaned when he saw that dark thatch of curls at the apex of her thighs. He kissed her stomach, all the way down low to that tender skin beneath her belly button. Then he forced her legs apart, his cock pulsing, his stomach muscles getting impossibly tight as he looked at his friend like this for the first time. He felt her try to close her legs, try to move away from him.

He wasn't going to let her get away with that.

She might have orchestrated this little camping trip. Might have thought she could conduct a seduction. And he was seduced; there was no doubt about that. But she wasn't in charge. Not now. Hell no.

He leaned forward, breathing in the scent of her. Musk and female and everything he craved. His mouth watered, and he leaned forward, sliding his tongue over her slick flesh, flicking that sweet little clit with the tip of his tongue. She gasped, her hips bucking off the bed, simultaneously moving toward him and away from him. He held her fast, grabbing hold of both hips, drawing her roughly against his mouth where he could have his fill and maintain control of the movements.

She tried to twist and ride beneath him, but he held her fast, pleasuring her with his lips and his tongue, pressing his fingers deep inside of her until she cried out, until her internal muscles pulsed around him.

"Knox," she said, his name thin and shaky on her lips, her entire body boneless. And that satisfied him. Because it had been a long damn time since he'd had a woman, and there was a deep satisfaction to making her come that he couldn't even describe.

He could do that to her body. This need, this skill existed inside of him, and the desire to practice it was there. He'd left that need boxed up inside of him for years. In a stack in the corner of his soul. Anything that wasn't work, anything that wasn't breathing.

Right now, this felt like breathing. And he didn't simply feel alive. He felt like Knox.

He wanted to do it again. Again and again. He wanted to make her scream his name. But she was reaching for him, urging him up her body, urging him to kiss her again. Who was he to deny her?

He was going to give her everything.

Everything he had.

He settled between her thighs, kissing her deeply. He wanted this to last longer. Wanted to go on. But he just didn't possess the control. He needed to be inside of her. And he needed it now. He could only take so much satisfaction from her orgasm without desperately needing his own.

He pressed the head of his cock to the entrance of her body, found her wet and ready for him. Then he slid himself upward, drawing his length over those slick folds, teasing her a little before moving back to her entrance and thrusting in hard.

Then he froze as she tensed beneath him. As she let out a cry that had nothing at all to do with pleasure.

Somehow, Selena was a virgin.

Selena tried *so* hard not to be a baby when the sharp, tearing pain moved through her. He had just made her feel so good. And really, she wanted this. She wanted him. But the invasion of his body into hers hurt and she hadn't been able to keep back the cry of shock when he had entered her.

Screaming in pain was probably not the best move on her part. A pretty surefire way to kill the mood.

Knox froze, looking down at her with anger written all over his handsome face.

She felt him start to move away from her, felt his muscles tense as he prepared to pull back. So he could stop touching her. So he could run out into the desert in the late afternoon and take his chances with the sun and snakes rather than with her. But she didn't want him to go.

So she clung to him, desperation probably leaving marks behind on his skin, digging her nails into his shoulders and kissing him fiercely, rocking her hips against his, ignoring the pain. She didn't want him to stop. It was too late anyway. Her virginity was gone. The hard part, the scary part, was over.

She didn't want to stop. Not now.

He tried to pull away again but she moved her hands down, clapping them over his muscular ass and holding him to her. She shook her head, her lips still fused to his.

He said nothing. Then he just continued on, slowly withdrawing from her body before thrusting back inside. He shuddered, lowering his head, his forehead pressed to hers. And she recognized the moment where whatever reservations he'd had were washed away by his own tide of need.

She'd had an orgasm already; he had not.

"Yes," she whispered as he began to move inside of her. As he began to establish a steady, luxurious rhythm that erased the pain she had felt only a moment before.

She wrapped her legs around his narrow hips, urging him on, chasing the pleasure she had felt before. And it began to build, low and deep inside of her, a band of tension that increased in intensity, drawing her closer to a second release. But this one seemed to come from somewhere deeper.

This time, when she shattered, it was just as he did, as his muscles tensed and his body shuddered, as his own orgasm washed through her, his thick, heavy cock pulsing as he spilled himself into her.

And when it was over, they lay there gasping, and she knew she was never going to be the same again. That there was no getting anyone out of her system. That her need for him would never change.

But along with that realization came a deep sense of peace. One that she was sure would vanish. But for now, she clung to it. For now, she clung to it and him, because reality would hit soon enough.

And she was in no hurry.

Because she had a feeling as soon as the afterglow receded there would be questions. She had a feeling there were in fact going to be quite a few follow-up questions. And what she really hadn't thought through in this moment was that there were going to be a lot of questions about Will.

She closed her eyes. Of course, she had already alluded to the fact that their marriage wasn't everything it seemed. So maybe Knox wouldn't be completely shocked. Maybe.

Well, even if he was—maybe that wasn't the end of the world. Maybe it was time to share the truth with him. She had closed him off. And now… Now he had been inside her body. So maybe that time was over. Maybe she just needed to go for it.

There was only one way to find out.

"Yes," she said, finding courage from deep inside that she hadn't realized existed. "I was a virgin."

He swore and moved away from her. She looked over at him just in time to see him scrubbing his hands over his face in what one might be forgiven for assuming was despair.

She folded her hands and rested them on her bare stomach, staring up at the canvas ceiling. "I assume you have queries."

"Yes," he responded. "I have several."

"Well," she said. "My marriage to Will wasn't real. I mean, we were never in a relationship."

"Never?" He treated her to a long hard look.

"No," she said. "We were never in a relationship at all. It was purely to help me get the trust-fund money."

"Why didn't you come to me? You could have picked either of your friends to help you out with this and you asked him?"

Panic fluttered in her breast and she took a deep breath, trying to tap it down. She wasn't going to tell him that she hadn't asked because she couldn't face the possibility that living with him wouldn't have felt fake to her. She wasn't going to bring up her feelings at all. "I just… Look what happened with my friendship with Will afterward. Don't tell me I was wrong in trying to protect our friendship from problems like that. Choosing Will seemed necessary. Marrying him seemed like the only thing I could do to make sure that you and I were going to be okay. You were always more important to me, Knox. I just didn't…"

"That's bullshit, Selena," he said. "I know it is. Give me a straight answer."

"Why?" she asked. "I don't want to give you a straight answer. Because there is no good answer."

"I want the truth."

"Fine," she said. "I was afraid we would end up like this." She swept her arm up and down, indicating their nudity. "I didn't worry about that with Will. Not at all. It was just never like that between us. I never had those feelings for him."

"You had them for me."

"Yes," she said. "That's kind of obvious, considering we are lying here naked."

"But even back then?" he asked.

He'd already confessed to being attracted to her, but she hadn't handed out a similar confession. For her it felt so raw. So deep.

"I wanted you. But I knew I wasn't in a position to have you. I thought maybe someday… And then… marrying Will was a bad choice, Knox. And it's one I've never been particularly interested in interrogating. It ruined a lot of things."

"About the time you got divorced I was with Cassandra."

"Yes," she said. "In a lot of ways, I was grateful for that. Because it helped us preserve our friendship. I don't regret that neither of us made a move. I feel like it was actually better. I feel like if it had happened when we were young, we wouldn't have been able to… process this. We wouldn't have been able to separate the attraction from the friendship."

"And you think we can now?"

"I think we're both tired," she said, obviously. "I think we're both fatigued after spending a long time denying what we wanted. It's a pattern. In both of our lives. I'm not going to pretend to compare my struggle to yours. I'm really not. But…why fight this? We both wanted it. And for the first time, we're in a place where we can both take it. It was always wrong, and maybe in the future it will be wrong again. Maybe it will just naturally fade away."

"Is that what you really believe?"

"Yes," she said. "I do. I believe this is something we can work out. This is something we can have."

"But… Hell, Selena," he said. "You've really never been with another guy?"

"No. I was really busy. I was really busy growing the company and…"

"Yeah, usually that's the kind of thing people say when they miss a lot of coffee dates. Not when they just kind of forgot to have sex ever."

Now this, she could not be honest about. She was not going to have a discussion with him about how no man had ever seemed to measure up to him in her mind.

Because that was beyond sad.

"It really wasn't something that mattered to me. And then… Over the past few weeks with you…" She cleared her throat. "I'm attracted to you. I always have been. But it's not something I dwell on. I mean, you were married to somebody else. You had another life. And I always respected that. I did. What you had with Cassandra… I would never have dreamed of encroaching on it. I care about you like a friend, and I kind of want to tear your clothes off and bite you like a crazed lioness, and those two things are separate. But there was never any crazed lioness fantasies while you were married." That was a little lie. There was the occasional fantasy, but she had known she could never act on it.

He paused for a moment, then placed his hand on her. "So your attraction went dormant?"

"Yes," she said. "Your marriage was the winter of our attraction. It hibernated."

"Your libido hibernated," he said, his tone bland.

"Yeah," she said. "And my burrow was work. Work and friends and establishing my life in Royal." She let out a heavy sigh. "I never wanted to get married and have a family," she admitted. "My father was... You know he was difficult. And it's..." She knew it was time to share everything. They were naked, after all. They were naked and he had just taken her virginity, and there really were very few secrets left between them. But the last one was hers. She was holding it. She had to give it up.

"My father used to beat us. He was violent. His temper was unpredictable. We walked like there was broken glass under our feet all the time. Doing the very best we could not to bring that temper up. It was terrible. Terrifying. I will never, ever submit myself to that kind of thing again."

"So is that why you avoided relationships?"

"I would say that's why they weren't a priority. I'm not sure that I avoided them. I just didn't pursue them."

"You're being difficult."

"Yeah, well," she said. "I reserve the right to be difficult. I *can* be difficult now. That's the beauty of life on your own terms."

"And you think that's the key to happiness?" he asked, brushing his knuckles idly over her hip. It was a question void of judgment, but it made her chest feel weird all the same. Mostly because she'd never thought of it in those terms.

"It's a luxury. One that I appreciate. That's why I was so desperate to marry Will," she said. "Because I needed that money. Because I needed to be able to control my life. Because if I couldn't, then I was always going to be under my father's thumb."

"He *hit* you?" he asked.

"Yes," she said. "All the time. For anything. For attitude, disrespect. For not complying with his wishes when he wanted us to. We didn't have any control. We had to be the perfect family. His perfect wife. His perfect daughter. He didn't want me to go to college. He didn't want me to have any kind of autonomy at all. My grandfather is the one who helped me enroll in Harvard. But then he died. And I knew I wasn't going to find any more support. I wasn't going to have the resources for college. I was going to have to go back home, Knox, and I couldn't face that. I didn't want to need my father again. Ever. And I needed to get my hands on that trust fund in order to make that happen. In order to protect myself. To protect my mother. After I got it, I moved her out of the house. I installed her somewhere he couldn't get to her. I did everything I could do with my money to make sure we were never beholden to him again."

He shifted, tightening his hold on her. "I didn't know it was that bad." His words were like ground glass, sharp and gritty, and it gratified her to know that Knox was holding her tight with murder on his mind, because he couldn't stand the thought of her being hurt.

She was right to trust him.

"We all have our own struggles," she said, working to keep her tone casual. "I never wanted anyone to look at me like I was broken. Like I needed to be treated gently. I've always felt strong. Growing up that way, I had to be. But I protect what I have. I protect what's mine.

"You can see how our relationship, love, all of that never figured into my plans. I could never see myself submitting to a man controlling my life. To anyone controlling my life. To love controlling my life. Because that was my experience. It took so much for my mother to leave because she loved him, not just because she was afraid of him. Because part of her wanted to make it work. Wanted to find the man she had once known. The one who had made her fall for him in the first place. No matter how much I tried to tell her that man never existed, it was difficult for her to accept."

Selena took a deep breath before continuing, "She refused to press charges in the end. She used to cry. And say that I ruined her life by breaking up the marriage. By sending her to live in Manhattan, far away from him, and safely ensconced in an apartment there. She would think about going back to him, and it was only her fear that kept her away. She skips therapy all the time, no matter how many appointments I set up. I just… I never wanted to be that creature. Ever."

Knox grabbed hold of her chin, met her gaze. "You never could be."

She reached up, curled her fingers over his wrist and held his arm steady. "Any of us can be. At least, that's what I think. One step in the wrong direction and you're on that path, and at some point you're too many steps in, and you can't imagine going back. I've never thought I was above anything. I've never thought I was too good, too smart… Because that's not it. That's not what does it. We can all get bound up in it."

He looked genuinely stricken by that. "I never thought of it like that," he admitted.

"I know. It's human nature to want to believe people are at fault for their own bad situations. And often times they are complicit. But I don't think it was a fundamental personality flaw that made my mother stay with my father. It was fear of change. A fear of losing what she had. Because what if she ended up with less?"

"But she stayed in a house with a man who hit her daughter. You might be able to excuse that, Selena, but I don't think I can."

She looked away from him. "Sometimes I have a hard time with that. I won't lie to you. I can't have a relationship with my father. He's not a good man. He hurt me. He hurt my mother. He was made of rage that had nothing to do with us. I'm convinced it had everything to do with some kind of anger at himself. But whatever it was, it's nothing I want touching my life. So yes. I feel like I could be angry at her. Maybe I would even be justified. Because you're right. She did stay. Her fear was bigger than her desire to take action to get us out. In the end, my fear of living in that hell forever is what made me take action. And I just… We are out. And I don't have the energy for anger anymore. I want to have at least one relationship with one family member that isn't toxic. I want to heal what I can."

"That's pretty damned big of you," he said.

She laughed, lifting her shoulder. "Sure, but then, I also don't want to have a romantic relationship, so I'm emotionally scarred in other ways."

"I can appreciate that."

Silence fell over them and she allowed herself to fully take in the moment. The fact that she was lying there, skin to skin with her best friend. With the man she had fantasized about all of her life. She had told him everything. She had finally laid bare all the secrets she had been so scared to roll out. But on the heels of sharing everything came the revelation she had been working on avoiding. The real reason she had been afraid of confiding in him all this time.

It wasn't just that she cared for him. It wasn't just that she was attracted to him. She was in love with Knox McCoy, and she always had been. In love with a man she could never allow herself to have, because she had sworn that she would never get involved in those kinds of relationships.

And she was such a fool. Because she had been in love with him from the moment he had first walked into her life. She had thought she could keep him as a friend, and ignore the bigger feelings, the deeper feelings, but that was a lie. There was no avoiding it. There never had been.

But she didn't tell him that. She had let out all her other secrets and replaced them with another. One that she hoped he would never discover.

Because as horrifying as it was to admit to herself that she was in love with him, it would be even worse to have him know and have him reject her.

So she laid her head on his chest and focused on the rhythm of his heartbeat, on the way his skin felt beneath hers.

It wasn't love. But for now, maybe it was enough.

Nine

They finished out the trail ride the next day in relative silence. Knox was saddle sore, because it had been a while since he had ridden a horse. And it had been a while since he had ridden a woman. But he and Selena had definitely indulged themselves the entire night. He still wasn't sure what to make of any of it. Of the fact that he'd made love to his best friend, of the fact that she had been a virgin.

Yeah, he didn't even the hell know. But things weren't terribly awkward, which was a miracle in and of itself.

When they arrived back at Paradise Farms he noticed that Selena was pretty cagey with Scarlett as they deposited the horses and thanked her for the generous loan.

"She knew, didn't she?" Selena asked when they got back into the car and headed down the highway.

"Do you think so?"

"Well, I wonder, because she obviously knew the tent only had one bed."

He chuckled. "So you think she was trying to set you up?"

"I think she was trying to set *you* up," she said. "She thought you seemed sad."

"I am," he responded, his tone dry. The answer more revealing than he'd intended it to be. He had meant to make the comment kind of light, but it was difficult for him to keep it light these days.

"I'm sorry," she said.

"Don't apologize," he said. "There's no damned reason to. You didn't do anything. Nobody did."

"I'm not apologizing, not really. I'm just sorry that life is so messed up."

He huffed out a laugh. "You and me both. I'm not sure what you're supposed to do with a bunch of broken pieces," he said, the words torn from him. "When they're all you have left. When you had this full, complete life and then suddenly it's just gone. I don't know what the hell you're supposed to do with that."

"I don't either," she commented. "I really don't. I guess you try to make a new life, new things. Out of the broken bits."

"I don't think I have the desire or the energy," he said.

"What's the alternative?" she asked, her voice hushed. "I'm not trying to be flippant. I'm asking a serious question. If you don't rebuild, what do you do? Just sit there in the rubble? Because I think you deserve a hell of a lot more than that."

"What's the point? Everything you do, everything

you are, can be taken from you." He didn't know what had gotten him into such a dire place. He'd just had sex for the first time in years and now suddenly they were talking about the fragility of life. "All these things you make your identity out of. Husband. Father. Billionaire. They're just things. They get taken from you, and then what? It's like you said about your mother last night. You lose sight of who you are, and then you're just afraid of what will be left. Once you lose those titles that defined you then…then there's just nothing. That's how it feels. Like I'm standing on a hell of a lot of nothing. Somehow I'm not in a free fall…but I don't trust this will last. I don't trust that the whole world won't just fall apart again."

They turned up the dirt road onto her property and didn't speak until they were inside the house again. Then finally she turned to him, her dark eyes full of compassion. He didn't like that. The compassion. Because it was so damned close to pity.

"I don't know what to say," she said, when they got into the house. She looked at him with luminous eyes, and he could read her sincerity. Her sadness.

He didn't want either.

He reached out, grabbing hold of her wrist and wrapping his arm around her waist, crushing her to his body, because he couldn't think of anything else to do. He needed something to hold on to, and she was there, like she had always been. In the middle of that horrible breakdown that he'd had at Eleanor's funeral, she'd been there. And she was here now. There was a yawning, horrific ache inside of him, and she was the only thing he could think of that would fill it.

"I used to be a husband," he said, his voice rough.

"I used to be a father. And now I'm just a man with a hole inside, and I don't know what the hell I'm going to do to fix it. I don't even know if I want to fix it. I don't know who I am."

"I do," she said softly. She lifted the hand that was currently free and brushed her fingertips against the side of his face, tracing the line of his jaw. "You're a man, Knox. A man that I want. For now…can that be enough? Can you just be that for me?"

Everything inside of him roared an enthusiastic hell yes. He could be that. He could do that. It was actually the one damn thing he knew in that moment. That he could be Selena's lover. That he could satisfy them both. He didn't know what the hell was going on in the rest of the world, but he knew what could happen here, in her bedroom.

And so he picked her up, holding her close to his chest as he carried her to the back of the house and deposited her on her bed. He stripped them both of their clothes, leaving the lights on so he could drink his fill of her beautiful body. He was about to do to her what he had done last night, to force her legs open and taste her as deeply as he wanted to. But she sat up on the bed, moving to the edge and pressing her hands to the center of his bare chest.

"Let me," she whispered. She pressed a kiss to his pectoral muscle, right next to his nipple. "Let me show you. Let me show you how much I want you."

He tensed, his entire body drawn tight like a bow. She continued an exploration down his torso, down his stomach, and lower still until she reached his cock. She curved her fingers around him, leaning forward and flicking her tongue over the head. His breath caught sharply, his entire body freezing.

"I've never done this either," she said. He looked down at her and saw that she was making eye contact with him, her expression impish. "If you were wondering."

Of course he had wondered, because he was a man, and damned possessive even if he shouldn't be. And the fact that she was doing this for him, only for him, and had never done it for anyone else was far too pleasing a revelation by half.

She braced herself on his thighs and took him deeper into her mouth, arching her back and sticking her ass in the air. He pressed his palm down between her shoulder blades and tried to keep himself from falling over as she continued to pleasure him with her lips and her tongue. It was a hell of a thing, accepting pleasure like this. He hadn't fully realized what he'd been doing to himself all this time. Punishing himself. Taking everything away that he possibly could.

Sex. Leisure time. All of it.

He hadn't allowed himself to enjoy a damned meal since his daughter's funeral. It was all hurry up and then get back to work. Leave work and then exercise. Work the ranch. It was only during this past week while he'd been here with Selena that he had begun to get in touch with some of the things he had left behind. Things like the company of people he cared about. Like going to an event and seeing people you knew. Like how much he enjoyed the touch of a woman. And he didn't know what he felt about all these revelations—the knowledge that he'd been punishing himself and the fact that he had started letting go of that punishment this week.

Piece by piece.

He felt a sharp pang of guilt join with the overriding sense of pleasure she was pouring onto him with all that sweet, lavish attention from her mouth.

Need was roaring through him now, and it was almost impossible for him to keep himself in check. He knew he needed to, but part of him didn't want to. Part of him just wanted to surrender to this completely, surrender to her completely.

But no, she deserved better than this.

In the end, she deserved better than him, but he was too weak to turn her away.

He didn't have the power. And that was what it always damn well came down to.

That when it came to the important things, he didn't have the strength to make an impact.

But he could make it good for her. And he would take that.

"Not like this," he said, his voice rough.

He grabbed hold of her arms and pulled her up his body, claiming her mouth in a searing kiss, his heart pounding hard, his breath coming in fierce gasps. Then he laid her down on the bed, hooked her leg up over his hip and thrust into her deep and hard, taking her until they were both breathless, until they were both completely caught up and consumed in their release.

When it was over they lay together. Just a man and a woman. Who had wanted each other. Who had needed each other, and who had taken steps to act on that need.

It was simple. Peaceful. He let his mind go blank and just rested. Listened to her breathe in and out. Focused on the feel of her silken skin beneath his touch. The way her hair spread over his chest in a glossy wave.

It didn't last long.

Didn't take long before he remembered who he was. Who they were. Before he had to face the fact that even though he felt like he might have been washed clean by what happened between them, he was still the same. Deep down, he was still the same.

Selena curled more tightly against him and he wrapped his arm around her, relishing the feel of her warmth, of her feminine softness, of her weight against him. Those words, those thoughts, triggered terror inside him. So he pushed it away.

"Are you going to stay away forever again?" she asked, her tone sleepy.

"What do you mean?"

"I mean, this is the first time you've been back to Royal since...well, you know since what. You've been in Wyoming. I had to chase you down over there to even see you."

"I know," he said.

"Is that what we are going to do? Are you going to leave and put distance between yourself and Texas again?"

And between himself and her. That part was unspoken, but he sensed it was there. And that it was a very real concern.

"It's hard to be here," he said. Finally. "The life Cassandra and I made together was here. It was a good life. It's one that I could have lived till the end. This beautiful house… Our beautiful family. It was good. It really was. I made it. I had all the things you think you want when you picture reaching that perfect position in your life. Then it crashed into a wall." He shook his head. "Nobody likes to go back to the scene of an accident. And that's what it feels like to me."

"I can't even imagine," she said, her voice muffled. She buried her face against his bare shoulder and he curled his hand around the back of her head, holding her. It was strange, to touch her like this, so casually. As if it all hadn't changed between them just last night. Because touching her like this felt natural. It felt right.

"Grief is a hell of a thing, though," he said. "It doesn't really matter where you are. It doesn't really care. It's in a smell, a strange moment that for some reason takes you backward in time. It's seeing a little girl that's the same age as Ellie would've been now. Or a little girl the same age she was when she died. Just seeing people walking together. Couples walking through life. It's freezing in the grocery store because you've picked up a box of crackers."

He tried to laugh, but it was hard. "We carry these crackers in the store. You know, graham crackers. Organic, obviously. And they were her favorite." He cleared his throat but it did nothing to ease the pressure in his chest. "I can't walk by that damn shelf, Selena." The words were broken, tearing through him, leaving him bloody and ragged inside. "Because I remember the way she used to wipe her mouth on my shirt and leave a trail behind. She would just…ruin all these really nice shirts. It was frustrating, and I think it annoyed me, even though I never got mad at her. Because she was just a baby. Just a little girl." It was surreal. Lying there, talking about this. Like he was watching someone else do it. But if it was another man's life, it wouldn't have hurt so much. "I'd give anything—my damned life—to wash graham cracker out of a shirt again."

He felt wetness on his shoulder and he realized she was crying, and then he realized there was an answering wetness on his own cheeks. "I didn't need to stay away from Texas to protect myself. There's no shielding yourself from something like this. I can lose my shit over a fucking cracker."

She buried her face in his chest. "I wish I could fix it," she said. "And those are the most frustrating words I've ever said. Because they don't give you anything. And they don't fix anything."

"Between the two of us I think we have a lot of broken pieces," he said, clearing his throat.

"I guess so."

"I won't stay away this time," he said, moving his hand up and down her bare curves, down her waist, over her hip. "I don't think I could." He was quiet for a long time. "I haven't told anyone that story." She didn't have to ask which one. "I just kept all this stuff to myself."

And he knew it was why his marriage had ended, or at least it was part of the reason why. Because he'd gone inside of himself, and Cassandra had retreated into herself. And neither one of them had known how to find their way back to each other, and they hadn't had the energy—or the desire, really—to even begin to try.

"Thank you for telling me," she said. "Thank you."

"You said you felt like you hadn't done anything. But you have. You did. You gave me this. This memory. This moment. The first thing I've really enjoyed in years. That's not nothing."

"What are friends for?" She smiled, and then she kissed his lips.

And after that, they didn't speak anymore.

Ten

Knox spent the next week at Selena's house, and he didn't really question what he was doing. Yes, he had an inkling that he was avoiding his real life. That he was avoiding dealing with the charity event that his ex had organized, that he was avoiding the reality of life in general, but he didn't much want to focus on any of that.

The mystery surrounding Will's return hadn't been solved, but there had been no more fake letters and no attempts by anyone to contact Selena. Knox was leaving all of that to the investigators and Will's family.

Instead, he wanted to focus on this newfound layer of his relationship with Selena. Wanted to focus on enjoying the way things felt again. Sex. Food. He and Selena were enjoying a lot of both.

And he was still helping her sort out her property.

Slowly, though, because he really wasn't in a hurry to finish. He was working out in the shed, while Selena took care of some business things in the house, when his phone rang.

It was from a number he didn't recognize, so he picked it up just in case it was a business call. "Hello?"

"Knox," the voice on the other end said.

Cassandra. The impact hit him like a punch to the stomach. And his initial response was rage. Absolute rage that she was intruding on this peaceful moment in his life. On this new thing that was happening with him.

He didn't want to hear her voice. Not while he was standing here in Selena's shed, mounting a new shelf so she had adequate storage.

"I don't know this number," he said.

"I got a new phone," she responded, her voice tenuous.

"Why did you call?"

And he felt like an ass for being impatient with her. For being such a jerk, because it wasn't like she had ever done anything to him. They had never really done anything to each other, and that had been the problem in the end.

"You never responded to the invitation for the Ellie's House fundraiser," she said.

"Did I need to? I wrote a check."

"I want you there," she said. "Ellie's House is really important to me. It's the only thing that makes me feel like what I went through—what we went through—wasn't completely pointless and cruel. I want this to be important to you. I want you to be there. To lend your connections. Your appearance matters."

"Don't say it like that," he said. "Don't say it like the charity isn't important to me. Like *she's* not important to me."

There was a long pause on the other end. "I didn't mean it like that. I really didn't. I did not call to have a fight with you, I swear."

He shifted, looking out the door of the shed at the field and trees off in the distance. The leaves blowing in the breeze, the sun shining down on it all. Like the world wasn't really a dark and terrible place. Like he wasn't being torn to shreds every time he took a breath. "We didn't fight while we were married. What's the point in fighting now?"

That produced another long silence. "There isn't one." Cassandra took a breath. "It would mean a lot to me if you could come. And I need to tell you something. Something that… I don't know how to say. I don't know…where to begin."

His chest tightened. "What?"

"Knox… I… I'm getting married."

He had not expected that. Neither had he expected the accompanying feeling of being slapped across the face with a two-by-four. "What?"

"I met someone." Something in her voice changed. Softened. Warmed. Happiness, he realized. He hadn't heard it in her voice in a long time. Certainly not when talking to him. "I didn't expect it. I wasn't looking for it. I didn't even want it. But he's… He makes me happy. And I didn't think I could be happy again. I have purpose with Ellie's House, and… I really want you to come. And I want you to see him. To meet him."

"I'm sorry—why the hell would I want to meet your

fiancé, Cassandra?" he asked. He could feel his old life slipping away. Moving into the distance.

Or maybe she was moving on and life was going past him.

"You don't love me," she said. "You're not *in* love with me, anyway."

That wasn't even close to being part of the visceral, negative reaction to her announcement. That much he knew. He didn't want Cassandra. He'd had her, they'd had each other, and they hadn't tried to fix things.

There was something else. Something he couldn't pinpoint. But it wasn't about wanting her back.

"No," he said.

"But we still care about each other, don't we? We were together for ten years. It's such a long time. Our whole twenties. It was you and me. We went through something... You're the only other person on earth who will ever know how I feel. You're the only person who experienced the same losses as me. You'll always matter to me for that reason. I just need you there. I need this closure. Please come."

Those words hit him hard. And somehow, he found that he didn't have the strength to turn her down. "Okay."

"Bring somebody," she said. "I mean it. Find a date. Find...something. We deserve to be happy."

After that, they got off the phone, and he struggled with his feelings about what she'd said. Because at the end of the day, he wasn't entirely sure he deserved to be happy.

He stumbled out of the shed and went into the house. Selena was sitting in there, her dark hair piled

up on top of her head in a messy bun. She was holding a pen in her mouth and staring down at her laptop.

She was so damned beautiful he could barely
breathe. "Hey," he said.

She looked up and she smiled at him, and it felt like
the sun coming out from behind the clouds. Which,
for a man who had spent the past two years in darkness, was a pretty big thing.

"Do you want to come to a charity thing with me?"

"Sure," she said, giving him a strange look.

"It's Cassandra's thing," he said.

"Oh," Selena said, her expression cautious. "For
Ellie's House?"

He frowned. "You know about that?"

She bit her lip. "About the foundation, yes. I wasn't
invited to any charity event. But I sent some money
in a while back."

He cleared his throat and shoved his hands into his
pockets. "Well, she told me to bring a date."

The corners of her lips turned upward, just slightly.
"Then I'm happy to fulfill that role."

"Great," he said, trying to force a smile.

It was only later that he questioned the decision.
He realized he was committing to bringing Selena to
a public function, as his date. Which had less to do
with how it might look—he didn't care, and anyway, it
was well established that they were friends—but that
he was bringing her along as a plus-one to his grief.
That he was basically submitting himself to showing
it all to the public.

But it was too late now. He'd already agreed. He'd
already asked her to come with him. He was just going

to have to get a handle on himself. To get some of his control back.

Because everything was moving in a direction he wasn't sure he liked. All that was left to do was try and keep a handle on himself.

Knox acted strange for the next week. Which was not helped at all by the fact that Selena was starting to feel a little bit strange herself.

She was trying not to dwell on it. Was trying not to dwell on anything other than the good feelings Knox created in her. Who knew how long all this would last? She didn't want to waste any time being upset or worried. Didn't want to waste time being hypersensitive to his moods or to her own.

There was way too much good happening. And she knew it was temporary. So she planned to just pull herself together and enjoy.

She tried to shake off her lethargy as she looked in the mirror and finished putting her makeup on. She was just so tired. She didn't know if it was because of the lack of sleep since Knox had moved in, or what. Stress, maybe, from the upcoming event for Ellie's House.

Because as much as she knew that he wasn't making a statement by bringing her, it still felt momentous that he'd asked her to come with him. He would probably be annoyed with her for thinking that. But she was coming to an event with his ex-wife and his ex-wife's fiancé. An event for a charity his ex-wife had created for the daughter they had lost.

He could have easily gone by himself. And Selena had a feeling that a few months ago that was exactly what he would have opted to do. Since he had been doing things on his own for the past couple of years.

The fact that he'd reached out to her was probably why he was acting weird. The intensity of the whole situation. She really couldn't blame him.

She checked her reflection in the mirror and had a momentary feeling of uncertainty. And then a flash of jealousy followed closely by a bite of guilt.

She had to wonder if he might compare her to his tall, blonde ex, who was more willowy than she was curvy. And Selena wouldn't really be able to blame him if he did. She and Cassandra were so different. The idea of standing next to Cassandra and playing a game of compare and contrast had been making her feel ill.

Of course, that wasn't what was going to happen. And Cassandra had always been very nice to her.

It'd been strange when she and Knox had gotten divorced, because Selena had genuinely liked her. As much as you could like the woman who had ended up with the man of your dreams, *obviously*.

But as Selena had recused herself from having those kinds of dreams, she'd never really been angry with Cassandra. Knox being married had always been both a relief and a heartache. There was really no other way to describe it. A relief because that feeling of *what if* had abated slightly since there had been no more *what if* left. But also it had just burned sometimes. Knowing he was with someone else. That he'd loved someone else.

But she'd never let herself dwell on it. She hadn't been able to be with him romantically, not when a relationship like that would have required risk and a trust she hadn't been willing to give. But she'd also needed him in her life, and she wasn't about to let something like a marriage come between them.

Now, had Cassandra been a bad wife, Selena wouldn't have been able to stand for it. But Cassandra had always been great. Exactly the kind of woman Selena thought Knox should have been with. So getting all bent out of shape about Cassandra and comparisons now was just pointless.

She twisted her body slightly, frowning as she smoothed her hand over the front of her fitted gold dress. A strange sense of disquiet raced through her as she adjusted herself in the halter top. Her breasts hurt. Like they were bruised.

That was very, very strange.

She knew of only one thing that caused such intense breast tenderness and…no. That was ridiculous. Except her breasts had never been tender before. Her eyes dropped down to her stomach. She looked the same. She couldn't believe…couldn't believe there could be a baby in there.

And the first time…she and Knox had forgotten condoms. That had been in the back of her mind, niggling at her consciousness, ever since. At the time, it had been lost in confessions of her virginity and the deep pain he'd expressed when talking about his daughter.

But the fact remained…the condoms had been forgotten.

The stomach she was currently scrutinizing felt as though it dropped down to her toes.

She could not be pregnant. Well, she could be pregnant—that was the trouble. She really could be. She and Knox had unprotected sex and she was… Well, she was late.

"No," she said to her reflection, bracing her arms on the dresser. "No," she said.

"What's going on?"

She turned around to see Knox standing there wearing a suit and a black tie, and if her stomach hadn't already been down in her toes, it would have done a full free fall.

"Nothing," she said, turning around quickly, still holding on to the dresser. "I just was afraid that I couldn't find my earrings. But I did."

"The ones you're wearing?"

"No," she said, grabbing for another pair on top of the cluttered dresser. "These."

And he kept staring at her, so she had to change into the earrings that she had already decided against. She took out the pair that looked absolutely perfect with her gold dress and sadly discarded them on the top of the dresser. Then she put the others in, smiling. "See?"

"Right," he said, clearly not seeing a distinction between the two. Because he was a man. Which was the only reason that her excuse actually worked. Because otherwise he would know that the other pair was clearly better.

"Are you ready to go?"

"Yes," she said.

"I got us a room at the hotel where the charity event is being held. You know, so that neither of us has to be the designated driver."

He was keeping his tone light, but she definitely sensed the hint of strain beneath it.

"Sounds good," she said.

At the mention of alcohol, she realized that she actually couldn't bring herself to drink a glass of champagne before she knew for sure.

Before she knew for sure if she was pregnant.

Oh, she was going to pass out. She really was. She wasn't sure how she was supposed to get through tonight. She needed to sneak away from him and get a test.

This wasn't happening.

It wasn't fair.

It definitely couldn't crash into the event tonight, because the event was way too important. For the memory of his daughter.

Suddenly, Selena was sure she was going to throw up.

"Are you okay?"

"I guess," she said. "I'm nervous." She opted to be honest about part of her problem so she could leave out the big, scary part. "I haven't seen Cassandra since your divorce. And the two of us are… You know."

"She's engaged," he said.

"It's not her that I'm worried about."

He frowned. "Are you afraid I'm going to see her and want her? Instead of you?"

"I don't know," she said, lifting a shoulder. "Yes."

"I'm not harboring secret feelings for Cassandra," he said. "We'll always be… We're linked. She and I created a life together. And then we both had to go through the experience of losing it. Losing Ellie. So it's not the same as if we were sharing custody or something. But…"

"I'm all right with that. I mean, I get it. I really do. And I am not upset about that at all. I just… She's prettier than me," Selena said finally.

He frowned. "You are the prettiest damned woman, Selena Jacobs," he said. He reached out and brushed his fingertips across her cheek. "I… I haven't felt this good in a long time. And the fact that I still feel pretty good even with all of this Ellie's House stuff looming on the horizon… It's a testament to you. I don't long for my marriage. The man who was married to Cassandra doesn't exist anymore. That's the only real way I can think to explain it. We changed too much and we didn't change together. Nobody's fault. It just is. But the woman she is now has found a different man. The man I am now wants you. Nobody else. I can't even compare the two of you. I don't want to. You're you. You always have been. You occupy a special place in my life no one else ever has."

Her heart felt swollen, like it might burst through her chest. It wasn't quite a declaration of love, but it almost was. He put his arm around her and started to guide her out of the bedroom, and then they headed to the driveway, where he got into the driver's side of her car and started down the road that would take them to downtown Royal for the event.

This felt right, being with him for this event to celebrate his daughter's memory. She had to wonder what that meant. She had been so convinced that there was no future between herself and him. Had been utterly and completely certain that the two of them could have nothing but sex and friendship.

But they were in some different space where all those pieces had woven together, and her feelings for him were so big. So deep and real. She just didn't know where they were anymore. And she wondered why she was resisting at all. Because when she had decided she wasn't going to have a husband and children, when she had decided that love wasn't for her, that idea had been attached to an abstract man. Some version of her father who might someday betray her.

But this relationship she'd started wasn't with an abstract man. It certainly wasn't with anyone who resembled her father.

It was with *Knox*.

Knox, who had been one of her best friends for all of her adult life. She trusted him, more than she trusted just about anybody. She wasn't afraid of him. She wasn't afraid of loving him. He was a safe place for all those feelings to land.

And if she was having his baby…

She had no idea what to make of that. Had no idea what it would mean to him. She knew he'd said he didn't want to have a relationship again, but what if they were having a child? What would that do to him?

Suddenly, the whole situation seemed a lot more fraught than it had a moment ago. Just one moment of peace, and then it had evaporated.

Surely he would want another child, though—if she was really pregnant. He had been a wonderful father, and it wasn't as if a new baby would replace the little girl he had lost.

Her brain was still tying itself in knots when they arrived at the hotel. Cars and limousines were circling the area in front, valets taking the vehicles away to be parked, doormen ushering people inside. Knox stuck his black cowboy hat on his head and smiled at her, and then the two of them got out of the car and headed into the hotel. She clung to him, mostly because she thought if she let go of him she might collapse completely.

And not just because of those strange feelings of jealousy she'd had earlier. No, not at all. It had very little to do with that. It was just…everything else. Suddenly, what she and Knox were doing, what they were sharing, felt too big.

They made their way into the lobby of the hotel. It was art deco with inlaid geometric designs on the floor reflected in gold on the ceiling panels. There was a banner hung over the main ballroom, welcoming the distinguished attendees to the first annual fundraiser for Ellie's House.

But it was the picture on the stand, right in the entry of the ballroom, that stopped her short and made her breath freeze in her chest. It was a photograph of a little girl. Beautiful. Blonde.

With the same gray eyes as her daddy.

She was lying in a field with her hands propped beneath her chin, yellow-and-purple wildflowers blooming all around her.

Selena's heart squeezed tight and she fought to take a breath. She clung even more tightly to Knox, whose posture was rigid. She sneaked a glance at him and saw that he was holding his jaw almost impossibly tense. It hurt her to see that picture. In memoriam of a child who would be here if life was fair. She couldn't imagine how it was for him.

He paused for just a moment, and she looked away as he brushed his fingertips lightly over the portrait. It felt wrong to watch that. Like she was intruding on a private moment. On a greeting or a goodbye. She wasn't sure.

He straightened, then began moving forward. She rested her head on his shoulder as they walked, and she had a feeling they were holding each other up now.

The ornate room was filling up, but it didn't take long for her to spot Cassandra, her blond hair pulled back into a bun. She was all pointed shoulders and collarbones, much thinner than she had been the last time Selena had seen her. But as beautiful as ever. Cassandra had always been a stunning woman, and tonight was no exception. She was wearing an understated black dress, with a ribbon pinned to the top.

She rushed over to greet them, her expression harried, her face a bit pale. "I'm so glad you made it," she said. She took a step forward, like she was ready to hug Knox, and then thought better of it. Instead, she reached into her clutch and produced two ribbons, pressing them into Knox's palm. "If you want to wear these."

"Thank you," he said.

"Hi," Cassandra said to Selena.

Selena broke the awkwardness and leaned in, embracing Cassandra in a hug. "Hi," she said. "It's good to see you."

Cassandra looked between them, her expression full of speculation, but she said nothing. Instead, she just twisted the large yellow diamond ring on her left hand.

"Is your fiancé here?" Knox asked.

"He was," Cassandra said. "I sent him out to get me some new nylons because I put a run in mine. He's good like that."

"He sounds it," he said, a slight smile curving his lips.

"Well," Cassandra said. "You know me. If there is a nylon in the vicinity I will cause a run in it."

"I'm glad you have someone to get you a new pair," he said.

"Me, too." After a beat of silence, she said, "I'm sorry—I have to go back to getting everything in order, but I'll find you again later tonight."

"You're gonna make tons of money," he said.

"I hope so," she said. "I hope we do. I hope I am part of making sure that in the future this doesn't happen. Not to anyone." Cassandra's blue eyes filled with tears and she looked away. When she looked back at Knox, her smile was in place. "Sorry. I have to go."

She turned abruptly, brushing her hands over her face, her slim shoulders rising and falling on a long breath. Then she strode forward resolutely, mingling with the other people who were starting to fill up the ballroom.

Selena could only be impressed with the way that Knox handled himself the whole evening. He had pinned the ribbon that Cassandra had given him proudly on his lapel, and Selena had done the same, to the top of her dress. And she did her very best to keep her focus on what was happening around them. Ellie's House—Ellie's memory—was simply too important for Selena to get caught up in her own worries.

There was a buffet, which Selena noticed Knox never went near. And she made a point of acting like she hadn't noticed. But when the band started to play, she asked him to dance.

He surprised her by complying.

He swept her into his arms, and for the first time

in hours, she felt like things might be okay between them. "This is a wonderful tribute," she said, softly.

"Yes," he responded, the word clipped.

"I'm sorry." She lowered her head. "I said the wrong thing."

"No. It's just…still hard to accept that my daughter needs tributes. I guess I should be more used to it by now."

"No. Don't do that, Knox. You were caught off guard earlier."

"It was a nice picture," he said, his voice rough. "I remember the day it was taken. Out at the Jackson Hole ranch where we used to take picnics. I don't… I don't even like to remember. Even the good times hurt."

Selena didn't say anything. She just rested her head against his chest and swayed with him on the dance floor. They didn't speak much for the rest of the evening. Knox focused on talking to potential donors, rather than to her. But Selena was used to these types of events and it was easy for her to go off and do the same, to make sure she did her part to bring in money for the charity.

Cassandra gave an amazing speech about the importance of medical research, and the progress that was being made in the effort to treat childhood cancers and other childhood diseases. She talked about the function of the charity, how they donated money to innovative research teams and to housing for the various hospitals, so families could stay near their children while they received treatment and not be buried under the financial burden.

Selena found that she could only be impressed with

Knox's ex-wife. She couldn't be jealous. She was just proud. And it seemed…okay then, that Knox would always have a connection with Cassandra. It seemed important even. Selena certainly wanted to be involved in supporting this effort with Ellie's House, and she thought it was amazing what Cassandra had done with her grief.

As the clock drew closer to midnight, Selena hit a wall, so tired that she was barely able to stand. Knox, on the other hand, was still moving dynamically around the room, stumping to have more checks written. It was amazing to watch the way the fire had been lit inside of him since they had arrived. Clearly he had a desire to make all of his family's suffering count for something. To make the loss count for something.

Suddenly she felt so nauseous, she thought she might collapse. Fuzzy-headed. Sleepy. It could just be stress and fatigue. It had been a crazy few weeks and a hard evening. She was just so overly…done.

She walked over to Knox and touched his arm. "I need to go to bed," she said.

He gave her a cursory glance, obviously still focused on the event. Which was fine with her. She imagined he would want to stay till the end. She *wanted* to stay; she was just going to fall over if she tried.

"I'll see you up in the room," he responded.

If he was disappointed about the fact that she would be asleep when he got there, rather than ready for sex, he didn't show it. But then, he was busy. And she could appreciate that. She could more than appreciate that. It was good to see him passionate about something, especially something involving his daughter's memory. Good to see him involved.

Selena slipped out the back of the ballroom and wrapped her arms around her midsection as she walked through the lobby. She felt so awful. So tired she thought she might fall asleep where she stood.

And though it *could* be stress and fatigue.

Or something a lot scarier.

There was only one way to find out whether or not she was carrying Knox's baby.

Maybe the timing sucked, and she should just go to bed. But now that she started thinking about the possibility again, she couldn't wait. Not another minute, and certainly not until tomorrow morning.

She stopped walking, pausing for a moment in front of the concierge desk. Then she took a tentative step forward.

"Is there a pharmacy close by?"

Eleven

Knox felt guilty about letting Selena leave the party without him. But he was engaged in a pretty intense conversation with a local business mogul about donations and ways to raise awareness, and he felt…like he was able to do something. Like he could be something other than helpless.

Tonight, Cassandra made much more sense to him. She had thrown herself into this. At first, her drive had been difficult for him. Because every reminder of Eleanor was a painful one. But now, after participating in the fundraiser, he understood.

Looking around at all of this, he couldn't help but understand. She was doing the only thing she could. Her mother's heart compelled her to let their daughter live on somehow, while Knox had been consumed in the grief.

He hadn't had it in him to take that kind of generous approach. To make sure what had happened to his daughter didn't happen to anyone else. But he had found it tonight. He had found something that he had thought long gone—hope. Like there was a future in this world that was worth being part of.

And that made him feel...like a little piece of himself had been recovered. A piece he had thought he might never access again. A piece that allowed him to be a part of the world, that allowed him to enjoy being alive. To enjoy the taste of food. The touch of a woman. The desire to accomplish something. Anything.

And, yes, the fundraiser had made a difference, but the catalyst for this change was all Selena.

As the night wore on, the crowds began to thin out, and finally, he was left with Cassandra, who sat up on the stage. She looked exhausted, and she looked sad.

"You did a good thing," he said, walking over and taking a spot next to her.

"Thank you," she said, treating him to a tired smile. "But I know."

"Isn't this exhausting?" he asked.

"What?" she asked. "Charity events?"

"Reliving this all the time," he said.

"I do anyway," she said. "So why not make something of it? This charity helps me feel like I'm moving on. Even though it all...stems from her, losing her. I don't know how to explain it, really. Like I'm taking the tragedy and making something positive with it."

He looked across the room and saw Cassandra's fiancé, who was helping with cleanup. He seemed like a good man. A great man. One who had jumped into all of this without having known Ellie at all, but who supported the charity just because it meant so much to Cassandra.

It occurred to Knox then that the truth of the matter was that Cassandra *was* a hell of a lot more moved on than he was.

And he didn't know what to feel about that. He didn't know how to reconcile it. He didn't know if he *wanted* to move on.

And yet moving on was what he had just been thinking about. That experience of beginning to enjoy life again.

Was that what she had now? Could she be thankful to be alive? Was she able to love this man? And not be afraid of loss?

Part of him still wanted to hold on to the past. Wanted to fight against blurry images, fading pain and the normalcy he was starting to feel on some days. Wanted to fight against the past slipping away. He wanted to go back out front and stare at that portrait of his daughter lying in a field of flowers. To memorize her face.

He just didn't want to forget.

He didn't *want* to come out the other side of this grief.

Suddenly, he felt like he was sliding down into a dark pit, and he had no idea what in hell to do about it. If he wanted to do anything about it at all. He had no idea what to do with any of these feelings. Had no idea what had happened to the good feelings from a few moments before, and even less of an idea about why he resented having those good feelings now.

Grief didn't make sense. All of the guides talked

about stages and moving on. For him, it wasn't stages. It was waves, coming and going, drowning him. The memory of his child acting like a life raft in his mind.

How the hell could he move on from his own life raft?

Cassandra had said earlier that he was the only person who had been through what she had been through. And that was true. But now he was sitting here alone with these feelings. She had moved on. And there was no one. No one at all.

It scared him.

What would happen if they both went on with their lives like Ellie hadn't existed? If she became only this monument to a greater cause, instead of the child they loved so much.

And suddenly, he needed to get out of there. Suddenly, he needed to find Selena.

He knew she was asleep, but he needed her.

"I'm going up to bed," he said, and if his departure seemed sudden, he didn't much care. He walked out of the ballroom and headed through the lobby, getting into the elevator and checking the key in his wallet to see which room he and Selena were in. Then he pushed the appropriate button and headed up to their floor.

He got to the room and pushed the key card into the door, opening it slowly. When he got inside, Selena was not asleep as he'd expected.

She was sitting on the edge of the bed, her head bent down. She looked up, her face streaked with makeup and tears and a horrific sense of regret.

"What's going on?" he asked. "I thought you were going to sleep."

Then he looked down at her hands. At the white stick she was clutching between her fingers.

The look on Knox's face mirrored what she was feeling.

Terror. Sheer, unmitigated terror.

But even through the terror, she knew they could do this. They would get through it as they had every other thing life had thrown at them over the years. They would make it work together.

She trusted him, and that was the mantra she kept repeating to herself, over and over again.

She had given Knox her heart slowly over the past decade. And now he had all of it, along with her trust.

She loved him.

She always had. But sitting there looking at the test results, she knew she was in love with him. The kind of love built to withstand. The kind that could endure.

She loved him.

They could weather this. She was confident they could.

"I'm sorry," she said. "I didn't want you to find out like this."

She had fully intended to talk to him tomorrow, but then she had ended up sitting on the edge of the bed, unable to move. Completely and utterly shell-shocked by what was in front of her in pink and white.

The incontrovertible truth that she was pregnant with Knox McCoy's baby.

She had cried, but she wasn't sad. Not really. It was just so much to take in, especially after spending the evening at the charity event. Especially after seeing the portrait of his daughter by the door and witnessing all the small ways grief affected him. The small ways that loss took chunks out of him over the course of an evening like this.

Now he was finding out about this. It just seemed a bit much.

"You're pregnant," he said.

"Yes. We didn't… We forgot a couple of times," she said, her voice muted.

That first time, down at the camp.

That second night, in her room when they had talked about Eleanor and graham crackers and her heart had broken for him in ways she hadn't thought she could recover from.

"I can't do this," he said, his voice rough.

"I mean…" She tried to swallow but it was like her throat was lined with the inside of a pincushion. "A baby isn't tea. I can't…not serve it to you. I can't… Maybe this is our sign we have to try something real, Knox."

The words came out weak and she despised herself for them.

"I can't," he said again.

Her heart thundered so hard it hurt. Felt sharp. Like it was cutting its way out of her chest.

"We *can*," she said. "We can do this together, Knox. I know that it's not…ideal."

"Not ideal?" he asked, his words fraying around the edges. "*Not ideal* is a damned parking ticket, Selena. This is not *acceptable*."

Anger washed through her, quick and sharp. At him. At herself. At how unfair the whole world was. They should just be able to have this. To be happy. But they couldn't because life was hard, and it had stolen so much from him. She hurt for him; she did.

But oh, right now she hurt so much for herself.

"I'm sorry that the pregnancy is unacceptable to you, but it's too late. I'm pregnant."

"Selena…"

"I love you," she said. "I didn't want to say that right now either. I didn't want to do it like this, but… Knox, I love you. And I know that I've always said I didn't want a husband and children, but I could do it with you. If we are going to have a baby then I can do it. I *want* to do it."

She straightened her shoulders as she said the words, realizing just then that she was committing to her baby. "I… I want this baby."

He looked at her for a moment, his eyes unreadable.

"Then you're going to have it on your own."

She felt like she had been blasted through with a cannonball, that it had left her completely hollowed out. Nothing at all remaining.

Pain radiated from her chest, outward. Climbing up her throat and making it feel so tight she couldn't breathe.

"You don't want this?"

"I can't."

She felt for him. For his loss. She truly did. But it wasn't just her being wounded. It was their child. A child who was losing a chance at having him for a father.

She had thought…

She had no idea how she could have misjudged this—misjudged him—so completely.

She'd thought…if she knew one person on earth well enough to trust them it should have been him.

This was her nightmare.

But it wasn't just heartbreak over losing the man she loved, over losing the future she'd so briefly imagined for them before he walked into their suite.

No, she was losing her friend.

And bringing a child into the heartache.

"So that's it. You don't want to be a father again." Dread, loss, sadness…it all poured through her in a wave. She felt like she was back in the river with him, but this time, he was pushing her under instead of holding her up. "You don't want me."

"Selena, I already told you. I've had this. I've had it, and I lost it, and I cannot do this again. There is no mystery left in the damned world for me. I know what it's like to bury my child, Selena. I will not… I can never love another child like that. Ever."

She had trusted him.

That was all she could think as she stood there, getting ripped to shreds by his words.

As a young woman, she had been convinced that the hardest thing, the most difficult thing in the world, was enduring being beaten by a man with his fists. Her father had kicked her, punched her while she was down.

But this hurt so much worse. This was a loss so deep she could scarcely fathom it. This was pain, real and unending.

She couldn't process it.

She pressed her hand against her stomach. "Then go," she said, her mouth numb, her tongue thick. "Go. Because I'm not going to expose my child to your indifference. I'm not going to be my mother, Knox. I'm not going to have a man in my child's life who doesn't care about them."

"Selena."

"No. You're the one who said it. Why couldn't my mother love me enough to make sure I was in the best situation possible? Why didn't she protect me? Well, now I'm the mother, the one making choices. I'm going to love this baby enough for both of us. I'm going to give it everything I never had and everything you refuse to give it. Now get the hell away from me."

He was operating from a place of grief, and she knew it, but he was an adult. She knew full well that her duty was to protect her child, not Knox's emotional state.

She was sick, and she was angry. And she didn't think she would ever recover.

"I just can't," he reiterated, moving toward the door of the hotel room.

"Then don't," she said. "But I don't believe the man who pulled himself up out of poverty, got himself into Harvard, stood by me as a good friend for all those years and came to Will's funeral, even though it was hard—I don't believe that man can't do this. What I believe is that you're very good at shutting people out. You go into yourself when it gets hard, rather than reaching out. Reach out to me, Knox. Let's do this together. I don't need it to be perfect or easy. We have a bunch of broken pieces between us, but let's try to make something new with them."

"I can't." He looked at her one more time with horribly flat, dark eyes, and then he turned and walked out of the hotel room, leaving her standing in a shim-

mering gold ball gown, ready to dissolve into a puddle
of misery on the floor.

There was pain, and then there was this.

Knowing she was having her best friend's baby.
And that she would be raising that baby alone.

Twelve

He drank all the way back to Jackson Hole. He drank more in the back of the car as his driver took him back to the ranch. And he kept on drinking all the way until he got back to his house and passed out in bed. When he woke up, he had no idea what time it was, but the sun was shining through the window and his head was pounding like a son of a bitch. He was also still a little bit drunk.

Best of both worlds.

He could hardly believe what had happened earlier. It all seemed like a dream. Like maybe he had never gone to Royal and had never gone to a funeral for Will that hadn't actually happened. Like maybe he had never slept with Selena. He had never gone to that charity event in honor of his daughter. And then Selena certainly hadn't told him she was pregnant with his baby.

Because why the hell would she be pregnant with his baby since certainly they had never really slept together?

And they certainly hadn't been living together like a couple. Playing house, reenacting the life that he had lost. A life he could never have again.

He got up and saw half a tumbler full of scotch sitting on the nightstand. He drained it quickly, relishing the burn as he fumbled for his phone. He checked to see if he had any missed calls and saw that he didn't. But he did see that it was about three in the afternoon.

He frowned down at his phone for a long moment, then scrolled through his contacts. "Hello?"

"Cassandra," he said, the words slurred.

"Knox?"

"Yes," he said. "I am drunk."

"I can tell." She paused, because clearly she wasn't going to help him with this conversation. She wasn't going to tell him why he had called. He wished she would. He sure as hell didn't have a clue. Didn't know why he was reaching out to her now when he hadn't done it during their marriage.

When he hadn't been able to do it when it might have fixed something.

"Are you all right?" she pressed.

"Fuck no," he said. "I am not all right."

"Okay." Again, she gave him nothing.

"How come you're happy?" he asked. "I'm not happy. I don't want to be happy. What happens if both of us are happy and we forget about her? We forget how much it hurt? And how much she mattered?"

He heard her stifle a sob on the other end of the line. "We won't. We won't."

"What if we do?" His heart felt like it was cracking in two. "I don't want to replace her. I can't."

"You won't," she said. "You won't replace her ever. Why would you think that?"

"Selena is pregnant," he said, "and I don't know what to do. Because it's like I traded our life in for a new version. That's not fair to anyone. It's just not."

His words didn't make any sense, but all he knew was that everything hurt, and he couldn't make sense of any of it.

There were no words for this particular deep well of pain inside of him.

"You're not," she said, her voice cracking. "You're *not*."

"I'm sorry," he said. "I think I called to be mad at you. For being okay. For moving on. But now I'm just sorry. I should've been there for you. Maybe we should have been there better for each other."

"Maybe," she said. "But I didn't want to be."

Silence fell between them. "I didn't either."

"I loved our life," she said. "And it took me a long time to realize that I think I loved our life more than we loved each other. And when we lost Ellie… It wasn't that life anymore. And what we'd had wasn't enough to hold us together."

"Yeah," he agreed, her words making a strange kind of sense in his alcohol-soaked brain. "Yeah, I think so."

"You need to find somebody you love no matter the circumstances. Not just someone you love because she fits a piece in your life. Because she fulfills a role. Not a wife—a partner."

"I'm afraid," he said, the words ripped from somewhere down deep.

Cassandra laughed, soft and sympathetic. "Join the club. Believe me. Nobody is more afraid than me. I mean, maybe you. But it's hard. It's hard to open yourself up again. I think so… I think you already did. I think you're already in love. So don't keep yourself from it. That's not protecting yourself. That's just punishing yourself. And if that's what you're really doing…you need to stop."

"How?" he asked. "How am I supposed to stop punishing myself when I'm here and she's gone? When I couldn't protect her? How am I supposed to move on from that?"

When Cassandra spoke again, her voice was small. "You have to move on from it, Knox, because she isn't here anymore. And as little as either of us could do for her when she was ill, there's nothing we can do for her now. There's nothing you can do by holding on to your grief. She doesn't need you anymore. She doesn't need this from you."

He couldn't speak. His throat was too tight, his chest was too tight and everything hurt.

"Selena *needs* you," Cassandra continued. "The child you're going to have with her needs you. And you're going to have to figure out a way to be there for her, for this child, or you really aren't the man I met all those years ago."

He couldn't speak after that. And Cassandra let him off the hook, saying goodbye and hanging up the phone.

Because he wasn't that man. He wasn't. He didn't know how to be. He didn't want to be. He was changed. Hollowed out and scarred. Like a forest that had been ravaged by wildfire, leaving behind nothing but dead, charred wood.

Selena needed him.

Cassandra's words continued to echo through him. Selena needed him. Not Eleanor. Eleanor was gone, and it was unfair. But there was nothing he could do about it but grieve. And he knew he would do that for all of his life. There was no way to let go of something like that. Not truly. But maybe there was a way to learn to live. To live with the grief inside of you, to allow good memories to come back in and take residence alongside the pain.

To let love be there next to it, too.

Maybe moving on wasn't about being the man he used to be. Maybe it was about doing what Selena had said. Maybe it was about making something new out of the broken pieces.

Selena needed him. Their baby needed him.

He was beginning to suspect he needed Selena, too. That without her he was going to sink into the darkness forever.

The question was whether or not he wanted to let in the light.

Selena had gone to the doctor to confirm her pregnancy after securing someone else's canceled appointment, and then had gone to Paradise Farms to visit Scarlett and see how baby Carl was doing. While she watched her bright-eyed friend play with her new baby, Selena felt a strange mix of pain and hope.

She had made choices to protect her baby. To protect this little life growing inside of her that she already loved so much.

Watching Scarlett brought it all into full Technicolor. Made impending motherhood feel real.

"Do you like it?"

"What?" Scarlett asked, looking up from Carl's play.

"Being a mother."

"That's a funny question."

Selena lifted a shoulder. "I'm in a funny mood. Indulge me."

"Yes. Although there are periods where I'm so tired I just want to lie on the floor and sleep." She shifted her hold on the baby and looked down at him, smiling. "And I have done that. Believe me. Sometimes I ask myself why I made this choice. Why I decided to have a baby before I had a life. But… I do like it. Adopting Carl has been the most rewarding thing I've ever done. Even though sometimes it's really hard. But I love him. And adding love to your life is never a bad thing."

Selena tapped the side of her mug of tea, looking out the window. "I like that. It's adding love."

"And a lot of work," Scarlett said. "Are you thinking about adopting?"

Her friend was likely joking, judging by the lightness in her tone. Because Selena had never given any indication she had an interest in adopting a baby. In fact, she was probably the least maternal person Scarlett knew. There was no way to ease her friend into this. No way to broach the subject gently.

So Selena figured it was time to drop the bombshell. "No, I'm not thinking of adopting. I'm pregnant."

Scarlett stared at Selena in shocked silence, opening and closing her mouth like a fish that had been chucked onto dry land. When she finally recovered her ability to speak, it came out as a shocked squeak. *"What?"*

Selena looked down into her teacup. Tea leaves were supposed to tell the future. Her Yorkshire Gold only contained the reflection of her own downtrodden expression. "It happened on the camping trip."

"Damn," Scarlett said. "I guess those tents really are romantic."

"Romance wasn't required," Selena said, grimacing. "It was more than a decade of pent-up lust."

She sighed and leaned back on the couch. "But he's not ready for this. He doesn't want anything to do with me."

Scarlett frowned. "He doesn't? That's just… I don't know him that well, but everything I do know about him suggests that he's a better man than that."

"He is," Selena said. "He's a good man. But he's also a scared man. He's not doing a very good job of handling his fear. It just got all messed up. I found out I was pregnant the night we were at the gala fundraiser for the charity his ex-wife created in honor of their daughter. He freaked out. And I kind of don't blame him. The night was an emotional marathon."

Her eyes filled with tears, and her throat felt strange, like she had swallowed a sword, making it painful to breathe. "I only just found out I was pregnant and I got it confirmed today. And while I was sitting there waiting for the lab results to come in I just… It already hurt to think that I might lose the baby. That maybe I wasn't really pregnant or something had gone wrong with the first test. I don't even have a little person to hold in my arms yet and my love is so big. Knox lost a child… I'm angry at him for hurting me. But I can't fathom what he's gone through, the grief he feels. And as much as he deserves it, I can't even hate him for walking away."

"You don't need to hate him," Scarlett said. "You might need to punch him in the junk."

"I don't want to do that either. Okay. I want to do it a little bit. But I just… I'll do this parenthood thing by myself. You're doing it, right? I'll raise the baby. I can take care of us. I have plenty of money. My child is never going to want for anything."

Scarlett looked down at Carl and stroked a finger over his downy cheek. "You're going to be a good mother."

"You say that with a lot of confidence."

"Because I know you. You'll probably be tired, and you'll probably make mistakes. I know I'm making mistakes all the time. But it all comes back to the love. Love covers a whole lot of things, Selena. I truly believe that."

"I just wish love could cover this." Tears she hadn't even been aware of began to slide down her cheeks. "I love Knox so much. I want him. For me. For the baby. But I also just wish he could have had a different life. Even if it meant losing him, I would give him a different life. But there's nothing I can do to ease his grief."

"Sure there is," Scarlett said, looking surprised.

"What?"

"Go after him."

Like it was the most obvious thing. And maybe to her fearless, confident friend, it was. But Selena was different. She didn't think she could survive getting turned down again.

"He doesn't want me to go after him," she said. "He walked away. He said he couldn't be a father to this baby. He said he didn't love me."

Scarlett shook her head. "Because fear makes you stupid. And that's exactly what *he's* letting happen. But you're letting him hide. You're letting him give in to it. Don't let him. Or at least make him tell you no again. Come on, Selena. He can be a coward all he wants, but you're not a coward. Make him look you in the eye in the light of day and say he doesn't want you or the baby. Make him tell you he doesn't love you. And then make him tell you he's not just saying no because he's afraid."

Selena's heart thundered faster. It hadn't even occurred to her that it might not be over. That there might be something she could do to fix this. "But if he rejects me…"

"Then he rejects you." Scarlett shrugged, looking pragmatic about it.

Selena closed her eyes. "I never wanted to be that woman. That woman who was such a fool over a man. My mother… She stayed with my father even though he was awful. Even after she left him, she missed him. The man who abused her, Scarlett—she said she missed him. I just don't… I don't want to be that person."

Scarlett frowned. "I can understand that. Really. But you know, hopefully, if you go make a fool of yourself for him, he'll make a fool of himself for you at some point, too. If you're going to be together for your whole lives, then there should be a lot of chances for both of you to chase each other down. For both of you to be idiots over love. I guess that's the big difference, right? Your mother was the one doing all of the giving, and your father did all of the taking."

Selena bit her lip. "It would never be like that with Knox."

"Well, there you go," Scarlett said, extending her arm out wide. "It's not the same."

Selena shook her head and sighed deeply. "No. I guess it's not." She put her hand on her stomach. "I don't feel in any way emotionally prepared for this."

"Well, good," Scarlett said, laughing. "Because if you did, I would have to break it to you that you're actually not. It would be up to me to tell you that you are in no way prepared. No matter what you might think."

"It's that different?"

Scarlett nodded. "Harder. Better, too."

Like love in general, Selena supposed.

She stood up, wobbling slightly, her balance off. She blamed the last few days.

"I have to go," Selena said.

"Where to?"

"I have to fly to Wyoming."

Thirteen

Knox had spent the rest of the day hungover and then had spent the next day working out on the ranch. Doing what he could to exhaust himself mentally and emotionally while he got all his thoughts together.

He had been pretty determined about what he wanted to do regarding Selena, but he had to be sure he was going to say the right thing. Because when you told a woman you didn't want her you had to prepare a pretty epic grovel.

He wasn't going to do anything to cause Selena more pain than he already had. And he had a lot of digging to do to find the right words. Through the dark and dusty places inside of himself.

He'd been restless and edgy in the house, and he'd decided to go out for a ride on the property. He urged his horse onward through the field, and he continued on to the edge of his favorite mountain. One with jagged rocks capped in snow that reached up toward the sky, like it was trying to touch heaven. Something he wished he could do often enough.

He wasn't a man who liked graveyards. But then, he supposed no one did. He just didn't find any peace in them. No, he found peace out here. With nature. That was when he felt closest with Ellie.

He looked around at the wildflowers that were blooming, little pops of purple and yellow against the green. Life. There was life all around him. A life to be lived. A life to enjoy. Maybe even a life to love, in spite of all the pain.

It was like that picture of Ellie. Sitting right here in this field surrounded by flowers.

He knew he wouldn't find her here, and yet he'd needed to come to this place. He'd avoided riding out here for the past two years.

Today had seemed like the day to go again. The last time he'd ridden out to this field, the last time he'd seen this view, he was a different man with a different future.

A man who'd known who he was and where he was going.

Now he was a man alone. Struggling to figure out what came next. If he could heal. If he wanted to heal.

An image of Selena flashed into his mind, of her hurt and heartbreak that night in the hotel room. She needed him. She needed him now.

Selena wasn't gone. Selena was here. And they could be together.

"I've got to figure out how to find some happiness, baby," he said, whispering the words into the silence.

Whispering the words like a prayer. "I'm never going to forget you. I'm never going to stop loving you. But I'm going to learn how to love some other people, too. I'm going to take some steps forward. That doesn't mean leaving you behind. I promise."

He closed his eyes and waited, letting the silence close in around him. Letting himself just be still. Not working. Not struggling or fighting. Just existing. In the moment and with all the pain that moment carried.

The breeze swirled around him and he kept his eyes closed, smelling the flowers and the snow, crisp on the air as it blew down from the mountaintop.

That was assurance. Blessed assurance.

Letting go didn't mean forgetting. Moving forward wasn't leaving behind.

And in that moment, as he took a breath of the air that contained both the promise of spring and the bite of winter, he realized it was the same inside of him, too. That he could contain all of it. That he could hold on to that chill. That he could welcome the promise of new life.

There was room for all the love. For the bitter. For the sweet. For everything in between. There was no limit, as long as he didn't set it.

He knew what love could take away. He also knew what it could give. He had despaired of that for so long. That there were no mysteries left available to him. That he knew all about the heights of love and the lows of loss.

But he realized now that he had the most powerful love yet ahead.

The love he chose to give, in spite of the knowledge of the cost.

He just had to be brave enough to take hold of it.

He got down off his horse and bent to pick the brightest, boldest yellow wildflower. He held it between his thumb and forefinger. Ellie's flower. Just like in that picture. He stroked his thumb over one petal and a smile touched his lips.

He put the flower in his shirt pocket, just over his heart, and looked at the view all around him. A view he hadn't allowed himself to enjoy since he'd lost his daughter. A place that was full of good memories. Good memories he'd shut away so they couldn't hurt him.

But they were part of him. Part of his life. Part of her life. And he wanted them. Wanted to be able to think of her and smile sometimes. Wanted to be able to remember the joy loving her had given him, not just the sorrow.

That was what he'd forgotten. How much joy came with love. Of course, you couldn't choose what you got. Couldn't take the good without risking the bad.

But you could choose love. And he was ready to do that.

It was time to walk forward. Into the known and the unknown.

And as long as Selena would have him, he had a feeling it was going to be okay.

He closed his eyes and faced the breeze again, let it kiss his face. Then he mounted the horse and took off at a gallop across the field, heading back toward the homestead.

He got his horse put away and strode out toward the front of the house. He needed to get his private plane fired up, because he had to get back to Texas, and he had to get back fast.

After what he had said to her, a phone call wasn't enough. He needed to go and find her. And he needed to tell her. To tell her he was sorry. To tell her they could do this. They could be together.

To tell her that he was done running.

There was something big, something fierce expanding in his chest. Something he hadn't felt in a long time.

Joy.

Selena.

And almost as if those feelings had brought her out of thin air, he looked up when he reached the front of his house and there she was. Standing in the center of the driveway, looking small and pale and a little bit lost. Selena Jacobs didn't do lost, and he had a feeling he was the cause of that desolate look on her face.

His heart clenched tight, guilt and love pouring through him.

"What are you doing here?" he asked.

She lifted her chin. "I came to get you."

"You can't be here to get me. I was about to get on a plane to go get *you.*"

Her bottom lip wobbled. "What?"

"I don't know what you're here for, Selena. But you have to hear me out first. Because I have to tell you. I have to tell you about everything I've realized. It's been a hell of a time."

"Yeah," she said, her tone dry. "You're telling me."

"I'm sorry," he said. "I'm sorry that I hurt both of us, but most especially you. I'm sorry that I did so much damage. I was afraid to move on. Because…

because of the guilt. I just… The guilt and the fear. It isn't that I don't want the baby. It isn't that I don't love you. I do. I want you, and our baby, so much I ache with it. I want so much that it scares me, Selena, because I haven't wanted a damn thing in years. I haven't let myself want anything. Not even food. Because wanting, needing, *loving*, in my experience has meant devastation. I can't come up with another excuse. It's just that. I am so afraid that I might lose you someday. That if I love you too much, want to hold you too close, that something will happen, and I'll have to face that dark tunnel again. I couldn't survive it, baby. I couldn't. You've meant everything to me for a long time. And now, wanting you as a lover, loving you as a woman, I know that the loss of you would destroy me. The loss of our life. The loss of our child…

"But I can't live that way. I can't live in fear. I can't live holding on to only bad feelings to try and protect myself."

He walked toward her, took her hands. "I called Cassandra. Drunk off my ass. She said something to me… She was right. She said you have to love the person you find more than you love your life together. What Cassandra and I had felt perfect. But only as long as it *was* perfect. Once that fractured, we couldn't put it back together. We didn't want to. We loved what we had more than we loved each other. But when I fell in love with you, Selena, we had nothing. Nothing but those broken pieces. And what you said… I think it's the way forward. That we put these broken pieces together and we make something new. I can't go back. I can never be who I was. But I can try to be something new. To be something different. I can try to be the man you deserve."

She said nothing. Instead she sobbed as she threw her arms around his neck and clung to him, her tears soaking into his shirt. "Seriously?" she asked, the word watery.

"What seriously?"

"You really want to do this?"

"I need to," he said. "I need you. I realized something today, walking around the property. Winter and spring exist side by side here. It's been winter inside of me for a long time. And there's a part of me that's afraid of what letting go of that means. That it means I don't love Ellie enough. Or that I didn't."

"Of course you loved her enough," Selena said. "Of course you do. I know that in our lives together I want to honor that. This baby, this child, is never going to replace what you lost."

"I know," he said. "That was what I realized. I can make room in my heart for both of them." He reached into his pocket and removed the yellow flower, holding it out for her. "This is us. This spring. New life. A new season. I want to make room inside of me for that. I want less cold. Less fear. More of this."

"Please," she said, smiling and taking the flower from his hand. "Yes, please. More spring. A lot more."

"I love you," he said. "I love you knowing that love is the most powerful thing on earth. That having it makes everything brighter, that losing it can destroy your whole world. I love you knowing what it might cost. And maybe that's a strange declaration, but it's the most powerful one I've got."

He cupped her chin, lifted her face to meet his.

"When you're young, you get to dive into things headlong. You get to embrace those big, scary feelings not knowing what might wait for you on the other side. I know. But I want to choose a life with you. More than anything, I want to love you. If you want to love me." He let out a long, slow breath. "You know, if you still can love me."

"I do love you," she said. She held on to his face, met his eyes. "I love you so much, Knox. And the thing is, I could never tumble headlong into it when I was younger because I was scared. But I've grown up. I trust you. And trust has always been the key. I know what kind of man you are. I was afraid of love for a long time, but I was never afraid of you."

"But I hurt you."

"Yes," she said. "You did. But you were hurting, too. You didn't hurt me because you were a bully or because you enjoyed causing me pain. You did it because you were running scared. I get that. But that doesn't mean I'm not going to make you pay for it later."

"Oh, are you?"

"I am." She smiled. "I'm going to make you give my skin-care line preferential shelving in your supermarkets."

"Corporate blackmail."

"Yes," she said, "corporate blackmail. But it could be worse. It could be sexual blackmail."

He wrapped his arm around her waist and drew her up against his body. "Honey," he said, "you couldn't stick to sexual blackmail."

"I sure as hell could," she said, wiggling her hips against him. "And you would suffer."

He leaned forward and nipped her lower lip. "You would suffer."

"Okay," she said, her cheeks turning pink. "Maybe I would."

"Will you marry me, Selena? Marry me and make a new life with me? I'll never be the man that I was. But I hope the man I am now is the one for you."

Her smile turned soft. "He is. Believe me," she said, "he is."

"So that's a yes?"

"Yes," she said. "I never thought I would walk down the aisle for real. But, Knox, if ever I was going to, it had to be with you."

He looked down at Selena, at the woman he had known for so many years, the woman he'd gone on such a long journey to be with.

"Right now," he said, "this moment… It can only ever be you. You're the one worth being brave for. You're the one who made me want to start a new life. And I'm so damned glad that you did."

"Me, too," she said and then squeaked when he picked her up off the ground and held her to his chest.

"I'm also glad that you saved me a flight," he said, heading back toward the house with her in his arms.

"Well, I'm glad to be so convenient."

"You're more than convenient," he said. "You're inconvenient. You made me change. Nobody likes that."

"Oh dear," she said, "however will you punish me?"

He smiled. "I'll think of something."

"You've always been my best friend," she said, hours later when they were lying in bed together, thoroughly sated by the previous hour's activities. "And now you're more. Now you're everything."

"I'm happy to be your everything, Selena Jacobs. I'm damned happy that you're mine."

He kissed her, a kiss full of promise. A kiss full of hope for the future.

And he smiled, so happy that for the first time in an awfully long time he had both of those things.

And more important, he had love.

Epilogue

A child's laughter floated on the wind, and Selena ran to keep up with the little figure running ahead of her. She had long, dark hair like her mother, and it was currently bouncing with each stride.

She had her father's eyes.

Selena's husband was lingering behind her, his speed slowed by the fact he was holding their new son.

Selena turned to look at them both. Knox was clutching the five-month-old baby to his chest, his large hand cradling the downy head. Knox was such a good father.

He was caring, and he was concerned, and he had a tendency to want to rush to the doctor at the very first sniffle, but she couldn't blame him. And watching the ways in which their children had opened him up… it made her heart expand until she couldn't breathe.

"Carmela!" Selena shouted. "Slow down."

Their daughter stopped and turned to look at them, an impish grin on her three-year-old face. She stopped, in the field of yellow-and-purple flowers, with the snow-covered mountains high and imposing behind her.

Selena turned back and saw that Knox had stopped walking. That he was just standing there, staring at Carmela.

Selena took two steps back toward him and put her hand on his forearm. "Are you okay? Do you need me to take Alejandro?"

"No," he said, his voice rough.

Carmela was turning in a circle, spinning, careless and free out in the open.

Knox couldn't take his eyes off her. He was frozen, his expression full of awe.

"What is it?" Selena asked.

"I just can't believe it," he responded. "That I have this again. This chance to love again. To love her. To love him." He brushed his hand over baby Alejandro's head. And then he turned those gray eyes to her. His desire for her was hot, open. It made her shiver. "To love you."

He leaned in and kissed her, and she shivered down to her toes.

"I remember feeling like I had nothing," he said. "Nothing to hope for. Nothing to hold. And now... I have hope. I have a future. And my arms are full."

Selena wrapped her arms around him and rested her head on his chest. "My best friend knocked me up on accident," she said. "And all I got was...this whole wonderful life."

He kissed her one more time, and when they parted she was breathless. Then the two of them walked on toward their daughter, toward the future. Together.

* * * * *

Don't miss a single installment of the
TEXAS CATTLEMAN'S CLUB: THE IMPOSTER.
Will the scandal of the century lead to love for these rich ranchers?

THE RANCHER'S BABY
by New York Times *bestselling author*
Maisey Yates.
RICH RANCHER'S REDEMPTION
by USA TODAY *bestselling author*
Maureen Child.
A CONVENIENT TEXAS WEDDING
by Sheri WhiteFeather.
EXPECTING A SCANDAL by Joanne Rock.
REUNITED... WITH BABY
by USA TODAY *bestselling author Sara Orwig.*
THE NANNY PROPOSAL
by Joss Wood.
SECRET TWINS FOR THE TEXAN
by Karen Booth.
LONE STAR SECRETS
by Cat Schield.

Holy. Hell.

Damon stopped on the stone driveway leading down to the wrought iron gate.

A woman stood outside the heavy bars, her fingers clutching the filigree that surrounded the house number in the center of the entrance. She was the right height. Even from this distance, he could recognize those dark brown eyes. The delectably full lips. The hair that had once been sun-streaked blond was now a shade of honey-gold pinned back in a way that showed hollows under cheeks formerly rounded with good health. Her frame was thinner. Her skin paler. And her expression was wary, lacking the vibrant self-confidence of the capable businesswoman he remembered.

Yet there wasn't a single doubt in his mind.

"Caroline."

He forced himself into motion again, even though he had no idea what he would say to his long-lost wife.

* * *

Claiming His Secret Heir
is part of the McNeill Magnates trilogy:
Those McNeill men just have a way with women.

CLAIMING HIS
SECRET HEIR

BY
JOANNE ROCK

MILLS
BOON

First Published in Great Britain 2018
By Mills & Boon, an imprint of HarperCollins*Publishers*
1 London Bridge Street, London, SE1 9GF

© 2018 Joanne Rock

ISBN: 978-0-263-93586-8

51-0118

To you. Yes, you, my reader.
Thank you for choosing this book to read,
and for spending some of your valuable time
with me. Whether you're reading one of
my stories for the first time, or you've read
many of my books over the years,
I appreciate you more than I can say.
I hope our shared love of romance brings
us together again down the road.

One

Steeling herself against the January chill, Caroline Degraff stood outside the gates of the Los Altos Hills mansion that would have been hers and wondered how to get in.

Her grip tightened on the wrought iron fence separating her from the French château-style home she'd helped to design but never lived in. Caroline guessed that she would already be visible on the property's security footage. Too late to turn back now from this crazy idea to show up unannounced.

Prepared to deceive the husband she'd once loved.

But she had to know the truth about the powerful man on the other side of this imposing enclosure dotted with motion-detecting cameras. The man she'd married eleven months ago but hadn't seen since their honeymoon, tech company mogul Damon McNeill. Her father, a well-known investor in Silicon Valley projects, had hated Damon even before the marriage. He'd sent Caroline into Damon's California-based social media software business, Transparent, as an entrepreneur in residence—a common practice in tech start-ups that could benefit from an outside business perspective— in the hope she'd find weaknesses Damon's investors could use to oust him from the CEO position. Except Caroline had fallen in love with Damon rather than give her father the scathing scouting report he'd craved.

She hadn't known until that time in her life how cold and manipulative her father could be. He'd called Caroline a traitor and refused to attend the wedding, preventing anyone else in her family from doing so, as well. That had hurt her deeply, but she'd been so in love with Damon, it hadn't mattered. The weeks they'd spent together in Italy for their honeymoon had been the happiest days of her life.

Then she'd travelled briefly to London on her own after the honeymoon. From there things got fuzzy in her mind. She remembered she'd argued with Damon on the phone because she'd seen her father while she was in London. But she also remembered returning to this very house overlooking San Francisco Bay. She'd never even seen Damon that day, and she'd been trying not to notice too many details of their new, custom-built home so they could enjoy it together when he got home from work. Then, while she'd been staring out over the Bay, she'd heard him enter the house.

Only it hadn't been him. After that, her memories of the ordeal were totally blurry. But she knew that day had been the beginning of a months-long nightmare. She'd been kidnapped and held for a ransom Damon never paid. He'd never informed her father at all. He hadn't even reported her as missing; the story was absent from all the news sites she'd scoured online.

Grinding her teeth together, she felt the old signs of fear and claustrophobia, the racing heart and cold sweats. These were the physical symptoms of panic attacks she'd been working for weeks to overcome with the help of a good therapist. She still wasn't able to shake the effect of weeks spent scared and alone, captive in a remote village somewhere on the Baja Peninsula, with guards who treated her humanely enough, but never let her forget that they would kidnap one of her younger siblings, too, if she didn't do as she was told.

Thoughts of Damon rescuing her had gotten her through the nights. Along with the comforting knowledge of their child growing inside her. A child she hadn't even been able to tell him about before the abduction.

"Ma'am?" A young man called to her through the wrought iron fence, making Caroline jump back from the scrolled gate. "Can I help you? Is the call button acting up out there or is the main house not answering?"

Her heart thumped so fast and so hard she couldn't speak for a moment. Everything felt frozen while her pulse rate skyrocketed and the guy with a man-bun, and carrying a pair of gardening clippers, came closer.

Who would ever believe she had graduated with honors from a prestigious East Coast business program when she couldn't even find her tongue to answer a simple question? Who would guess she'd helped her investor father to make millions on the two other tech start-ups she'd recommended he buy, back before her life fell apart?

These days, Caroline didn't even trust her memory of what happened yesterday, let alone last year. She'd been drugged a few times during her captivity with roofie-style pills that made past events fuzzy. Between that and vicious bouts of morning sickness, her health had been in serious decline by the time her captors rowed her out to a remote island and left her stocked with enough food for a month, unguarded and alone. Thankfully, the drugs hadn't harmed her baby, but she'd been too ill to try looking for help. When she'd regained enough strength to do so, just two months before her due date, a fisherman had found her and contacted her father.

"Ma'am?" The gardener tossed aside a handful of dead roses and set down his heavy trimmer. With just a tee on, he seemed oblivious to the chill in the air. "If you go around to the back entrance, I can let you in the service gate."

Caroline swallowed down the panic as she remembered her therapist's affirming words. *You are strong and capable. Trust your instincts.*

"Is Mr. McNeill home?" She had to see Damon. To learn for herself if he'd only married her to win a favorable review of his company for the sake of the investors. Was it just to cling to his CEO position for another year and keep control of Transparent?

Had her charismatic husband duped her completely, even going so far as to marry her for profit?

Or had her father been feeding her lies from the day he'd quietly brought her back to one of the family homes in Vancouver to deliver her baby? Damon had made it impossible for her to contact him directly—his cell phone was disconnected and he wasn't responding to emails. Calls to his office weren't returned, although she had been too afraid to leave her real name, worried her father would find out she'd gone behind his back and contacted her husband. All along, her father had insisted Damon wanted nothing to do with her, and her internet searches seemed to support that. Her father had shown her a tabloid article that speculated about how Damon's grandfather had recently required his heirs be married for one year to inherit a portion of the McNeill legacy. Caroline hadn't even known Damon was related to those McNeills, one of the richest families in New York, but now she wondered if their marriage had been purely for business reasons.

But she'd certainly discovered a few disconcerting clues in the last two weeks that made her think her father could be manipulating her. Transparent had a board meeting one week from now, and she wanted to learn the truth before her father maneuvered Damon out of his CEO position.

"I think Mr. McNeill is here today, but you need an appointment to see him." The gardener peered at her curiously, perhaps wondering why any guest of a multimillionaire tech genius would show up at the gate with no vehicle and dressed more like domestic help.

She'd debated her strategy until she felt ill about it. But there was no other way. Damon had abandoned the cell number she had for him and wasn't responding to her other attempts to contact him. He hadn't launched a public search for her or filed a missing person report. If it was just about her and their marriage—maybe Caroline would simply walk away and start over.

But she had their six-week-old son to think about. And if there was any chance that what she and Damon had shared was real, she needed to understand what happened. Why he was carrying on his life as if she'd never existed.

"He'll want to see me." She hoped. She didn't have to fake the nervous tremble of her fingers as she fumbled in the back pocket of faded jeans and removed the tattered piece of paper her sister had found hidden in their father's den. "I want to ask him about this."

The document looked like it had gone through the washer and dryer a few times. Or maybe it had fallen into the Pacific with her once, when she'd tried to escape her captors. Caroline genuinely didn't remember. She'd suffered amnesia during the ordeal, but her memories were coming back.

Not that Damon McNeill needed to know.

"A marriage certificate?" Squinting at the washed-out ink, the gardener scratched the spot under the man-bun, shifting the dark hair side-to-side. "For Mr. McNeill?"

"I'm Caroline Degraff." She pointed to the name on the second line, trying to recapture the sense of shock she'd felt when her sister first showed her the paper.

She hadn't recalled the marriage for weeks after her father rescued her, yet he'd never mentioned it until she confronted him. He'd tried to keep her isolated from her family so she wouldn't learn the truth. Her mother was dead, her younger brothers at boarding school and her sister had been at university in the States. What else had he kept from her about her marriage? About Damon? Her therapist had gently suggested that Caroline had been subjected to gaslighting.

The gardener's gaze flicked up from the paper. "You're Mr. McNeill's wife?"

Her throat went dry. She remembered enough about Damon to know he might never forgive her for this deception she had planned. But if he'd been the one tricking her into romance in the first place, what would it matter?

She was going to fake amnesia to find out what he

had to say about her disappearance. She had to know for sure if her father had been lying to her about her husband.

"I'm honestly not sure." She allowed all the doubts and fears of the last months to come through in her voice. That much was not an act. "We'll have to ask him because…" She bit her lip and blinked back the swell of emotion before she spilled out a lie that was crucial to getting the answers she needed for her child. "I don't remember."

"What did you just say?" Damon McNeill pressed the pause button on the video he'd been watching on the big screen in the downstairs media room.

He'd asked not to be disturbed while he watched a hacker's demonstration of how to unlock the security on the software Damon's company was bringing to market in the spring. The hacker had found legitimate issues Damon's technical team would need to patch. If he asked his own staff to troubleshoot, he would have gotten thirty-page reports that gave him the all-clear to go into production. Ask a twenty-two-year-old who busted complex digital coding for the thrills and the cash? He got results in forty-eight hours.

Except he'd have to rewind the video to the start now, because he couldn't keep his focus on the demonstration when he was getting calls from the housekeeping service. Damn it. He'd only hired outside help to get the house ready to put on the market since he didn't want to keep the place he'd barely set foot in since construction had finished a year ago.

Caroline had loved their Los Altos Hills home, spending weeks with the architect to get the design just right. And yet she'd disappeared from the property

mere hours after setting foot in it for the first time after
it was completed. That was more than enough reason
for him to want the house gone from his life forever.

"Mr. McNeill, there's a woman at the gate." The head
of the maid service had arrived this morning to personally oversee the housecleaning and stage photos for the
Realtor. "She says she's your wife."

The phone slid from his hand, dropping halfway
down to the chair before Damon slapped at it, stopping the descent by pinning the cell to his chest.

He went motionless, holding the device in place
while keeping his heart in his rib cage at the same time.

What. The. Hell.

"What kind of joke is this?" He knew Caroline
couldn't be out there. He'd hired private investigators
to find her. He'd paid a ransom to someone claiming to
have kidnapped her. He'd searched half the world for
her himself, convinced something had happened to her
even though her wealthy and powerful father insisted
Caroline had simply found Damon unsuitable and no
longer wished to be married.

Stephan Degraff had said Caroline wished to travel
and was entitled to her privacy, a story that was upheld
by the occasional hits on her credit card. An apartment
rented briefly in Prague. A used car purchased in Kiev.

Damon had never bought it.

He shot to his feet.

"No joke, sir." The housekeeper's voice was cool and
modulated, as if she'd grown accustomed to disagree-
able clients long ago. "She has a marriage certificate
with your name on it and she looks like the photograph
I'm staring at over the mantel. Shall we open the gate?"

Caroline on his doorstep after her father insisted
she'd seen the error of her ways in marrying Damon

and had walked out on him for good? Not damn well likely.

"I'll be right there." Damon was already charging toward the door. He shoved his way through with one shoulder. "Find the number for the local police, in case we need to send this crackpot a message about what happens to people who play pranks like impersonating my wife."

Cold fury roared through him. Caroline had been gone for ten and a half months. He'd chased false leads all over Europe, tracking withdrawals from her bank account and use of her credit card, trying to find her. All the while her father insisted she'd left her marriage and wished to be left alone. But then a ransom note had shown up weeks later, which he saw as proof she'd been kidnapped. But the police had never believed the kidnapping theory, insistent the ransom note was sent by someone who took advantage of her disappearance by demanding cash for her safe return.

Damon had gladly paid, transferring money to an offshore account on the appointed day. He'd never heard from the so-called kidnappers again.

Pounding his way up the stairs to the main floor, he couldn't wait to see who would have the nerve to pull a prank like this. He barreled through the handcrafted double doors that had delayed their move-in date by two weeks and stalked down the stone walkway covered in dried leaves that led to a fountain imported from India.

He hated all of it. And he rarely had an outlet for any of the fury that had seethed in him for weeks—fury that was a welcome change from the old fears for Caroline, the guilt that he hadn't done more to find her and the stark sense of loss…

Holy. Hell.

He stopped on the stone driveway leading down to the wrought iron gate.

A woman stood outside the heavy bars, her fingers clutching the filigree that surrounded the house number in the center of the entrance. She was the right height. Even from this distance, he could recognize those dark brown eyes. The delectably full lips. The hair that had once been sun-streaked blond was now a shade of honey gold and pinned back in a way that showed hollows under cheeks formerly rounded with good health. Her frame was thinner. Her skin paler. And her expression was wary, lacking the vibrant self-confidence of the capable businesswoman he remembered.

Yet there wasn't a single doubt in his mind.

Caroline Degraff had blindsided him the first time they met, igniting an incendiary passion that made him overlook every need for caution. Her father coveted Damon's company, but it didn't matter. Stephan Degraff had sent his smart, exquisite daughter to spy on Damon's operation, possibly to undermine him and oust him from his own company. But who cared? Damon would have given up everything—*everything*—to have Caroline.

Just when he'd thought he'd won her forever, after a honeymoon so beautiful that it hurt to recall, Caroline had vanished. She took her wallet and her car, a bag of clothes and a few prescription pills, all signs that, according to the cops, meant she left of her own volition. Her powerful father had convinced the police his daughter was entitled to her privacy and that she would file for divorce in her own time. The fact that Caroline left behind her wedding ring seemed to support the theory. Local law enforcement refused to file a missing person report, leaving Damon on his own to locate her. He'd been advised by multiple private investigators and the police not to talk to the media, so he hadn't. A story had been leaked to the press at one point, but her father had forced the news outlet to print a retraction. His lone effort to reach out to the public—discreetly asking for any information about her from the employees who had worked with them both at Transparent—had resulted in that ransom note.

Yet he never saw Caroline again.

Until now.

It occurred to him he'd stopped moving toward her. That he'd been staring at her like he'd seen a ghost for long, drawn-out moments, his head flooding with memories while his fingers ached with the need to touch her and see if she was real.

"Caroline." He forced himself into motion again, even though he had no idea what to say. Had she left him? Was she here for that divorce her father promised she would one day demand?

She backed up a step from the gate as he neared. She wore jeans with threadbare knees and faded thighs that hugged her subtle curves. A gray wool sweater with fat toggle buttons kept the chill out; the temperature was in the midfifties, with a cold breeze blowing off the bay. She wore no makeup, her face looking younger even as the expression in her eyes seemed far older than he remembered. She looked wary. Cautious.

And, if he read her expression correctly…confused. She appeared bewildered by his appearance even though *she* was the one who had shown up on *his* doorstep.

"Damon McNeill?" she asked, her arched eyebrows knitting together as she pursed her lips.

Just what the hell was she asking him? He noticed

that one of the guys on the landscaping crew was hovering nearby, a crinkled piece of paper in his hand.

Damon pressed a button on his phone to open the electric gate and stared down the gardener while the bars slid silently to one side. "You can leave now. Water the roses or whatever."

"Sure thing." The guy nodded fast and seemed grateful for an excuse to leave, but first he ambled closer and handed Damon the faded, worn paper. "She said she found this."

Damon would have stuffed it in a back pocket to focus on Caroline, but the gold seal in one corner caught his eye.

Their marriage certificate.

"I don't understand." He moved closer to the wife who had once held his heart. The woman who now stared at him like a stranger. "Why did you bring this?"

His pulse pounded hard. He braced himself to hear the words he dreaded. The news that she wanted to end their marriage legally. Forever.

Alone on the private road that led to the mansion, she stuffed her hands in the pockets of the oversized sweater she wore, the fabric hugging her body tighter at the movement.

There'd been a time when he would have picked her up off her feet and wrapped her in both arms. Even not knowing where she'd been, what had happened or why she'd come back now, Damon still wanted to kiss her more than he wanted explanations. Something about her body language, so hesitant, restrained him.

"You're Damon." She seemed to seek confirmation, her brown eyes flecked with gold scanning his face, as if calculating the sum of his features. "I saw your photo online, but you look so much like your brother. Cameron."

Half brother, he silently corrected her while his brain tried to make meaning out of the nonsensical words.

"It's been less than a year since you saw me last. Do I look so different now?" He'd kissed her for long minutes in the airport in Florence, hating to part from her after the honeymoon. Their home in Los Altos Hills—this house—hadn't been completed yet. So she'd gone to see a friend in London while he flew back to the States for business that couldn't wait. Business he'd come to regret sorely in the last ten months, especially since they'd argued during the time they'd been apart and he'd always wondered if that had been the reason she left.

As it turned out, she hadn't just been seeing her friend, after all. She'd gone to the UK to make amends with her father, who would give anything to take control of Transparent. Stephan Degraff's plans to oust Damon were about to come to a head one week from now at the final board meeting before the product launched.

Had Caroline been helping her father take over Damon's company from the start?

"I don't remember." Her eyes were haunted. Scared. Unsure. "I've been in Mexico. With amnesia. I remembered my name two months ago, but it's taken time to recall more than that." She glanced up and away from him. Shut her eyes for a long moment before she began again. "I've had this paper ever since I woke up in a fishing village on the Baja Peninsula. But at the time, I didn't even know that name was mine."

Damon could not have been more stunned if she'd been the ghost he'd first imagined. Amnesia? A bracing gust of wind sucked the breath right out of him.

"You don't remember me? Us?" He tried to envision what this meant for them. Behind him, he heard the sprinkler system switch on.

"Nothing." She shook her head slowly, a wave of her honey-gold hair bumping her cheek. "I looked you up online weeks ago, but I've been scared to come because there was…no mention of me being missing. No photos of us together." She lifted her shoulders in an awkward shrug. "I thought maybe the marriage certificate was fake. Or that we divorced and you'd moved on—"

"No." He'd been living in a state of suspended animation without her. Hell, he couldn't call it "living" at all. He'd spent his time chasing leads about her all over the globe, incapable of "respecting her privacy" the way her father had demanded. "I've searched everywhere for you."

He wanted answers about where she'd been. If she'd been kidnapped or if she'd left him of her own free will. His private investigators had spent endless hours chasing down fake leads for her whereabouts—it was as if she'd wanted to purposely disappear, or someone had spent significant time making it look that way.

He still had her wedding rings that she'd left behind.

But he remembered reading somewhere that chasing memories wasn't good for an amnesia victim. And didn't the fact that she was suffering from amnesia suggest she'd been through a trauma already? The need to protect her—to make sure nothing else hurt her—overrode everything else. He needed to keep her safe and get her healthy.

And, selfishly, he couldn't help but see her return as a second chance.

If she'd left him, she didn't remember.

Once she was well and whole again, Damon had a chance to rewrite history. To show her they could be good together again.

To win her back.

"I don't know where I've been. My memories should come back in time." She pulled a hand from her sweater pocket and smoothed aside the wave of hair that brushed her cheek. For a moment, he could see the old Caroline in the gesture. The vibrant, flirtatious woman who had captivated him the moment she strode into his office, demanding a position on his team. "But until they do, I'm not sure where to go. I've been at a shelter the last two nights."

The idea appalled him. How long had they been in the same state while he'd been lost in alternating bouts of grief and bitterness, not knowing what had happened to her?

"You were right to come home." He stepped closer, careful to give her space but needing to touch her.

She flinched and backed up a step, reminding him that they might be married but they were still essentially strangers in her mind.

She just needed time. Something he was more than happy to give her since he was determined to help her remember how happy they'd been together before that one stupid argument. And, hell, if she *hadn't* been happy, he'd make her remember something better than that.

"You belong here, Caroline," he assured her. "Always."

Two

To keep her guilty conscience at bay, Caroline sank deeper into the thick cushions of the hanging daybed on the second-floor patio and thought about her son—her whole reason for lying her way into Damon's home.

Lucas was safe with her sister, Victoria, in a carriage house Caroline had rented for them nearby. She'd paid in cash and used a fake name to ensure their father wouldn't find them. She'd timed their trip to coincide with his business visit to Singapore, but she doubted their absence had remained a secret past the first forty-eight hours, which meant he could be learning about their defection anytime now. Would he guess that Caroline had run straight to Damon in Los Altos Hills? Would he be worried about their safety and send the police?

She had no idea, but she knew Lucas and Victoria would be safer in the carriage house than with her. Victoria swore that their father had purposely tried to keep her from seeing Caroline while she was recovering from her ordeal. Her version of events since Caroline's return—so different from her father's—had been the impetus to see Damon for herself. To find out if he loved her or if he'd only married her for expediency's sake.

Still, she found it difficult to accept that her father coveted Transparent so badly that he would use her as a pawn. She'd been kidnapped, after all. How could Damon have kept that a secret from her family? Her father would have reported her missing if he'd known, but he said that her bills—cell phone, car payments, the mortgage on a small apartment she maintained in Manhattan—were being paid consistently, even during the times when she'd been a captive.

How was that possible? Someone was lying to her, or else she really was going crazy.

Caroline stared into the leaping flames in the stone fireplace and tried to relax before Damon returned. He'd started the blaze to ward off the late afternoon chill as the sun set over San Francisco Bay in the distance. The view was beautiful and the patio heater nearby sent bonus warmth her way. As if the blankets she burrowed under weren't enough. Damon had dragged half the linen closet outdoors when she professed a desire to sit on the patio, extending her the courtesy he might give an invalid.

Which made sense, considering he thought she was suffering from amnesia. And she still did suffer from it, of course. Just not to the degree she pretended.

While she waited for him to return with their dinner, she closed her eyes and reminded herself this was absolutely necessary. She couldn't think of any other way to find out if he had only wed her for material gain, or if he'd genuinely cared for her. And she refused to introduce him to Lucas until she knew for sure. For now, all she knew for certain was that her husband hadn't come for her when she'd been kidnapped. Her captors said he didn't pay the ransom and didn't want her back. While she had no reason to trust them whatsoever, her father's version of events supported this.

He'd sworn he hadn't known she was missing until that fisherman discovered her. But something didn't add up, and she knew her father would lie to further his own ends—of course he would. He hadn't even breathed Damon's name in his house when she'd still been confused about her ordeal and couldn't remember who the father of her child was. How could her dad do that? He'd always been manipulative, relentlessly steering Caroline in the direction he wanted. But she'd drawn the line at allowing him to tell her who she could—and could not—marry.

She would learn all she could in the next two days, and then she would tell Damon the truth. Two days was her limit for being apart from Lucas. But if there was a chance she and Damon could have a future together, she would introduce him to Lucas personally and maybe they could be a family. If it turned out that Damon had never loved her and married her for self-serving purposes?

She would hire a lawyer and sue for full custody through formal channels. She had her own money, accounts solely in her name. She'd changed all the passwords on them last week after discovering someone might have accessed them to pay her bills while she'd been held captive. If necessary, she would hire a financial investigator to help her track what happened there. But her balances were still healthy from her years of nonstop work before she'd met Damon. And right now, she cared far more about her personal affairs than her bottom line.

"Caroline?" Damon asked quietly from the opposite end of the patio, a tray of food in his hands. He must have come up the outdoor stairs; she'd been so caught up in her thoughts, she hadn't heard. She would need to be more careful, more on guard in the future.

He waited there now, balancing the heavy, domed silver platter. With his dark brown hair and deep blue eyes, her husband shared the features of his equally handsome brothers she'd met at their wedding. Damon was slightly taller than Jager and Gabe, though, his six-foot-three frame well-proportioned. And whereas his younger brother, Gabe, possessed an easygoing nature that made him quick to smile, Damon was serious, often pensive and intense. More like his driven older brother, Jager, who managed the brothers' businesses while Damon and Gabe both tended to follow their passions. Damon had always been deeply passionate about his work, he could lose track of the hours spent on business, and he told her once that she was the only woman who'd ever intrigued him enough to get him to spend time away from his company.

He'd had the same effect on her, enticing her out of her office to savor a sunny day or breathe in a cool breeze off the Santa Cruz Mountains.

"Yes?" She straightened from her slouch, propping herself higher on the back pillows so they could share the daybed like a sofa.

A spark arced and popped from the stone fireplace.

"Just checking to make sure you hadn't fallen asleep." He headed her way with the tray, settling it on the low tile table nearby. He'd changed from his earlier cargos and tee to a lightweight black wool sweater and gray trousers. The winds off the bay were chilly now that the sun had gone down. "Are you sure you'll be warm enough out here?" He checked the setting on the patio heater and held his broad palms out to test the temperature. "We can take dinner inside, if you prefer."

"This is perfect, actually." She remembered those early days of recovering her memory when she had grounded herself in the everyday, simple things to anchor her. Enjoying the feel of a warm bath. Stroking the furry back of her sister's cat, Socrates. "I saw a physician about the amnesia in Mexico and she said that surrounding myself with the familiar will help me to recover my memories." Caroline smoothed a hand over the cashmere blanket that Damon had given her earlier, her heart picking up pace as she prepared to dig for information. "I'll bet I spent a lot of time on this swing."

Damon settled on the edge of the cushion beside her, the warmth of his sudden nearness making her senses come alive. She'd forgotten the way he smelled—the musk and spice of his aftershave that sent a flood of pleasurable memories to her brain. Of shared kisses. Incredible sex. Orgasms. Curling into his side afterward and having him stroke her back until she fell asleep.

Her body tingled at just the thoughts.

"None." His blunt response was so at odds with everything she was feeling—the word as stark as his expression. "This house was still being built while we were on our honeymoon in Florence and the Tuscan countryside. We never spent any time here."

She held her breath, waiting for him to say something about the day she'd been abducted. The only day she'd ever stepped inside the completed house. The events of that afternoon were still fuzzy in her mind. Her father had insisted she was planning to leave Damon that day, but she couldn't remember why.

When he continued, however, his attention had returned to the tray of food. "I've only been in town for a few days myself, so I'm afraid the meal offerings aren't as extensive as I would have hoped for your return." He tugged off the silver dome and set it on the stone patio, revealing two empty plates and a cold cut platter. "I called for a grocery delivery and a catered meal for later, but for now, this is the complete contents of the refrigerator."

"The turkey looks good." She leaned forward to make half a sandwich for herself, but Damon politely waved her away.

"Let me." He cut open a small roll and stabbed two slices of meat with the knife. "For months, I would have given anything for the chance to do something for you. See you. Touch you. Bring you dinner."

She swallowed back the knot of emotions his words tangled inside her. What she wouldn't have given to have him there when she'd been scared and alone on that island in Mexico, too ill from her pregnancy to even walk outside and look for a neighboring village.

"What did you think happened to me?" She couldn't help the rasp of her voice that betrayed the pain she kept hidden inside. Clearing her throat, she tried again. "I mean, as I told you, there is nothing about me being missing online."

It was as though she'd simply ceased to exist after their wedding.

He set down the plate with her sandwich on the coffee table before settling his hand on her knee through the blanket. It was the first time he'd touched her since she arrived and it affected her as much as she had feared it might.

"Are you sure you want to talk about this now? So soon after arriving?" He caressed her knee with his thumb through the thick layers of cashmere and wool, the intimacy seeming so easy and natural for him.

As if he truly cared about her.

"I have driven myself crazy trying to piece together the past on my own. I'm hoping you'll help me fill in some of the blanks in a way that will be less stressful."

His blue eyes locked on hers in the firelight, searching.

Could he read her better than she realized? Did he have any inkling that she might not be telling him the whole truth? Never in her life had she felt so unsure of herself as she had these last few months. She used to be so steady and self-assured. Now, everything her father had told her about her past contradicted what she had believed about it.

"I definitely don't want to add to the stress of remembering." Damon returned to the tray and finished making her turkey sandwich, which he passed over before pouring her a drink—water with a twist of lemon. "I did a quick scan online about amnesia recovery while the housekeeper put together the meal, and it said that the senses can sometimes trigger memories more easily. Hearing a song or smelling something familiar can help, like your physician said."

Thinking about the flood of memories from the scent of his aftershave, Caroline would say the doctor had been spot on.

"If I never lived here, maybe there's nothing to be gained by me staying here." She had allotted two days to solving the mystery of Damon. She couldn't afford to waste time. "Is there somewhere else that might be more meaningful?"

Nibbling on her sandwich, she watched him make another for himself, the muscles in his forearm shifting and flexing as he reached for cheese slices and fresh tomato. She'd fallen for him hard and fast the first time—getting engaged after knowing him for only six weeks and marrying him a month after that. She needed to be more cautious now, to learn all she could about him.

"You lived in a hotel when you first came to town to research Transparent. I had a smaller house close to the company in Mountain View." He leaned back against the cushions lining the daybed swing, keeping a foot on the patio floor to anchor them.

Caroline was grateful both for the darkness and Damon's focus on keeping the daybed from rocking, which took his attention away from her while her face flamed with memories of time spent at his place. How many nights had she languished in his bed there before their wedding? They'd made love in virtually every room. Also, the sauna. The pool house...

She didn't dare ask him about that home. Her voice might betray her.

"Did we have dates anywhere significant? Special?" She frowned, trying to remember how it felt to have no frame of reference for conversations about the past. When her amnesia had been at its worst, she'd asked questions constantly. "Or maybe we should visit the business, if that's how we met."

Would seeing her office help? They'd worked in the same building.

But she needed to be careful. Damon was a very smart man. Brilliant, even. She'd been fascinated by his mind and his innovative ideas for Transparent even before they'd met. One misstep in her ruse could ruin her cover story for being here.

"We went hiking in the Santa Cruz Mountains once." He studied her with a clear blue gaze that missed nothing. "And you were fixated on the Winchester Mystery House for a while. We had picnics in the gardens while you kept an eye out for ghosts."

His unexpected choice of memories touched her. Those outings were such brief pockets of time they'd spent together compared to the long hours they'd invested in his business and, later, trying to deal with her father.

Her driven, focused father would have hated that she'd gone ghost-hunting. Did he know she'd ever done something like that?

"Do you remember?" Damon asked suddenly, making her realize she'd been quiet a beat too long, thinking about how thoroughly her father had schooled her to think like him, to fill her days with work the way he did.

"No." She shook her head quickly, returning her gaze to her plate. "I'm just surprised to imagine myself ghost-watching. It hardly sounds like the hobby of a businesswoman."

She'd been a different person with Damon, though. Their courtship had been a revelation. It hadn't just been about love. It had been about play. Fun. Laughter.

Things she hadn't really taken the time to savor in a life full of goals set ever higher ever since childhood, from violin recitals to debate team championships to achieving perfect test scores. Then, after graduating from college, it had been about obtaining a lucrative position in a New York financial firm before joining her father's company. Her father had trained her to focus on work relentlessly, while Damon wasn't afraid to enjoy himself.

"I think you liked the diversion of something whimsical after the stress of long days at the office." He took a bite of his sandwich and seemed to reconsider the answer. "Then again, maybe you were just trying to give *me* a diversion after the long days at the office. We never did see any ghosts."

And his sense of whimsy had faded, she recalled, toward the end of their honeymoon when her father had urged her to come to London to help him with a takeover of a UK company. She'd been excited for the chance to end the standoff with him. Damon had been stunned she would even consider it. In the end, she'd told him she would head to London anyhow to see a friend and at least meet with her father. It had been an unhappy way to wind up their romantic Italy trip.

But could it have really been the end of their marriage?

"Then let's try again." She still hoped their son could one day see the more lighthearted, loving side of Damon. Provided it ever existed outside her hopeful imagination. "Let's go back to a place with happy memories."

The next day, with Caroline in the passenger seat of his white Land Rover, Damon pulled into the Los Trancos Preserve in the mountains above Palo Alto. The woods were close to the house, easy to access from the home they'd built together.

It seemed like a million years ago now. Their dating. Their marriage. Even her disappearance. Last night, after she went to bed, he had reopened his old investigation notes from those frantic first few months she'd been gone. He'd taken his time reading over everything again, looking for new clues now that he knew she'd been in Mexico. All of the evidence he'd found on her whereabouts had led him to believe she was in Europe. She'd deposited money in her account in London and used an ATM card in Prague, Paris and Venice. Her credit card had been used for a room in a Barcelona hotel, but when his PI had shown her picture around the place, no one on staff recognized her.

Had someone been impersonating her? At the time, he'd guessed she wanted to disappear and had paid someone well to cover her tracks. Whatever the case, it was as much a mystery as ever. While he was inside the house retrieving food for Caroline, he'd also messaged the PI his half brothers had used to find him when he'd been traveling Europe looking for her on his own. At the time, he had ditched his cell phone so as not to be distracted with work calls or requests from his family to return home. He'd bought a burner and focused on following Caroline's trail, but he'd come up empty handed.

Bentley, the investigator who had located Damon when Jager and Gabe got fed up with his disappearing act, was excellent. But unfortunately, he'd been hired by a branch of Damon's family he would rather forget. Damon's father, Liam, had left their mother when they were kids and Damon, Jager, and Gabe had no use for the guy. But recently, their grandfather, Malcolm Mc-Neill, had made it his mission to reunite all of his grandchildren, even the illegitimate branch. Damon might not have much use for all the new blood relatives in his life, and most especially not his father, but he could appreciate the value of a good PI. Maybe Bentley would figure out what a whole team of investigators had failed to the first time around.

Just what the hell had happened to his wife?

Talking about the good times with her last night had felt surreal, like the experiences had happened to someone else. He'd been trying so damn hard to forget her, and now? She'd forgotten all about him instead.

If that meant she forgot all about her bastard of a father, Damon didn't mind the sacrifice one bit. He hoped the subject of Stephan Degraff wouldn't surface between them today since Damon knew he wouldn't be able to scrounge a single positive thing to say about the guy who was still fighting to take control of Transparent. Her father was on a mission to turn the rest of the investors against Damon so they could pull in a more experienced CEO to run the company.

Over his dead body.

"Are you sure you feel up to this?" Damon asked Caroline as he switched off the Land Rover. "We could always go for a Sunday drive instead."

She was as beautiful as ever, but her pale skin and thinner frame made her seem frailer somehow. Or maybe it was simply because he knew she'd suffered a trauma that had given her amnesia. He didn't want her to exhaust herself. He'd suggested she call a doctor first thing this morning, wanting to know what a professional had to say about her condition, but she'd been adamant she was well enough. When he hadn't backed down, she'd conceded to a visit tomorrow if they could have one day together first.

He'd been hard pressed to argue. He was having a tough time just letting her out of his sight. Tomorrow would be soon enough.

"I'll be fine." She gave him a smile that threw caution to the wind. He remembered it from when they'd climbed the bell tower in Florence and she'd challenged him to see who could scale the four-hundred-some steps faster. "The fresh air and exercise will be good for me."

He still wanted to wrap her in cotton and keep watch over her for days, but he nodded.

Leaving the picnic basket in the back, he locked his door before stalking around to her side and helping her down. He only touched her briefly, putting his hand on her forearm to steady her while she hopped out, but it reminded him how long it had been since he'd touched a woman. Touched her. Even when he'd thought she was never coming back, he hadn't consoled himself with someone else. In his mind, he'd still been married.

He watched Caroline take in the sights, her head turning as she studied the oak woodland and grassy knolls, the combination of forest and rolling hills scented with bay leaves and the cool, damp earth. The sun shone warmly enough for a southern California winter day, but little light penetrated the thickest patches of trees nearby.

Dressed in a dark blue running suit and a pink tee she'd found in her closet, she started toward the closest hiking trail, her new white sneakers fast on the well-worn path.

"Ready?" Her ponytail swung around her shoulder as she turned back to see him.

"Which way looks good?" he asked, curious if she had even a subconscious memory of the place.

"It seems sunniest in that direction." She pointed toward the grassier path heading south.

He followed her, discreetly lifting branches out of her way when low boughs seemed too close to head height. For the most part, however, the trail was wide open and the preserve was quiet save for an older man taking his Dalmatian for a walk.

When they reached a high spot with a view of the Bay, Caroline dropped down to a flat rock and zipped her jacket up midway. Damon sat beside her, admiring the view from the peak, and all the time debating if he should ask her more about her ordeal or if he should focus on making new, happier memories. Before he could decide, she turned dark brown eyes his way.

"You said you searched everywhere for me." Her voice was quiet. Serious. "Why didn't you report me missing?"

The wind whistled through the tree branches overhead, a lonely sound that echoed through him.

Yesterday, when they'd touched on this subject, he'd been too stunned by the realization that she didn't remember him to focus on the question. Now, he heard the hurt in her voice. The doubts underlying the question. She had hesitated to come back to him, thinking he might have "moved on."

Which gave him no choice but to bring up her father.

He ground his teeth at the very thought of the man.

"Your father showed the police proof you'd been in touch with him. He said you'd left the marriage of your own volition and said I should respect your privacy." He studied her expression, trying to interpret what she might be feeling at that news. "Do you remember much about him?"

"No. I've made progress since those first days where I didn't recognize my own name. I can visualize my family, as well as college and the jobs I had after I graduated. But I don't really remember anything about why I came out to Los Altos Hills. The last apartment I can recall clearly was in New York City." She drew her knees up to her chest and wrapped her arms around them. "I can remember that I worked for my father, and

I have a few memories of my childhood, but not much about him personally."

Just his luck, she hadn't wiped out all memory of Stephan Degraff. Just of Damon.

"Then you might recall your close relationship with your father," he ventured carefully. "How often the two of you spoke." Stephan Degraff counted on Caroline's business advice for his investments, calling on her any-time day or night if he had a question. The guy was re-lentless. Manipulative. And then, a disturbing thought occurred to Damon. "I'm surprised you didn't go to him first if you didn't recollect anything about me."

"I—" She hesitated, a mixture of emotions evident in her eyes. Guilt. Worry.

"It doesn't matter." He covered her knee with one hand, not wishing to upset her. "I'm glad you came here."

"But my father told the police that I left you? Was it you who called the police?"

"You texted me when your plane landed after you re-turned here from London." He wasn't going to mention the argument they'd had about the UK trip. "It didn't make sense to me that you would contact me then, only to pack up and leave me."

"Of course not." She shook her head, ponytail swing-ing. "Unless we'd been unhappy?"

"Right after the honeymoon?" He removed his hand from her knee to withdraw his phone and tapped open the gallery of images he'd saved. "Scroll through a few of those and see if they look like pictures of unhappy people."

She shifted positions, lowering her knees to glance over the photos of them on the Ponte Vecchio, seated at their favorite café for morning espressos, in front of the Uffizi Gallery, at the top of that bell tower they'd climbed. Most of the images were of her smiling and him kissing her cheek, but in a few of them, you could see them both grinning. Wildly in love.

Or so he thought.

"My God." Her finger swiped faster, sending pictures spinning off the screen, one after another. "Did you show these to the police? To my father? What did they say?"

Her voice quavered. Her whole body seemed to tremble. *Damn it.*

"I'm sorry." He wrapped an arm around her shoulders and gently slid the phone from her hands. "I didn't mean to upset you. We'll figure it all out, okay? Just relax."

She shook like a leaf. He couldn't understand what, precisely, had her so troubled. But he didn't want to rile her more.

"This is too important for me to relax." Edging away from his touch, she shot to her feet and paced around the small lookout spot. "Would you be able to put me in touch with the officers you spoke to? The police who supposedly talked to my dad?"

"Supposedly?" Getting to his feet, he frowned. Defensive. "You don't believe me?"

She tipped her head to one side. Thinking. "I've invested a lot of time struggling to piece together the past. I don't want to worry that the perspectives I'm hearing are biased. I'd like to know what a neutral party has to say."

"Of course." He reached for her again, needing to offer some kind of comfort when she was clearly rattled. "Caroline, it's not good for you to be so agitated. Let's think about something else. Something happier."

"Why would you believe I left of my own free will if we were so happy?" With her lips pursed and her eyebrows scrunched in confusion, she stared up at him waiting for answers he didn't have.

Okay. Answers he didn't want to share.

"Every couple argues. When your father said you'd been contacting him regularly, I assumed I must have missed something, but you'd be home soon." He didn't want to delve into this now. Not when his whole purpose today had been to relive good times.

"And when months went by?" She peered up at him, frustration simmering in her clear brown eyes.

"I took solace from the knowledge that you loved me once and you'd love me again." He dropped his palms on her shoulders, drawing her closer. Wanting her to feel the connection that still stirred inside him every time she was near. "I knew what we shared wouldn't just disappear. I hired private investigators to find you myself."

He could feel her swift intake of breath. A mixture of wariness and some warmer, answering emotion flared in her eyes, but she didn't move away.

The wind stirred the leaves at their feet and whirled around them. To Damon, it felt like it was drawing them closer.

"I'd like to show you what I mean." He teased a touch along her jaw, testing the softness of her creamy skin, breathing in the faint scent of roses.

He wanted to take his time, to soak in the feel of her, the warmth.

If she remembered nothing else, she had to remember this.

Slowly, he grazed his lips along hers, the barest brush of mouths. Of breath. He tipped his forehead to hers, standing still, waiting.

When her fingers curled into his shoulders, her nails softly pressing through his sweater and tee, Damon's blood surged in a heated rush. He ground his teeth against the bolt of hunger and forced himself to step back. He simply took her hands in his and caressed and kissed them.

"That proves passion is still there," she said finally, her voice expressing the same hunger he felt. Yet she backed up another step and slid her hands away from his, tucking them into her pockets. "But what about love?"

Three

Late that night, safe in the master suite that Damon had wanted her to use during her stay, Caroline called her sister on a burner phone to check on Lucas.

Her Mexican captivity had been frightening and lonely, but the experience had taught her about making herself difficult to find. The men who'd held her went through cheap, pay-by-the-minute phones like candy, opening new packages of them every week. They were perfect for contacting their colleagues and not leaving a trace. When Caroline left Vancouver with her son and her sister three days ago, she'd purchased similar devices at a few different places along the way, driving almost to Montana to cross the border discreetly.

Illegally.

But since they were US citizens anyhow, she didn't feel as guilty about that as she did about deceiving Damon. Assuming, of course, that he really did love her. Even before the toe-curling kiss he'd given her on the hiking trail, those honeymoon photos he'd shown her had gotten to her. Could that kind of happiness be faked? She knew she'd been in love with him. But the pictures had her almost believing he sincerely felt the same way for her.

Almost. And she needed to be absolutely certain.

Because if Damon was being forthright about what they'd shared and about her father's role in not reporting her missing—that meant her dad was guilty of... She didn't even want to think about it. If that was the case, her father had far more to answer for than simply withholding the truth about her husband.

Earlier in the evening, she'd attempted to phone the two police officers Damon had spoken to, but neither was on duty. Surely Damon had to feel confident they would back up his story if he provided their names so readily?

Her sister answered the phone on the third ring, sounding flustered or maybe scared. "Caroline? Are you okay?"

Victoria's worry fueled her own. Caroline sat up straighter.

"I'm fine. Are you safe? Is Lucas okay?"

She could hear Victoria huff out a breath on the other end, relaxing. In the background, the laugh track from an old sitcom added an odd note to their tense greeting.

"We're good. He's fast asleep in the other room and I have the baby monitor right next to me so I can hear if he so much as sighs."

A pang of longing stabbed Caroline in the chest. She wished she were holding her infant son right now, the warmth of his small body comforting her and giving her strength after this stress-filled day.

"I miss him so much. Thank you for taking care of him." She drew a steadying breath herself, padding over to the California king–size bed to slip between the luxurious sheets. She propped herself on down pillows stacked against the leather bolster. The room's color scheme of tans and creams was so neutral it felt like an old sepia-toned photograph. "Have you seen anyone? Heard anything?"

They'd both been worried their father would have them followed. Or he'd cut short the Singapore trip to come after them himself. It didn't matter that they'd crossed the border in secret; Stephan Degraff would probably guess Caroline's ultimate destination. Her father knew she was upset that he'd withheld Damon's name from her when she'd been confused and suffering from amnesia.

At the time, her sister had been doing a semester abroad program for her degree and hadn't been aware of what was happening. Victoria had some flexibility in her schedule this semester to work on her master's thesis, but she was due back at Stanford by the end of the month.

"It's been quiet. I haven't left the carriage house and I've kept the blinds drawn, like we talked about. I've got enough diapers and formula for a whole week, I think."

"I'll be back long before then." She briefly relayed to Victoria what she'd learned from Damon, ending with the news that an officer from the Santa Clara County Sheriff's Department was supposed to return her call in the morning.

After a long silence, Victoria let out a low whistle. "My God, Caro, I don't even know what to say." She swore softly. "Because if your husband is telling the truth, that means Dad is—"

"Dangerous?" She barely breathed the word, not wanting to believe it herself.

When her sister scoffed, Caroline shifted against the pillows, flipping the cream-colored sheet up higher against her red floral nightshirt.

"Dad might be controlling," Victoria mused aloud, the laugh track still rolling from the television in the background. "Hell-bent on winning, even, but that doesn't make him dangerous."

Right. This was the father who'd pushed them on the swing when they were girls and used it as a fun physics lesson. The same dad who took them camping and taught them how to tell which plants were poisonous. He might have had high expectations for his daughters, but Caroline had never had reason to doubt his love.

"How could he not have been worried if Damon told him he thought I was kidnapped?" She felt like she was missing pieces of a bigger puzzle. "Why wouldn't he have at least looked into the possibility? Was he that angry with me that I married someone he didn't approve of?" She thought back on the last few months in her father's house. At first, she'd been ill. But as she gained strength and her memories began returning, she'd told him she'd been abducted. "Furthermore, why didn't he call the police when I told him what I remembered about the men who held me against my will?"

"But Damon said Dad told the cops you'd been in contact with him shortly after you were taken," Victoria said carefully. "Maybe that's true and you still have gaps in your memory from the drugs?"

"I do have gaps in my memory. I know that." Frustration simmered, but how could she expect other people to believe her version of past events when she had so many doubts of her own? "But I didn't imagine that house in Mexico or the rotating staff of guards who stood watch every day for months."

A shiver chilled her skin and she burrowed deeper in the covers, tugging the khaki-colored duvet up over the sheet. She reached a hand out of the blankets long enough to tap the remote for the gas fireplace. The flames leaped higher inside the pale-river-stone hearth. The house was quiet and she wondered if Damon was still awake. He'd kept things light between them after their kiss, his behavior toward her solicitous, polite... caring, even. But he'd seemed determined not to revisit conversation topics that could "agitate" her and he'd reminded her over dinner that she'd promised to see a doctor tomorrow.

For the amnesia she didn't really have. The last holes in her memory now were drug-induced and, her doctor said, might never return.

"Okay." Victoria turned down the television on her end of the call. "But what if the gaps in your memory are bigger than you realize? What if you were a captive for weeks and not months? Isn't there a chance Dad could be telling the truth about having contact with you at first? Maybe you just don't remember that you left Damon—like Dad said—because it was too upsetting."

Her chest constricted. She wasn't sure if she resisted the idea because she still cared about her husband, or because she wanted her son to have a relationship with his father. Or both.

"Why wouldn't I have told you if I left my husband?" Caroline asked, tracing the buttons on the fireplace remote with her thumbnail.

Victoria was her closest confidante and had been since they lost their mother to an overdose of prescription opioids five years ago. Actually, she'd been closer to Victoria since well before that, as their mother had struggled with depression for years before her death. Caroline and Damon had that loss in common; his had died when he was young. At least she'd been close with her father. Damon's dad had stopped visiting his illegitimate sons before Damon was a teen, choosing to be a father to his offspring by his legal wife rather than Damon and his brothers.

"Just guessing, but I was buried in coursework that semester, so maybe you held off because of that." She seemed to hesitate and for a moment Caroline heard nothing but the soft hiss of the flames in the fireplace before Victoria continued. "Or maybe you were keeping me out of it since Dad asked you to keep your distance from me when you chose to marry his business enemy."

It was all speculation of course, since Victoria couldn't know Caroline's reasons any better than Caroline did. A wave of fatigue hit her.

"But I remember someone entering the house. And it wasn't Damon." She had to have been kidnapped. She remembered being frightened that day.

"You were drugged," Victoria said softly. "There's a reason they give benzodiazepines to patients to forget about surgery. It makes things fuzzy and confusing. Time bends. That's not your fault, Caroline."

Right. Her physician had said the same thing. But that didn't make it any less scary or infuriating.

Before she could say as much, however, she heard a baby's cry on the other end of the call. She sat up straight in bed, poised to help before reminding herself that she wasn't in the same house as Lucas.

"Guess it's time for the midnight bottle." The crying quieted for a moment; Victoria must have turned down the volume on the baby monitor. "I'd better go."

"Okay. Wish I was there." Caroline wanted her baby with her. Always.

She hated that she had to deceive people—her father and her husband, too—just to find out who was telling her the truth.

"Soon. Be safe, Caro. And good luck." Victoria disconnected, leaving Caroline feeling more alone than ever.

Tomorrow, she'd have to find a way to divert Damon from her doctor's appointment. She would go in person to the police station if she didn't hear from the officers first thing in the morning. Her future was riding on what they had to say. Because once she found out if Damon had been telling her truth, she would confront him with her own: that although she couldn't remember if she'd left him or not, she knew without a doubt she'd been held against her will for some of the time.

Damon had been the man she'd missed then, the one person she'd yearned to see. No drugs could make her forget how much she'd loved him once. Too bad she was no closer to knowing if he'd felt the same about her. Worse, she feared that even if he had returned those feelings at one time, she might have destroyed that love forever by keeping their child a secret.

"I've got a simple solution for all your problems, brother," Damon's younger brother told him in their Skype call at dawn.

Well, dawn West Coast time. Where Gabe sat, on the back patio of the Birdsong Hotel near the McNeill family compound in Martinique, it was already late morning. Exotic birds chirped in the palms swaying behind him, the whole image like an eighties pop-art painting full of pinks and turquoise.

"My missing bride finally returns home and doesn't remember me. Her investor father wants to kick me out of my own company. I found a glitch in the new software we're about to launch. And our older brother is happy just to sell off everything and get out of Dodge so he can spend time with his new wife." Damon sat in the breakfast nook off the kitchen, one of the few rooms in the gargantuan house that didn't echo when he had a phone conversation. Also, he'd chosen this spot since it was close to the stairs from the master suite, and he needed to stick near Caroline. "Now, explain to me how you could possibly have a solution to all those problems."

Gabe had surprised him with the call this morning after Damon texted him the night before, asking for his opinion on the potential sale of Transparent. Their older brother, Jager, wanted the sale to happen so they could start over and get out from under the pressure of investors who wanted to control the direction of the company.

Namely, Stephan Degraff.

Damon couldn't let go yet. He was grateful to Jager for leading the company while Damon had searched for Caroline. But now he was ready to return his focus to the technology he'd developed. Technology he believed in. He wasn't selling. And he wasn't allowing Stephan Degraff to unseat him from the board, either.

"Go to New York," Gabe informed him simply, spreading his arms wide as he rocked back in a purple-painted lounge chair, as if the answer was obvious. "Call on the new family relations and see if the McNeills will put their legendary money where the old man's mouth is. Granddad says he wants us to be part of the family. Let him dust off the wallet and buy out Degraff to prove it."

"Spoken like the baby of the family." Damon leaned back against the leather banquette cushion and toasted Gabe with a mug of black coffee. "It doesn't gall you even a little to go begging for a handout?"

"Who's begging? Degraff would sell out his own kid to take over Transparent and the dude is worth a fortune. Clearly there is capital to be gained from your software idea." Gabe shrugged, his sunglasses glinting with the reflected noontime glare. "Although, to be honest, I only invested because we're related."

"Generous to a fault, you are." Damon shook his head, content to let Gabe ramble on about his assessment of "Granddad" following a recent phone call. But Damon's thoughts lingered on something else his brother had said.

How much would Stephan Degraff "sell out" Caroline to obtain control of Transparent? What lengths would he go to?

A year ago, Damon had told himself that it didn't matter what Stephan did because Damon's love for Caroline surpassed everything else. But what if Stephan hadn't just sent Caroline to Transparent for business reasons—to be Damon's entrepreneur in residence? What if Caroline had come to get close to Damon personally, as well?

The idea was ridiculous. She was a beautiful, brilliant woman. She would have never married him solely because her father wanted to spy on Damon's company. But the fact that she'd disappeared right after the honeymoon, coupled with the fact that she'd returned now, claiming to have no memory of the marriage, right at a sensitive time of transition for the business...

Across the kitchen, he saw the door of the master bedroom open silently. He closed his laptop with no warning to Gabe, not wanting Caroline to overhear the discussion. Damon watched her as she stepped onto the bamboo floor, her shoes in her hand, as if she wanted to make as little sound as possible. She was fully dressed in fresh clothes she must have found in the closet. A cranberry-colored purse was slung over the shoulder of a shawl sweater that swung around her knees. Her gaze was on the door.

Leaving?

"Good morning."

He startled her so badly she dropped the shoes she'd been carrying, brown leather boots that clunked heavily to the floor. Damn it. How had he let his brother's comment twist him around to think the worst of their relationship? He knew Caroline better than that. Didn't he?

Shoving to his feet, he was across the room and at her side. Picking up her shoes and setting them neatly by the kitchen island, he reached to steady her arm.

"I'm sorry, Caroline." He smoothed a touch along her shoulder, remembering the feel of her lips against his the day before. "I should have given you a warning."

"No need." She waved off the apology, her high ponytail brushing her shoulder when she moved away. "You live here. I'm the newcomer." She tipped the cell phone in her hand to show him. "I'm on hold with the local police department. I'm trying to speak to the officers you mentioned yesterday."

"I thought they were going to call you when they went on duty?" He had been with her when they'd left a message at the station the day before.

"Shift change is at seven a.m. I thought I'd try to reach them before they head out for the day." Her attention shifted to the call and she tucked the phone against her cheek. "Yes, I'm here. I'm holding for Officer Downey."

Damon watched her pace the kitchen, her outfit a swirl of rich colors reflected in stainless steel appliances. She must have been transferred to the officer she wanted because she gave her name and the details of why she was calling, checking notes that she pulled from her purse to read him approximate dates Damon had given her yesterday.

Having his story checked was a strange sensation. Long before he'd dreamed up the idea for Transparent, he'd been a successful businessman. In Martinique, where he and his brothers owned a marina and a historic plantation home available for private parties and corporate retreats, he had a reputation for being a fair employer and a generous contributor to local causes. In Silicon Valley, he was a man people listened to. He filled lecture halls when he spoke at prestigious universities about digital progress.

But the woman he'd given his heart to had to verify his story with the police. Was that normal for amnesia sufferers? He added it to the list of things to ask the specialist, who'd made time to see her today when he called in a favor from a friend.

For now, he distracted himself by making a fresh pot of coffee for Caroline while she quizzed the cop on the other end of the phone.

"Thank you so much," she finally said, her brown eyes darting Damon's way. "I appreciate knowing more about what my father said." She seemed to hesitate as she listened to the officer. She shook her head even though he couldn't see her. "No," she finally said. "Not yet. But I will contact you as soon as I'm ready to come in to give a statement."

Caroline thumbed the off button and tucked her phone in her bag. Was it his imagination or did she take her time? The suspense was killing him.

"You need to give a statement?" he asked after a moment.

She slid the purse strap off her shoulder and laid the bag on the gray granite counter of the island. Licking her lips, she eyed him warily, ignoring the coffee mug he'd set out for her.

"I suffered amnesia, Damon." Her chin was tilted, her posture defensive. "But I've recovered more memories than I led you to believe when I showed up here two days ago."

That…was not what he'd expected.

Two days ago, he'd been sure she'd only come to see him to obtain a divorce. He braced himself for that news now, his whole body tensing.

"Why would you do that? Mislead me into thinking you didn't remember what happened between us?" He hated that he hadn't been a better husband. That he'd allowed her father to come between them when he'd known from the start that Stephan Degraff only wanted to get his hands on Transparent.

He couldn't believe that Caroline had been a part of her father's plan to usurp him all along. Refused to believe it.

"I needed to know why you didn't report me missing." The hurt in her eyes seemed real enough. "It didn't make any sense. Besides, my father told me—"

"Your father?" His worse fears were confirmed. She'd been talking to that bastard all along.

Cold filled the hollow pit in his gut.

"He found me in Mexico. Helped me to locate a doctor to treat my amnesia—"

"When?" Damon regretted the harshness of his tone, but it was as though his heart had been ripped right out of his chest. Forcing his voice lower, he took a steadying breath. "Exactly how long have you and your father been playing me, Caroline? For two days? Or from the very beginning?"

Four

Caroline closed her eyes for a moment, giving herself a chance to think about her child. If Damon had truly loved her at one time, she owed it to Lucas to find out. Those photos from the honeymoon had filled her dreams the night before, stirring the slimmest hope that she and Damon could find some kind of happiness again.

Assuming the connection hadn't been faked the first time.

She ached for the deep love she'd seen in those photos. But as she opened her eyes to meet Damon's frosty blue glare, she wondered if she could ever find it again. He rose from the dining table in the breakfast nook, leaving his phone and laptop abandoned on the sleek hardwood surface as he stalked toward her. He stood on the opposite end of the island from her, almost as if that was as close as he could bear to be.

"My father doesn't even know I'm here," she told him

when she felt steady enough to respond to his accusation. She was walking a thin line here, being truthful about her father, but being dishonest about her amnesia and not sharing about the baby. "I've been struggling to remember what happened this past year and I have reason to believe Dad was thwarting my efforts more than helping them."

Damon's head tipped back, the subtlest evidence that her words hit him like a blow. "So you don't deny it? You ran to your father when you left me?"

"I was abducted from this house ten and a half months ago, Damon. I was upstairs in the spare bedroom I planned to make into my office when someone came in." She hadn't set foot in that room on this visit, afraid she would have a panic attack if she recalled what happened next. The day was blurry in her mind, but she recalled suffocating fear. "That's why I need to make a statement to the police. I was kidnapped, and yet the police never believed I was in any danger."

He laid his broad palms on the island's granite countertop. Once upon a time, he'd put his hands on her, as often as possible. Now, he'd rather keep them splayed on cold stone than touch her.

One more hurt among so many others.

"You just spoke to the police, so you know that's not true. I called them the same day. I came home and when you weren't here—" He stopped himself and shook his head. "It was your father who said you had been in contact with him. He convinced the cops you were fine."

"And that's why I'm going to the police and making a formal statement." She still held the notepaper in her hand with the dates, times and names of law enforcement officials Damon said he'd spoken to about her whereabouts. "Someone came into this house, put a hood over my head and drugged me. I ended up in Mexico and after being captive in various places, I was abandoned in a house on the Baja Peninsula in Mexico. By then, I'd been drugged multiple times, and I could no longer tell what month it was, let alone what day."

She had been so frightened. All the more so when she'd discovered she was pregnant, since her worries were twice as big for the baby she carried. She'd been terrified the drugs were hurting the precious life inside her. Even through the amnesia, fear for her child's health was the one coherent thought she'd retained. She'd asked her father for multiple pediatricians to assess Lucas's health and make sure he was okay.

Damon's hands flexed against the granite. "I'll take you to the police station myself. They said the ransom note was a hoax, but maybe now they'll see things differently."

Could she trust him? She wanted to, which made her all the more cautious. "The guards told me you didn't give them the money." She'd been deflated that day. It had been a turning point in those lonely weeks of captivity. Because even though she knew to be skeptical of what they told her, she believed they would have released her if Damon had given them the exorbitant sum they'd requested.

"They lied to you. I wired the full amount to an overseas account as requested." He slid his hands off the counter and walked slowly toward her in his socks. He still wore the same clothes as the night before, a black tee and cargoes, tipping her off he'd never been to bed. "I would have paid it twice over to get you back, Caroline, but I didn't trust the cops when they said it was a hoax since you had been in touch with your father and you were still paying your bills—the mortgage on your New York apartment, a car payment on the Mercedes, a few things you kept in your own name after the wedding."

"You paid the ransom?" She swallowed hard, her thoughts shifting again as she discovered yet another new piece to the puzzle that kept changing.

Damon stopped a foot away from her, his strong shoulders too enticing in the morning light slanting into the kitchen. How easy it would be to lean on him. To share the burdens and the confusion. To let him sort out the mess that she couldn't figure out no matter how hard she tried.

"I have proof. I kept meticulous records. I hired private investigators to follow leads." His blue eyes bored into hers, and she had the sense that he was seeking holes in her story. After all, he had just accused her of deceiving him with her father's blessing. "The police can have everything my team discovered."

"I'm sure that would help." Her mouth was dry. Had it been a mistake to reveal all of this to him and not to the police first? She'd been so romanced by those damned honeymoon photos that she'd hoped—maybe—she could have more trust in Damon than her father.

"Someone laid a very deliberate false trail, Caroline." He spoke slowly, articulating the idea simply and clearly, as if she was as addle-brained as she'd pretended to be when she showed up. "Do you understand what I'm suggesting? Someone spent a great deal of money making it look like you hadn't been abducted."

She understood what he was saying—and whom he was accusing—but she couldn't believe it. "My father would never knowingly subject me to harm, if that's what you're getting at."

"How can you be so sure? You must have your doubts

if you left without telling him where you were going. You came here, to me, even knowing that he wouldn't approve." Damon inched closer, just enough to lay a hand on her shoulder. "So if you're not still playing a game with me, you must distrust him."

She traced the pattern in the gray granite countertop, thinking. She needed to tell him about Lucas. The time had come. "After I was kidnapped and drugged, I truly suffered a bout of amnesia. I was ill. I didn't know who to trust."

"You went to your father."

"At the time, I didn't remember you."

Damon studied her, no doubt weighing her words.

"What made you change your mind?" he asked, his hand falling away from her.

She missed his touch, even when they were at odds. Even when she didn't know if she could truly confide in him.

"My father never mentioned you. He didn't say one word about me being married, even though I was confused about— I couldn't remember anything." She had told her father about the pregnancy, but he claimed not to know anything about who she'd been dating before the kidnapping, suggesting the father of her child was a one-night stand. She had been devastated when she learned the truth. That she'd had a husband who would be hurt to have missed out on their child's birth. "But then my sister came to see me. He couldn't keep me isolated forever. She gave me the marriage certificate. I guess my father had a copy in his office."

It hadn't occurred to her to wonder why. She'd had a lot of other worries in her head and in her heart at that time while she struggled to remember her past.

"Victoria told you the truth." Damon nodded, a satisfied gleam in his eyes. "I've never met her, since your dad forbade anyone in your family to attend our wedding." His jaw flexed. "But of course, you remember that now, don't you?"

"Yes. Victoria's revelation was a big help in recovering more of my memories." Caroline paced around the kitchen island, not trusting herself around Damon when she felt this magnetic draw to him. "And the therapist who was helping me with the amnesia suggested I'd been a victim of gaslighting. She didn't openly accuse my father. I think she believed that maybe my captors had been the ones to feed me lies and withhold information." Caroline hadn't wanted to believe she could be susceptible to suggestion and misinformation, but once Victoria revealed the truth, Caroline had to face the reality that her father no longer had her best interests at heart. "And by then, I knew that it was my father who didn't want me to remember you."

"If any other man hurt you this way…" Damon didn't finish the thought.

He didn't need to.

"Damon." A fresh dose of anxiety poured through her. "I came here because I had suspicions about my father, but I also didn't trust my memories where you're concerned. That's why I pretended to have amnesia to a greater degree than I really do. To see what you'd say."

She tried to gauge his reaction, studying his expression. The kitchen was brightly lit now that the sun had risen well above the horizon. Birds chirped in a nest outside the window near the sink, providing an incongruously cheery soundtrack to the most difficult conversation of her life.

"You should have gone straight to the police." His jaw was set, his shoulders tense. "Do you have any reason to believe those kidnappers won't come after you again? My God, Caroline. You took an incredible risk if you believed me capable of such a thing." He speared a hand through his dark hair, ruffling the long layers shaggy for want of a cut. "Sure, now you know it wasn't me. But you could still be in danger from whoever took you."

"I wanted to see you face-to-face, for myself. To come to this house and see how it felt. What else I might remember." She closed the space between them, leaning against the kitchen island where he still stood. "Maybe that was reckless of me. I'm doing the best I can with the unimaginable things that have happened to me. Who could possibly prepare for what I've been through?"

"We need to talk to the cops. Now." He charged toward the door leading to the three-bay garage.

"Damon, wait." She needed to tell him about Lucas before things went any further and they got law enforcement involved. "There's something else you need to know first."

He stopped. Turned. "Whatever it is, the police will surely want to hear it." He picked up his set of keys from a rack of hooks near the door. "I think you'll be telling the whole story a few times today. The trail for those bastards who took you has long gone cold, but the sooner we can get law enforcement after them—"

"Damon." She followed him, pausing just inches from him. "Please. This is important." She took the keys from his hand. Set them on the bare desktop of a built-in workstation near a wall of cookbooks. "There's another reason it took me so long to get back to you."

"And we can sort through all of it after you give your statement to the police."

There was no way to put this but to simply say it. So she did.

"I was pregnant when they kidnapped me." She had wondered more than once what his reaction would have been like if she'd gotten to tell him the news months ago.

For a moment, he was utterly expressionless. "Pregnant?"

"Yes. I—"

"But you said you were drugged. Didn't those bastards know you were pregnant?" A dangerous light entered his eyes. His nostrils flared.

"*I* didn't even know at first." She blinked fast. Took a deep breath. "But he's fine, Damon. I had our son—a perfectly healthy baby boy—six weeks ago."

Five

The news staggered him.

Damon stared at Caroline, uncomprehending. They had a son. And she'd been lying to him on every level imaginable. The sting of betrayal tainted what should have been the happiest news of his life.

He had a *son*. But the woman he'd loved hadn't trusted him enough to tell him. She'd gone to her lying, conniving father rather than turning to her husband.

"Damon?" Caroline's voice was tentative.

He realized he'd backed up a step. That he'd somehow dropped onto one of the leather bar stools at the kitchen island while the baby bombshell tore away any hope he'd had that he could salvage the love he'd once had for his wife.

"Where is he now? Our son?" The word tripped awkwardly off his tongue.

"Safe. Victoria helped me and Lucas leave my fa-

ther's house." She blinked rapidly, no doubt hearing the
edge in his voice. "I rented them a small house nearby.
I made sure it had a security system. We paid cash and
she has the doors locked in case my father tries to have
us followed."

Damon felt his fury rising. He would decimate
Stephan Degraff's business interests. Ruin him finan-
cially. And that was just for starters. He would follow
Gabe's advice and make peace with the rest of the Mc-
Neills—his grandfather and half brothers—to leverage
their business influence if that's what it took to bank-
rupt Caroline's father.

But first, he needed to prevent himself from falling
down the emotional rabbit hole after this latest betrayal
from his wife. He had a son to think about.

"We must have conceived during the honeymoon. I
didn't know I was pregnant for the first two weeks that
I was a captive." She licked her lips, speaking quickly
as she straightened a white cup hanging from one of
the wooden hooks over the coffee bar. "I didn't have a
pregnancy test to confirm it, so it was only a guess for
a few weeks, but once I started having morning sickness, I knew for sure."

His brain reminded him he had a role to play here.
He was a father now. Protector to a vulnerable child and
a wife who could still be the target of a kidnapper who
hadn't been caught. He would be a better father than
his own worthless DNA contributor had been, so when
push came to shove, he would do right by his child and
Caroline, too. But it was damned hard to know the right
words to say when he didn't trust the mother of his baby.

"We'll talk on the way to the police station." He
picked up the Land Rover keys again, determined to get
a statement on file so the police could launch the inves-

tigation that should have started months ago. "We need to get the ball rolling to find the person responsible for your disappearance. Then, I want to meet my son, hire a security team, and ensure you are both protected 24/7."

Shoving to his feet, he went to the door to the garage and held it open for Caroline. She hurried to follow him, hugging her sweater around her while he helped her into the vehicle. She kept up a steady stream of words as they drove to the Los Altos Hills police station, telling him about the house her father had taken her to in Vancouver for the last five months, and the doctor she'd worked with for her amnesia.

But it was a one-sided conversation. Damon listened with half an ear, still not sure if he could trust what she was telling him, all the while wondering if he should assemble a private team of mercenaries to hunt down whoever had taken her and his unborn child.

For now, he settled for escorting her into the local police station so she could give her statement formally and they could begin legally searching for whoever had abducted her.

They spoke to a detective together and then filled out more paperwork separately. The police assured him they would interrogate her father for providing false information about his contact with Caroline. Damon sincerely hoped that was a felony crime worthy of prison time, but didn't mention as much to his wife. He needed to get a grip on his emotions and figure out his next move.

First, he'd see his son. Bring everyone back to the Los Altos Hills house. Hire security. After that? He would take his family to New York and solicit aid from multibillionaire Malcolm McNeill before the Transparent board meeting. As for Caroline, he couldn't afford to alienate her no matter how much her deception had cost him. More than ever, he needed to get her wedding ring back on her finger so they could raise their child together. If that meant using the attraction between them to his advantage, he would not hesitate. Lucas's future was too important.

He sat with her through her interview with two different officers, one from the Los Altos Hills Police Department and another from the Santa Clara County Sheriff's Department. She kept her composure well, even when she described her kidnappers leaving her alone for weeks while she'd been ill and suffering from dehydration and morning sickness.

The police said they would assign more drive-bys to keep an eye on the property, but Damon had his doubts about the sheriff's department keeping his wife and child safe.

Now, while they waited for an official copy of her statement before leaving the station, Damon reached for her hand and squeezed it. He refused to let her betrayal destroy their marriage.

"I'm eager to meet Lucas after this," Damon said quietly as a uniformed officer wheeled a bicycle past them, a skinny teen trailing behind and muttering curses. "I'll do everything in my power to make sure you both feel safe with me."

The suburban police station had been quiet for most of the morning, but as it neared noon, activity picked up. A young couple came in hand-in-hand to report a stolen car. A confused older woman was released into the custody of a middle-aged man who offered his arm to her for support while they walked out to his car. As Damon watched the two of them leave together, one supporting the other, it occurred to him how at one point he'd found that kind of loving relationship. But it had been a lie.

Unaware of his thoughts, Caroline leaned forward in the molded plastic chair beside him. "The house has better security now than it did a year ago, judging by that massive electronic gate out front, so I'm sure we'll be safe with you. We can pick up Victoria and Lucas as soon as I turn this in." She flipped over the manila folder she was holding. "I miss my baby so much, I don't want to wait another minute."

"*Our* baby," Damon corrected in a tight voice. "Of course you want to see him. And I want to meet him." Just the thought of that moment hit him in the chest, making each breath hurt as though glass shards were being raked through his insides. "But since your father will look for you here first, I would like to move you and Lucas somewhere safer." He stopped himself as the detective reappeared to take their paperwork. Damon rose to his feet, never relinquishing Caroline's hand.

He would at least play the role of loving husband. He needed her to acknowledge him as Lucas's father and work with him to create a stable environment to raise their child.

After receiving assurances that the department would do "everything possible" to find Caroline's kidnappers, Damon drew her out of the police station and into the noonday sun. Her long shawl swirled around her knees, her high-heeled leather boots clacking on the asphalt as they walked toward the Land Rover.

"Where did you have in mind?" she asked as he helped her into the SUV.

"For starters, I'd like us to take a trip to New York City." He had to restrain himself from buckling her in with his own two hands. What he'd really prefer was an armored car and a few Secret Service guards, but he settled for watching her fasten the seat belt before he closed the door.

"My father knows I kept an apartment in Manhattan," Caroline said as he joined her in the vehicle, where she already had the directions for the rental house she'd taken for her sister and their son pulled up on her phone. "Dad might look there after he strikes out at the house in Los Altos Hills."

"You wouldn't be staying at your apartment." Damon turned the key in the ignition and pulled out of the parking lot, more than ready to put the cops behind them for the day. "I have family there that I never knew about. Family that's been reaching out to my brothers and me to join the fold. We could stay with them."

Caroline remained silent for a long moment. Damon turned onto a road that led them toward the bay.

"We can stay somewhere else, of course." Damon tried to gauge her expression, realizing she might have lost her ability to trust him to the same debilitating degree that he had lost all trust in her.

They needed to find a way to move past that. Fast.

"My father knows about your connection to the New York McNeills. He showed me an article about your half brother proposing to a ballet dancer he'd never met before, and the public speculation that Malcolm McNeill's will requires his heirs to be married in order to inherit." Caroline folded and refolded her copy of the police statement in fidgety hands.

Her fidgety bare hands.

He needed to put that wedding ring back on her finger where it belonged.

"Does that bother you?" He wasn't sure what to make of her nervousness. "Are you familiar with that family?"

Last year, Damon's father, Liam McNeill, had revealed the existence of his secret sons to his legal heirs and to his father, the wealthy patriarch of the McNeill family and founder of McNeill Resorts, a global hotel chain.

Now, Malcolm had made it his mission in life to bring Damon, Jager and Gabe into the family and make them full heirs. Damon hadn't wanted any part of the reunion until today, when he discovered Stephan Degraff had tried to cheat him out of his son. He was open to leveraging the McNeill muscle for the sake of revenge.

"I've never met any of the McNeills, but my father suggested that Malcolm's will was the only reason you married me, since there are strong tabloid rumors suggesting that he's demanded his heirs be married before inheriting. My father believes you married me to claim your inheritance."

Anger simmered that Stephan Degraff would stoop to that level to undermine their marriage, but by now, it certainly wasn't a surprise. Damon needed the police to dispense justice to his bastard of a father-in-law, sooner rather than later.

"That's not true. I didn't even know I was related to Malcolm when we wed." His grip tightened on the steering wheel. How many more times would he have to have his word verified by the police? "My half brother flew out to Los Altos Hills to introduce himself while I was searching for you in Europe. I didn't learn about the family connection until a private investigator hired by my grandfather located me and convinced me to return to the States a month ago."

On the other side of the Land Rover cab, Caroline gave a small sigh. Of relief or disbelief? He couldn't read her as easily as he once could. She put up major boundaries now.

"Damon, I'm truly sorry. I know this is hard for you. Please remember I have holes in my memory that made it so much easier for my father to persuade me. It's still difficult to sift through my life and trust my gut." She put the police report aside and double-checked the GPS on her phone before settling the device in front of the map screen built into the dashboard so he could see where they were going. "But I promise you, I am trying to make sense of what happened. Maybe it wouldn't be a bad idea to go to New York. A change of scenery might be good for both of us."

The audio on the GPS alerted him his final turn was ahead.

Time to meet his son.

And as much as he couldn't wait to hold his child in his arms, Damon couldn't help but wish that the circumstances were very, very different.

Anxious to see her baby again, Caroline texted Victoria as they pulled up to the carriage house she'd rented for her sister and son. Before she could open the door of the Land Rover and race inside to hold Lucas again, Damon placed a hand on her knee.

It was a touch designed purely to slow her down. She could tell by his body language that he had withdrawn from her. Ever since she'd told him about the baby, Damon had been cooler toward her. Yes, he'd accompanied her to the police station and said all the right things about protecting her and Lucas. But she could feel his retreat as surely as a cold front coming off the Pacific.

"Let's take a look at the cars parked nearby first," he suggested, adjusting the rearview mirror for a better view of the street. "Make sure we don't see one of your father's vehicles, or anyone who looks like they're sitting idle and keeping an eye on the place."

Her stomach cramped; it worried her that she hadn't thought to do so on her own. What if her memory loss was affecting her judgement more than she realized? The possibility made her think she might need to rely on Damon more, for Lucas's safety. "Good idea."

"I'm going to hire full-time security for you and Lucas as soon as we get home, but until I've got a team in place, we need to be careful."

"Right." She nodded, a fierce wave of protectiveness surging at the thought of someone trying to take Lucas away. "Thank you for thinking of that."

"If I had any idea you might be at risk, I would have done it a year ago." He let himself out of the SUV and came around to open her door.

She took the hand he held out to her and met his gaze as he helped her down to the sidewalk. A pleasurable frisson danced over her skin from the contact. Because he'd offered to protect her? Or maybe because for the first time since she'd returned to Los Altos Hills, she wasn't keeping secrets from him?

Whatever it was, the sensation reminded her of a time before their relationship had become a casualty of her kidnapping. But telling Damon the truth about how she was hiding his son from him had driven a wedge between them, thwarting any attempt to salvage their marriage.

When Damon let go of her hand, he placed a palm on her back, guiding her up the stone path to the two-story brick carriage house. His touch was impersonal, perfunctory. It was the same courtesy he'd extend to anyone in a weakened condition. So she needed to stop feeling pleasure at the contact, and at the way his leg sometimes brushed hers.

Ahead of them, the blinds were all drawn on the oversize lower windows, as Caroline had requested. But her sister must have had a way to see outside because the heavy wooden front door swung wide open before they even had a chance to knock.

"Caroline!" Victoria wore black-and-pink plaid pajama pants and a gray Stanford tee, her dark brown hair in a ponytail drooping sideways, the tail tickling along Lucas's forehead while the baby slept in her arms. "Thank God you're here. I saw someone's shadow near the kitchen window about an hour ago and I panicked, thinking Dad found us."

Victoria gave her sister a one-armed hug, skillfully keeping her precious cargo safe on the opposite side of her body while she squeezed Caroline tight. Damon's gaze went to the baby, but he didn't reach for Lucas yet.

"I'll go look around back. You should go inside and lock the door behind you." Damon shifted away, taking another wary glance around the quiet yard. There were no houses close by, just the huge, three-story stone home that went with the carriage house. The property bordered a park with a playground on one side where a couple of young mothers pushed preschool-aged children on the swings.

"Oh, wow." Victoria edged out of the doorway a bit to watch Damon as he strode away. "He's even hotter in person."

Too bad Caroline's very hot husband had retreated from her in every way possible.

"Agreed," she said, gently lifting her son from Victoria's arms, savoring the warm weight of his tiny body wrapped in a blanket covered with elephants. "We can ogle him from a window though, once we're inside."

For a moment, Lucas's face scrunched like he was about to cry, but then he settled in against Caroline's chest, his tiny hand stretching and flexing before relaxing against his face. She kissed his temple, rubbing her cheek along the silky down of dark hair that covered his head. He smelled like baby shampoo.

While she cuddled him, Victoria watched Damon from one window and then another, discreetly peering through the blinds. The house had been beautifully restored, with the original pine floors buffed to glowing. A wrought iron chandelier hung from the exposed joist ceiling in the living room, where a fire burned in the stone hearth. Blue baby blankets and equipment were strewn around, making the place looked lived-in, but not messy. Then again, maybe seeing all of her child's things simply made her happy, so she welcomed the sight of baby chaos.

When Damon came back around to the front entrance, Victoria was waiting to open the door again for him. Caroline watched him as he stepped inside and drew the bolt behind him.

"I'm Victoria, by the way." Her sister stuck out a hand to introduce herself, planting herself in front of Damon. "Caroline's sister. And I'm going to start packing so you can meet the kiddo."

"Nice to meet you." He gave a clipped, polite nod, even though his eyes were completely locked on Lucas. Damon could be charming when he chose to be, but he'd always been reserved around women, as if his smart brain was too busy thinking about his next revolutionary tech idea instead of flirting.

Caroline wondered if any woman had turned his

head in the past months that he'd thought she'd left him. The idea sparked a jealous heat that she didn't want to acknowledge right now. Not when she needed to introduce him to his son.

Listening to her sister's footsteps as she retreated up the stairs, Caroline brought Lucas over to meet his father.

"Damon, this is Lucas." She turned her body so that her back was to her husband, giving him the best view of their sleeping child from over her shoulder.

She could feel Damon go very still behind her. Peering around to look up at him, she spotted the awe in his expression. The wonder. The feeling resonated with her. Weeks after giving birth to Lucas she still experienced that same sense of amazement every time she looked at their baby.

"He's perfect." Damon brushed a hand over Lucas's downy head. "Thank you for bringing him to me. For taking a chance on trusting me again." He made no mention of trusting her in return. "I will keep you both safe."

"I know you will." She just wished she felt more sure of his reasons for marrying her. He had said he didn't even know about his grandfather, let alone the dictate that the McNeill heirs marry to inherit, when he'd proposed to her. But after all that had happened in the last months, she would need to work to recover her faith in their bond. "Do you remember why I named him Lucas?"

Damon traced the sleeping infant's features, running his thumb along one barely-there eyebrow, his fingers along one baby-fat cheek. "We came up with names the day we decided to throw away your birth control pills, right after the wedding."

"I know we were just sort of goofing around that night, but—" With the baby cradled against her, her shrug was awkward. "It was the only thing I had to go on for choosing a name."

"I wasn't joking that night." He slid around to face her, putting his arm around her shoulder to draw her closer. "Chloe for a girl. Lucas for a boy."

"Good. It was hard naming him on my own, when I was still so unsure of so much." She felt some tension slip out of her shoulders that she hadn't realized she'd been feeling.

"I would never question a decision you made for our child when you were ill, alone and had no support." He cupped her face in his hand, his tone grave, his gaze cool and remote despite the supportive words. "I'm damned sorry I wasn't there for you. For both of you."

She nodded stiffly, not wanting tears to spoil a moment that should be happy.

"Thank you." She attempted a smile to lighten the mood, but couldn't quite manage it. Instead, she lifted Lucas higher and edged her arms closer to Damon. "Would you like to hold him while I help Victoria pack up his things?"

"Yes." He reached for the baby, sliding one arm under Lucas while using the other to carefully cradle him. "It's past time I got to know our son."

Caroline lingered, unable to tear her eyes away from the sight of their baby finally nestled in his father's arms. Heart in her throat, she could hardly speak. She bit her lip hard to collect herself.

"You look like a natural." She tucked the blanket around Lucas's toes, her knuckles grazing Damon's bicep.

"Gabe had a son last spring, while you were…away."

Damon's jaw tensed. "His girlfriend gave him full custody before breaking things off a few months afterward. I got to hold Jason a few times." Turning his attention back to Lucas, Damon pushed the blanket away from the baby's face. "The boys have a strong resemblance."

"All the McNeill males do." She had seen the photos of his half brothers Quinn, Ian and Cameron in the article her father had shown her. Their blue eyes, dark hair, and tall, athletic builds were strikingly similar to Jager, Damon and Gabe's.

"Lucas won't lack for cousins. Cameron just adopted his wife's daughter, Isla." He glanced back up at Caroline. "You'll meet them when we go to New York."

"How soon?" She was nervous about her father finding them. To work off some of the anxiety, she started picking up the baby items strewn around the living area. A soft rattle with a puppy face. An empty bottle. "And do you think it's safe for Victoria to return to school?"

"We can leave for New York as soon as you're ready. I'll hire security for Victoria for the next six weeks to make sure she's safe. I can have someone in place to accompany her by late this afternoon if she wants to drive back tomorrow."

Caroline nodded, grateful for the way he easily accepted responsibility for her sister.

Victoria hurried down the stairs with a pink duffel bag over one shoulder, her tennis shoes half on and untied. "Whoa. Whoa. Whoa. Let's not get too carried away making plans for other peoples' lives, okay? I don't need a keeper, thank you very much." She paused at the bottom of the stairs to shove her feet more fully into her shoes, jamming the laces down inside with her socks.

Caroline carried the empty bottle over to the sink

and washed it. "I couldn't live with myself if something happened to you because of me. You can handle a bodyguard for a few weeks until we figure out who kidnapped me and why." She'd never forget the way her captors had threatened her siblings. Those threats had frightened her far more than anything they'd done to her. "I'm scared enough about our younger brothers, but the police promised to get in touch with their boarding schools to make sure they were on alert."

"Seriously?" Victoria let her bag fall to the floor with a thunk. "I've got way too much research to do this semester. I'll be lucky to ever leave the library. And I'm going to be stuck with some muscle-head goon?"

She was twenty-four years old to Caroline's twenty-eight, but sometimes Caroline felt decades older.

"You might come to appreciate muscle if it saves you from being dragged away from your home and held against your will." Caroline shoved the clean bottle into the diaper bag along with a few baby towels. "Trust me."

Victoria hesitated. "I know, but—"

Barreling past her sister, Caroline headed toward the door, unwilling to hear complaints about the extra protection they all needed. "Once we have the car seat and the porta-crib, we'll be all set to go."

"I can get them." Damon passed her the baby, his hand grazing her breast and setting off a riot of sensations. "Wait here and I'll pack the vehicle."

Their gazes met, heat sparking in a whole other, unspoken conversation going on between them. What a crazy moment to recall that her obstetrician had okayed her to resume all normal activity at her last visit. The printed patient summary she'd taken home had specifically referred to physical intimacy. Clearly, her body had gotten the message.

"I—" She couldn't even remember what they'd been talking about. "Er. Okay?"

If there were any doubts in her mind that they were both feeling the spark, they faded away at the heated look in Damon's eyes. Was it the deliberate, calculated seduction of a man who wanted to keep his family together? Or was he feeling a genuine attraction? The hitch in her breathing made her heartbeat skip.

"Good." He pressed a kiss to her cheek, using it as a way to speak quietly into her ear. "I'm very ready to take you home."

Six

After cueing up the playlist Caroline had requested on the house's built-in state-of-the-art sound system, Damon adjusted the settings so that the nursery was the only room to hear the classical lullaby music. Tapping the app on his phone, he turned down the volume, settling on a barely-there level so Lucas could fall asleep to the soft symphonies.

Meeting his son had helped him to quiet some of the anger still simmering inside him over his wife's deception. Seeing the boy's face had raised the stakes. He couldn't afford to fail at this marriage. So while he had no intention of giving over his heart to Caroline again, he would fulfill his obligations to her. He would be attentive. Solicitous. And he would damn well be passionate. His attraction to her hadn't dimmed.

They'd all been busy since returning home from the rental house with the baby and Caroline's sister. Damon had spent time researching private security firms, call-

ing friends for recommendations before settling on a
company based in San Jose. It had been started by a
former local sheriff with the help of the tech guru who
owned a digital security firm called Fortress. Damon
used the system on his own properties and had been
impressed with Fortress's founder, Zach Chance, who
had given him some welcome input on start-ups in Silicon Valley when Damon first arrived in town. Damon
liked having a personal connection to the business at
a time when he was questioning who he could really
trust in his life.

Once he'd signed a contract and emailed it back, it
was less than an hour before the first shift team arrived.
They upgraded some of the exterior security systems
on the Los Altos Hills property, then divided the protective detail so two people would remain with Caroline and Lucas at all times, and one guard would go to
Stanford with Victoria.

They were all scheduled to leave in the morning,
with Damon, Caroline and the baby on a private flight
to New York, while Victoria made the short drive to
her university. Now that the arrangements were set,
Damon could relax enough to help put his son to bed
for the first time.

His son.

Rejoining Caroline over the porta-crib in a room
they'd designated as the nursery, Damon watched as she
expertly laid the swaddled bundle on the freshly washed
sheets she'd pulled out of the dryer a few minutes ago.
Dinosaurs cartwheeled around the border of the blanket. Lucas's baby hand clutched the satin trim of the
cover, his grip sporadic and unintentional. He seemed
to be at an age where he flexed his fingers simply to

make use of them. His stare was vacant and sleepy for a moment before he closed his eyes again.

"He's a miracle," Damon said earnestly. He continued to watch the baby drift into a deeper sleep, his tiny hand falling lightly on the mattress beside his nose. "I need to make up for a lot of lost time with him."

"You could always...take the late shift for his next feeding," Caroline offered haltingly, as if she wasn't sure how much labor to share. Or how much he wanted to take part in parenting.

No doubt about it, they were tentative around each other now, though she did seem more relaxed since they'd retrieved the baby. It was obvious that motherhood made her happy. She might not have feelings for him anymore, but Damon had no doubt that she loved their child profoundly. She practically glowed when she looked at Lucas.

Damon wasn't sure if that was a normal connection, or if her attachment was all the stronger because of what she'd gone through during her pregnancy. He'd read her official statement, the detached summary of facts not doing justice to the hell she must have gone through. The fear. Loneliness. Confusion. Of course, there was no "statement" for him to read about her experience afterward with her father. How much had Stephan Degraff added to his daughter's fears by keeping her in the dark about her marriage? How could anyone let their daughter think she was alone in parenting a newborn when she had a husband desperately searching for her?

"I'll gladly take the late shift." He relished the quiet time in the dim nursery with her now after a day that had come at him from all sides. "It will give me a chance to get to know him."

"I'm going to take you up on that." She moved toward the night-light and switched it to a lower setting. "Having Victoria babysit him the last two days has helped me catch up on rest, I think. I feel better than when I left my father's house."

"All the more reason to secure some help with him." Damon had brought in two potential nanny candidates and asked Caroline to interview them while he dealt with the security team. Caroline had liked them both, but insisted she wanted to care for Lucas on her own. "An extra caregiver could give you much needed time to recover from the pregnancy and the ordeal you've been through."

He followed her to the door and closed it partially behind them while Caroline paused in the hallway to pull up the nursery monitor's video feed on her phone.

"I realize that." She tucked the phone in the pocket of her shawl sweater, flipping her ponytail behind her shoulder. "But I like caring for him myself. Being with him."

"And I admire that. But you'll have more energy to enjoy him if you're taking good care of yourself. But we can debate this another time." He opted for a strategic temporary retreat on the subject rather than risk backing her into a corner. Damon pointed toward the second-story patio that she liked, hoping he could persuade her to unwind with him for a while. He needed to make his case to recommit to their marriage. "I had some of that herbal tea you like brought out near the fire pit if you want to stargaze before bed."

"You did?" She tipped her head to one side to look out toward the patio where flames leaped from the copper bowl. "That sounds good, actually. Thank you."

Her careful politeness bothered him. It reminded

him of his own hesitation. No doubt about it, there was an awkwardness between them now. A cool wariness behind the facade.

"We have a lot to talk about before tomorrow." He pushed open the French doors from the master suite's sitting room that led to the patio. "But I don't want to wear you out."

"I'll be fine." She stopped to look up at the sky, tipping her head back to see the stars while a cool breeze blew the hem of her sweater against him. "So much happened today, my head is still spinning."

There had been a time when he would have wrapped his arms around her to steady her. To kiss her until they were both breathless and ready for more.

"Mine, too." He limited himself to putting a hand on her waist, gently guiding her toward the daybed swing where he'd piled blankets in deference to the cold night air. "I found out I had a son today."

Her guilty wince made it clear she was still feeling wary around him.

The patio heaters were humming, along with the fire. Decorative stonework along the low walls of the exterior was punctuated with built-in propane torches. The effect was medieval, making the home look all the more like an old French château.

"I'm sorry that my father's lies cost us the chance to be together for Lucas's birth." She stopped in front of the daybed and held the chain to steady it while she sat down.

The glow of firelight played along her skin, brightening her cheeks.

"Yes. They did." Damon took his time unfurling the blankets and tucking them around her, not wanting to get sucked into a conversation about Stephan Degraff.

Damon needed this time to mend his relationship with her. Regardless of what her motives had been in hiding Lucas from him, or deceiving him about her condition, Damon needed to win her over. Earn back her trust so they could move forward in parenting their son. Together.

He would not raise his own child in the type of unstable environment he'd known growing up.

"I don't how Dad could have done that to me. Was he trying to teach me a lesson for marrying someone he didn't approve of?" She slipped off her boots and tucked her feet under her on the swing, sitting cross-legged. She laid her phone on the cushion beside her, leaving the video feed from the nursery monitor on. "Or did he hope I'd just forget about the marriage forever if he pretended it didn't exist? Did he really expect you would never find out I was still alive? God, what if one of us had wanted to get married again. Would he have just stood aside and allow a bigamous union?"

"Tough to know what he was thinking." Damon took the spot beside her then leaned forward to retrieve the insulated tea carafe. He poured two mugs of the stuff even though he wasn't much of a tea drinker. Anything to get her to stay here with him for a little while.

And since bashing her father wasn't going to get him anywhere with her, he would remain diplomatic. For now. Sooner or later, she would have to discover his plans to ruin Stephan Degraff. By then, Damon intended to have their marriage on far more stable ground.

She wrapped her hands around the gray stoneware mug and sipped the steaming hot drink. He took the opportunity to change the subject. Setting down his cup, he reached into the pocket of the sports jacket he'd worn for his meetings with the new security team members and took out her wedding ring set. He held the rings up to the firelight so she could see.

"One of the pieces of evidence the police pointed to in support of your father's claim that you walked out on me was the fact that you left this behind." He'd had the princess-cut diamond engagement ring and the matching platinum-and-diamond wedding band custom-made for her.

He studied her expression carefully, trying to assess what he saw there. Nostalgia? Maybe. But there was wariness, too. Had she taken it off when she got home that day, planning to leave him?

"I wondered where they went." Caroline set down her tea on the stone rim of the copper fire bowl, then reached to touch the glittering band, tracing the outline with one finger. "I thought they were stolen from me while I was drugged."

Taking her other hand, he dropped the rings into her palm and the diamonds sent tiny refractions glinting in the dark.

She stared down at the rings, making no move to put them on her finger.

"Do you think you were wearing them that day?"

She peered up at him, surprised. "I would have worn them on the plane coming home from Heathrow. I'm sure I had them on when I was taken from the house."

"The rings were on the top of the bureau in my closet. As if you left them there deliberately for me to find."

"I suppose I could be wrong." She shook her head slowly. "I was given a lot of drugs during those first two weeks. More when they moved me a month after that. But I'm not sure I'll ever recall exactly how that day played out when they took me."

He ground his teeth in frustration, knowing he

needed to get past it fast if he wanted to fix things with Caroline. He wanted the ring on her finger, needed her commitment to this marriage to provide a healthy and happy childhood for Lucas.

"You may never recover all your memories," he reminded himself as much as her. "But I hope you'll consider working with a new therapist in New York. Recalling those lost memories isn't just about the two of us. It's important for Lucas."

Caroline rubbed the two rings against one another, sliding the platinum-and-diamond pieces back and forth between two fingers.

"You can't imagine how badly I want answers." Her brown eyes reflected the glow of the fire as she glanced up at him. "I need to know what happened, so yes, of course I'll meet a new doctor."

In this much, at least, they were on the same page.

More than that, he recognized the vibrant energy and determination in that statement. It was a flicker from the past; for a moment, he spied the woman he'd fallen in love with inside this stranger who'd returned to him.

"Good." He closed his hand around hers where she toyed with the rings, stilling the movement long enough to take the jewelry from her. "Then, with your permission, I'd like to return these to where they belong."

Wordlessly, she watched him line up the bands and hold them over her left hand. The swing swayed gently beneath them, lulling them to forget some of the angst of their hellish day. Still, a furrow wrinkled her brow just above her nose, as if she couldn't quite decide.

He tipped her chin up with his free hand, needing to see that fire in her eyes again.

"All I'm asking for is the chance to start over." He

spoke gently, knowing this had been tough on her, too. He didn't know how much he could trust her, but he damned well needed to try to move past her betrayal. "To try and be a couple again." He nudged the phone beside her, the video feed from the nursery brightening for a moment to show their sleeping child. "For Lucas's sake."

He knew it was the final words that persuaded her. She gave the slightest nod before returning her gaze to her bare finger as he slid the wedding band set back into place.

Memories of the vows they'd spoken hit him hard. He could hear her voice from the past promising to love him forever and always. For the rest of her days.

He'd believed her absolutely.

Disillusionment left a chill the roaring fire couldn't touch. Having accomplished his goal for the night, he celebrated the victory by placing a cool kiss on the back of her hand just above the rings. He was ready to finish his drink and retire for the night, to figure out his next move once they got to New York.

And yes, to take his time staring at his child and wrapping his brain around this massive change in his life.

Straightening, he was surprised to see the soft glow of heat in Caroline's eyes, the relaxed parting of her lips. He watched in stunned fascination as she canted forward. Toward him.

All around them, the night sounds intensified. A few brave birds called out and the logs crackled and shifted, casting sparks on the stone patio deck nearby. Caroline's breath puffed against his lips for one sexy exhale before her hands clamped his shoulders.

He had a moment to breathe in the strawberry scent

of her lip balm. Then her mouth landed on his with a delicate and wholly unexpected kiss.

Caroline didn't know what came over her.

Simple attraction to her husband? Or was it a memory of true love inspired by the wedding rings he'd carefully slid into place on her left hand?

She didn't know. But the compulsion to get closer, to test the swirl of complicated feelings sending pleasure to every atom of her being, was too strong to ignore.

How long had it been since she'd experienced something so...delicious?

Her tentative exploration of Damon's lips didn't last long. A breath. An instant. Then his hands came around her waist, drawing her whole body toward him, as if he could encompass all of her with one squeeze of his powerful arms.

The pleasure she'd been feeling multiplied ten times. A hundred times. Being pressed up against her husband's muscular warmth sent tingly sensations everywhere from her breasts to her thighs, with the most potent concentration deep inside her. Being in his arms, kissing him, felt more like coming home than crossing the threshold of this colorless mansion ever had.

This, she recognized.

This, she remembered in her body more than her brain.

How else could she account for the sudden, reflexive *need*? Her hands tunneled into his dark hair, and she craved more. More of the kiss and the man.

He accommodated her instantly, pulling her fully across his lap. Her thighs draped over his, her hip pressed intimately to his arousal. The chilly night air blew lightly on her back, but it didn't cool the heat their bodies generated where they touched. Damon kissed her with a slow thoroughness that undid her. She dropped her hands to his chest, wanting to feel the thrum of his heartbeat, to see if the rhythm was as unsteady as hers. Or maybe just to reassure herself this was no fevered dream or wishful memory.

Damon McNeill in her arms was the real thing.

She broke the kiss, needing to feel that addictive slide of his mouth on her neck. Behind her ear. Down to the base of her throat. She didn't know if she steered him there or he simply understood everything she wanted. Arching into him, she let the heat build, not questioning it. Needing it.

He said he wanted to start over, didn't he?

Was it madness to begin again this way, right here and now?

For the first time in months, she didn't have to struggle to remember. She could simply be. Feel.

Savor.

She tugged at the buttons on her sweater, needing to feel his kiss on her breasts. He thumbed aside the bra strap as she exposed it, his hands working seamlessly beside hers…

Until the wail of Lucas's cry filled the night.

The nursery monitor feed blinked to brighter life on her phone, the audio as clear as if they were standing right next to the crib. Caroline lurched forward, off Damon's lap.

He stood beside her.

"Get your rest, Caroline." He placed a kiss on her forehead. "I want to go to Lucas."

She couldn't argue since she'd already teased him about taking the late feeding. Damon deserved to spend time with Lucas after she'd kept him to herself these last weeks. Logically, she understood that.

But as she watched Damon walk away from her, she got the sense that he hadn't just left to be with his son. He'd left to get away from her and what was happening between them. Because no matter what he said about new beginnings, she knew he didn't trust her.

And it was possible he didn't even love her.

So no matter how blissfully sensual his kisses made her feel, she would be wise to keep her guard up around her husband.

Seven

By late afternoon the next day, Damon sat beside Caroline in the back of a limousine taking them from the airport to his grandfather's home on the Upper East Side of Manhattan. Lucas snoozed in a car seat across from them while their security guard rode up front with the driver. Malcolm McNeill insisted on sending the Mercedes limo for them, even though he was out of the country on business. When Damon had called his grandfather to let him know they were going to be in New York City, the old man had urged them to stay at his house since it was fully staffed and none of the McNeills were in town for the next three days.

Damon had accepted since he needed to meet with his grandfather as soon as possible to discuss the McNeills taking over Stephan Degraff's stake in Transparent. He'd closed the house in Los Altos Hills that morning, but asked his Realtor not to put the property on the market yet. His life had changed drastically since Caroline's return. He now had his wife and his son to consider, making the Silicon Valley condo he'd rented out of the question because it was too small. Plus, there was her long-term safety to consider. As much as he wished they could hole up back on the family property in Martinique, he knew she wouldn't go for that.

But sooner or later, he wanted his son to meet Jager and Gabe.

Now that his brothers were recognizing their father's relatives as family—though not their father himself, if Damon had anything to say about it—Damon needed to get used to the idea that he had half brothers. And he'd soon have to introduce Caroline to them. Their son deserved a stronger sense of family than he and Caroline could provide. And he had no intention of allowing Stephan Degraff anywhere near his child.

"I'm anxious to see your grandfather's home." She shifted in her seat, straightening her long wool coat to cover her legs as she peered out the window. The car sped up on a curving road through Central Park. "If it's as big as you say, it's got to be one of those turn-of-the-century mansions on the Upper East Side."

He pulled his gaze up from her legs, from the spot where her tall leather boots met the hem of her knee-length skirt. He'd thought about their kiss all night, wondering if it had surprised her as much as him. Not that he was caught off guard by the heat or the passion. He expected as much when they touched. It had always been that way between them. What had stunned him was how engaged she'd been in the kiss. The touches. He'd missed that about her. The woman who'd returned to their doorstep, claiming not to know him, was more circumspect. But something had reawakened her more

impulsive side and he wondered how long it would take
for him to see that side of her again.

"The McNeill home is impressive." With an effort, he
focused on her words instead of the attraction. Damon
wasn't as much of an architecture aficionado as Gabe,
who was bringing his historic hotel back to pristine life
in Martinique. But he'd been around enough five-star
properties across the world to appreciate something like
the McNeill mansion. "It has six floors, not counting the
staff rooms and kitchen on the basement level. There's
an entrance to the park across the street."

"How long did you spend there?" She smoothed her
hands along the folded leather gloves on her lap, her
wedding rings glinting in the dull winter sunlight.

He'd been glad to see the bands back in place today
when she'd awoken from a long rest. Damon had kept
his word where Lucas was concerned the night before,
walking the baby around the house when he cried and
settling him down after the midnight bottle. He'd enjoyed the time to study the boy's features and get to
know him even though the feeding had interrupted one
hell of a moment with Caroline. There would be more
heated moments. Soon.

"I only stayed there for a few days last month after
my grandfather's private investigator found me over
in Europe." He'd been in a dark place at the time, convinced Caroline had either left him or was being held
against her will. "My brother, Jager, had been looking
for me. I'd saddled him with the responsibility of over-
seeing Transparent while I was away and he was beginning to have trouble explaining my absence to investors.
I threw out my cell phone though, not wanting to deal
with any of it." A foolish act. "If only I'd kept it, maybe
we would have been together sooner."

The car slowed for another light. A few heavy snowflakes began to fall, lightly brushing the windows on their way to the ground. The city was expecting major winter weather tonight, and he would be glad to get his family settled for the night.

It still floored him to think about having a family of his own.

"At least we're together now, and Lucas is safe." Her dark gaze landed on the baby as the little boy stretched and sighed. "Thank you for making sure Victoria got to school safely, too." She checked her phone and then set it aside. "I told her to text me if she heard from Dad, but she said everything seemed fine at her apartment."

Damon nodded. "I'm receiving updates from her protective detail, as well. They retrieved a few books and personal items from the building on campus, and moved her temporarily to a spot with more security. Just until the police finish investigating your father's role in this."

They could only do so much to hide Victoria if her father wanted to see her, but at least she wouldn't be easy to find.

"I'm more concerned about protecting her from whoever kidnapped me. My captors threatened to come after my siblings if I didn't cooperate." She turned her attention back toward the sleeping infant. "I want them safe, and Lucas, too." She tugged at the green striped quilt she'd laid over the car seat to keep him warm, lifting it higher.

Damon wanted to tell her to prepare herself for the possibility that her father was more involved in her kidnapping than she realized. But perhaps Caroline herself had asked for her father's help in freeing her from marriage to Damon and simply didn't remember. Better to keep his misgivings to himself and let the police work on it.

And his private investigators. He'd called Bentley—the PI who'd located Damon when he'd been wandering Europe looking for Caroline—with an update the night before when he'd been pacing the floor with Lucas. Like Damon, Bentley was suspicious of Stephan's role in Caroline's disappearance.

Until he had proof, however, Damon's revenge against Stephan would wait. He'd spend his time assembling all the pieces necessary to ruin him so he would be ready to act when the time came.

For now, Damon would focus on solidifying his relationship with his wife. After last night's heated kiss, the plan was very, very appealing.

Two hours later, Caroline wandered through the sixth-floor solarium of the stunning house that belonged to Damon's grandfather. Snow fell in a dizzying haze on the glass roof, which was illuminated by the ambient light from Central Park on the opposite side of Fifth Avenue. The building faced East 76th Street, but she could see the park from here.

Lucas had already been settled in his own bedroom across from hers on the fifth floor. She was touched to see the steps the household staff had taken on short notice to ready the room for a baby. They kept a crib in storage, apparently, and had set it up for them. It had been in use often as of late, since Cameron McNeill, one of Damon's half brothers, had recently adopted his wife's daughter.

Caroline had gotten the full scoop from two fresh-faced staffers who were pursuing advanced degrees in early childhood education—young women recently retained to work part-time whenever Malcolm McNeill hosted the grandchildren he hoped would soon fill his home. Like the Mercedes limo he'd sent to the airport and the home he'd opened to Caroline and Damon unconditionally, the extra caregivers were another way Malcolm proved extremely generous and thoughtful.

Caroline hadn't wanted to deprive the young women of the new charge they seemed excited to care for. When she'd left him in the nursery, he was on a blanket in the middle of the thickly carpeted floor, surrounded by blocks and rattles, his every coo and cry tended to by Marcie and Dana. Curious, she now took out her phone to see the nursery monitor feed, and the group was just as she'd left them. Classical music played while Lucas stared up at a baby gym, the young women flying stuffed toys above him to keep him entertained.

Nearby, the elevator doors swished open, alerting her to company. Caroline turned from the view to look out into the hallway through the open door.

Damon approached her, his strong shoulders backlit by the sconces flanking the elevator. He'd changed from the suit he'd worn for their flight. The gray jacket and dark jeans were more casual, the white shirt with no tie a staple look for him. He'd traded his black tie-up dress shoes for boots.

He looked good enough to eat. No doubt that's why she felt the need to study every inch of him. She was willing to bet he smelled great, too. She had dreamed of that sandalwood and spice scent when she'd been apart from him.

"Is everything all right?" he asked, edging around a café table in the center of the solarium. "I've been looking all over for you."

"I'm fine." She lowered herself to sit on a bright-blue

modern sofa in front of the window looking down onto the street. "This is like being at the drive-in theater. Only the show playing is *New York in a Snowstorm*." She gestured to the wide view framed by long glass panels.

Just hearing Damon's footsteps on the tile floor made her skin hum with awareness. How was she supposed to be on her guard around him with no baby in her arms to care for? No distractions of any kind?

Her main goals in New York were keeping her child safe and finding out if Damon had married her out of self-interest. The former seemed easier now with a full-time bodyguard devoted to Lucas. And the latter? She wouldn't be able to discover much until Malcolm McNeill returned to the town house. Or maybe Damon's half brothers. In the meantime, her husband had made it clear he wanted to start over. Be a couple again.

The memory of his words last night slid over her senses like a caress, making her shiver.

"I can light a fire if you're cold." Damon hesitated at the edge of the sofa, pointing toward the hearth on the other side of the room.

"No, thank you." She realized her mistake as soon as she said it, since he took the opportunity to sit down beside her, bringing all that masculine appeal within inches of her. If she'd taken him up on his offer to build a fire, she would have had more time to build her defenses. "You can see the view better this way. That's why I didn't bother to turn a light on."

"I wondered why you were sitting in the dark." He kept his attention on the snow coming down, the fat flakes gathering up in the corners of the windowpanes, outlining the view with a frosty border.

"Just soaking up a side of New York I've never seen.

The year I worked in the Financial District, I lived down there and barely ventured north of Canal Street." She clung to a neutral conversational topic, safe terrain after the emotional toll of every exchange the day before. "My building was in an old part of the city, but construction was completed the year I moved in. It couldn't be more different from this place."

The neo-Renaissance mansion that housed the McNeill patriarch was a turn-of-the-century masterpiece. It even had its own Wikipedia page.

Damon shifted to make himself more comfortable, extending his arm along the back of the sofa just behind her neck. Not touching her. Just…so close. She breathed in the light hint of sandalwood.

"How did you like living here?" he asked, and she felt the warmth of his gaze on her even though she kept her attention on the living snow globe outside the window. "I don't think we've ever talked about that. I know you grew up in San Francisco. Got your degree in Boston. What did you think of New York City?"

"I loved it." She remembered the joy of earning her own paycheck, and a good one at that. "Coming from a wealthy family, I always felt a bit guilty for having nice things that I didn't earn for myself." She had noticed at college the vast difference between kids who were sent to the prestigious school because of their family name and finances, versus the handful of students who were genuinely brilliant and there on scholarship. "But when I lived in New York, I had a sense of independence that I'd never really felt before. I got the job on my own merit and did it well."

She'd always thought she would return, in fact. She'd kept her apartment on Spruce Street and sublet it since then.

"What made you give it up?" Damon asked. He trailed a finger along her shoulder, a light touch with a powerful impact through the simple cashmere sweater dress she'd changed into after the plane trip.

Keen awareness of that touch made it difficult to concentrate. But did he touch her out of desire? Or a more calculated need to reset the relationship button?

"My father asked me come work for him and help him choose which businesses to invest in." At the time, she'd felt obligated to fulfill the request since she couldn't have afforded her college education on her own. "I felt underqualified, and worried he only gave me the job out of family loyalty, but I helped him turn an excellent profit on the two companies he invested in before I got involved in the deal with Transparent."

She hadn't thought much about returning to her career since leaving Mexico. And yes, she wanted to be a full-time mother to enjoy every moment with Lucas that she could. But would it restore some of her personal confidence, her faith in herself, if she worked on a part-time basis?

"If we hadn't started a relationship, would you still have recommended your father invest in Transparent?"

"Without question." She had recovered her memories of the earliest part of their dating first, and she felt certain about her answer. "I knew within the first week that I would endorse it. There was a good energy in the building. Everyone really bought into your ideas." She hadn't recommended it that quickly, of course, spending time on the due diligence to make sure the market forecasts and business plans made sense.

But she'd had a strong instinct about the company early on.

"Were you concerned that I wouldn't be the best CEO to take the company to the next level?"

Straightening, she shook off the allure of his touch and the cozy sensation of watching the snowfall. "Should I look back at my notes? Because I'm getting the impression that there is more to your questions than just casual conversation."

"You still have your notes?" He lifted a dark eyebrow.

She met his gaze, but she detected only curiosity. Professional interest. She felt a new buzz along her skin that had less to do with attraction and more to do with her work. She'd forgotten the excitement of being a part of a new project, and helping to bring a brilliant idea to life.

"Of course. I did extensive research on your software, from the technical production plans to marketing." She hadn't given much thought to Transparent since her marriage. So much had happened in her personal life— from the kidnapping to becoming a mother—that her job was the least of her concerns. But there'd been a time where she lived and breathed her career. "And you must remember that I shared those reports—over a year ago—with my father, since that was part of the terms of his investment."

"Certainly." Damon nodded thoughtfully and she recognized that look of deep concentration. When he turned back toward her, his gaze hardened. He was all business. "I had my software tested by a hacker recently, and he discovered a few holes I need to plug before we release it."

"I'm confused. What does that have to do with my old notes?"

"Nothing." Damon shifted closer, the blue leather

cushion creaking softly as his knee brushed against hers. "But if I know the extent of the research on Transparent your father has access to, I might be able to shift the final product to ensure he can't ambush it once it hits the market."

"He wouldn't—" She stopped herself as she saw Damon's gaze darken. Even in the dim glow of light reflected from the street lamps outside, she could see the glint of frustration in his eyes. "Okay, maybe he would."

"Do you really believe that, Caroline? Or are you just saying it for my sake?" His words were clipped, his tone brusque.

"I understand that he resents you for marrying me." She didn't comprehend the depth of her father's fury with Damon, however. She remembered his adamant refusal to attend their wedding. "I know he was frustrated with you before we even met, because you wouldn't accept his help or expertise—only his financial support."

"I made it clear that's all I needed."

She recalled how Damon's intractable ways angered her dad. "He's used to being a valuable asset when he supports a new business."

Damon abruptly rose from the couch. He stalked the short distance to the windows overlooking the street. "Not to me. I wouldn't let him beat me at business. But then it got much, much worse when he realized I'd won you, too."

The words hit her with unexpected force. She shot to her feet to face him.

"I'm not a prize for the taking, Damon." Fuming, she folded her arms.

"And that's not how I see you. But make no mistake, your father views your affection for me as a betrayal." He shook his head. "I don't understand it, but nothing else can explain the way he tried to shut me out of Lucas's life. The way he misled the police when you disappeared."

Caroline didn't want to believe it. Her head hurt just thinking about all the ways her dad had tried to keep her and Damon apart. Had her therapist been correct when she gently suggested she'd been a victim of gaslighting?

Had her father tried to undermine her recovery from amnesia by lying about not knowing the father of her child?

"I don't claim to understand his motives. But I know I won't be manipulated anymore." She leaned closer and lowered her voice. "Not by him. And not by you."

"I'm trying to protect you." Damon's hands moved to her shoulders, his touch gentle. "And I'm ensuring Lucas's future is secure by introducing Transparent to the market in the most successful way. The company is his legacy."

Some of the anger thrumming through her eased. She understood his point.

"I want that, too." She'd always hoped for Transparent to succeed. She'd been a fan of the concept even before her father had gotten involved with the company. Now, there was far more riding on Damon's public launch, since Lucas would one day inherit whatever his father built.

"Do you?" He let the question hang between them for a moment. "Because if you want the business to succeed in spite of your father, I would appreciate it if you would share your notes. I need to know how much inside information he has."

"I'll do it." She bit her lip, hating being torn between someone she'd felt loyalty toward for the last twenty-plus years of her life and the man she'd married. "If you can tell me how it makes any sense for Dad to sabotage a business that he has an enormous stake in."

"I think revenge has become more important to him than walking away with a profit this time. Especially when he has investments in plenty of other lucrative ventures."

He let go of her shoulders, so that it was only his powerful words that kept her close to him.

"You think he wants revenge enough to ruin his own grandson's future?" She didn't want it to be true. But she couldn't deny all the ways her father's actions had hurt her in the past year.

"Lucas is a McNeill now." Damon straightened. "He might not feel any loyalty to our son."

But she knew for certain Damon would protect their child no matter what. Even if he didn't love her.

"Very well." She nodded, her mind made up. "I'll send you all of my research. Everything that I shared with my father."

Eight

Damon hated that Caroline was under such tremendous stress. Thank goodness she'd agreed to his idea for a break from it all, a chance to unwind and let the pieces of life slide back into place.

"I didn't think sledding was possible in New York City," Caroline called to him as they crossed Fifth Avenue the next morning, a bodyguard trailing them.

Her cheeks were pink from the cold, her brown eyes bright as they trudged the snowy path already worn from early morning visitors to the park. She wore black ski pants and a bright aquamarine parka with a pair of insulated boots left behind by another guest of his grandfather's. The maids had produced the clothes within minutes of his asking about winter gear. Caroline had brought her own gloves and a white knit hat for the trip, so she'd been well equipped for the outing he'd suggested. He wanted to smooth things over between them after the talk about her father last night.

While she'd complied with his request and sent him the files he'd asked for via email before midnight, Damon had sensed that she was upset. No doubt, she wished things had turned out differently in regard to her father. But in time, she would have to see that Stephan Degraff was far more ruthless than she knew.

"It's the City that Never Sleeps, not the City that Never Plays." Damon juggled the brightly colored inflatable tube under his arm, an item he'd had specially shipped from a local seller capitalizing on the snowstorm. He hoped his own son would one day be as industrious as the teen who'd showed up at the mansion this morning on a fat-tire mountain bike, five more sleds strapped to a wagon on the back.

"But are there hills?" Her gaze swept the bright terrain where a flood of early risers built snowmen along the park paths.

"Seriously?" He draped his free arm around her shoulders to steer her where he wanted to go. "You didn't ever leave your office while you lived here?"

She gave him a sheepish grin and he was glad he'd come up with the sledding idea. He hadn't enjoyed needling her about her father last night. More than anything, he wanted to start their relationship over and cement things between them as a couple. But he had a duty to protect his investment at Transparent, too, for investors but also for his family's financial security. With the public launch around the corner, he needed to ensure the product was protected from Stephan Degraff.

"I told you, I was very focused on work. I loved my job consulting for entrepreneurs. I would have gladly stayed in that field for years if my father hadn't tapped me to help with his venture capital investments." She pointed to a group of evergreens with boughs weighed down to the ground from the snow. "This is all so pretty."

Damon liked the feel of her under his arm, the scent of her shampoo right through the crocheted wool cap she wore.

"Seems like a good time for you to have some fun." He remembered how easy it was to be with her in Italy on their honeymoon. Not just because they'd been in love and eager to spend every second together. But because simple things made her happy. She was unpretentious despite her family's wealth. She'd counseled struggling women entrepreneurs through her work in the financial industry, helping female business owners win grants, negotiate complicated financial regulations and win more capital backing. Damon had always considered her work history a far cry from her father's business interests even though she'd stepped into Transparent as his representative.

Damon had been impressed by her savvy from the first day. She'd been helpful without being overbearing. She'd genuinely facilitated his company's move forward.

"I will admit, Lucas appears to be in very good hands." She held up her phone in front of Damon as they passed a vendor selling hot chocolate along with hot pretzels. A small crowd clutched steaming foam cups.

Her nursery app showed the two college grads his grandfather had hired. Lucas sat in a baby bouncer on the floor while one of the young women—Marcie, he thought—danced an impromptu ballet to the classical music playing, using a stuffed elephant as her partner. At the same time, her colleague assembled a baby swing in the middle of the room. Wide-eyed, Lucas kicked happily in his seat.

Damon could rest easy leaving their son behind when Lucas had a second security guard assigned to his safety.

"He certainly seems entertained." They trooped through fresh powder to one side of the path as a troop of kids ran by them, squealing and throwing snowballs. "I asked the caregivers to bring him to the park after we finish sledding. In another hour, the plows will have swept through again and it should be easy to push the stroller on the paths." He could see the crowd at the top of Cedar Hill already. "We'll trade off the sled for a baby and a winter picnic. The girls might enjoy trying out the tube once we're done."

"That sounds great and—oh! Look!" Caroline halted as they turned a corner and got a good view of Cedar Hill crowded with sledders.

A mish-mosh of music drifted up from competing external speakers on a variety of electronic devices. An eighties tune, pop music and some sort of funky electronica overlapped with squeals and laughter even as the fresh snow muted the sounds to a dull, vibrant hum. Toboggans, plastic saucers and a few pieces of cardboard all carried people down the hillside.

"New York sledding at its finest." He let go of her shoulders to hold up the inflated tube. "Are you ready to set the new land speed record?"

"Very." Caroline tugged her knit hat lower on her ears. "Let's show them how it's done."

He watched a family at the bottom of the hill tip their sled into a snowbank, upending the whole group.

"Have you been sledding before?" He knew she'd spent most of her childhood in southern California, but her father's wealth had probably allowed for ski vacations.

"I've gone tubing behind a boat." She dug a pair of sunglasses out of her pocket and slid them on her nose. "How different can it be?"

She headed toward the highest crest where a few groups of people took turns careening down the hill. Damon took a moment to give their security detail a thumbs-up, letting the guy know they would remain in this location for a while. Then he followed Caroline.

"Seriously? You've never ridden a sleigh down a hill?" Damon wended his way through a mob of parents supervising smaller children on sleds, following Caroline to where a group of teens filmed one another using an empty refrigerator box for a makeshift snowboard.

"This will be a first." She flashed him a smile and pointed out an available spot for the inner tube.

He laid it in the snow. "Didn't you take the obligatory rich-kid trip to the Alps as a teenager? There must be some sledding hills somewhere in all those mountains."

His own teen years had been marked by his mother's death and the emptiness it left behind. He and his brothers had worked their asses off to make something of the property that had been their legacy, the historic plantation house and land in Martinique. They'd kept a portion for living space and they'd turned the rest into an exclusive corporate retreat and private party facility. The income had helped fund his start-up.

"Any cold-weather trips we took were devoted to ski lessons." Caroline seemed to track the progress of a young woman on a tube similar to theirs, watching as she sped down the hill and no doubt cataloging the technique. "My father considers skiing, tennis and golf the most 'business-friendly' sports that any upwardly mobile executive should know."

"Right. Remind me to brush up before I meet you on the links." It should come as no surprise that Caroline had been groomed to take over the man's business interests from an early age, but it bugged Damon to think that Stephan Degraff couldn't be bothered to let her have any fun as a kid.

Time to remedy that.

"Have any pointers?" She dropped down onto the tube and took a seat in the middle.

"Sure I do." He sat down behind her and straddled her. "Be prepared to get close," he said into her ear through the knit hat.

The feel of her curves nestled against his lap reminded him how very much he wanted to visit her bed again. And the ski pants she wore were sexy as hell. He resisted the urge to hug her hips with his thighs—if only for a moment.

"Um. Duly noted." She reached over his knees to grip the handles on either side of the tube. "How do we get going?"

Damon already had his hands planted on the snow behind them. "When we get better at it, I'll get a running start and hop on. But for now, we'll just focus on getting down the hill."

"No land speed record this trip." She nodded. "Got it."

"Ready?" Planting his gloved fingers deeper in the snow, he did something similar to crunches with the tube, letting the sled slide up and down on the slight incline as a warm-up. He flexed his arms and damned if he didn't find himself hugging her hips with his thighs.

It did help him move the sled. The fact that he enjoyed it mightily was a bonus.

"Ready!" She leaned forward, her skiing skills

clearly paying off as she pointed them in the right direction on the slope while Damon pushed off with one last shove.

Their combined weight helped them to gain momentum. The inner tube was the perfect choice for the soft conditions. Snow sprayed up from either side, dotting their faces and covering their legs. Caroline whooped with joy as they passed a teenager on a thin plastic sled. With her competitive nature, she clearly loved the thrill of it.

They were almost at the end of the run when they hit an icy patch and picked up speed, spinning sideways and out of control. Tipping precariously, Damon let go of the handles to hold on to Caroline so he took the brunt of the fall. They ended up in the same snowbank as the family he'd watched earlier.

A cloud of snow dusted up from their landing. His shoulder was buried deepest, with Caroline's spine curved against his stomach. Her hips still nestled against his.

"Are you okay?" He shifted his leg off hers.

She shook gently against him.

"Caroline?" A moment of panic punched him in the chest. Had she gotten hurt?

He shouldn't move her if she'd landed badly...

But then, she straightened up on her own, laughter wracking her slender form. Her cap was perched cockeyed on her head, her one cheek red from being pressed in the snow. A crust of icy flakes covered her collar and the side of her hat.

Even her glasses were crooked.

"That was the best!" she managed between laughs that—in his defense—sounded a lot like sobs.

"You scared me." He slumped back against the snowbank while a sled full of little kids tumbled out a few feet away from them.

Four of them were on their feet almost before they'd finished falling, charging back up the hill on short legs while the youngest of the group screeched at the others to wait for her.

"I didn't mean to frighten you." Caroline pulled the glasses off along with the hat. "My favorite part was the out-of-control three-sixties we were doing at the end."

"You're a madwoman, that's why," he said dryly, his heartbeat only just now slowing back down after the nanosecond when he was convinced she'd broken her neck.

"I mean it. I loved it." She shoved the glasses inside her inner coat pocket. "Let's do it again."

He watched her shove to her feet to dust off the excess snow and a little more of his tension melted away. Because not only was she safe, but she was also having fun.

That put him one step closer to his goal of winning her back this week. Before he removed her father from his business and their lives.

Caroline's legs were sore from climbing the hill again and again by the time Marcie and Dana arrived with the baby carriage and a picnic hamper on an old-fashioned sled with red metal runners. She noticed the careful eye Lucas's bodyguard kept on the trio, as did the security guard who had trailed her and Damon all day. An inconvenience, perhaps, but it gave her peace of mind. The two young women traded the baby and the picnic provisions for the inner tube, promising to meet them back at the McNeill home in two hours in case they were needed.

Inside the carriage—a fancy stroller with multiple settings for pushing a baby—Lucas was dressed in a tiny winter papoose with a hood. The outfit looked like a dark, insulated bag with a zipper up the front, leaving plenty of room for his legs to kick freely inside. The hood tied with a ribbon under his chin and had tiny dark ears sewn on top, making him resemble an elfin mouse. Or maybe a mousy elf.

Whatever it was, he looked adorable with his bright blue eyes and gummy smile. A reflex smile, according to the baby books she'd read, but so cute nonetheless.

"Are you still up for a winter picnic?" Damon asked, propping his aviators on top of his head.

He practically oozed sex appeal in his dark jeans, red flannel shirt and insulated gray vest. It was West Coast grunge meets New York style. His boots and hiking socks were as snow-covered as hers, but despite the cold, he'd unfastened his vest an hour ago, impervious to the chill in the air now that the sun was shining brightly.

"I'm game." She pointed toward a quieter section of the huge park, away from the hill that had gotten far more crowded since they'd first arrived. "I hope there's plenty of food in there since I've worked up a major appetite."

Damon pulled the sled toward where she pointed. The snow had settled and packed down a bit, making the trekking easier. The baby carriage had rugged wheels, making it easy to handle, if a bit slow. The noise receded the farther they got from the sledding.

"You think Lucas will be okay? It's not too cold for him?" Reaching into the carriage, Damon brushed a knuckle along the baby's cheek.

"Not at all. I'm glad he's getting some fresh air after

all the travel yesterday." She noticed that only one security guard trailed them now that they'd reunited with their son. The other guy must have returned to the town house until his next shift.

"The outfit is very cool." Damon gave a light tug on one dark mouse ear. "You think he's a bear?"

"A bear?" She tilted her head sideways. "I thought it was a mouse papoose."

"McNeills are not mice," he announced definitively.

"Why am I not surprised?" She spotted a clearing in a thicket of trees off the path where the snow wasn't quite as deep. "How about over there?"

"Good eyes." Damon steered the sleigh in that direction. "Do you want to switch and have me push the carriage?"

"I've got it." The mild strain in her arms felt pleasant after months of being inactive. "I'm really looking forward to getting back in shape after the pregnancy."

"You look beautiful." He rested his hand lightly on the middle of her back before dropping a kiss on her hair.

"Thank you." His words warmed her as much as the touch. "But it will be nice to build up more endurance again. I guess it's a good thing babies aren't mobile for the first months."

"I'm here to help you," he reminded her as they reached the clearing. He lifted the picnic hamper and slid out a folded blanket. "I hope you remember you're not in this alone anymore."

He shook out the waterproof blanket on the snow—plastic on one side, wool plaid on the other. She watched him line up the sled at one end of the blanket before he knelt in the snow to open the picnic hamper. All the while, Caroline rocked the carriage gently, tilting it back and forth. Thankfully, their bodyguard sat outside the trees, keeping an eye on the hill below to make sure no one intruded on their space. She didn't feel "watched," per se, although she felt certain the guy kept an eye on them somehow. The team Damon hired seemed very skilled at maintaining a discreet presence.

"I know that I'm not alone any longer, and I'm glad for that." She debated lifting Lucas out of the baby carrier, but then changed her mind, putting the brakes on the contraption and facing the carrier toward the blanket so they could keep an eye on him.

"Are you ready for the winter picnic to end all picnics?" Damon asked, waiting to open the picnic basket until he had her attention.

He shoved his gloves into the pockets of his vest. His dark hair had a few fresh snowflakes coating the top where he must have brushed against one of the evergreen boughs.

"Do you know what's in there?" She peeled off her own gloves, ready to eat. "I can't imagine what a winter picnic entails, so my expectations are fairly low."

"I packed this myself. And believe me, my expectations run permanently high." He tipped open the lid with a flourish. "I present to you, the Post-Sledding Woodland Feast."

Caroline felt her eyes go wide. Crammed inside the huge basket were two brightly colored thermoses and insulated mugs, a red-and-white-checkered tablecloth, a wooden cheeseboard with fresh fruits and cloth-covered cheeses, a tray of shrimp on ice, a stack of Sternos and a lighter, a bag of huge, homemade-looking marshmallows, a tin of graham crackers, chocolate-covered strawberries…

"And champagne!" Her gaze finally reached a bottle of a highly recognizable brand of bubbly inside a champagne bucket. "Is that even legal?" She glanced around, half expecting a park ranger to issue a citation.

"Alcohol in the park is regulated, but not prohibited, so no one will bother us unless we start causing trouble." Grinning, he gestured for her to have a seat on the blanket. "Get comfortable and I'll serve us."

She did as he asked, her eyes still on the stuffed hamper.

"You packed this?" It was a feat of engineering, the way everything was stacked and prepped.

"The technical mind is good for more than designing software, you know." He pulled out fondue sticks and set them beside the Sterno cans so they could toast their own marshmallows. "And under the champagne is a bottle of whiskey if you'd rather doctor up the hot chocolate." He produced a smaller basket with airline-sized bottles of Jameson and Baileys, plus a variety of add-in flavors from vanilla and almond to butterscotch.

"You have outdone yourself." She glanced up into the carriage to check on Lucas. Surrounded by trees on three sides, their picnic spot felt safe and surprisingly private considering the view of the mayhem near Cedar Hill and the row of emerging snowmen lining the biggest walking trail less than fifty yards away.

"I will admit, it's been hell keeping a lid on the surprise all day." He found two small hurricane lanterns and placed candles inside them even though the sun still shone brightly outside. Then, he uncapped one of the containers of cocoa and poured her a mugful. "Here. You can add what you like while I work on the seating."

He scrambled around to the back of the blanket where he used one arm to scoop a pile of snow under the edge of the wool plaid. It took her a moment to understand why he wanted a big lump of snow under the spot where she was sitting. But then he covered it up again, packing the pile into a U-shaped curve to create a support for her back.

"Genius," she announced, settling into the snow seat with her mug of hot chocolate, the picnic spread out at her feet. "It really is the picnic to end all picnics."

"I'll drink to that." Damon poured his own hot chocolate and settled on the blanket beside her. "Here's to our first real day as a family."

She met his blue gaze, his eyes all the more crystalline in the bright sun. He'd taken considerable time and trouble to make the day perfect for her, and Lucas, too. While she'd been sleeping late to catch up on rest, he'd been ordering a special sled and packing the perfect picnic.

"To family," she echoed, softly clanking her pewter cup to his.

Tipping the drink to her lips, she savored the complex swirl of flavors. She hadn't added much alcohol, just enough to give a pleasant jolt of warmth on the way down. The almond and vanilla notes were especially good, and the melting homemade marshmallow she'd set on top was a gooey bonus.

She was about to compliment the first beverage course, but when she turned to him again, she felt a flash of heat from the simmering look he gave her. His mug remained untouched, his attention fixed on her mouth.

He was very still.

"What?" Self-conscious, she set her cup aside in the snow. "I have marshmallow all over my face, don't I?"

Her hand went to her nose, but Damon caught it. He'd set his own drink aside, too, freeing his hands.

"Let me." He canted closer, his focus shifting to her eyes.

The heat ratcheted up so much it was a wonder they weren't melting snow.

She could feel her heartbeat quicken, the answering spark she'd always experienced with this man. Time and distance hadn't broken it. Even forgetting him completely for weeks on end hadn't erased the response she had to him.

By the time his mouth brushed hers, she had somehow crept closer to him, her hands slipping under the vest he wore to rest on the flannel shirt over his chest. His heart sped quicker, its rhythm synchronized with hers in a dance she remembered all too well.

He tasted like whiskey, a straight shot that imparted a stronger burn than any drink. She let the feel of his kiss fill her whole body, the nerve endings coming to life from the roots of her hair to the most intimate heart of her being. His tongue coaxed and toyed with hers, slowly at first. Then harder. More demanding.

Her pulse pounded faster. She breathed in the sandalwood of his aftershave and fresh pine all around them, her senses all attuned to the pleasure to come.

Until Damon slowed the kiss again.

Stopped.

Pulled back just a fraction of an inch.

Caroline's fingers clutched at his shirt, holding him. Wanting him.

It took a long moment for her to return to the moment and the picnic. The feast he'd carefully planned for her. The bodyguard protecting them, who'd no doubt gotten an eyeful. Dragging in gulps of cold air, she hoped the winter chill would put out some of the fire inside. She forced her fingers to unclench from where she gripped his shirt. Thank goodness they were in a public park with a baby in the carriage beside them or she might have toppled him onto his back and lost herself in the feel of him.

"You had a little bit of marshmallow," he explained belatedly, reaching up to graze her upper lip with his thumb. "Right here."

Even now, his touch sparked a powerful need.

"Then I'll have to be careful with my next taste." She picked up her mug for another drink, grateful for something else to focus on besides Damon's touch. The way he looked at her.

"No need," he assured her, reaching toward the sled full of food to drag the cheese board closer. "The pleasure was all mine."

His wolfish grin was very male. And even as he goaded her, she knew her defenses would never hold if he kissed her again.

Nine

After sledding and a picnic, Damon thought Caroline seemed more relaxed. They'd made a plan for dinner in front of the fire in her suite, a location he didn't even have to lobby for since she wanted to stay close to Lucas and his room was on the same floor as hers. Her bedroom had a sitting room with a table, and she'd suggested it would be more relaxing to have a simple meal up there as opposed to the formal dining space.

That she *wanted* to unwind around him seemed like a personal victory.

He pushed the baby's carriage across Fifth Avenue while the bodyguard who accompanied them pulled the sled with the picnic hamper and leftovers. Damon hadn't wanted Caroline to overexert herself, and it had been a busy day already.

"So I'm going to feed Lucas while you relax for a little while." He reminded her of the plan as they approached the huge town house. "Just text me when you're ready for dinner and I'll have it brought up."

"Thank you." She hugged her arms around herself. The temperature was dropping now that the sun had dipped low on the horizon. "It was fun getting outdoors today. It made me realize how long I've been cooped up inside, between caring for Lucas and being sick."

Damon didn't remind her that she'd been a prisoner in her father's home as much as she had been in Mexico. He hoped with time she would comprehend the depth of her father's betrayal. Did she understand that Damon would never allow Lucas to be near Stephan Degraff again?

"Speaking of which, I confirmed an appointment with a highly respected local therapist for you tomorrow." He unlocked the door to the town house, unwilling to bother the staff inside. Besides, they had enough witnesses to private conversations with the security lurking behind them. "Maybe she'll have new ideas for helping you recover your memories and your health."

If Caroline recovered her full memory, it would go a long way in convincing her to stay away from her father. Assuming, of course, she was genuinely committed to starting this marriage over. He had at least ruled out his concern that she might be conspiring against him with her father. Damon believed she was invested in discovering the truth.

"Thank you." She stepped inside while he held the door for her. "I'd like that."

He barely had time to savor that small triumph when the bodyguard who'd been stationed at the house stalked into the foyer, a paper in hand.

This one was Wade, he recalled. The guy had an impressive scar on the side of his neck and a don't-mess-with-me demeanor that Damon appreciated in a protector.

"Is everything all right?" Damon's eyes darted to Lucas and Caroline, and he reassured himself they were still right there with him. He reached into the baby carriage to lift his son from the seat so he could cradle him in his arms.

Behind him, Caroline slid off her boots and left them on a mat to one side of the entry. She padded closer in stocking feet as she unzipped her bright parka.

"There's been no activity to report here," Wade assured him. "But it's a different story back at the Los Altos Hills house." He passed Damon the paper while Caroline stood by him to peer over his shoulder. "The security cameras caught this guy on film shortly before he asked one of the groundskeepers if you were in residence. He took off without giving his name."

"It's the fisherman who rescued me." Caroline's arm brushed against his as she tilted the photo toward her for a better view. "I'm sure of it."

It damn well couldn't be a coincidence.

"This guy?" Damon gave the black-and-white print-out to her so she could look more closely. "This is the same man who pulled you out of the water off the coast in Mexico?"

"Yes." She nodded. "But I don't understand why, that is, how he would find me. Unless—" She went very still. "Do you think he found out something about who kidnapped me? Or where I was being held?"

The bodyguard appeared ready to offer more information, but Damon held up a hand to delay his input, wanting to hear what conclusions Caroline reached on her own. If she was close to a breakthrough with her memories, he didn't want to stifle it.

When Caroline's dark eyes met his, he tried to help her think through the possibility she'd suggested.

"It seems unlikely a fisherman living south of the border would make a trip to the US to find you." He articulated what she had to be thinking already. "Furthermore, you didn't remember me at the time, let alone your married name. So he wouldn't know to look for you at the Los Altos Hills house."

Her face paled. She shook her head.

"You think he works for my father." She thrust the photo back at Damon and spun away, pressing the heels of her hands against her closed eyes. "That he worked for my father even then. Which would mean he didn't save me at all. He just acted out another part of some elaborate drama my father created to keep us apart?" Straightening, she relaxed her arms and opened her eyes. "Why would he ever do that? He's not a madman, Damon. He's just—"

She couldn't quite fill in that blank.

Damon resisted the urge to do so himself, since he had a wealth of names to label the bastard, but none of them would line up with whatever fairy tale Caroline concocted in her mind to account for her father's behavior. One day, she would be able to see her father's actions for what they were—calculated, self-serving and, yes, unbalanced.

It was bad enough Stephan had thwarted an investigation of Caroline's disappearance. If it turned out that he had masterminded her kidnapping? He was going to prison, no question.

"What else were you able to find out about him?" Damon asked, turning back toward Wade.

As much as Damon wanted to comfort his wife, her safety came first. He lifted Lucas higher against his chest, kissing the baby's downy head while the little boy stretched sleepily.

"His name is Theo Bastien." The bodyguard pulled out a phone and seemed to read from his notes. "He's a French-Canadian transplant who moved to Vancouver two years ago, when his employment history shows he started as a chauffeur and groundskeeper for Stephan Degraff, who keeps a rental home there and visits frequently."

At Caroline's muffled cry, Damon interrupted the report. "Whatever you need to make sure the properties are both protected, it's yours. For now, I'd like a copy of the information to go to Officer Downey at the Los Altos Hills police department."

"We've already called it in," Wade assured him. "The police still haven't been able to locate Degraff to interview him."

"Thank you." Damon dismissed him with a nod and waved over the head housekeeper waiting on the periphery of the huge foyer. The McNeill mansion had no lack of personal servants. "Would you find Marcie and let her know Lucas is ready for a bottle? I'm going upstairs with my wife and we'll take dinner in her suite in two hours."

"Of course." The woman nodded, her face a professional mask as she accepted the squirming six-week-old, easily cradling him against her starched gray livery. "Your security team suggested we don't open the door to anyone but uniformed police officers or McNeill family members." She lifted a dark eyebrow, seeking confirmation.

"Correct." Damon tightened his hold on Caroline, feeling her trembling right through her warm winter clothes. "And please be as vigilant at the service entrance. No delivery people past the gates."

"Certainly. I'll remind Marcie to stay in the nursery where you can monitor the little one." The woman spared a brief smile for the wriggling baby before turning on one quiet heel and disappearing down the hallway that led to the service elevator, the bodyguard behind her.

With Lucas cared for and the home well-guarded, Damon could turn his attention to Caroline. His plans for winning her back tonight would have to be deferred after the devastating revelations she was still trying to process. He steered her toward the elevator, hugging her close to his side.

A few minutes later, Caroline swayed on her feet inside the suite's lavish dressing room, her brain pinging with too many worries, thoughts and fears to name them all.

Could her father really have arranged to have her kidnapped? Her head throbbed with as much pain as her heart to think about that while she searched for a clean tee and pajama pants—comfort clothes. It seemed easier to believe she'd walked out on her husband than that her father would be so cruelly calculating.

People ended relationships all the time, after all. And she had been arguing with Damon when she was in London before she flew back to the Los Altos Hills house. What if the holes in her memory had steered her all wrong? What if she hadn't been kidnapped? Maybe she'd asked for her father's help in walking away from the marriage...

That scenario made her head hurt less, but her heart protested just as much. She had been wildly in love with her husband, and no amount of secrets or betrayals could dim that fact. Stepping into warm blue flannel pj pants, she reminded herself that she'd seen evidence of her happiness in those honeymoon photos. The joy in the pictures couldn't be faked.

She ran a brush through her hair and tapped her phone to pull up the video feed of Lucas in the nursery. The baby curled against Marcie while the young woman sat with him in a rocker, the lights dim. The fresh air had tired them all out today.

Stepping out of the dressing room, she found Damon in front of the fireplace in the small sitting room. He'd rearranged the furniture a little so the gray couch was closer to the hearth where he'd built a real fire from the supply of logs in a wrought iron grate. An elaborate white mantelpiece was decorated with a relief sculpture of figures in ball gowns beside a carriage, surrounded by servants with torches lighting the way.

Pivoting from the grate with a poker in his hand, Damon watched her move toward him.

"I just wanted to stay long enough to build a fire and make sure you are okay."

The authenticity in his voice washed over her. He truly was a kind and thoughtful man underneath the intense, work-driven exterior. If Damon had done nothing wrong in all this, and her father bore the full brunt of the blame for what happened to her, she couldn't begin to imagine how hurt her husband must have been at her disappearance.

He had missed out on so much by not being a part of Lucas's birth. And if she didn't handle things well moving forward, if she couldn't sort through what had happened and recover some additional memories, she ran the risk of hurting him all the more. Yet she ached everywhere whenever she tried to force herself to remember.

"It causes physical pain to think about my father…" She couldn't even finish the sentence. Her eyes stung, but that pain was minor in comparison to how her head throbbed.

"Then don't think about it." He set aside the wrought iron poker and rose to meet her. He laid his hands on the part of her upper arms exposed by her tee. "Are you warm enough in this?"

"Kind of." She wasn't. "Actually, I don't think there are enough sweaters to ward off the sort of chill I'm feeling anyhow."

"Come and sit." He tugged her phone from her hand and propped it on the arm of the sofa before gently pushing her onto the seat cushion directly opposite the blaze in the hearth. "I'll get you a blanket."

Drawing her feet up underneath her, she double-checked that she could still see the nursery video feed. Marcie had moved the camera so that it was closer to the crib, where Lucas now slept with his favorite dinosaur blanket.

"Here you go." Damon returned with a snowy white quilt for her, and he draped it around her so that it covered all of her from the neck down.

"Thank you." She caught at his hand where he'd tucked the quilt closer to her chin. "Lucas is already sleeping if you want to stay with me a little while longer."

She needed him, ached to have his arms around her to help bear a burden she still couldn't wrap her brain around. She could not hurt this man any more than she already had.

"I don't want to keep you from your rest." He leaned closer to her, stroking a thumb over the back of her hand. "I know you must be exhausted."

"I'll never sleep with so much on my mind." She snaked a hand out from the blanket and gripped his arm, drawing him toward her on the sofa. "Please."

They could find comfort in a physical connection, at least. She would not deny them that.

"I know you don't want to think the worst of him." He dropped onto the cushion beside her. He'd taken off the vest and flannel he'd worn for sledding, leaving just his gray tee between her hands and his warm chest as she nestled closer to lay her head on his shoulder.

"He's my father. My only living parent." She bit her lip as soon as she said it, knowing he didn't have a relationship at all with his remaining parent. "Didn't it hurt sometimes when you first made the decision to cut your father out of your life, even knowing he hadn't treated your mother fairly?"

She stared into the flames in the hearth, which provided the only light in the room now that the sun had fully set for the evening. She felt the steady thrum of Damon's heart beneath her ear. He slid his arm around her, stroking her hair where it lay on her back.

"I was twelve. It wasn't a decision so much as a fact of life. Dad wasn't coming back and Mom was sick of his pretending he would ever leave his wife to be a part of our family. She made the decision, not me."

"But what about later? After your mother passed and you could have contacted your father again?" she prodded, honestly needing any guidance she could get to figure out how to excise a parent from her life. "I mean, how can you go from loving someone to deciding not to love them anymore?"

Her eyes stung when she spoke the words aloud. Because that was where things stood for her now. She'd have to find a way to un-love someone who didn't have her best interests at heart. But after a lifetime of looking up to her dad, that wasn't going to come easily.

"By the time my mother died, it wasn't hard to hate my father. We blamed him for not being there to help her through the chemo." His voice was rough and he cleared his throat. "For forcing her to move halfway across the globe far from her family. Hell, we blamed him for everything."

"But it was your mother's idea to move far away, right? He never knew she had cancer." She tried to remember the bits that he'd shared with her long ago about his family. He wasn't a man who willingly shared much personal information.

Damon McNeill might be a tech genius and an ambitious businessman she admired, but he kept his emotions in check and his past closely guarded.

"My brothers and I didn't see it that way. My father was a serial cheater with a whole other family. It was Liam's fault that Mom felt like she had no options. I believe she secretly hoped that a drastic move might shake up her lover and force him to realize he loved her." His shoulder lifted a fraction beneath her cheek. A subtle shrug. "When it didn't work, she lost some of her joy. Her will to live. The cancer found a victim without much fight left."

Caroline kissed his chest, rubbing her cheek against him there. "I'm so sorry you lost her at such a young age." She lifted her head, straightening so she could see him. "No wonder you didn't want to see your father afterward. I don't really want to see mine, either. Although I guess a part of me still wants to just ask him why?"

The fire popped and crackled in the hearth, the flames leaping higher as a windy gust blew over the chimney, making a whooshing sound. The shifting of logs stirred the scent of wood smoke.

"Maybe one day you'll be able to. But until we can be sure you're not in danger around him—and that you're not putting Lucas in danger—you'll have to settle for whatever answers the police can shake loose from this investigation." Damon's response was careful. Considered.

And she could read between the lines enough to know he didn't ever want her to have anything to do with Stephan Degraff again. But what about her brothers who were still in his legal care? She couldn't simply write them off. Or worse, leave them in the custody of a man who might not have their best interests at heart.

Wouldn't she need to maintain some kind of dialogue with her family because of them?

"I'm hoping the police find him soon." There had been no news today outside of the report from the security guard about the inquiry at the Los Altos Hills house. "He'll have to put in an appearance at the Transparent investors meeting this week, won't he?"

She felt Damon's shoulders tense. His hand stilled on her back.

"If he's going to follow through on his plans to oust me from the CEO position, yes." The muscle under one eye ticked, and he seemed to weigh the merit of saying anything more. Finally, he let out a gusty breath. "I realize you have a stake in this business, Caroline, but considering all you've been through, I'm hoping you don't feel the need to be a part of a contentious board meeting."

"You're right I have a stake in Transparent. And I will have a lot of guilt and responsibility to bear if my father succeeds in railroading you out of the business before the launch." She'd convinced her dad to invest heavily in the company because she believed in Damon. Now, her husband could be pressured into vacating his seat if Stephan convinced other investors that they would make money with a more seasoned CEO at the helm.

A bloodless, professional executive who took a huge salary to mine the business's assets for the sake of a fatter bottom line.

"I won't let that happen." Damon gripped both ends of the blanket around her shoulders. "Thanks to the notes you shared with me last night—all your research into the business—I know what Stephan knows. That gives me an edge."

Her head throbbed again as she remembered happier days with her father. He'd been so proud when she'd been accepted into a prestigious business program for her master's. She had always thought of him as her biggest champion. What happened to that man?

But her business know-how—the degree and experience her father had helped give her—provided her with unique insight into the situation now. "You won't have enough of an advantage to regain control. His share is significant, Damon. Even if he can't convince other investors to remove you, he's not going away. He added a right of first refusal clause into your initial contract with him so he could invest more in Transparent."

Stephan Degraff had put himself on a track to rule the company with that restrictive clause.

Yet Damon tipped his chin up, a gleam in those deep blue eyes.

"The McNeills can afford to buy him out."

The realization of his calculated move shouldn't have

surprised her. Maybe if she wasn't recovering from amnesia and childbirth, she would have seen it sooner.

"Of course." Understanding dawned more fully. "So you're not in New York City to join the family fold. You came here purely for business reasons."

"And safety purposes. I wanted to get you and Lucas out of Los Altos Hills." He smoothed his fingers over the embroidery on the edge of the quilt, and no matter how frustrated she felt that he'd kept this secret from her, she still wished his hands were on her instead of the blanket.

The picnic and sledding had eroded her defenses. She wanted the comfort of his arms, his kisses that made her forget everything but him.

"So you're not interested in being a part of McNeill Resorts? Inheriting the McNeill legacy?" She took some small comfort that at least he hadn't married her to fulfill the requirements of Malcolm McNeill's will the way she'd once feared.

"Transparent is the only legacy our son needs. And it's one I built with you at my side." The heat in his eyes, the fierceness of the words, convinced her.

He might have hidden his deeper motive for traveling to New York, but perhaps he'd only wanted to shield her from more of her father's schemes. She absolutely believed Damon was the kind of man who would want to build a corporate empire all his own—something apart from his wealthy father and grandfather. She understood that desire a little too well. With the benefit of hindsight, she sure wished she'd put more separation between her work and her dad's company.

But right now, she didn't want to look backward.

"Then you really want us to be a team again." She plucked Damon's hand from where he played with the quilt binding, holding it between hers. "We would need to be stronger than we were before all this happened." She was a different woman now. A mother.

And things were far more complicated.

He watched her with an almost predatory stillness.

"I thought I made that clear the night I put your rings back where they belong." He used his free hand to lift her left one to his mouth.

He kissed her ring finger just below the wedding band set. The feel of his lips on her skin incited awareness. Promised pleasure. And yes, added to her fears about where all this was heading.

She worried about the board meeting. Her memory. Their future. But for now...she could savor this moment with him. This one thing they had that had always been perfect.

"You said you wanted us to start over." She remembered that night so clearly. His invitation had mesmerized her into an explosive kiss. "That you wanted us to be a couple again."

"I do." His fingers aligned with hers before he pivoted his palm a few degrees, bending his fingers into the spaces between hers. An act suddenly intimate.

He stole her breath.

She had to lick her lips to speak again, her mouth gone dry. "Then I think it's time we lived up to those words."

Ten

There had been a time in his relationship with Caroline where those words would have scorched Damon's skin, launching a blistering encounter against the back of a door, the top of a desk, or anywhere else they happened to be. They'd spent weeks on their honeymoon indulging every erotic impulse, driving each other crazy over expensive dinners, only to race back to the hotel before dessert so they could peel one another's clothes off.

But he couldn't afford to let that instinct take over quite yet. Not when his future—his family—hung in the balance of this marriage.

"What about your health?" He hadn't talked to her about her visits with the obstetrician. They'd spoken about the amnesia. About Lucas's well-being after the way Caroline had been drugged while pregnant. "Are you sure it's safe for you? So soon after giving birth?"

He had to grit out the words, doing his damnedest to

ignore the blaze of heat climbing his back, the need for her stronger than ever after so long apart.

"My doctor in Vancouver said I could resume all normal activity." She walked her fingers up his forearm, a teasing invitation to touch her that worked so well he felt the first hint of sweat bead along his shoulders.

"How can you be certain that means—"

"I asked," she interrupted, a sure sign she was feeling the effects of holding back every bit as much as him. "Point blank."

Her gaze dipped to his mouth.

Yeah. Game over.

He speared a hand through her long, silky hair, angling her head for his kiss. Her quick intake of air caused her breasts to brush against his chest, that sexy gasp of surprise only fueling his fire.

She tasted like marshmallow and strawberries, her lips soft and yielding. The kiss sealed them, drawing her body closer to wrap all over his. He didn't know if he did that, or if somehow she did, but the blanket fell away as her breasts pressed to his chest, the subtle curves molding against him. Even through their two tees and her bra, he could feel the tight points of her response, which echoed the same fiery desire that had been riding him for days.

Consumed with the need to see her, feel her, he broke the kiss enough to scrape aside the cotton V-neck, to shove away the lace of the bra enough to taste one rosy-pink peak.

Her fingers curved along his shoulders, scraping lightly as her head fell back. Her spine arched, giving him more access, her throaty moan vibrating on a sizzling frequency he could feel like a physical stroke up his sex.

He unclasped the hook in the front, freeing more of her. With impatient hands, he skimmed the clothes up and off of her, baring her to his view in the firelight. One tousled strand of honey-gold hair curled down her neck to land between her breasts. Her body was different—the curves fuller, the tips darker—than he remembered. And even more tempting.

With that visual reminder, he took a deep breath. Told himself to be careful with her no matter how much they both wanted this.

"Let me take you to bed." He slipped one arm beneath her and another around her shoulders. "We should go slow. And you should be comfortable."

He said it to himself as much as her. A stern reminder to the possessive hormones urging him for more. Now. Faster.

For her, he would shut that voice up.

"I dreamed of you all the time." She whispered the words while he cradled her against his chest, scooping up her phone to bring with them before carrying her from the sitting room to the sleeping area of the suite. "Before they drugged me too much to remember. I dreamed about you holding me, just like this."

She rubbed her cheek against him, her eyes closing in a sweep of dark lashes. He hated that he hadn't been there for her when she needed him. When she'd been frightened, and alone, and expecting his baby.

He kissed the top of her head, pausing at the edge of the king-size poster bed. Holding her steady, he used two fingers to sweep back the snowy white duvet and lay her on the sheets, resting her head on the thick down pillow. He tugged off his shirt and his dark denim pants before sliding into bed beside her.

"It's not a dream anymore." He trailed his fingers

down her cheek to tip her chin up. "We're together now. And I'll never let anything happen to you again."

A small smile curved her lips and she sidled closer to him, her hands smoothing down his chest, slowing at his waist.

"I don't want a bodyguard forever." She kissed his shoulder, her tongue darting out to flick along the spot she kissed. "I'd settle for you making the sexy parts of my dreams come true."

He stilled her questing hand and flipped her to her back.

"I'm being careful with you, Caroline." He splayed his hand on her bare stomach, his fingers spanning narrow hips to cover the place where she'd carried his son. "At least this first time."

"I'm not fragile." She burrowed her hand beneath his to untie the drawstring on her pajama pants. She used the loosened ribbons to snake along his arm. "If there's one thing this year has taught me, it's that I'm stronger than I knew, Damon McNeill. And I want this." She arched up to kiss him fully on the mouth. "You."

He closed his eyes, a shuddering sigh rushing through him.

"I can fight myself, but I'll be damned if I can fight you, too."

Her smile—full of victory and feminine wisdom—torched the last of his restraint.

Kissing his way down her body, he dragged her cotton pajama pants down and off, admiring the way her skin looked in the glow from the fire across the room. Bronze flickered with shadow along her pale flesh and black lace panties. He hooked a finger in the skinny expanse of elastic on her hip and peeled that last layer away.

Her smile faded a moment before he dipped his head

to kiss the dark triangle above her thighs. She shifted her legs, one smooth calf grazing his shoulder. Her skin smelled like roses—a body oil or soap maybe. Everything about her was familiar and yet different, too.

But the way she tasted…perfect. Just like he remembered.

She made tiny, helpless sounds as he kissed her intimately, losing himself in the feel of her slick heat. She twitched and wriggled, her hips rocking for a moment, her back arching. Then, she went utterly still.

He remembered that, too.

He didn't let that slow his pace. He gripped her thighs. Steadied her. She came apart with sweet cries, her fingers gripping the sheets and twisting as the spasms rolled over her. When the last seemed to have its way with her, he tasted his way up her hip. Her stomach.

Caroline was having none of it, though. Her hands were surprisingly strong as she locked onto his arms and tried to pull him higher. He gave in to the wordless demand, prepared to please her thoroughly now that he felt sure she was relaxed. Healed.

And very ready for him.

"You did that on purpose," she accused him breathlessly before she kissed him, attempting to roll on top of him.

"Pleasured you on purpose?" he teased, nipping her shoulder as he let her take charge. "Is that a bad thing?"

"I thought we could…" she reached beneath the covers to peel away his boxers and finished dragging them off his legs with an agile foot "…you know. Find that peak together."

She straddled his thigh while she stroked him. The sexiest wife a man ever called his own.

"Sweetheart." He gripped her narrow waist, molded

his hands around her hips. "Your memory really has taken a hit if you don't recall how easily we can get right back to that high point again."

She gave him that smile again. The one he'd once planned to move mountains for.

"You're wicked. But you're right." She shifted her legs, positioned herself above him and took the sweetest revenge imaginable.

Time stopped.

Caroline was sure it did for one protracted moment as she reunited with Damon in the most fundamental way.

The night wrapped around them, everything dark and shadowy except for their bodies in the reflected glow of the hearth. Skin to skin. Heart to heart. She breathed in the scent of her soap and his aftershave. Her shampoo and the fragrant applewood smoke.

Damon's blue eyes locked with hers, communicating things he never shared in words. She couldn't possibly understand him. She knew this much, though. There was no denying their connection. It *had* to mean something. The longing for him. Craving him. Missing him.

In her mind and her heart, that added up to a new hope.

"Caroline." His voice was gruff with unfulfilled desire, reminding her he hadn't reached that finish point he'd already given her.

Gladly, she lost herself all over again, giving in to the feel of his hands on her hips as he guided her higher. Faster.

This was a language they understood. He made her feel beautiful. Sexual. Desirable. And she couldn't possibly get enough of him. She wished time would stop again so they could go on and on this way, relishing every shared breath and sigh. But now, the moments sped faster, driving her toward the inevitable as pleasure twined tight inside her.

Just as he'd predicted.

She tried to slow everything down, but she felt the gallop of Damon's heart, the rush of his need. She had no choice but to hang onto him. To brace herself for…

Sensation gripped her, tossed her in the waves of another heady orgasm that undulated through her again and again. She knew that his completion came at the same time as hers, felt the harsh tensing of his body and heard the guttural shout. Yet she was so lost in what she was feeling, she couldn't even find the will to peel her spent body off of him for long moments afterward.

She simply curled onto his chest, trying to catch her breath, comforted by the rhythm of his heartbeat beneath her ear.

In time, he turned them both sideways, easing her off him to lie next to him in the fading firelight from a blaze that needed stirring. It was early yet. They hadn't even had dinner. But it felt so right to be with him.

Naked. Fulfilled. Happy.

Save for one tiny thought at the back of her brain.

In the past, the aftermath of sex had always been a time for more intimate words. Another sort of connection they'd once enjoyed.

I love you, he might have once whispered in her ear, stroking her hair as she fell asleep. Now, the gentle glide of his fingers through the long strands felt strangely…quiet.

Forcefully quiet.

As if there was an effort not to say anything he might regret later.

Sleepily, she opened one eye to peer up at him, try-

ing to gauge his expression. Brow furrowed, he seemed
to concentrate on her hair as if the way he combed his
fingers through were of monumental importance.

Because he was busy telling himself it didn't matter
that he no longer loved her?

Probably she was reading too much into the moment. Even though the sex had been as earth-moving as
ever, they were still off in their conversational rhythms.
They'd been apart too long.

Caroline hoped that was all there was to it. Because
if her husband didn't love her anymore, it didn't matter how beautiful, sexual or desirable he made her feel.

It didn't even matter that they shared a child together,
although she would hurt more for Lucas's sake.

No. If Damon didn't love her, no power on earth
could make Caroline stay.

Eleven

Two hours later, Damon cradled Lucas in his arms and stared out into the snowy night through a window that overlooked Central Park to the west. Behind him, Caroline picked at the desserts after the small meal they'd shared in the sitting room of her suite, an informal affair to make it easier to spend time with the baby. His son blinked up at him with wide blue eyes, his expression content. His little face was so familiar now.

With his wife back in his bed, once more committed to being a couple, Damon should share that sense of contentment. Being with Caroline again reminded him that he was in reach of all his goals. Now that his family was secure, he could focus on his company. His son's legacy.

Except something was still off.

He could feel the disconnect between them now no matter that the sex had been so good it had left them nearly delirious, blissed out and languorous in the sheets together long afterward. Something was missing in their marriage. Something they'd had before and hadn't recaptured. He felt the loss all the more for having known her full love. The off-the-charts intimacy hadn't patched the hole left by the lack of trust.

Surely that was the missing piece. Questioning one another, the betrayals and secrets, had left them with a deep uneasiness no matter how hard they worked to be a team. Damned if he knew how to restore that bond.

A brusque knock on the door called him from brooding thoughts. Caroline set down her plate and moved as if to rise.

"I'll get it." He strode to the door, not wanting her disturbed.

He'd seen a marked improvement in her health since they'd been reunited and he didn't want to slow her recovery by stressing her any more. He enjoyed seeing hints of her competitive spirit return. Some of her natural joy.

Wade stood on the other side.

"Sorry to disturb you." The guy's black pants and tee were neatly pressed, but appeared to be off-duty wear, making Damon wonder if there was a problem.

"What's wrong?" Instinctively, he looked past the guard into the hallway, shifting Lucas to the arm farther from the door.

"You have visitors. We started to run a check on them before we bothered you, but the staff vouched for them. It's your half brother and his wife, Cameron and Maresa McNeill." He flipped his phone screen around for Damon to see.

Sure enough, Damon's doppelganger showed up on the screen—the half brother who looked most like him. "Yeah. We'd better let the family through the door or

I'll get booted out of here." He had thought Cameron was going to wait until tomorrow to show, but Damon didn't feel right turning him away when this was his grandfather's house.

Caroline arrived at Damon's side, her silky hair brushing his shirt sleeve as she joined him in time to glance at the photo of his relative.

"Just doing my job." Wade pocketed the phone and nodded an acknowledgment to Caroline. "The house-keeper wanted them to wait in the library, so I sent Joseph to keep a discreet eye on the third floor while they're here."

"Dismiss him, but thank you. We'll go down to them in a few minutes." He closed the door behind the body-guard, pivoting to face his wife. "I can make your ex-cuses. I'm sure they'll understand—"

"I'm eager to meet them," she surprised him by say-ing. "I'll just slip into a dress."

"Are you sure?" He would have discouraged her if Cam hadn't brought along his wife. He could hardly claim this was a brothers-only meeting.

"With my own family disintegrating, Damon, I look forward to connecting with yours." She was already moving toward the dressing room. "You might not care about nurturing a relationship with your grandfather and half brothers, but for Lucas's sake, I would like him to have the chance to be part of a bigger family."

Was that a positive sign? Maybe if Caroline felt more deeply connected to the rest of his relatives, he could finally feel like they were a team again. A real couple.

United.

"Very well. If you don't mind, I'll take Lucas to the nursery and go down now to greet them. Come down-stairs whenever you're ready."

"Thank you." She retreated into the dressing area.

No doubt she wanted to hurry along her preparations. That's probably why she'd seemed flustered.

But as he departed the bedroom suite where they'd renewed their marriage, he couldn't shake the sense that Caroline was still holding something back from him. Was she actively keeping secrets from him?

Or did she simply fear—as he did—that her uncovered memories might reveal deeper rifts in their marriage than he'd ever be able to fix?

Logically, Caroline understood that integrating herself into the McNeill family wouldn't magically make her feel like a real McNeill again.

But knowing as much didn't stop her from throwing herself wholeheartedly into a private conversation with her breathtakingly beautiful sister-in-law as they had after-dinner drinks in the third-floor library. Caroline acknowledged that she'd been too isolated by her father. Even during her time working in New York, away from him, she hadn't strayed far from her office. Maybe if she'd surrounded herself with a larger network, she wouldn't have been so susceptible to his control. She would make sure her son had more influences in his life.

Now, she and Maresa were able to speak privately on the couch while Damon and Cameron conversed on the other side of room behind the huge desk that dominated one side of the library.

"So your brother is really happy here?" Caroline asked, sitting beside Maresa McNeill on a huge leather sofa in the mahogany-paneled room surrounded by books and beautiful, antique, Chinese-lacquer panels hung on the walls between the windows.

There was a faint scent of leather and wood smoke

from yet another fireplace. Had Damon said there were nine in all? Eleven? Caroline sipped at her port wine and tried to focus on Maresa's story about her family's summer relocation to Manhattan. The woman had led an interesting, though difficult life, and had met Cameron while working as a concierge for one of the family's resorts in St. Thomas. Her mother had multiple sclerosis, and her brother had suffered a traumatic brain injury after a car crash during one of their mother's seizures. Apparently, both had found excellent health services and opportunities in New York City.

"My brother loves it here. He does landscaping work in a supervised program and is truly thriving." Maresa shifted on the sofa to face Caroline more fully, her amber-colored eyes striking against her darker skin tone. With her dark curls that ended in golden tips, she looked sun-kissed, even in the gray New York wintertime. "But enough about me. I insisted Cam bring me with him tonight so I could meet you. How are you feeling?"

"Fine." Caroline wasn't sure if anyone in this family knew about her ordeal being held against her will, or if the other woman was just curious about how her recovery from childbirth was going. "Damon took me sledding today in the park and it felt nice to be outdoors."

Maresa bit her lip. "Gabe said you had amnesia. Are you recovering any memories?"

"I may have remembered all that I can, but that doesn't mean I'm going to stop trying and hoping for more." She wasn't certain how much to share of her convoluted relationship with her father and the kidnapping she only recalled in pieces because of the drugs. "I'm seeing a new therapist tomorrow though, so maybe I'll learn some new strategies for digging through the hazy parts of my past."

"Good." Maresa reached over to lay a comforting hand on her arm. Her fingernails were painted a soft shade of lilac and a pear-shaped diamond surrounded by a halo of smaller diamonds glinted in the lamplight. "The important thing to know is that you're safe now and your husband loves you. I never saw a man so devastated as Damon when I met him last month—before you returned."

"Really?" she blurted before realizing that might come across as strange. But Maresa's words startled her, while also making her heart race. "I mean, I'm sure it was hard for him, but—"

Maresa leaned closer to lower her voice while Cameron and Damon looked over from across the room. "Honestly? I thought Damon looked haunted the first time I met him. He bears a resemblance to my husband, but there was a complete void in his eyes so different from how he looks now." She grinned and straightened, her gaze seeking the two men for a moment. "It's obvious he's found his happiness again. I'm so glad for you both."

Caroline's heart squeezed around the words, and the idea of her husband being that hurt by her disappearance. Could Maresa have read him correctly? Caroline was unsettled by how desperately she wanted to believe Damon's feelings ran that deep. Still…she didn't know this woman well enough to show her insecurity about her husband's affections.

"I forgot he came here then—right after he returned from his trip to Europe." She knew that he'd been searching for her.

So even if Damon didn't profess his love to her now, didn't his actions during that horrible time prove that he loved her? Maybe she needed to dig deeper. To try harder to connect with him.

She'd just been so damn rattled by the way they'd laid silently together after making love.

Or what she'd thought had been making love.

With no promises of forever in her ear, no gentle words sweetly spoken, it didn't feel the same as before.

"Cameron likes him," Maresa confided. "And between you and me, I don't think he was prepared to like any of his half brothers. But he came here tonight with Malcom's power of attorney for the duration of the Transparent board meeting. They're prepared to help Damon however they can."

Caroline tensed at the mention of the meeting that was certain to be an ugly showdown between her dad and her husband. Two men she had once loved dearly. Now? She didn't understand her father, and she feared that Damon no longer returned her love. Whatever Maresa thought she'd seen in him—a new happiness—wasn't there as far as Caroline could tell.

"Malcolm won't be there when the board convenes?" She understood that Cameron would have his grandfather's authority, but she wondered if it would be as effective as having Malcolm McNeill there himself, an internationally recognized face of corporate success.

"You haven't heard?" Maresa peered toward the men again before returning her attention to Caroline. "I'm sure Damon will tell you after we leave either way. But Malcolm is in Wyoming trying to make peace with the son who disowned him long ago."

"Liam?" She had no idea there was a rift between Damon's father and grandfather.

"No." Maresa shook her head and took a small sip of her port. "The *other* son that he never speaks about. Donovan."

Maresa filled her in on a few more details, but Caroline's brain was stuck wondering if Damon had known about this hidden branch of the family. Had he withheld the news from her?

It was one thing to make excuses for his reticence concerning his love for her after the way this year had torn them apart. But would he purposely shut her out of his private life now?

Then again, perhaps he didn't know about Malcolm's other son, either. There was a chance he was only just learning about it from Cameron, the way she'd just learned from Maresa. Perhaps they'd speak about it tonight and her fears that they would never heal the rift between them would be for nothing. She was simply rattled and unsettled because she was beginning to think she'd lost her chance at love.

Doing her best to dial back into the conversation, Caroline learned that Malcolm's ill health had made him decide to give the relationship with his estranged son one last try. Maresa assured her that Quinn, Cameron and Ian had all known about their uncle, but not one of them had ever met him since he'd been cut out of Malcolm's life when their father was just a teen.

There were McNeills all over Wyoming, successful ranchers who led a much different lifestyle than the real estate moguls, their East Coast relatives. Even the business news media failed to recall Malcolm's elder son when they wrote about him, a fact that explained why Caroline had never heard about those relations before.

As the evening came to a close and the men shook hands, Caroline thanked and hugged Maresa, a woman she would gladly view as a friend and ally down the road. Assuming, of course, Caroline remained a McNeill. Her gaze sought her husband's while they said their good-nights, wishing she could discern some small hint of the love Maresa had mentioned seeing in Damon.

When the door to the library closed behind Cameron and Maresa, who insisted they'd find their own way out, Caroline couldn't deny the pleasant shiver she felt as her husband wrapped two arms around her from behind and drew her back against his chest.

"You look so beautiful." His breath warmed her ear when he spoke. "I haven't been able to take my eyes off you all night."

Awareness stirred. Her pulse quickened at the feel of his whisker-roughened jaw against her neck as he bent to kiss her there. And yes, maybe she was far too willing to let go of the fears that had plagued her all evening. She needed this chance to be with him. To search for some hint of the love she wanted to feel in her marriage again.

"You appeared to be deep in conversation with your brother," she accused lightly, a secret thrill racing through her that he'd noticed the extra care she'd taken with her appearance.

"Not from the moment you set foot in the room." His hands skimmed her sides, lingering on her waist. "All I could think about was how soon I could get you out of this dress."

The fitted black dress was deceptively modest with a Nehru neckline that kept the bodice well covered. It was sleeveless, however, with a sexy cutout along one shoulder so that from the back it was decidedly racier. The asymmetrical crepe hem was knee-length on one side and thigh-grazing on the other. Silver snaps up one side gave it a rock n' roll edge.

And yes, she'd worn it with Damon in mind. They'd purchased it together from a design house in Italy on their honeymoon, and he'd liked it then, too. She'd brought it to New York with her, hoping it would bring them some of the romance and happiness of that time. Sure enough, the garment had worked some of its magic already.

"I seemed to recall you liked the snaps when we picked it out." She gripped his hand and steered it south along one hip where the silver snaps began.

His fingers brushed her bare thigh where the fabric ended, and she could feel his appreciation for the outfit pressing against her. She rolled her hips against him, only too glad to let the heat of this moment burn away everything else. She didn't know how much time she had left with Damon. She would damned well store up every moment of pleasure she could.

"I want you. Now." He flicked open a snap and she felt the cool rush of air against her thighs where the fabric slid open, almost to her panties.

"What if someone comes in?" She didn't know if the staff would be cleaning soon.

Then again, the feel of Damon's strong hand palming the front of her leg made her knees too weak to walk anywhere. Desire rushed through her. Hard.

"There's a private card room in back." He spun her around, taking her hand to close the distance to an entrance she hadn't noticed before, an opening disguised by one of the decorative lacquer panels. "This door locks."

They entered and he flipped on a light switch that illuminated a wine rack in the back of a circular red room with a long, mahogany bar. At the center sat a leathertopped poker table with five club chairs. The sound of a bolt sliding into place sent a ribbon of anticipation tickling its way up her spine.

Turning to face Damon, she watched his blue eyes darken to midnight. There was a naked hunger in his gaze that, for a moment, she swore had to be more than just physical need. It had to be.

They both craved this with a passion that went beyond sex.

Then, his hands were on her again and her brain switched off. He wrenched open the rest of the snaps on the dress in one easy swipe, baring her body. She'd worn red silk panties but no bra, her B-cups supported enough by the dress.

And now they were well supported by her husband's hands. His fingers roamed her curves, smoothing around the nipples and then gently plucking them, kissing each one in turn. A moan simmered from her and she pressed herself to him, arching up on her toes to position the V of her thighs closer to the hard heat of the ridge in his trousers.

His answering growl gave her another private thrill, stroking her feminine ego along with the fire inside. She wrapped her arms around his neck, desperate to be even closer. He lifted her up against him, steering her hips where she wanted them most, snug to his arousal.

He only left her there for a moment though, until he deposited her onto the heavy poker table, laying her on her back so her legs dangled off one side. The cool leather felt good against her back while she admired the view. He wrenched off his shirt, revealing the sculpted muscles she loved to touch. Then his hands moved lower, working fast but carefully as he unbuckled the belt and undid the buttons that kept him from her. She thought to repay him in kind, slipping a hand into her panties to give him access, but he halted her with an iron grip that gentled almost instantly.

"I'd like to." He whispered the word against her stomach before he dragged the silk down a few inches with his teeth.

More shivers danced over her. She tossed her head from one side to the other, ready for release, her hair tangling beneath her for a moment before he cupped her sex and touched her.

There.

The spasms were fast and hard, the orgasm a shock of sudden pleasure she hadn't been ready for. Her nails scratched against the table and he helped her ride the waves. When she had almost caught her breath, he entered her.

Fully.

Lost and clinging to him, she said his name like a mantra. Wrapping her arms around him, she could only hold on, the pleasure so intense. She kissed his face, savored the stubble-rough jaw and finally locked her ankles around him to hold him deep inside her.

He moved faster. Slower. He unwound her arms long enough to kiss her breasts again. When he took her mouth, he kissed her with devastating softness. Sweetness. Thoroughness.

All the while, he built a steady rhythm inside her that stole her breath.

When the second orgasm shook her, she saw stars behind her eyes. She hugged him tighter, feeling his release in the tensing of every muscle. Sensation drenched her, tugging her deeper into love.

So much so, she realized as consciousness slowly returned, that the mantra she'd been repeating against his skin all that time wasn't just idle sweet words.

It was: *I love you. I love you.*

The echo of the sentiment still hung in the small

room, as if the words circled above their heads now that she'd said them aloud. Maybe hearing what Maresa had said, that Damon loved her, had given her the courage to say it tonight.

To hope he would say it back.

A year ago, it would have been perfectly normal for her to expect to hear it in return. But now, the room remained unnaturally silent except for their breathing.

Had she really said that?

Wrenching open her eyes, she peered up at him in the dimness only to see his gaze dart away as fast as hers alighted on him.

Her heart deflated along with all the hope she'd been feeling. Damon didn't love her. He was only with her to hold his family together.

They didn't speak about it as they dressed in silence, even though Damon tenderly kissed her temple and retrieved her clothes for her, even though he kept an arm around her as they walked to the elevator and rode it upstairs to their bedroom suites.

She would stay with him through the board meeting. Make sure she did everything in her power to help him win Transparent away from her father. But after that, she would have to walk away from this man who didn't trust her enough to love her anymore.

Twelve

Three days later, Damon understood in no uncertain terms that he'd screwed up irrevocably. As in, there was no going back. He'd wrecked things with Caroline beyond repair. His chest ached with the knowledge as he watched her from the railing of the second-story patio of the house in Los Altos Hills. They'd flown back from Manhattan the day before to be in Silicon Valley for the Transparent board meeting today. Now, she jogged toward him as dawn broke to the east, her golden hair catching the slanting sunlight while Wade, the bodyguard, kept tabs on her from a mountain bike.

She'd told Damon over dinner last night that she was working on her endurance so she could start pushing Lucas in a baby stroller while she jogged. And that had been about as much conversation as they'd shared since his colossal misstep with her that night in New York in the card room.

I love you, she'd told him.

And what did he say in response?

Nada. Zero. Zip.

He'd frozen up like a kid with his first girlfriend instead of a man intent on winning back his wife. He'd felt himself lock down at the notion of putting his heart in the line of fire again after the way she'd withheld Lucas from him when she returned. She'd believed the worst of him, thinking he didn't care that she'd disappeared.

"Dude?" His brother Gabe called to him from a seat at the patio table where he was shoveling down his second plate of eggs. He'd flown in from Martinique with his nine-month-old son so he could attend the board meeting. Jager was in the air now, scheduled to arrive before the ten o'clock start time. "Have you heard a word I've said over there?"

Damon forced himself to drag his gaze away from his wife. If he hadn't thought of a way to fix his mistake by now, chances were good he never would. There were some moments in life when a man didn't get a second chance, and he would have to live with that. Too bad the realization crushed the air out of his lungs until he could hardly draw a breath. Why hadn't he been able to simply return the words that might have kept her by his side forever?

He must still love her deeply or he wouldn't have felt like he was free-falling into an abyss these past two days. The problem was, when she'd said those sweet words he wanted more than anything, he hadn't been certain they were true. How could she know how she felt when she didn't even remember their whole past? When she wasn't 100 percent certain if she'd walked out on him or if she'd truly been forcefully taken from their home?

She'd turned to her father when she was pregnant with his child. Hadn't she felt any of that love for Damon then? He stalked back toward the table where Gabe sat with his son Jason squirming on his lap. The kid was already a handful, crawling all over the place, climbing anything and everything, with a willful disposition tempered by the cutest grin imaginable.

"Honestly?" Damon tried and failed to remember a single thing his brother had been saying to him as he gladly plucked baby Jason off Gabe's lap so the guy could finish his eggs in peace. "I'm more than a little distracted today."

He set his wiggly nephew down on the rug in the middle of the patio deck so the kid had some room to scoot. Would Lucas look like this in another seven months? He didn't want to miss another day of his son's life, yet if he didn't fix things with Caroline…

He couldn't even fathom the future.

"Yeah. No kidding. And I'm trying to adjust to the time change when I've barely slept for days after the latest nanny quit, but I'm still making an effort to converse like a normal human being." Draining the last swig of orange juice in his glass, Gabe scraped his chair back from the wrought iron table. "I've been trying to tell you that you're an idiot to delay talking to her."

"And tell her what?" Damon sidestepped Jason's path as he crawled like his diaper was on fire toward some red blocks that Gabe had brought out of the nursery with him. "The truth? That I didn't trust her enough to believe she loved me?" He shook his head. "That's only going to make her pack her bags faster."

He'd tried to speak to Caroline's therapist back in Vancouver, to solicit the woman's advice for talking to her, but the doctor had held firm that she wouldn't discuss any issues that could compromise Caroline's privacy.

"No." Gabe rose from his chair, his white button-down and tan cargo shorts about as formal as the guy ever dressed outside of a meeting like the one they'd have to attend today. His work at the Birdsong Hotel definitely ran to the informal. But there was nothing casual or relaxed about his expression now as he stalked toward Damon. "First thing you do is let her know you love her. Fix that screw-up before anything else, because I guarantee you, that's killing her."

Gabe stood shoulder-to-shoulder with him, watching over Jason as the baby tried to eat one of the fat red blocks. Damon was grateful for the distraction from the topic since the accusation his brother had just leveled had found its mark.

"I think she's angry more than anything." He knew because she'd hardly spoken to him. But she was harder to read now than before her disappearance. His wife was quieter. In the past, if she was upset with him, she would have told him why in no uncertain terms.

And since that night in New York, he'd buried himself in work, preparing for his appointment with the Transparent investors. With a wince of guilt, he realized how quickly he'd fallen into that old pattern. Back when she'd gone to London to make amends with her father, he'd been upset and had retreated to his office on the West Coast. He had regretted not talking to her more rationally then, yet now he followed the same path. Avoidance.

"Is that how you'd feel if someone you loved left you hanging when you put your heart on the line? Angry?" Gabe shook his head. "I'm not saying I have the best instincts where women are concerned, though. Maybe

I was never lucky enough to find a really good one." He scooped Jason off the floor, lifting the baby high over his head long enough to make the kid smile. Then he swooped him down low, while the boy squealed happily. "All I know is you don't just sit back and watch while a woman like Caroline walks away."

His brother started to leave, shaking Damon out of his thoughts.

"Gabe." He appreciated his younger sibling's insights, especially now when Jager was so happy with his own wife that Damon would never ask him about this. "What if she eventually remembers what happened that day she disappeared? What if she wakes up one day and recalls that she left me because she wanted it to be over?" He had played the scenarios over and over in his head, grappling with those fears that he wasn't a good husband. But how would he ever be a better one if he didn't change? "Maybe she didn't run into trouble with the guys who abducted her until she had set up a life apart from me."

Gabe stalked back toward him, his expression stark. In contrast, Jason kicked and drooled, gumming one finger while he grinned.

"Wake up, brother." Gabe spoke the words just inches from Damon's face before he leaned back. "None of that matters. Or if it does, count yourself lucky you got another chance with someone who loves you *right now*. Today. That's a whole lot more than most people get."

There was a wealth of feeling behind the words, making Damon wonder what kinds of hell his brother had dealt with that he knew nothing about.

That was a conversation for another day, though. Right now, Damon needed to head into the office for the professional battle of his life. With any luck, the police would be there afterward to ask his father-in-law all the questions about their investigation he'd avoided while he was overseas.

It was probably too much to hope that Stephan Degraff would be dragged off to jail then and there for giving false statements to the police. But if it came to seeing Stephan behind bars or keeping Caroline, Damon knew what he would choose.

Because his brother was right. Damon might not deserve a second chance with her, but since he'd been fortunate enough to get one, he needed to try and convince her they were worth it.

He just hoped it wasn't too late.

Caroline paced outside the penthouse boardroom of the Transparent building later that morning, trying to time her entrance to the most important business meeting of her husband's life.

Her husband. For now.

She stopped short, her gaze moving from the stunning view of the Santa Cruz Mountains outside the reception area windows down to the wedding band set on her fingers. Pausing at one of the floor-to-ceiling windows, Caroline indulged herself for a moment, staring at the diamond, tilting it this way and that to catch the best light and refract it so that little rainbow squares danced across the polished bamboo floors.

Damon needed her help today, even if he didn't know it. He'd allowed her to ride into the office with him and his brother, Gabe, although he'd insisted she wait outside the meeting with her bodyguards. They'd brought two, knowing that her father would be in attendance. But Damon had asked her not to sit in on the contentious conference, even though her former job title would have given her every right to do so.

She understood that he might see her as a distraction today when he needed to be on top of his game to out-maneuver her father. What Damon didn't understand was that he had no chance of beating Stephan Degraff without her help. Her father was hellbent on revenge. She saw that now. Stephan would do anything to thwart Damon if only for the sake of proving to her that Damon wasn't worth her time.

Her love.

Her father was wrong about that. Damon was the worthiest man in the world for that honor. If only he loved her back.

Yet to help make things right for her husband, she would have to be the one to maneuver her father. She could convince him to sign that paper and give Damon the ultimate win. But Damon wasn't going to like it one bit.

Not that it should matter now. He'd already broken her heart with his profound silence following her declaration of love. Except, foolishly perhaps, she didn't want to hurt him any more than she already had. Keeping his child a secret from him had been more than he should have to bear.

Behind her, the elevator chimed. Her bodyguards didn't move, and yet she could feel their readiness for anything.

"Mrs. McNeill?" A familiar police officer stepped off the elevator onto the top floor, his dark jacket and plain blue tie setting him apart from most of the staffers at Transparent. From the coders to the front office workers, the company embraced a more relaxed, West Coast vibe.

"Officer Downey." She strode forward to shake his hand. "My husband made sure I wasn't in the building when my father entered, but he's in the boardroom now." She pointed to the meeting space where Damon had been joined by his brothers Jager and Gabe, plus his half brother, Cameron.

Beyond the McNeill men, there were five other attendees, including her dad. An administrative assistant sat off to one side, taking notes. They could see the proceedings through the clear glass wall on one side that gave the meeting room a mountain view, but still allowed the light to spill into the interior reception area.

Fortunately, her father's back was to her.

She needed to steel herself to face the man who had ruined her marriage and tried to keep Damon from his child.

"We've spoken at length with the man who asked for your husband at the Los Altos Hills house a few days back," the officer informed her, peeling off his aviator shades and tucking them in his pocket. "We have some good leads on two of the suspects we believe served as your captors in Mexico. Once we speak to your father, we'll know more. But I will warn you, it appears your father has business ties to both of them, as well."

She wanted to ask him if he thought her dad could have really masterminded the kidnapping of his own daughter, but she knew he wouldn't answer such a thing. How could anyone have suspected that? She'd known her father was controlling, but she'd never guessed he would try to erase her memory to keep her away from Damon. Whatever her father did, if she couldn't prove it and see him punished, she would have to find a way to live with it. To move past it.

"Thank you." She nodded, needing to keep her

thoughts on the task in front of her and not her spiraling emotions. If she wanted her father to sign over his stake in Transparent, she needed to put on a hell of a show in that boardroom. "If you'll excuse me though, I think I see my cue to enter the meeting starting right now."

She watched as Damon shoved a contract in front of her father. He was passing over the buyout offer with incentives to sell his stake to the McNeills. There were terms Stephan Degraff would never agree to.

Unless she made him.

"Are you sure?" Officer Downey stepped forward, as if he would follow her into the meeting. "I can go with you."

"I'll be fine." She tried for a gracious smile, all the while knowing how important timing was for the entrance. "I have two bodyguards and you can see me through the window."

Her heart beat faster in fear of her father, of what she might discover. Damon would be angry about this. But the end would justify the means.

She hoped. It was the best way she could think of to make amends for not finding her way back to him sooner. She peeled off her wedding ring set and slid the diamonds into her purse.

She couldn't afford to think about those vows right now when she was about to break them in spectacular fashion.

"I would have to agree to the sale, and I never will." Stephan Degraff had the nerve to smile as he refused to even glance at the agreement in front of him. It was a small, fake-apologetic smile that Damon wanted to punch into next year.

He wouldn't, of course.

He wasn't going to lose his cool in the boardroom, especially now when the stakes were higher than they'd ever been before. The safety of his wife and his child rested in the balance.

It was just because of the hell this pale, perfectly groomed man had put Caroline through that had Damon imagining all the ways to exact revenge. How dare the bastard show his face after lying to the police about Caroline's disappearance. The guy had always been somewhat of a Silicon Valley enigma, focusing on start-ups that other investors hadn't even heard about before, beating his competition to the punch. Damon suspected that had far more to do with his daughter's business savvy than his own. The value of Degraff's portfolio had skyrocketed once Caroline had joined his company. And the bastard had paid her back by sabotaging her marriage. Her health.

Risking the life of his own grandson in the process.

The knowledge made Damon tense with icy rage, but he had to get through this. Had to turn the tide before the man succeeded in robbing him of his company.

Everything about Stephan Degraff was meticulous, from his perfectly centered double Windsor knot to the way he put down his pen at a ninety-degree angle to the top of his legal pad every time. He was a perfectionist who took things too damned far.

"Has it occurred to you that it's generous of the company to offer a buyout now when you might be sitting in prison this time next week, without any way to tap into the rewards of your investment at all?" Damon ground his teeth while Gabe kicked his shin.

Little did Gabe know how much he'd restrained himself already.

"Prison?" The bastard lifted an eyebrow, his lips pursing in a smirk. "I hardly think so."

"The terms are generous," Cameron McNeill stepped in smoothly, redirecting the conversation away from prison time and giving Damon a moment to get his fury under control. "And this way you're not tied to the launch of the new product for a payout. You must realize we can continue to stall the launch if we can't agree on terms."

There was grumbling around the dark cypress wood table from the other investors, none of whom wanted to wait another day for their investment to appreciate, let alone months.

Damon didn't care. He needed control of his business. And now, even if Degraff agreed to stop trying to boot him out of the CEO seat, it was no longer enough. Damon needed the backstabbing prick gone.

He lifted his eyes toward the glass wall separating the meeting space from the reception area, and glimpsed Caroline talking to the cop who was working on the investigation into her disappearance. Damn it. What was she doing in such a visible spot? He'd hoped she would wait in one of the offices. What if her father saw her?

The need to run out of the meeting and take her somewhere safe was making it impossible to concentrate.

"I know that you're trying to remove me." Stephan Degraff flipped his black Montblanc fountain pen in the other direction, oblivious to his daughter standing so close to him on the other side of the glass. That damn pen remained perfectly perpendicular to the edge of his pad, but was now facing the other way. "I understand that you don't want me to have a role in Transparent. But you've taken my daughter. You won't take my stake in the business."

Damon hadn't even processed that remark when the conference room door swished open. The click of her high heels had an authoritative sound as Caroline entered and made her way across the room.

Stunning every single person in the room.

Her hair was brushed to shining silk, a shade lighter than it had been just the day before. He hadn't noticed that in the car on the drive over; he was too distracted thinking about the meeting. In fact, even her clothes were different from the things she'd worn earlier in the week. This was Caroline Degraff, executive in charge. Her stiletto pumps made her tower over the table. Her white fitted dress had been tailored to the leaner frame of her body.

"Don't be ridiculous." She kept her eyes on her father as she entered the room. "Damon hasn't taken me, Dad." She smiled warmly at him. The dutiful, perfect daughter, reunited with her lying bastard of a father.

Betrayal stabbed Damon.

Dad? That's how she thought of the scum who had lied through his teeth about her disappearance? This was the same man responsible for keeping Damon from his son. Had she been lying to Damon all week? He could not imagine how she could still be loyal to this miserable excuse for a human being.

His brain couldn't comprehend it. He watched her drop into the empty chair beside Stephan Degraff, who almost looked like he'd seen a ghost. Had he not expected to see Caroline? Or was he expecting to see a different version of his daughter, the weak and confused amnesiac he'd tried to manipulate for his own ends?

For once, Damon could identify with her smarmy father. He didn't know what to believe, either, but he sure as hell understood what it meant that she no longer wore her wedding ring. She'd made sure the whole room would know where her real allegiance lay.

Bile burned his gut.

"Caroline." Stephan Degraff gripped his pen harder, clearly trying to compose himself. "You're here."

"Of course." She smiled that high-wattage grin that Damon remembered from the honeymoon photos. "Where else would I be? I'm all about protecting the family interests." She passed him her pen, a Montblanc that matched her father's except it was silver. "I've had the benefit of reading the agreement ahead of time, and the terms are very generous, especially considering how we know about the glitch in the launch product."

There were more murmurs around the table. Was she talking about the security issue Damon's hacker had found? The one she knew Damon had already patched?

He straightened in his seat, trying to follow whatever she was doing. Damon might not comprehend her motive, but one thing was certain. Having her father sign that paper benefited Damon.

Not Stephan.

And Caroline knew it better than anyone.

"McNeill, is that true?" a worried voice asked loudly over the fray. "Is the launch product flawed?"

That seemed to be the concern around the table for anyone who wasn't a McNeill or a Degraff. They didn't want to think their investment had gone belly-up because of a glitch.

Thankfully, Gabe responded for him while Damon watched the drama play out between Caroline and her father on the opposite side of the table. Stephan Degraff stared at her in wonder, like he'd recovered the most precious thing in the world to him.

To a certain extent, Damon could empathize. He

hadn't wanted to lose her, either. But he sure as hell wouldn't kidnap or drug someone he cared about to force them into staying loyal to him. That wasn't love. That was obsession.

"You really think I should sign, Caroline?" Stephan Degraff took the pen she'd given him, his hand poised over the contract.

For the first time since he'd entered the room, the bastard appeared confused. Conflicted. Something in his tone of voice revealed how much he wanted his daughter to be on side.

Damon held his breath.

He wanted Caroline on *his* side, too. And in that moment, he realized how much more important it was to win her than Transparent. He'd been battling so hard to keep his company when all along what he should have been fighting for was the woman herself.

Caroline slid the papers out from under her father's elbow, flipping to a back page. "I do. This is very fair to the Degraff interests. We need to protect our investment and get out before Transparent tanks." She slid the contract back under his pen and leaned closer to touch the bastard's arm. "I know how important our family is to you."

It was all Damon could do not to launch over the table and tear her away from Stephan. But one thing was becoming clear. She wasn't betraying Damon at all, no matter how it appeared. The deal wasn't going to help the Degraff interests one bit.

She was playing her father for all he was worth to make sure he signed the paper that gave Damon control of Transparent.

"There is nothing more important." Sweat beads popped along the man's pale forehead as he swore the words like an oath. "I would do anything to keep our family safe, Caroline. I'm glad you know that."

A smile stretched the bastard's thin lips as he stared up at the daughter he must care about in some twisted way.

Then Damon watched his primary investor scratch his name in ink on the contract and tossed down the pen like a gauntlet.

Damon almost couldn't believe his eyes. He heard someone—his brothers, maybe—trading discreet high-fives. Then Jager clearly told one of the other investors there was no problem with the launch and that it was as hack-proof as possible.

Cameron rose from the table and went around to shake Stephan's hand. "Since you've sold your shares to me, Mr. Degraff, I'll have my attorney escort you out so he can sign the funds over while the rest of the investors finish up the meeting."

"Of course." Stephan nodded, though he watched the byplay around the table uncertainly, as if becoming aware he may have missed something. "I look forward to being done with the McNeills." He held out an arm for his daughter. "Caroline?"

Damon held his breath. He couldn't allow her to walk out of this room with that man. Their marriage may have fallen apart, but he would never let anything happen to her on his watch.

"I need to stay a bit longer, Dad," she told him gently. "Just to hammer out a few details about my own stake in the company." She opened the file folder that had been in front of the empty seat at the table, which contained a projected timetable for the new product launch. "I'll be along shortly."

With her perfect posture and thoughtful scrutiny of

the pages in front of her, she gave every appearance of being all business. But Damon saw the way the blue vein in her neck ticked like mad, the pulse tapping triple time.

He was an idiot. And he wasn't worthy of the woman who'd just handed him the biggest business victory of his life after he'd hurt her. He wanted to roar with fury at himself as the rest of the room cheered Degraff's departure. Everyone but Caroline, of course, who turned sad eyes to watch Officer Downey escort her protesting father into another room.

Thanks to her, Damon had regained control of Transparent. But he couldn't imagine a more hollow victory when he'd lost her in the process.

"Congratulations, brother." Cameron McNeill hauled Damon to his feet and pulled him in for a bear hug. "We're going to make beautiful business together, mate."

Damon nodded. Thanked him. But when Gabe thumped him on the back and pointed to the conference room door closing, Damon realized his wife had made a quiet exit.

Shit.

He scrambled toward the door.

"Excuse me." He clapped a hand on Jager's shoulder, the brother who'd taken the reins at this company plenty of times in the past. "Jager will finish the meeting. I have to go."

Thirteen

A uniformed officer and a female detective Caroline hadn't met before whisked her father away before she even arrived in the reception area. She met her father's cold, furious gaze as he backed stiffly into the elevator cabin, flanked by his two escorts.

Lifting her chin, she allowed herself to meet his eyes without flinching. To let him know she'd recovered—if not her memory, damn it, her dignity. Her self-respect.

It was a small consolation considering everything else she'd lost this week. A love that she'd once thought was strong enough to overcome anything. Her husband.

Her chest had ached more each day following the cold ending to their encounter in the card room. Now, the hurt and hollowness inside would have brought her to her knees if not for Lucas. She still had a precious son to mother and her love for her child would have to keep her strong.

"Caroline." The deep rumble of Damon's voice sounded behind her in the reception area.

She turned around to find him closing in on her, his steps muffled by the Aztec-patterned rug in the lobby. She glanced into the meeting room where Damon's older brother Jager seemed to be leading the meeting, all eyes turned toward him.

"Shouldn't you be in there?" She wondered what he thought of her performance in the conference room. Was he going to rebuke her for pointing out the flaw in the software to the conference room at large? She wanted to believe he'd seen through her guise of camaraderie with Stephan, but then again, Damon didn't trust her much anymore. Maybe he would see that calculated risk she'd taken as yet another betrayal. "Your meeting is still going."

He joined her near the windows overlooking the Santa Cruz Mountains, in the corner farthest from the small reception desk where an administrator sat with a Bluetooth in one ear as she tapped her computer keys.

"I've waited too long to talk to you already. Jager can finish up in there without me."

"Your investors need your guidance. Your reassurance." She understood all too well about how fickle investors could be. Her father got antsy at the slightest hint of unease in a company that he'd backed. "I thought it was worth leaking the information about the software glitch to convince my father I had his best interests at heart."

"You've given the remaining investors the best possible reassurance already by relieving the board of the one consistently dissenting opinion." His blue eyes searched hers. "I wish you'd been there to receive the thanks we all owe you for making that deal happen."

She felt a spike of relief that he'd recognized what she had been angling to accomplish. They still understood each other at some level, at least.

"You knew what I was doing then?" She flicked a thumb over the empty place on her ring finger, remembering how bare that spot felt.

"I'm not going to pretend I didn't have a moment of…" He seemed to search for the right words. Behind them, the phone rang, and his brow furrowed. "Look, Caroline, I really need to talk to you, but not here. Could we go to my office?"

Her mind traveled back a year to late nights working on plans for the company when they would lock his office door and take a break from the job in the most rewarding way possible. She wasn't sure she could sit in those chairs where they'd made love.

Not now.

"How about we speak in my office instead?" Maybe it was the business victory with her father making her feel newly emboldened. She guessed that when the adrenaline let-down kicked in, she was going to have to start dealing with the hurt and regret of discovering her father had gone to criminal lengths to separate her from Damon. But she couldn't think about that right now if she was going to negotiate a future apart from Damon.

She needed to work from a position of strength before her heart broke the rest of the way.

"No problem." Damon nodded. "You still have a key? I'm sure the cleaning staff have maintained it, but I haven't been in there since the day I let the police go through your things."

His words helped her to recall how much he'd been through, as well. This year had been so painful for them both. She reached in her bag and withdrew her key ring before leading the way down the hall.

Despite her outward bravado, her hands were a little unsteady as she worked the lock and opened the door. She turned on the lights to the penthouse corner office, a spread that equaled his in amenities.

Only now, of course, the administrator's seat out front was vacant. Caroline hadn't worked a day at Transparent since she'd departed for her honeymoon, but the space was precisely as she remembered. Unlike the rest of Transparent's hypermodern offices, she'd chosen to complement the views from the floor-to-ceiling windows with bookshelves on every other wall. White linen swags draped along the tops of the shelves and the windows. Her cream leather office chair sat behind an antique desk, which was painted another shade of eggshell and hand-rubbed for a distressed effect. Birch branches stood in a wooden pitcher in place of flowers on one corner of the desk.

Here, the books, the framed photos, and the stunning mountain views provided all the color. A framed photo of Damon and her sat prominently on one bookshelf. The two of them seated together on a park bench in the gardens of the Winchester Mystery House. She wore a blue dress with white polka dots, a fanciful, romantic sundress with a fuller skirt than she normally chose. Wide-set straps showed off the necklace she'd bought in the gift shop that day, a glass daisy inspired by one of the windows in the home.

Seeing that necklace—a piece she hadn't seen in months—brought back a flood of new memories. The streak of thoughts through her head came so fast it almost hurt. She reeled back a little from the photo, the day of her kidnapping returning to her mind.

"Caroline?" Damon was beside her, his hand on her waist. Then, he shifted it to her shoulder when she still wobbled. "Are you all right?"

"My father was there." She blurted the worst of it, needing to share the burden of those painful moments. "My God. He was in our house that day they took me."

"Sit down." He guided her into a spot on the love seat near the windows, the stiff white denim fabric yielding under their weight as they sat down together. "You remembered something?"

Just two days ago she'd sat across the room from a therapist in New York who'd told her she might never recover her memories. But now, new information flooded her neuropathways, making connections throughout her brain in a way that felt like her whole head was lighting up.

"The necklace I'm wearing in that photo." She pointed to the picture of them on the park bench. "I was wearing it on the flight back from London."

Damon left her side for a moment to retrieve the image for a closer look. Lowering himself back to the loveseat, he set the silver picture frame on the low table near a stack of books on gardening.

"I bought you the replica of one of the daisy windows you liked." His full attention returned to her, his hand smoothing light, comforting circles between her shoulder blades. "It was just a fun, lunchtime trip to get out of the office. I put daisies in your hair that day, too."

Her heart hugged the memory close. How could she lose this man now when she was only fully appreciating how much he'd meant to her?

"Right. It was a happy time and I liked wearing that daisy." She closed her eyes, remembering. "I heard someone in the house a couple of hours after I got back to the Los Altos Hills place. I hoped maybe it was you, coming home early to surprise me, because who else enters a house without knocking?" She shook her head, her chest tight. "I guess I'd left the door unlocked though, and the security system hadn't been hooked up yet."

"I was furious with the security company when I realized there were no cameras going the day you disappeared." Damon nodded, his expression grave. He looked impossibly handsome in his navy suit and custom tailored shirt. "I fired them for not having everything up and running when you returned. Then I hired a whole new company to redo every bit of the job."

She thought back to Maresa's insistence that Damon had been a wreck without her. How could it be too late to recover their love if it had run so deep? She dragged in another steadying breath.

"When I went downstairs, my father was in our house. He'd flown here the day before me, hoping to convince me to leave you since he hadn't managed to do that when I saw him in London." Her fingers clenched into fists as the time washed over her, blooming in bright red bursts of pain. His cruelty had been shocking. Painful. "I was angry to see him, but I attempted to be civil even though he'd brought two goons with him I didn't know. I thought they were his private security. I didn't realize until later they were there for me."

She no longer needed the police to tell her the role her father had played in her disappearance. She remembered.

A gust of air from the ventilation system sent a chill through her and she shivered.

"I'm so sorry I wasn't there to protect you." Damon

brushed his hand over her hair where it trailed down her back. "So damned sorry."

"I would have never guessed he would try something so…" She shook her head, then steadied herself by looking into Damon's eyes as he patiently let her find her way through wave after wave of emotions. "He went ballistic about the necklace." That had tipped her off to the heartbreaking—terrifying—realization that Stephan Degraff had moved from eccentric and controlling to full-on obsessive. "He said cheap trinkets were beneath me. He ripped it off my throat." Her hand went to her neck, remembering the scrape of his nails on her skin as he took it. "He wrestled off my wedding rings, too. I was screaming so much, one of his guards had to restrain me."

Damon hugged her closer, his lips brushing her temple. "The police have him. You'll never have to deal with him again, I promise you, on my life, I promise."

"I know." She breathed deep, trying to regain that sense of strength she'd felt after she tricked her father into signing away his share of Transparent, but she found herself needing Damon's support to sustain her through the past steamrolling over her. "I told him to leave, but he refused. He said he would have me committed for unstable behavior. Then those goons grabbed me and—" Things got a little hazier after that.

"It's okay," Damon soothed. "Take your time. You're safe. I have you."

She tried to slow down her breathing, needing to press through before the fog once again overtook the memories. "They gave me a drink in the limo, trying to make me calm down even though they'd tied my hands. My father had already left in his own car while I went with the two muscle-heads. By then I was truly terrified. I took the drink and didn't scream because they said they could get one of my siblings next, but that's how they drugged me the first time."

"Your father must have stayed behind to leave your wedding bands and pack a few of your things." Not letting go of her, Damon pulled his phone from his pocket with his other hand. "I'm going to text Officer Downey that you have additional evidence so he knows to keep your father in custody."

It would be so easy to tip her head onto Damon's shoulder. To soak in every bit of comfort she could from his presence. But she knew walking away from him would be even more harder if she gave in to that impulse now.

"Thank you." She straightened, telling herself to keep it together. "I know you wanted to talk to me privately, and instead, I've dominated the conversation completely." Her heart ached for her husband and the love they used to share.

He set his phone aside. "What you remembered was too important to risk delaying. I couldn't be happier for your sake that your memory is coming back. I can't imagine how frustrating it's been for you missing pieces of the past."

He took her hand. Squeezed. She had to close her eyes to prevent herself from overthinking the simple gesture. She wanted it to mean so much more.

"Thank you for understanding," she said finally, her throat dry, her eyes burning with tears for her failed marriage. "But please, tell me. What did you want to talk about?"

Nodding, he shifted beside her. "I wanted to see you alone to ask you for another chance to prove to you that I love you and trust you. I—" He took a deep breath, his blue eyes darker with emotion. "I know that doesn't mean much for me to tell you now, after you've proven your loyalty beyond all doubt." He shook his head. "I should have told you before. I never stopped loving you, Caroline. Not even when it hurt the most."

It scared her how much she wanted to believe him. So she stuffed down all the hope that wanted to dance to life inside her to focus on what he was saying. She needed to be sure.

"Why should I believe you?" She felt tears sting the backs of her eyes that she would need to question him after he'd told her the words she'd longed to hear. "I have to ask, Damon, because you've had days to return the feelings I shared with you. And instead, you retreated into your work and pushed me out."

She couldn't be married to a man who didn't share her love. She had thought Damon was so different from her father. Open and warm. Ready to play and let work slide sometimes to simply enjoy life and be. The daisy necklace had reminded her of that. Of the simple pleasures.

Like winter picnics in Central Park? a contrary voice inside her asked. Maybe she had seen signs of his playful side since her return. But she needed him to trust her, too.

Outside her office, she heard voices in the reception area. The meeting must have broken up. But Damon didn't move to join them.

"Things happened so fast between us when we fell in love." His knee brushed hers as he spoke, a warm stroke of wool-gabardine on her bare knee. "I probably should have questioned it more at that time, but it was the most exciting, passionate love I'd ever experienced, and I couldn't wait to just make you all mine."

"Me, too." Her throat burned at the thought of losing that. Still, he'd said that he loved her. "That's how I felt."

"But maybe we didn't take enough time to really think about how we could fit together long-term. When we argued after the honeymoon, it felt like the end of the world to me. That's the only reason I could believe for a second that you'd walked away on your terms and left me. I figured I hadn't lived up to my end of the fairy-tale relationship and I lost you." He stroked a strand of her hair that lay on the shoulder closest to him.

Her scalp tingled.

Maybe his love was still there after all?

"I couldn't wait to see you and make up with you when I got home." She knew that for certain. "But even if I was upset, I wouldn't just walk out. For better or worse, Damon, my father did raise me to be the kind of woman who works hard at everything. And I would never give up on something so easily."

"I should have known that. And when you came back…" He shook his head, the emotions and regret evident in his eyes. "I was ready to do anything to make you stay forever. To fix anything I'd messed up the first time. So when I realized you'd been keeping secrets—"

"For Lucas." She wanted to be clear about that. "I couldn't risk revealing him to you until I knew for sure what your feelings were toward me. My father has been feeding me a diet of lies for months, showing me stories about the McNeills and telling me you married me to inherit—"

"None of it was true." His jaw tensed, showing a streak of pride and stubbornness that she admired. Something about his expression made her imagine what Lucas would look like one day. Would he take after his father with that same McNeill pride?

Would she be with them both to see that day?

The hope she'd stuffed down before grew back stronger. More insistent.

"I know that now. But between the drugs and being ill and having amnesia, I questioned everything. Every. Single. Thing." She realized that no matter what the outcome of this conversation, she loved him as much—more—than ever.

"That's what a good mother would do." He stroked a hand along her arm. "I'm sorry, Caroline. I understand now that you had to make the call to put Lucas first while I was still concentrating on us—fixated on why you left. I'm trying to catch up to be a good father."

"And you are." She liked seeing him hold their son. Kiss the baby's silky hair. "I trust that. But what I really want to know is, what's next for us?"

Of all the risks she'd taken today—maneuvering her father into thinking she was on his side, gambling with Damon's company in front of his other investors—this one was the biggest. Because Damon McNeill still held her heart.

"If I had my way, we would go to the police station right now to tell them everything you've remembered. While you give your statement, I'd work on making arrangements to have legal custody of your brothers shifted over to you so that we can help them through this." His hand moved to her knee. "My father went missing from my life at their age, and I know how confusing that will be for them."

Tipping her head to Damon's shoulder, she couldn't wait another moment to take the comfort he offered. Not when he said the most beautiful things. She appreciated that he would think of her family—her father's sons—in that way.

"You're right. Thank you for considering my brothers' needs." She kissed his shoulder through his jacket. No matter what, Damon was going to be an amazing role model. And maybe, her heart hoped, he would be so much more.

"I think we should pull them out of school. Let them spend a few weeks with us here, or maybe in Martinique. That's a good place for kids." He frowned as he seemed to weigh two important choices. Then he lifted his head. "Maybe we ask them?"

"I think that's a great idea." She felt a smile from deep inside her, confidence gathering along with the hope. This feeling couldn't be wrong. She remembered it from those heady weeks when she'd fallen in love with this man. They clicked. They fit together.

Damon nodded. Then he took both her hands in his, turning to face her more fully on the sofa. "But first, I want to ask you to forgive me for not telling you how much I love you. Today, yesterday, and every day since I met you." He stroked the backs of her fingers. "I was tongue-tied and stupid that night you said it to me. My brain was stuck wondering how you could feel that way about me. But not for a moment of that time did I not love you back." His voice lowered, the emotions behind the words so evident she couldn't believe she hadn't heard them before. "Please believe me."

The rightness of the moment, the truth of their happiness, flowed over her. Comforting her. Assuring her. Making her heart whole again.

"I do." She kissed his cheek, let a tear of happiness roll unchecked down her face. "I believe you. Because whether you say it or not, I feel your love all around me right now. It's been there all along, I was just too afraid to believe it. It's in the thoughtful things you do for me and the way you took care of Victoria with the bodyguard. Or putting my brothers' care before anything else today."

"I would do anything for you. I knew it in that board meeting that I'd rather lose the company a hundred times over than lose you for even one more day." He kissed her fallen tear and both of her closed eyes. "Will you do one thing for me, my sweet Caroline?"

"What is it, my love?"

"Will you let me put your wedding rings on again?" He took up her left hand and kissed the bare third finger. "I keep putting them right here and they keep disappearing."

She laughed. "Yes." Digging in her purse, she couldn't help the relieved laughter that kept coming. Everything was going to work out for her and Damon and their family. "But you have to admit I had a good reason for taking them off this time."

"The best." Smiling, he took the two bands from her and slid them into place. "You slayed me back there when you walked into the meeting and took charge."

She flexed her fingers, admiring the sparkle of diamonds in the sunlight through the huge windows, the sense of rightness filling her.

"It will always hurt—what my father did to me." There would be a hole in her heart that nothing else would fill, but she looked forward to connecting with Damon's family. To finding more role models for her son, and to strengthening her own support network with friendships like she'd started with Maresa. "But it felt good to shut him out of Transparent forever."

"You are an incredible woman on every level, Mrs. McNeill." He leaned closer to kiss her neck. "I'm going to have the most stunning daisy necklace made for you to replace the old one."

Her skin heated where he kissed it. "I actually really liked the gift shop trinket." She skimmed a hand under his jaw to cup his face and looked in his blue eyes.

"You want another necklace from the gift shop?"

She thought about why the impromptu present had pleased her so much the first time.

"For my whole life, I was taught to be the best. That second wasn't good enough." She'd been trained from early childhood and she was ready to break free of the mold. "I don't want to strive for perfection anymore. I want to know that our love is strong enough it can bear a misstep and we'll trust in each other to get through it." She warmed to her theme, imagining a future by Damon's side. "I want to take spontaneous walks in the middle of the workday and not feel guilty about it. I want to play. To have fun. To just be."

"I can do all of that." He wrapped her up in his arms. "I can play and have fun, I swear. But I'm still going to work my tail off not to make any more mistakes with you."

"Just love me the way I love you." She felt confident saying it because she knew it would be returned in full. Maybe even with interest. "That's all I need."

"I'm so glad to have my wife back." He kissed her lips. Slowly. Thoroughly. "You can't imagine how happy that makes me."

Actually, she had a very good idea because it made her glow inside to be reunited with him. But for now, she simply closed her eyes so she could feel the love all around her.

Epilogue

One month later

Damon bent over the portacrib and settled his son onto the sheet covered with smiling blue jellyfish. Two weeks ago, he'd relocated his whole family to a private bungalow at the Birdsong Hotel, the property his brother Gabe owned in Martinique. He'd felt the need to solidify the new, expanded family dynamic that included Lucas, Caroline and Caroline's two younger brothers. Even Victoria had requested a leave of absence from her university program to join them for a week. New McNeills and honorary McNeills filled two bungalows of the Birdsong, giving them time to play together on the shore of the Caribbean, safely away from the headlines about Stephan Degraff back home.

As Damon watched Lucas huff out a sleepy sigh, his arms flung wide in that careless, baby way, Damon's heart filled with love. Again. The way it did dozens of times a day as he marveled at how full his life had become in such a short time. He'd gone from a year of devastated loneliness to having a beautiful wife and three sons. One by blood, two by law.

He wouldn't be able to adopt the boys, as much as he would love to, since their father would never sign any more paperwork that would benefit Damon. But Caroline's brothers knew they would always have a real family now, and they were excited about the idea of attending public schools and being under the same roof as their sister and baby nephew.

Damon turned on the nursery monitor for Lucas's nap even though he wasn't venturing far from the crib. He didn't mind sitting on the deck of the bungalow with the baby monitor while he watched Caroline cavort on the beach with her siblings. Damon double-checked the video feed on the nursery monitor before he dimmed the lights so his boy could rest and dream of happy times.

Stepping out of the baby's room, Damon wandered out onto the patio to find his brother Gabe already there, sprawled on a deck lounger, a silver bucket full of ice and bottled beers at his feet. Flowers bloomed on either side of the deck, spilling bright petals around them like a private luau. Gabe had been remodeling the property for years, recently hiring a landscaper to redesign the gardens.

"Don't try to tell me there's no drinking on duty," Gabe warned him, popping the caps off with a bottle opener. "I know you're committed to being a good dad, but one beer is allowed during naptime."

"Is that right?" Damon dropped into a lounger, his eyes already moving to the beach beyond to see where Caroline and her siblings had gone.

"They're right there, Mr. Overprotective." Gabe pointed down the beach to where the four of them were dragging paddleboards onto the shore.

The two boys were having squirt gun wars at the same time, shooting each other while running for cover in the bushes that spilled onto the beach.

"I'm still getting used to life without bodyguards." Damon had let the security detail go once he knew Stephan would be in prison for good.

Or at least until his sons were over eighteen.

But after having Caroline disappear on him once, it wasn't easy relaxing his instincts.

"I know, bro." Gabe clapped him on the shoulder and then tipped his bottle to Damon's. "And you're dealing with everything like a champ."

"I don't want to be so protective I drive Caroline away." He had spent every second with her since the day she'd regained her memory, hardly daring to believe that she was back. Whole.

His.

Getting to know her all over again made every day happier than the one that came before. And seeing her as a mother made him so damn proud he thought he'd burst with it.

Gabe laughed. "Yeah. I don't think that's happening. That woman loves you something fierce."

Lifting the beer to his lips, Damon relaxed into his seat, inhaling the sea air. "I'll drink to that."

"You're a lucky man." Gabe's words were wistful, hinting at a wealth of mixed emotions beneath the surface.

Gabe's ex-wife had been pregnant when she decided she didn't want to be a mother. Soon after she gave birth, she'd walked away from the baby and left the marriage. Now, Gabe's ten-month-old son, Jason, was well-loved but motherless. Damon knew it broke his brother's heart. The boy was currently napping back at Gabe's place tended to by a nanny.

"I am, at that. Thank you for letting us crash here for a few weeks." Damon straightened in his seat, seeing Caroline head their way while Victoria retrieved a huge plastic water gun to chase her brothers. "I hope it's not…awkward."

"More than anything, I want Jason to experience having a family." Gabe picked at the beer label with his thumbnail. "You're giving him that and I'm glad about it." He peered up, seeing Caroline wrapping a towel around herself as she walked closer. "In fact, I'm so grateful, I'm going to do you a favor and keep watch on your nursery monitor if you want to take some downtime with the missus."

Damon grinned. "I've got a better idea." Getting to his feet, he held out his arms to his beautiful wife, hauling her close to kiss her cheek. "I'll keep the nursery monitor while you go show the Degraff crew how to win a squirt gun war."

Gabe raised an eyebrow. "I do have the mother of all water guns in the shed."

"I seem to remember you trying to blast me with it on my last visit."

Setting aside his empty bottle, Gabe shot to his feet. "You're on."

Caroline called after him. "Victoria is craftier than she looks."

Gabe was already out of sight when he shouted back, "I love a worthy opponent."

Damon turned his attention to the woman in his arms, still damp from her paddleboard adventure. She smelled like coconut sunscreen and sunshine; her lips were salty when he kissed her.

"Not as much as I love you," he told her. "I hope you're not getting tired of hearing that."

"I can't hear it enough." She trailed a touch along his cheek, cooling his hot skin with her fingers. "And I want to make love to you and hear you say it again and again." She kissed the words into his skin as her lips traced a path along his jaw. "But first, I want to stare into our son's crib together and marvel at what a miracle he is."

Damon's throat closed with emotion. He was a lucky man to have the love of this strong, incredible woman who'd been through so much. Who'd fought so hard to reunite their family and have a future together.

"Sounds like another perfect day."

"Another happy day," she corrected him softly. "That's all I want."

"One lifetime of happy days, coming up." Damon would move mountains to give them to her. Picking up the baby monitor, he walked with her into the bungalow to retreat from the sun. To have her all to himself for a little while. "I promise."

* * * * *

If you liked this story of the McNeill family,
pick up these other
MCNEILL MAGNATES *books from*
Joanne Rock!

THE MAGNATE'S MAIL-ORDER BRIDE
THE MAGNATE'S MARRIAGE MERGER
HIS ACCIDENTAL HEIR
LITTLE SECRETS: HIS PREGNANT SECRETARY

as well as reader favorite
SECRET BABY SCANDAL
Available now from Mills & Boon Desire!

MILLS & BOON®

Desire™

PASSIONATE AND DRAMATIC LOVE STORIES

A sneak peek at next month's titles...

In stores from 11th January 2018:

- **For the Sake of His Heir** – Joanne Rock *and*
  Rags to Riches Baby – Andrea Laurence

- **Rich Rancher's Redemption** – Maureen Child *and*
  Between Marriage and Merger – Karen Booth

- **His Temptation, Her Secret** – Barbara Dunlop *and*
  The Baby Claim – Catherine Mann

LET'S TALK

Romance

For exclusive extracts, competitions
and special offers, find us online:

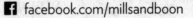

▪️ facebook.com/millsandboon

📷 @millsandboonuk

🐦 @millsandboon

Or get in touch on 0844 844 1351*

For all the latest titles coming soon, visit
millsandboon.co.uk/nextmonth

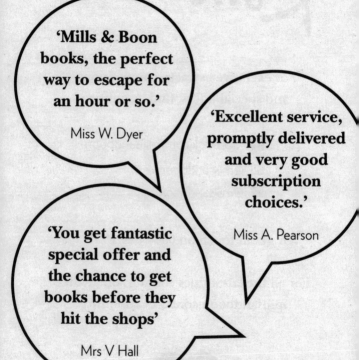